"How dare you, Sandoval Parrish?"

Tess took a step forward, thrusting her chin out. "I wouldn't be in this situation if it weren't for your desire to curry favor with that unprincipled killer!" She was too angry to care they were alone and she was very much at his mercy.

Sandoval's head snapped back as if she had slapped him, and he paled. For several endless moments they stared at one another. "You're right, you wouldn't. You have every right to think the worst of me. The best thing you can do is trust me."

"But *why*, Sandoval? What do you hope to gain?" she demanded, self-control slipping, tears of outrage and fear suddenly threatening to spill over onto her cheeks.

"I can't tell you that, Tess," he said. "You may not believe this, but I'm not a bad man."

Something about the softness of his tone and the kindness in his eyes was her undoing, and Tess gave way to her tears. Then suddenly he was holding her…

Laurie Kingery

and

Louise M. Gouge

The Outlaw's Lady

&

Love Thine Enemy

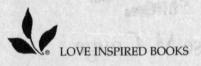 LOVE INSPIRED BOOKS

Recycling programs
for this product may
not exist in your area.

ISBN-13: 978-1-335-47360-8

The Outlaw's Lady & Love Thine Enemy

Copyright © 2019 by Harlequin Books S.A.

The publisher acknowledges the copyright holders
of the individual works as follows:

The Outlaw's Lady
Copyright © 2009 by Laurie A. Kingery

Love Thine Enemy
Copyright © 2009 by Louise M. Gouge

www.Harlequin.com

Printed in U.S.A.

CONTENTS

Laurie Kingery is a Texas transplant to Ohio who writes romance set in post–Civil War Texas. She was nominated for a Carol Award for her second Love Inspired Historical novel, *The Outlaw's Lady*, and is currently writing a series about mail-order grooms in a small town in the Texas Hill Country.

Visit the Author Profile page
at Harlequin.com for more titles.

THE OUTLAW'S LADY

Laurie Kingery

God is our refuge and strength,
a very present help in trouble.
—*Psalms* 46:1

To Elaine English, my agent, with grateful thanks
for helping me to keep on believing in my writing,
and to Tom, as always.

Author's Note

The town of Chapin, in Hidalgo County, Texas,
mentioned in this book is the present-day Edinburg.
The name was changed in 1911.

Chapter One

Rio Grande Valley
Texas, 1880

Tess Hennessy stared down through the darkness at the image taking shape before her in the chemical bath. The photograph she had taken of the Spanish mission-style home in which she lived was to be a present for her parents on their anniversary tomorrow. She had captured it at a moment when the lighting was perfect, with the noon sun directly overhead so that the palm trees didn't cast their shadows over the house. She smiled, pleased at her work. They would love it, especially after she mounted it in the elegant oak frame Francisco, her helper, had prepared. She'd have to sneak out here to her developing shed after they returned from the party tonight, no matter how late it was, so that the picture would be ready for gifting tomorrow.

If only it were as easy to see her future develop before her as it was to develop a photograph. Her mother, she knew, expected her to marry. But what man would want to marry a girl who had an unladylike pastime that involved messy, finger-staining chemicals and long sessions in a darkroom?

Was there such a man? If only she could submerge one of her collodion plates into the chemical bath in the basin before her, and see his image take shape...

"Tess! Tess! Where are you? Now, where can that girl have gone, Patrick? I specifically *told* her we were leaving for the barbecue at one o'clock...."

Oh dear, she'd lost track of time again. It was so easy to do when she was immersed in photography, her passion. "Mama, I'm in the darkroom, developing a picture. Don't come in, please—"

But it was too late. Sunlight suddenly flooded the little shed by the barn as Amelia Hennessy burst in.

Tess groaned. Her mother's untimely arrival had just ruined the photograph.

"Tess! What are you doing in here?" her mother cried. "We have to leave for the barbecue, and you're not even dressed. Look at you!" Her mother spoke as if she expected Tess to look down and be surprised that she was wearing her serviceable navy skirt and waist.

Behind her mother she could see her father, looking sympathetic and uncomfortable, his eyes appealing with Tess to comply so peace could be restored.

She would have to give her parents an IOU for their anniversary present and take the photograph again. Her father would understand and apologize privately to Tess for not stopping his wife before she'd burst into her darkroom.

Amelia Hennessy tapped her foot, her face tight with impatience.

"I *am* ready to go," Tess replied in a level voice, wishing she could avoid the inevitable confrontation.

"Surely you weren't thinking of wearing *that* at the

Taylors' barbecue?" An imperious finger indicated Tess's utilitarian clothes, in contrast to her own elaborately lace-trimmed dress with a fancy, bow-topped bustle.

Tess took a deep breath, praying for calm. She *did* want to obey the commandment that instructed her to honor her parents, and with her father that was easy. No matter how often she explained to her mother what was important to her, however, Amelia Hennessy seemed incapable of understanding. Tess shot a look at her father, but though his eyes were full of sympathy, he said nothing.

"Mama, I'm not going as a party guest, but to *work*. I told you the Taylors hired me to take the photographs of them and their guests. The developing chemicals can be messy, and with all the bending and stooping while posing the subjects, what I wear is apt to get dusty and stained, so it's hardly practical of me to wear a light-colored, frilly dress."

Her mother sighed and put her slender fingers up to her head as if she felt a migraine coming on. "Tess, I do *not* understand you!" she said for surely the thousandth time. "You're a beautiful girl—or you would be, if you'd take some trouble to put yourself together. You could make a brilliant marriage, but you'll never do it if you insist on spending so much time on this little *hobby* of yours. You're always at your little shop in town. I don't know why your father ever let you take it over when James passed away. And when you're not photographing, you're drawing. Patrick, *say something* to your daughter to make her see sense!"

Patrick Hennessy put one hand on his wife's shoulder, the other on his daughter's, and smiled the charming smile that usually mellowed his wife's anxious reaction to his daughter's individuality.

"Yes, she *is* a beautiful girl. Thanks be to God, our last chick in the nest got your looks, Amelia—especially your blue eyes, and only my red hair," he said, with a quirk of amusement that lifted the corners of his mouth and eyes. "When—and *if*—" he added, with a hint of steel "—she's ready, our youngest has only to crook her finger to have any man she wants. But she's not a brainless belle with no thought but how many beaux she can collect. If she wants to be a photographer and carry on for James, I don't see the harm."

Amelia Hennessy's lips thinned and she sighed again. "You never do, when it comes to Tess, Patrick, but she's already twenty and she's going to end up an old maid, you mark my words."

"I always do, Amelia," he said, giving his wife an affectionate peck on the cheek. "But an old maid? Nonsense. Our Tess is the prettiest girl in Hidalgo County. A man would be a fool to think otherwise if he had eyes in his head. And now, we'd better leave or we really will be late."

Tess sighed, too, knowing the battle was only postponed, not won, and followed her mother out of the shed. As she left the dimness, the tropical heat of the Rio Grande Valley washed over her. For a moment she envied her mother's lightweight dress, low cut over the shoulders.

In front of them stood two carriages, the open victoria, with its matched bays and driven by Mateo, and a smaller vehicle that resembled a Civil War ambulance, covered on all sides and in back by heavy canvas and pulled by Ben, the same mule that had once pulled the wagon for Uncle James. Tess had requested that her photography wagon be ready at the same time as her parents' vehicle, and Mateo had done so.

"We're going to be the laughingstock of the party with that wagon following us," Tess heard her mother grumble as her husband assisted her up into the carriage.

"Horsefeathers," her father scoffed. "They'll be lining up to have their pictures taken, and Tess will be very popular indeed."

"If it comforts you to think so," her mother sniffed. "But I just wish Lula Marie had had the decency to ask me first before hiring our daughter. I would have forbidden it."

"Sam talked to me," Patrick Hennessy told his wife. "I said it was all right." There was a warning note of finality in his voice. Tess heard no more objections. She climbed into the driver's seat and gathered up the reins.

Her heart warmed with love for her father. He'd always supported her dreams, God bless him. She loved her mother, too, and knew despite her mother's fretting about her future, that the feeling was fiercely reciprocated.

Tess understood that her mother had grown up in a simpler time. She'd been a belle in the truest sense before the charming Patrick Hennessy, an Irish immigrant, had swept her off her feet. Everyone said she was marrying beneath her, but apparently she had known what she was doing. Starting from scratch, Hennessy had built his empire in south Texas until he was one of the richest cattlemen in the state, even after the Civil War.

If only she could convince her mother that she, too, knew what she was doing. Tess had grown up on her uncle James's tales of working as a photographer for the famous Mathew Brady during the war. She had

taken her first daguerreotype at her uncle's direction
when she was only seven. By the time she was fifteen,
she was working alongside him in his shop in nearby
Chapin whenever she wasn't away at school, and by the
time he died, he had taught her everything he knew.

Tess glanced backward into the wagon to assure herself that all her bottles of chemicals were safely and
securely bestowed inside. "Giddup, Ben," she said,
clucking to the mule. And the beast obediently took
his place behind the victoria for the short drive to the
Taylors' plantation.

"I tell you, Dupree, we're going to have to call the
Rangers in again to deal with these Mexican cattle
thieves like McNelly did in seventy-five," Samuel Taylor said, turning to the man sitting next to him. "He certainly showed Cortinas what was what."

"I'm sure you're right, Sam," Mr. Dupree agreed.
"I'm sick and tired of losing cattle to these bandits, not
to mention two of my best broodmares." He slapped his
hand on his knee as if to emphasize his disgust.

Tess threw off the heavy, dark canvas cover under
which she had been crouching and faced the two men she
had posed standing in front of their wives and daughters.

"Please, Uncle Samuel, Mr. Dupree. You must remain still, or you will be a blur," she pleaded, striving
for a tactful tone. She swatted at a horsefly that had
taken advantage of her coming out from cover to land
on her neck. "The exposure will take only a few seconds and then you may talk all you want."

"I certainly *hope* we'll be done so soon," Maribelle,
one of the Dupree daughters, complained. Like her sister, she was sitting at her father's feet with her skirts
spread out decorously in front of her. "I'm roasting here

in this heat, and without my parasol, the sun will *bake* my complexion, I'm sure. I don't know why we could not have sat on the veranda where it's shady."

Tess had already explained the need to use natural light, so she didn't bother to do so again. "Just another minute, Maribelle, and you can go back to the party. Just think, you and your family will always have this picture to commemorate the day."

Maribelle made a little moue of distaste, as if nothing Tess could create with her camera could possibly compensate her for her suffering, but then her eyes shifted to something behind Tess and her camera. Her eyes widened. Without turning her head, she spoke out of the side of her mouth to her sister. "Melissa, who *is* that?"

"Who is *who?*" snapped her sister, also irritable in the heat.

"Ladies," Tess begged. She had been about to duck back under the canvas again and take the picture.

"That man who just stepped off the veranda, the one who's now standing by the fiddlers' platform," Maribelle Dupree told her sister. "Don't look now, because he's looking this way, but my stars, he is quite the handsome fellow!"

"You know I can't see that far without my spectacles," Melissa whined, "and I could hardly wear them *here.*"

Involuntarily, Tess looked back over her shoulder, and saw just what had caught Maribelle Dupree's attention.

The man was tall, probably all of six feet, and whipcord lean. He wore no hat, and in the sunlight his hair gleamed raven-black and a bit overlong, brushing the collar of his white shirt in the back. His features were angular, his nose slightly aquiline. He held up his hand

to shade his eyes, peering around as if looking for someone or something.

What a fascinating face, Tess thought. What she
wouldn't give to photograph him, to try to capture those
angular planes of his face, that magnetism and sense of
determination that radiated from him.

"Oh, he's coming this way!" squealed Maribelle to
her sister. "Melissa, is my hair all right? Is it coming
loose in the back?"

"Girls, please," Taylor implored, just as Tess was
about to remonstrate with them again. "If you two chat-
terboxes could hush up while we get this picture done,
I'll present him to you."

Even as the girls squeaked blissfully and went into
their poses again, Mr. Dupree spoke up. "I'd rather you
didn't, Sam. I don't like what I've heard of the man.
They say Sandoval Parrish is two different people, de-
pending on which side of the border he's on."

Taylor blinked in surprise, then said, "Very well, a
father has that prerogative, after all. Now, if we could
let Tess take her picture? I believe there are several others who also want theirs done. Tess dear, thank you for
your patience."

"Of course, Uncle Samuel." Tess took one last, fleet-
ing glance at the object of the Dupree girls' attention.
The stranger had paused to accept a drink from a tray
proffered by a servant, and was now lifting it to his
mouth as he continued to look in their direction.

Had he seen her staring right along with the giddy
Dupree girls? Tess ducked under the canvas with the
same feeling a mouse must have as it darts into a hole
to escape the scrutiny of a hungry hawk. Half a minute
later, she had completed the exposure.

"I'm done now. You are free to move," she said, coming back out from under her cover. She watched the Dupree girls stroll away, their bustles swaying as they each took one last, longing look over their shoulders. Apparently they had lost their nerve and weren't bold enough to stay and hold Taylor to his promise of an introduction.

Tess wondered if the stranger was still standing where he had been, but she was much too busy now to look at him again. Carefully, she removed the glass photography plate from the camera and strode over to where her wagon stood parked in the shelter of three shady live oaks. Her darkroom while at a job consisted of a larger, dark canvas tent stretched over the square, shallow bed of the wagon, in which sat the developing bath. She had only ten minutes to develop the picture or the collodion in the plate would no longer be wet, and her efforts would have been in vain.

Tess wished Francisco, her assistant in the shop, could have come to the barbecue today to take care of the preparation of the collodion plates and the developing while she took the pictures so she could be done sooner. But he had told her he had to help his father today. She straightened her shoulders, reminding herself that Uncle James had often worked alone to photograph the aftermath of battles during the war. Whatever he had done in the hardship of the battlefield, she could certainly do at a barbecue.

"Tess, can you come out for a minute? There's someone here who'd like to meet you," Sam Taylor said, just after she had gone into the developing tent.

"I'm sorry, I'm afraid I can't right now, Uncle Samuel," Tess said, staying under the tent and using her metal dippers to lower the undeveloped picture into the dipping bath. "If I don't bathe this photograph right now, then hang it up to dry, the picture will be ruined. I'll have to be in here for a few minutes, I'm afraid. Why don't I find you when I'm done, before I start posing another photograph?"

Idly, she wondered who it was her godfather wanted her to meet. She feared her mother had infected him with her anxiety about the possibility of her daughter's spinsterhood. Tess hoped he was not trying his hand at matchmaking.

She heard a rich chuckle outside the tent. "Well, if the picture needs a bath, it needs a bath," an unfamiliar voice drawled. The voice was deep and accented in such a way to suggest that while Spanish was the speaker's first language, he was equally fluent in English. For a moment, she was curious about the possessor of such a voice. Then, when she heard nothing more, she assumed the men had taken her at her word and moved off. She had work to do, Tess reminded herself, and in the shadows of the dark canvas tent, she concentrated on producing the best image she could.

Minutes later, the photograph laid out on cloth and pinned into place so it could dry next to the others she had taken, Tess backed out of the tent. Before she left the party, she would have to brush a coat of varnish over the images to fix and protect them from the dust and moisture, but that could wait until all the images were dry.

"Ah, there she is, our lady daguerreotypist," Sam announced as she emerged.

Tess blinked, her eyes momentarily blinded by the brilliant sunlight after the semi-darkness of the tent. As her eyes adjusted to the afternoon light, her jaw fell open.

"Oh—it's *you!*" she said, before she could think.

Chapter Two

He watched with great interest as Tess Hennessy's lovely oval face went pale, then flamed as she realized what she had said.

"I—I mean, I didn't think y'all were going to wait right here!" One hand self-consciously flew to smooth her hair, which was coming down after brushing the overhead canvas too many times. Her gaze fled to Samuel Taylor, standing next to him.

Taylor stepped forward. "Tess, I'd like to introduce you to an old friend of mine, Sandoval Parrish. That is to say, *he's* not old, but our friendship is. Sandoval, Miss Teresa Hennessy, youngest child of Patrick Hennessy, my good friend who owns the land next to ours. I'm her godfather."

Parrish saw Tess blink as she heard his name. Sandoval, she would be thinking, a Spanish name, yet his last name sounds Anglo.

"I am pleased to meet you, Miss Hennessy," he said, and remembering that Anglo women thought hand kissing too forward, offered his hand instead. "My given name is from my Mexican mother. My surname, as well as my height, is from my father, who was an Anglo."

She colored again as if embarrassed that he had guessed her thoughts. "I see, Mr. Parrish. But you haven't taken your mother's name, too, as I understand most Mexicans do?"

He smiled, pleased that she knew of the custom. "Yes, my full name is Sandoval Parrish y Morelos, but it's much too big a mouthful, at least on this side of the border."

"And on which side of the border do you live, Mr. Parrish?" she asked.

Parrish cleared his throat. "I have ranch property on both sides of the river, Miss Hennessy, inherited from each side of the family."

He watched her eyes narrow at his noncommittal answer. She probably thought he was one of the many *Tejanos,* Texans of Mexican heritage, whose larger allegiance lay with Mexico. When it came to the test, Anglo Texans didn't trust them.

Ah well, it was a pity she seemed to feel that way, but maybe it was better. He hadn't known he would find the lady photographer so interesting, but if she didn't share the feeling, he could carry out his plan without distraction.

His suspicion was confirmed when she took a step back and said, "It was very nice to meet you, Mr. Parrish, but perhaps I'd better get back to my job. There were several other guests who wanted their photographs taken before I leave today."

Now Taylor took a quick step forward. "Now, Tess, I didn't mean for this barbecue to be all work and no play for you! The party ain't half over, so there's plenty of time for you to get to know Sandoval a little better. Why not let him get you some lemonade and y'all go sit down in the shade and get acquainted?"

"I… I really should do what you hired me to do before I stop to enjoy myself, Uncle Samuel," Tess protested, "or I can't take the fee we agreed upon." She pulled a folded sheet of paper from the pocket of her skirt and brandished it at her uncle, almost as if it were a weapon. "There are still several names on my list…."

"Actually, I was interested in having a photograph taken myself, Miss Hennessy," Sandoval said suddenly, "if you think you would have time today. If not, I could perhaps make time to come to the shop Sam tells me you have in town," he offered. "It would be a present to my mother, whose birthday is coming soon."

She hesitated.

"Who's next on that list?" Sam demanded, grabbing the paper away from her with the boldness only an old family friend could get away with. "Ah, Sissy Dawson. Why, she's much too busy flirtin' with Fred Yancy's youngest pup to be bothered sittin' still right now," he said, jerking his head in the aforementioned Sissy's direction. Just as he had said, Sissy was giggling and fluttering her eyelashes at a young man who looked utterly captivated by her antics. "Why don't you take Sandoval's picture right now?"

Her eyes darted to Sandoval, then back to her godfather. There was no way she could politely refuse. "I… I suppose I could do that," she said at last. "Very well, Mr. Parrish, please make yourself comfortable on that chair and I'll just prepare another collodion plate…"

"Tess, Lula Marie's motionin' for me to come over and meet somebody," Taylor said, "so I'll just leave you two together. Make Sandoval look handsome, mind— his mama thinks he is, and nothing I could tell her will convince her otherwise," he added with a chuckle, giving them a last wave as he strode away.

Tess started after his departing figure with obvious dismay.

"Relax, Miss Hennessy, I do not bite," Sandoval assured her, amused.

She stared at him, her lapis lazuli-blue eyes widening. "I never thought that you did," she began, but he interrupted her before she could deny it further.

"I will cooperate fully, better than any of your other subjects today, so you will be rid of me in half the time."

He enjoyed the flash of amusement that curved her lips upward. He liked the way her lower lip was fuller than the other, and the way she was biting it just now with straight white teeth as if to hold back a laugh. He wanted to make her laugh some more.

"Well, you'd hardly have to do much to behave better than those Dupree girls, Mr. Parrish. They were fidgety before, but once they spotted *you,* they became impossible."

Was it a test to see if he enjoyed the admiring glances of women? He'd seen the silly chits eyeing him, but they held no appeal. It had been this woman he'd come to meet.

"Ah, well, there's no accounting for taste, is there, Miss Hennessy?" he said lightly.

She met his gaze as if she weren't quite sure how to take his remark. "Just make yourself comfortable, Mr. Parrish," she said, gesturing toward one of the two ornately carved chairs she had been using all afternoon for her subjects.

"We have been introduced, Miss Hennessy. You may call me Sandoval."

Tess Hennessy did nothing to indicate she had heard him, merely moved the second chair away from the one in which he sat, and ignored his murmur that he could have done that for her. "I'll just be a few moments preparing the plate," she said, disappearing once more under the canvas hood.

"So you are called Tess, not Teresa, Miss Hennessy?" he asked, trying to keep her talking while all he could see of her, from his vantage point in the chair, was her navy-blue skirt. "It suits you."

"By my *family*. Uncle Samuel is my godfather, so he has that privilege, too." As you do not on such short acquaintance, he knew she meant. Her voice was muffled by the heavy fabric, but he didn't miss the starch in it. Sandoval smiled inwardly at her attempt to put him in his place. Tess Hennessy had the tart tongue to go with the fiery hair that the knot at the nape of her neck barely restrained anymore. He settled into a pose, staring back at the camera with a half smile. He let her direct him in how to hold his head, where to put his hands. When she announced that she was finished, he stood and told her he would pick up the finished product in three days at her shop.

"But...perhaps you didn't understand. I can have it done by the end of the day for you, Mr. Parrish," she said, taking a step after him. "It will come complete with a matte and protective folder."

"Ah, but your grandfather tells me one can also purchase frames at your shop, custom-made for the picture by your assistant. I would like a frame suitable for the picture, a gilt frame, if that is possible?"

"Of course, we can make such a frame for it," she said. "You said you will pick it up on Tuesday?"

Sandoval nodded. Had he imagined the slight heightening of color in her cheeks when she realized she would see him again? "Would late morning be convenient?"

"I'll expect you then, Mr. Parrish." Her voice was

brisk, businesslike. A prelude to goodbye. She stared
down at the notebook she'd taken out to note the appointment.

He wanted more than that from her, despite his re-
alization that mutual interest might complicate things.
"If you like," he went on, "I'd be honored to take you to
lunch at the hotel across from your shop. I'm told they
have good food." He said it to gauge her reaction to
him. Both of them would be many miles from Chapin
by then, if all went according to his plan.

Her chin jerked up again. "I… I don't know… I'll
have to think about it," she said.

"Very well, Miss Hennessy. Until Tuesday, then." He
felt her eyes upon him as he strode away.

"Aren't you done yet, Tess?" Amelia Hennessy
shouted through the heavy canvas of the developing tent. The sudden sound caused Tess to straighten
quickly and bang her head on the support post, exac-
erbating the pounding headache she already had. She
didn't know why her mother thought she had to shout,
as if the canvas were a six-foot-thick adobe wall.

"No, not quite, Mama, why?" Tess replied, purposefully vague, though she was brushing varnish on the
last picture. If she left at the same time as her parents, her mother would insist on critiquing the party
with her—who had worn what, who had been flirting
with whom, the quality and quantity of the food, and
so forth—which would require Tess to drive her vehicle abreast of the victoria. After spending most of a
day with social chatter droning into her ears, Tess was
looking forward to being alone with her thoughts. She
already knew what—or rather whom—she was going
to think about.

"It's late. Your father and I are ready to leave."

Under the canvas, Tess pushed an errant lock of hair off her damp forehead, feeling wilted and sticky. She resolved never again to accept any commissions that involved outdoor photography in the heat of a south Texas summer. It was no longer necessary to protect the photographs from the light, but remaining under the hood allowed her to protect the drying photographs from dust and insects.

"You go ahead, then," she said, praying her mother would do so without further questions. "I'll drive back when I'm finished. I won't be too much longer."

She heard Amelia loose a heavy sigh. "Very well, but be home before dark, won't you? Have Sam escort you."

Tess stifled the urge to remind her mother it was only a mile between the Taylors' place and Hennessy Hall. She was not about to ask Uncle Samuel to saddle a horse and escort her as if she were six years old and afraid of the dark. Would her mother ever treat her as a grown woman? Why, her sister Bess had been married at seventeen!

Tess was the youngest child, the only one left at home. Perhaps that explained her mother's overprotectiveness. She resolved to be more patient with her.

"You need your rest, Tess. Don't forget, church tomorrow, and your brother and his family are coming for Sunday dinner."

She always enjoyed going to the little church in Chapin they had always attended, and it would be good for her mother to see Robert and his family. They lived in Houston and weren't able to visit often. Having three lively grandchildren around would distract her mother, and surely Tess could gain some breathing room.

"Well, aren't you going to come out from beneath

that thing and tell your parents goodbye?" Amelia asked, her tone reproachful.

It wasn't as if they were going to be parted for more than an hour, but Tess deemed her last picture dry enough, so she obliged her mother by throwing the flap open and giving her mother an affectionate kiss on the cheek.

When she drew back, she found her mother staring at one of the portraits she had just finished and pinned up to dry. Sandoval Parrish's image stared back at them, his eyes dark and probing, as if he wanted to penetrate the soul of whoever gazed at the picture. There was definitely something about the man that disturbed Tess's peace, though she could not have said how, precisely.

Amelia's peace had apparently been disturbed as well. "Sam Taylor introduced you to *that man?* He must have done it when I wasn't looking. Why, I'm going to give him a piece of my mind," her mother said indignantly, snatching the picture from where it was pinned on the drying board and whirling around.

"Mama, it's not completely dry. Be careful!" Tess pleaded, following her and hoping she would not have to tell Parrish her mother had ruined the picture and he would have to sit for it again. She couldn't help glancing around to see if Parrish was still around and had heard her mother, but she saw no sign of him.

Her mother, however, had spotted her husband and Taylor standing by the hitched and ready victoria, and was already sailing off in their direction, her bearing rigid with indignation, brandishing the photograph in front of her.

"Mama, please, he only sat for a picture!" Tess protested, not wanting Uncle Samuel to be the victim of one of her mother's dramatic scenes. She knew better than to mention that her godfather had practically thrown the two of them together. She was also unwilling to admit—even to herself—that there had been more in Parrish's eyes than the mere politeness and cooperation a subject would give a photographer.

"Sam Taylor, what were you *thinking?*" Amelia demanded.

"What's wrong, Amelia?" Taylor asked, his face honestly confused. He looked to Patrick Hennessy for enlightenment, but seeing his friend looking as surprised as he was at Amelia's outburst, turned back to her. "Did I do something to upset you, dear lady?"

"As if you didn't know," Amelia Hennessy snapped. "Introducing *that man* to our youngest *daughter.* Why, everyone in Hidalgo County knows he's little more than a bandito!" her mother cried. "I could not believe my eyes when I saw him strolling around the grounds today as if he were as good as anyone else. Why on earth would you invite such a man, let alone introduce him to an innocent girl?"

Her father peered at the photograph, and when he looked up, his eyes were troubled. "So that's who that was. Sam, I hear tell he's rumored to be a compadre of Delgado himself." The questioning note in his voice echoed his wife's concern.

It was no light charge. Delgado was a notorious Mexican outlaw who raided Texas ranches along the Rio Grande, then ran back across the border with his loot—horses, jewelry, guns, sometimes even a rancher's entire herd of cattle.

"Don't believe everything you hear, Patrick," Sam protested. "I've known Sandoval Parrish since he was just a sprout, back in my days as a Ranger. You surely don't think I'd introduce my goddaughter to a bad hombre, do you? I'd ride the river with that man anytime."

Tess blinked in surprise. In Texas, saying a man was good enough to ride the river with was high praise. It meant he was as trustworthy as they came.

And saying it was enough, apparently, to leave her voluble mother speechless.

Seeing that, Sam pressed his advantage. "And like Tessie said, all she did was take his picture."

Tess smiled at the nickname, one she hadn't heard him use in years. But Amelia Hennessy was never speechless for long. Handing the picture back to her daughter, she said, "Tess is our youngest child, and I'll thank you to ask us before you introduce her to anyone, Samuel Taylor."

Samuel hung his head. "Yes, ma'am. I'm sorry, Amelia, I didn't mean t' ruffle your feathers."

Patrick sighed. "No harm done," he assured his friend. "As you say, she only took his picture."

"And a fine job she did, too," Sam said, glancing at it. "Not only Parrish's, but all the ones she took today. Everyone told me how pleased they were. I'm much obliged to your daughter, Amelia and Patrick. Tess, why don't you come up to the house and we'll settle up?"

The sun was sinking behind a distant line of mesquite when the mule pulled Tess's wagon off the palm-lined lane onto the main road. Despite her most diligent efforts to be on her way quickly, Uncle Samuel and Aunt Lula Marie had been in a buoyant, post-party mood and were loath to let her go until Tess finally insisted she must be on her way or her mother would make her father come back to fetch her.

Tess let Ben have his head, for the mule knew the

way home. It had been a very profitable day, Tess mused. With the money she'd been paid today, and the enthusiastic response she'd gotten from the guests that would surely lead to further business, she was that much closer to her goal of traveling to New York City. Portfolio of her best work in hand, she would waltz into the studio of the famed Mathew Brady himself and offer her services. He would be so impressed he'd hire her on the spot.

It was an idea that horrified her mother, who prophesied a dire end to a young lady who ventured anywhere into the Dreadful North, let alone a huge, wicked city such as New York. She would starve to death without the Protection of a Man to see that she ate only in Decent God-fearing Establishments, be accosted by rascals bent on No Good, and her traveling funds would be ripped from their place of safekeeping in the hem of her skirts.

"You have to remember that your mother lived through the War Between the States, darlin'," her father always reminded her. "And while the Yankees never penetrated as far inland as Hidalgo County, it seemed for a while they might. Then we got word of her cousin Lucretia being murdered by bummers during Sherman's March to the Sea. You're her last precious chick in the nest, Tess darlin', and she's anxious to see you married and settled."

"But I'm never going to marry. I want to do something more with my life."

"Darlin', darlin', never say never," her father advised. "Some nice young man may well come along and change your mind. And it's not impossible you might meet him in New York," he'd added, surprising her. "I came ashore there, fresh off the boat from Ireland some thirty-five years ago, and it wasn't so bad a place. If you must go, I'll have Robert escort you there."

Not if, Papa—when. And when she went, she was going alone. She loved her elder brother, but he was just as overprotective as Mama and sure he knew the only right way to do anything. Besides, he had a family to look out for. It would have been fun to have another girl her age along, but once they had become young ladies, all of Tess's school friends had become obsessed with beaux and clothing, and affected to swoon at the idea of leaving all that for some musty old photography studio up north.

One minute Tess's wagon was rolling alone along the shadowy, mesquiteand cactus-lined road; the next, figures like ghosts had emerged from the scrub and formed themselves in lines in front of her wagon and behind it. All of them, dressed in the simple, light-colored clothing of Mexican peasants, were pointing rifles or pistols at her.

Chapter Three

"Hola, señorita," a mustachioed fellow in the center of the road called out, smiling broadly. *"Buenas noches."*

Tess began to shake—not out of fear—or at least, it wasn't mostly fear, but rage. Less than a mile from home, she was now about to forfeit the fifty dollars for which she had labored all day to a handful of banditos. She would have given anything she had for a Winchester carbine in her lap right now.

"I don't have anything you want," she said, hoping she could bluff it out. "Just a camera and a wagon full of chemicals for developing photographs."

The mustachioed man translated her words to the others. Laughter rang out as Tess fumed. She hadn't been put here to amuse them! One evil-eyed man, standing on Mustachio's left, sniggered.

"You don't have anything we want? Ah, *señorita,* I am not so sure about that," he countered with an insolent grin that flashed white teeth against his brown skin.

Tess tried to stare him down with her haughtiest look, but failed. Rage was fast transforming itself into pure, unalloyed fear as she realized they could do anything they wanted with her—*anything*.

With a pang, she made the decision to surrender the fifty dollars and hope they would be content with that. The idea hurt her, but not as much as it would have to give them the camera and supplies. She switched to Spanish. She'd learned it early in a household run by Mexican servants. "All right, I will give you my money, if you're so desperate, but you must leave me my camera and the wagon. It's how I make my living."

The man smiled at her fluent Spanish, but his reply was not conciliatory. "*Señorita,* do you take me for a fool?"

"I—I don't know what you mean," she said, setting her jaw so her teeth wouldn't betray her by chattering. "You're not...are you saying you want the mule, too?" Ben had been at Hennessy Hall since Uncle James had died, and she hated the thought of handing him over to these outlaws. *God, please send someone along this road. Anyone. These men would flee if I wasn't alone.*

You're not alone. I am with you.

The bandito just smiled at her. "*Señorita,* it is good news that you have money—it is added luck for us. But it is not your camera, Señorita Hennessy, that we came for."

"How do you know my name?" Startled by that, the rest of what he said didn't register at first.

"The lady photographer? *Señorita,* you are famous along the Rio Grande."

She was getting very tired of his grin. "But I told you, I make my living with that camera. You can't take it!"

"Oh, but we can, *señorita,*" he said, almost apologetically. "We are, after all, *ladrones*—thieves. It's how we make *our* living."

Now, because he was toying with her, she was angry again. "Are you thinking to sell it? Don't bother—I very much doubt anyone between here and Mexico City would know how to use it!"

Señor Mustachio *tsk-tsked* at her. "*Señorita,* it is clear you have no high opinion of Mexicans." He shrugged. "What you say is true—we would not know how to use it. But *el jefe* has a fancy to have his picture made, as well as a picture history of his exploits, you see."

Nothing he was saying made sense, but she was willing to engage him in conversation as long as she could on the chance that someone might happen along to rescue her. "*El jefe?*" she echoed. "Who's that?"

"Our leader, *señorita.* Perhaps you have heard of him? His name is Delgado."

Delgado, the notorious outlaw her parents and others at the party had been talking about only this afternoon.

"But if none of you knows how to operate a camera," she said desperately, "or even if you did, how to develop the pictures…"

He beamed as if she had suddenly grasped the secret of their plan. "Then, obviously, you will have to come with us to take the pictures, Señorita Hennessy."

"C-come with you? Me? You're *loco!* I'm not going anywhere with you."

Mustachio laughed and said something in rapid-fire Spanish to his fellows. Despite the fury that sent the pulse throbbing in her ears, Tess thought she heard the word *pelirroja,* the same word she'd heard one of the Hennessy housemaids call her. *Redhead.*

As one man, they aimed their weapons at her again.

"You see, you have no choice, *señorita,*" he said.

"But do not worry. If you come with us, you will not be harmed. When Delgado has his pictures, you will be free to return to your home."

Tess had had enough of his carefree banter. "Well, that's just dandy!" she cried. "If you think for one cotton-picking moment I'm going to tamely disappear and frighten my mother to death, you'd better think again."

They were beginning to advance, guns still trained on her. Frantically she looked backward, then ahead, but there was no one on the road but herself and the bandits. With nothing else to do, she opened her mouth and screamed. *Please, God, let someone hear me!*

She had not guessed any of the bandits could move so fast, but in what seemed like the blink of an eye Tess had been yanked off the seat of her wagon by the evil-eyed man who had laughed at her. He stank of stale onions, garlic and sweat.

Tess went wild, screaming and kicking. She knew that one of her kicks must have connected with something tender when she heard the man grunt and loose his hold on her.

"*Bruja!*"

In that instant she broke free and, crazy with hope, began to run.

Tess had only covered a few yards when she was tackled by one of the bandits, knocking the wind out of her. Her cheek stung from sliding against a rough rock and her mouth was gritty with dust, but before she could gather enough air to scream again, Tess found herself gagged and bound at her wrists and ankles. In mere moments she was lifted into the bed of the wagon and laid out in the center, surrounded by her bottles of chemicals. She felt the wagon lurch forward and realized they were moving off the road and into the brush.

Where were they taking her? Would she ever see home again? If only she had listened to her mother and gone home when they had, or had Uncle Samuel ride along with her! Or were they so determined to capture the "lady photographer" that the presence of others would have been no deterrent, and might have resulted in her parents' murders? Now, bowling along over the rocky scrubland as night fell, covered by the heavy canvas, no one would see her being taken away from everyone and everything she knew. Her stomach churned with nausea and fear.

Tess began to sob, soundlessly because of the gag, but soon her inability to clear her nostrils made breathing too difficult to continue crying. Then she could only lie there, feel the lurching and jerking as the wheels rolled over the uneven ground, and watch the last hints of light disappear from the tiny chinks in the sideboards of the wagon bed. At last, exhausted by terror, she slept.

Tess woke because of a sudden absence of the rocking, swaying movement that had haunted her dreams. Were they stopping temporarily, or had they reached Delgado's hideout?

Before she could listen for clues to the answer, the canvas under which she lay was shoved back off the wagon bed, blinding her with a sudden blast of sunlight. With her wrists and ankles still tied, Tess could only clench her eyes tightly shut.

"Idiotas! Necios!"

The man went on yelling in Spanish so rapidly that Tess could only comprehend that someone was being berated. She assumed it must be Delgado. After all, he would not want his henchmen to manhandle the lady who was about to make him immortal. Now she kept

her eyes closed because she was afraid to have her worst
fears confirmed. The voice barked out another spate of
words, clearly a command, and she felt the bonds at her
wrists and ankles being severed.

Tess knew she could not shut out the reality of her
situation forever. As soon as she could shade her eyes
with one hand against the brilliant sunlight, she raised
herself on one elbow and peered at the speaker.

And saw with astonishment that it was not Delgado
or any other stranger, but Sandoval Parrish who stood
looking at her over the side of the wagon.

"You!" Before she could put together a rational, pru-
dent thought, she had struggled up onto her feet and
launched herself at him, fingers curved into claws.

He caught her easily before she could do any damage, and holding her wrists gently, but with an underlying steely strength, kept them pinioned against the side
of the wagon. His body was next to hers, rather than
directly in front of her, so that even if she were foolish enough to bring up one of her knees, she couldn't
hurt him.

"Calm yourself, Tess Hennessy," he said, in the same
soothing, low voice one would use to soothe a fractious
horse. "No harm is going to come to you."

"No harm?" Tess cried. "I've been kidnapped and
transported to who knows where, and my family has
no idea what has happened to me, and you call that *no
harm?* Sandoval Parrish, you are every bit the scoundrel my mother said you were!" There were no words
for the depth of her hurt and disillusionment with him.
To discover he was the one who had orchestrated her
kidnapping, when she had already been imagining him
coming to her rescue. "How dare you do this to me? I

demand that you escort me and my possessions safely home immediately!"

He gazed down at her, his dark eyes serious, but there was an amused little curve at the corners of his mouth that betrayed the fact that he was struggling mightily not to laugh at her.

"Tess, Tess, you are in *no* position to demand anything," he told her, and now there was no merriment playing about his lips at all. "As you have guessed, you are many, many miles away from your home, and only I stand between you and a camp full of very rough hombres indeed."

She looked beyond him and saw that what he was saying was too awfully true. There must have been a score, at least, of swarthy men in ragged clothing watching this interplay between Parrish and her, and each man looked more dangerous than the one next to him.

"How very comforting," she fairly spat at him. "And my name, as I told you before, is *Miss Hennessy.*"

"Miss Hennessy, then," he said in that musical, accented voice that seemed to caress her senses. "I would set your mind at ease about your parents. They have been left word that you are safe and will be returned unharmed."

"Unharmed if they raise a ransom, you mean? What sum are you demanding for me? Your men have already taken possession of the fifty dollars I earned from my godfather."

He raised an eyebrow, clearly surprised. "If money was taken from you, it will be returned," he promised, then called sharply over his shoulder, "Esteban?"

The man Tess had mentally named Mustachio stepped forward. "*Sí,* Sandoval?"

"Give the lady back her money. I told you nothing

was to be taken from her, and you have disobeyed. Just as you did by transporting her in such a position of discomfort."

Esteban smiled sheepishly at her and held out a small, cloth drawstring bag which clinked as Parrish took it from him.

"And there is no question of ransom, Te—Miss Hennessy," Parrish went on. "You will be staying among us for a time to take pictures of Diego Delgado and his men, and possibly some pictures of our adventures— though I understand the limitations of the camera make it impossible to portray us in the midst of action."

"No, I would have to pose you amid your stolen booty, afterwards," she hissed at him.

He shrugged, as if her intended insult did not touch him. "Once Delgado is satisfied that he has pictures enough to record his adventures for posterity, you will be escorted safely home."

All she could do was stare at him, her brain reeling at the implications of what he had said.

"I'll find a way to escape," she whispered at least, hating the shakiness of her voice. "If not with my camera, then without it. I won't stay here in a camp of outlaws, with only your promise to protect me."

He lowered his head so that his lips were mere inches from hers. "I would not advise that, Miss Hennessy. You are across the Rio Grande, in territory foreign to you, and you're clearly a *gringa.* Not only Delgado's men roam this land, but other *bandoleros* much less civilized than these, not to mention Apaches and Comancheros. As I have said, I will protect you from all harm. I make this promise before God, and I consider it a sacred promise. And one other thing you have said is wrong, Miss Hennessy."

"Oh, and what is that?" she asked.

"That God does not know where you are. He does know, Miss Hennessy—Tess. And if the promise of my protection does not comfort you, the promise that He always knows where you are, and will keep you safe, should give you all the assurance you need."

Chapter Four

$\sim$

He could tell by her sudden stillness that his words had made Tess think. She looked down, blinking. When she lifted her face again, her expression was calmer, though her blue eyes still flashed with defiance.

She's afraid, he realized. What woman wouldn't be, in these circumstances? But she doesn't want to show it. Most women would have swooned by now, or succumbed to a bout of hysterics. His admiration for her spirit grew.

"You're right, He does know where I am. And if you believe in God, how can you take part in something like this?" She made a sweeping gesture as if to include everything—her kidnapping, the camp and all of Delgado's men.

He allowed his face to show polite regret and shrugged. "A man must earn his bread in the best way he is able."

"Having ranches on both sides of the river wasn't enough for you?"

Inwardly he winced at her scornful tone, much preferring the spark of interest he had seen in her eyes at the barbecue. He wished he could take her into his confidence, tell her she had no reason to fear him, that he was on the side of justice, but it was too dangerous. There were too many eyes on them right now.

"Ah, where is the zest in that? There is no excitement," he said, knowing his words would make her more furious still, but that she would control herself because she knew she must.

"So being a *bandolero* is a sport for you?" Tess exclaimed, but didn't wait for an answer before asking another outraged question. "You never did intend to come and pick up your framed picture at my shop on Tuesday, did you?" she asked then. "That was just a ruse. And you probably don't even have a mother, do you? Much less one having a birthday soon."

"On the contrary, Miss Hennessy, my mother is very much alive, living on my ranch north of Chapin, and will be very pleased with the picture you have taken of me, frame or no frame. You do have it with you, don't you?"

She nodded sullenly, pointing into the wagon.

"And if you had not driven home by yourself, then yes, the appointment on Tuesday would have been necessary—although a kidnapping raid in broad daylight in a town, involving seizing you, packing up your wagon and hitching up your mule, would have been much more risky, not to mention difficult."

Again, she appeared to consider his words, and it was a long moment before she spoke again.

"Do you think that my parents will just tamely wait for me to return?" she asked. "You don't know my father. He'll have the Texas Rangers after you—maybe even the army!"

He couldn't help grinning at the irony of what she was saying, and knew she would take it as insolence.

Which she did. "You think I'm joking? Mister, you just took hold of a tiger's tail!" she cried.

"Miss Hennessy, don't you think if the *Rinches*—the Rangers—or the army were capable of catching us, they would have long ago?"

He thought she would have another retort for him, but just then he saw her look behind him, and heard footsteps approaching.

"Ah, our guest has arrived at last, eh?" Delgado remarked in Spanish.

"Sí, jefe," Sandoval said, turning to face the outlaw leader, and switched to English, which Delgado understood as well. "Miss Teresa Hennessy, may I present Diego Delgado, leader of our band, and the reason you are here."

He saw Tess's eyes widen as she beheld Delgado, who had dressed for the occasion in the spotless uniform of a Mexican *coronel,* which had been cleverly laundered of its bloodstains and mended by Delores, Esteban's old mother, to hide the bullet holes that had caused the uniform's sudden availability.

Delgado swept her a bow as courtly as any European count could have made.

"Señorita Hennessy, I am delighted you were able to join us, especially on such…shall we say 'short notice'?" His English was as flawless as Sandoval's, though more heavily accented.

"Mr. Delgado," she replied, "the pleasure is all yours. I am here very much against my will."

He stared at Tess for a moment as if he was not sure he had heard her correctly, and then he threw back his head and roared with laughter. "'The pleasure is all yours,' she says!" he exclaimed, slapping his side gleefully. "Sandoval, you said she was a feisty one and you were correct, amigo! *Ay, caramba,* I like her!"

Delgado's eyes gleamed as, coming toward her, he looked her up and down, as if she were an untamed mare that needed breaking, and suddenly Sandoval had to fight the urge to clench his fists. "*Jefe,* I have promised her she need not be afraid, for she will be safe among us," he said quickly, hoping Delgado would get the hint.

It seemed he did, for Delgado took a step back. "*Señorita,* you will be as safe here as in the midst of a church," he said, sweeping her another bow. "I, Delgado, have sworn it." He turned and repeated his words in Spanish for the benefit of his men. "Any man who touches this lady will answer to me, and will pay with his life, you understand, amigos?"

There was a resounding chorus of agreement.

Delgado turned back to Tess. "You see, they agree. You will be as their *hermana,* their sister." He made a gesture with his hand to indicate that he considered this problem solved. "And so you are here to take my picture, Señorita Hennessy? Why don't we start now, eh? Do I not appear magnificent in uniform?"

Now that her worst fears had been relieved somewhat, Sandoval saw the lines of weariness etched on her face. "*Jefe,* Señorita Hennessy has traveled a long way overnight bound and gagged. She has not eaten anything, I'll wager, since yesterday afternoon. Perhaps the picture taking could wait a little while until she has broken her fast and rested a bit?"

Delgado looked surprised. "But, of course! How remiss of me not to realize how tired she must be, and how hungry. Delores!" he called over his shoulder to the older woman who had been hovering nearby. "Cook

this young lady some breakfast. She is famished! And
then assist her to settle in. Get her some comfortable
clothes—Alma's will fit her, I am sure." His face darkened slightly as he said the last, and Sandoval knew
he was thinking of his last mistress, who had become
so jealous and demanding that Sandoval had finally
taken her back to the village from which he had lured
her. "Perhaps I can pose for the *señorita* this afternoon
instead? Until then, *señorita*," he said, bowing again.

Sandoval saw Tess nod uncertainly as Delgado
walked away. "Come with me, Miss Hennessy," he
said. "I hope you don't mind if your breakfast is a little
spicy. Delores makes the best *huevos rancheros* I've
ever tasted. Esteban will unhitch your mule and bring
your supplies to that adobe over there. It's where you
will be staying."

Now that the outlaw leader was no longer favoring
her with his bold stare, and the other outlaws were busy-
ing themselves elsewhere, Tess felt freer to examine
her surroundings as she followed Parrish to where the
old woman was stirring something into a skillet over
an open fire. Beyond them, flush against the high red-
rock walls that soared perhaps forty feet above them,
sat three adobe huts. One of them was large, and stood
on the left end of the row; the other two, including the
one Sandoval had indicated as hers, were smaller.

"That one's Delgado's," Parrish said, pointing to the
large one farthest from hers. "That one is mine," he
added, pointing to the one in the middle. "The rest of
the men sleep by the fire."

"So you really are Delgado's right-hand man," she
murmured. "No humble bedroll for Sandoval Parrish."
As she had expected, he only shrugged at her barb.

She was reassured by the fact that Parrish's building was situated between Delgado's and hers, but despite his earlier words, how safe was she, really, with Parrish?

Lord, protect me. She had a comforting sense of God's presence, but knew that sometimes evil things befell God's children for reasons they might never understand on this earth.

A creek, with a wooden plank bridge spanning it in the middle, mirrored the curve of the rock walls and served to separate the adobes from the rest of the camp. There were two corrals, one empty, one full of horses. Ben was now being led into the latter. Many of the horses had carried the men who had kidnapped her last night, but a tall, rangy black mustang she hadn't seen before pranced up now to challenge the newcomer, laying back his ears and snorting threateningly. Ben flattened his own longer ears against his skull, brayed and whirled around, lashing out with his heels. His hooves missed the mustang. The black horse turned and trotted away, still snorting.

Tess smiled, then saw that Sandoval was watching her. "My mule doesn't cotton to bullying," she said.

"And neither does his mistress, I'm thinking. Good for you, Miss Hennessy." They had reached the campfire now, and Parrish smiled at the older woman who turned to face them. "Delores, this is Señorita Teresa Hennessy, the photographer and our guest," he said in Spanish, then added, "and she speaks Spanish." He turned back to Tess. "It's a good thing, since Delores speaks little English."

"Mucho gusto, señorita," the older woman said, smiling warmly at her, then invited her to have a seat on a pile of old blankets behind Tess. Delores then turned back to the eggs, peppers, onions and tomatoes she

was cooking. The wind carried a whiff of the savory, spicy smell and all at once Tess realized how hungry she was. It had been probably more than fourteen hours since she had eaten.

She sank onto the horse blankets, her aching bones protesting at the long, bumpy ride, and smiled gratefully as the woman handed her a tin cup full of steaming hot coffee poured from a pot resting on hot stones within the fire ring. She caught sight of her dusty navy skirt as she drank, and was thankful all over again that she had been wearing sensible, modest clothing. She could only imagine how nervous she would have felt among these outlaws if she had been wearing the frilly, frivolous dress her mother had wanted her to wear.

She wondered what the clothes being loaned to her by the aforementioned Alma would look like, and if Alma would begrudge her the loan. She prayed the garments would be decent—if Delgado and Parrish thought she was going to parade around in revealing clothing like a cantina girl, they had better think again!

Minutes later Delores had deposited tin plates heaped with eggs and tortillas in both her and Parrish's laps, and refilled their coffee. Tess ate the spicy food ravenously, and saw out of the corner of her eye that Parrish was doing likewise. It was a surprisingly companionable moment. For a few minutes, at least, Tess forgot she was so angry with him for involving her in this strange situation.

After they both had finished, Parrish excused himself, and Delores took their plates away, returned and gestured for Tess to follow her into the small adobe building designated as hers. The wagon had been left right outside the door.

The door itself was a colorfully woven blanket,

which Delores pushed aside so Tess could enter, though the lintel was so low Tess had to duck her head. The room was bigger than it had looked from the outside. Thin, makeshift curtains that had obviously been a pair of dish towels covered a small window. The interior was divided into a larger and a smaller room by means of an ornate screen—where had he stolen that? The larger room contained nothing but a rocking chair—probably also booty—and a pallet on the floor.

Delores mumbled something, pointing at the screen, and went back outside.

Tess went and peeked behind the screen. Here she found a pallet with threadbare but clean sheets, a pillow and a light blanket, and a large brass-bound trunk. Lifting the lid, she found a small, purple cut-glass stoppered bottle lying atop several items of folded clothing. Unable to resist her curiosity, she wiggled the stopper until it came out and held it near her nose. The bottle was empty, but the perfume it had held had been musky and overpowering—not the type of scent a demure woman would use. Had this been Alma's? Where was she now? What had happened to her?

Restoppering the bottle and setting it aside, she pulled out the garments and examined them. There were two skirts, one a much-laundered, faded-brick red, the other of a dingy hue that must have originally been green. Beneath them she found two bleached-muslin blouses with gathered, bright embroidery-banded sleeves and drawstring necklines. There were also a pair of fine white lawn camisoles beneath them and a lace-trimmed nightgown.

The last items in the trunk were the most surprising—a tarnished, brass-framed hand mirror that had a diagonal crack bisecting the glass, a black lace mantilla

and a pair of combs. For all her practical habits when
it came to clothing, Tess wouldn't have been female if
the mantilla hadn't made her sigh with pure feminine
delight and reach out to wrap the garment around her
head. Instantly, she felt transformed into a woman who
was mysterious, unpredictable—fascinating!

Tess sighed and refolded the garment. It wasn't likely
she'd ever have occasion to wear it, unless perhaps Delgado compelled his band to attend church on Sundays.
The thought made her giggle.

It was getting increasingly warm as the sun rose
higher above the canyon. Tess supposed she had better
try on the borrowed garments so she would have something cooler to wear than the perspiration-dampened
clothing she had arrived in. Peeking outside, she saw
no one heading toward her hut, so she stepped back behind the screen and stripped off the dusty navy skirt and
waist and pulled one of the blouses over her head. The
soft, worn fabric felt soothing as it settled around her
shoulders. Tying the drawstring at the neck in a bow,
Tess studied herself in the cracked mirror, and supposed
the neckline was modest enough, though if the drawstring were loosened, it would sink lower around her
shoulders. The lower neckline of the blouse revealed
the small, gold cross necklace which she always wore,
reminding Tess that just as Parrish had said, God was
with her, even here in this outlaw camp.

Next she dropped the skirt over her head. It also fas-
tened with a drawstring. Alma must have been a few
inches shorter than she was, for the skirt revealed her
ankles, but she supposed if she kept her boots and stockings on, it would be all right.

She lifted the curtain again and gazed around the
camp, seeing a few men caring for the horses, but there

was no sign of Sandoval or Delgado. She wondered what Sandoval was doing.

Her brain ached with fatigue, her eyes felt heavy. The pallet looked so inviting. She hadn't slept soundly as the wagon had rolled over the uneven ground, and she was still tired. It wouldn't hurt to lie down until someone fetched her....

Chapter Five

"Is Francisco here?" Patrick Hennessy tried to sound calm, but he couldn't keep the anxiety from his voice. He exchanged a look with Sam Taylor, who had come with him. Sam looked as if he hadn't slept a wink last night, either.

"*Sí, señor,* I will call him," Francisco's father said, but before he could do so, the boy appeared at the door of their small house. He must have heard the approaching horses.

"*Hola,* Señor Hennessy, Señor Taylor," he said, smiling upward and raising a hand in greeting.

"Good morning to you, Francisco," Patrick said, but did not return his smile. "Francisco, Tess is missing," he said. "She never came home from Mr. Taylor's barbecue last night. The housemaid found a note in her room, saying she was all right, but it wasn't in her handwriting. Her mother is frantic, as you can imagine."

Francisco blinked and his eyes widened in alarm.

"Have you seen her?" Patrick asked.

"No, *señor.* What could have happened to her?"

Patrick could see his surprise at the news was genuine. The boy looked as worried as he felt. He had reason to be grateful to her. After all, Tess was his friend as well as his employer. She'd taught him an unusual skill, developing photographs and mounting them, passing on a gift her uncle had given to her.

"We don't know," Patrick Hennessy said, wiping a weary hand over his face. "We're just checking to see if she might have stopped here, or told you she was going anywhere. She…she didn't say anything about going to New York, did she?" His heart told him his daughter wouldn't sneak off like that, without even saying good-bye, but he had to ask.

The boy shook his head vehemently. "She wouldn't have gone to New York, *señor,* this I know. She told me she wasn't ready for that. She said she had to have something…." He clearly struggled for the English word. "A…a collection of pictures, do you know what I mean?"

"A portfolio?" Samuel Taylor asked.

Francisco seized upon the word. "*Sí, sí,* a portfolio. To show Señor Brady, the great master of photographers. She said she didn't have enough good pictures yet."

Patrick's gaze sought Sam's again as he considered the boy's words. He felt waves of apprehension dancing down his spine.

Patrick saw the boy move a step closer to his father, as if he feared the two men wouldn't believe him, and managed, through his worry, to also feel regret that he had caused the boy to be afraid. The Hennessys and the Taylors and most of their Anglo neighbors had always lived in harmony with the *Tejanos* among them, but prejudice and bigotry were not unknown among the Anglos.

"You…you haven't heard of anything unusual happening, have you, Francisco? Señor Luna?" Patrick persisted, including Francisco's father in his question.

"Anything happening, *señor?* What do you mean?"

"Anything like raiding," Taylor answered for Hennessy, his voice stern, uncompromising, like that of the Ranger captain he had been in his younger days.

"*Señores,* one of my neighbors tells me Delgado's men were seen last night, riding along the main road about sundown. This man, he did not challenge them, but hid so they would not see him."

The very thing Patrick had feared. "Oh, no," he breathed. "Not Delgado! How am I going to tell her mother Delgado took her?"

Sam still looked as worried as he, but he spoke quickly. "I never heard tell of any bandit troubling to leave the family a note, and in English, at that. I don't reckon Delgado knows how to write Spanish, let alone English. No, there's got t' be more to this disappearance than that, but I'll be cussed if I know what."

"We've got to go see the Rangers," Patrick said. "They have to go after her!"

"Miss Hennessy?" Sandoval called, standing outside the blanket-door, but there was no answer. "Tess, it's Sandoval." Still no answer, so at last he stepped inside the hut. As his eyes adjusted to the cool darkness of the main room, he saw she was not here.

Where could she have gone? Could she have been so foolish as to try to escape already? But where would she have gone? It was not as if she could climb the steep vertical wall of the canyon, or walk right past his compadres who were dicing in the shade, cleaning guns or caring for the horses.

And then, as he stood still in the semidarkness, he

heard the quiet, even sound of her breathing, beyond the blanket that divided the room. Moving quietly, he crossed the room in three quick strides and pushed the curtain aside to peer into the sleeping area.

Tess was lying on her side on the pallet, fully clothed in her new, borrowed garments, and fast asleep. One arm lay under the pillow, the other cradled her cheek. Her knees were flexed beneath the faded skirt so that only the tips of her toes stuck out. Her features were relaxed in slumber, the fear and anger that had marched across them earlier entirely absent. She looked so innocent....

As innocent as Pilar had looked before Delgado had ridden into Montemorelos, luring her into leaving with him. *As I live and breathe, Tess Hennessy, this will not happen to you,* he swore silently. He would not fail her as he had failed Pilar.

A wave of longing passed over Sandoval as he continued to look at her. He wanted to drink in the sight of her sleeping until she woke up, even if it took hours, but he knew he couldn't. Even if Delgado wouldn't become impatient and come looking for him, he didn't want to frighten her if she woke and found him staring down at her.

Sandoval stepped carefully and soundlessly backward, letting the blanket fall back into place across the doorway. He called again, louder this time: "Miss Hennessy? Tess? It's time to wake up. It's Parrish, and I've come to take you to Delgado. He's ready to have his picture made."

He heard her utter a quick, involuntary cry of alarm and the pallet rustled. Sandoval imagined her pushing herself up into a sitting position and stretching, perhaps trying to remember where she was.

"I... I guess I fell asleep," he heard her murmur. "Wh-what time is it?"

Sandoval smiled to himself. There were no clocks in the canyon hideout. The banditos rose with the sun and, when not going raiding, ate and slept when they wanted.

"Late afternoon, Miss Hennessy. You slept through lunch. But no matter. I am sure you needed the rest after your journey, and Delores will be making supper before long."

"Oh! I—I didn't mean to sleep so long! I'll be right out."

He forced himself to sound casual, even disinterested. "Take your time, Miss Hennessy. Delgado merely thought you might want to take advantage of the afternoon light," he said, stepping back outside. "With your permission, I'll have Esteban and Manuel pull your wagon of supplies over in front of Delgado's hut."

She joined him three minutes later, one side of her face still faintly imprinted with the mark of the wrinkled pillowcase, and tendrils of escaping hair curling around her face. "Your new garments become you," Sandoval told her. It was the truth. Her dark-blue skirt and long-sleeved blouse had masked the delicacy of her bones and her womanly form. Her neck was long and elegant, rising above the gleaming, golden cross necklace he spotted just above the drawstring. She was more beautiful in these simple garments than most women would be in satin and lace.

He swallowed with difficulty, trying to look away. "I hope they are comfortable?"

She nodded, gazing down at them. "I daresay they're more practical than what I wore here."

"One might almost think you a *señorita* in a Mexican village, were it not for this," he said, reaching out and touching the thick plait that ran halfway down her back. "It's an unusual color for a *mexicana*." He saw her blush then, and let go of her hair. What had he been thinking, to take such a liberty?

Then she looked very directly at him and asked, "Who's Alma?"

The question surprised him so much that he replied in the same straightforward way. "Delgado's former mistress. Why?"

She blinked at the information, but went determinedly on. "These are her clothes. I was wondering if she minds my borrowing them. Is she here somewhere?" She peered beyond the little creek as if she expected the woman to be standing just beyond it, glaring at her.

"She is no longer with us, Miss Hennessy," he told her.

Tess gasped. "He killed her? Why?"

He could have kicked himself for phrasing the information that way as he saw the color drain from her face and her eyes widen. "No! I meant that she and Delgado are no longer together," he said quickly. "The last I heard she was living in a village somewhere in the state of Zacatecas."

"What…what was she like?" Tess asked. "Was she beautiful? Why did she leave?" Her blue eyes, alight with curiosity, made her face even more appealing.

"Very beautiful. But very temperamental. She didn't leave willingly. Delgado got tired of her jealousy and her scenes, and left her there with a promise to visit her often. He's never gone back."

Tess looked thoughtful, and perhaps would have asked more, but at that moment Delgado stepped out of his adobe, once more dressed in his fancy Mexican colonel's uniform, complete with ornamental rapier at his side.

"Ah, there you are!" he called, catching sight of them. "Come, come, Señorita Hennessy. I know you will not want to lose the light."

It was many hours till sundown, but once Delgado was ready to do something, there was no gainsaying him, and they walked toward his hut, just as Esteban and Manuel arrived to move the wagon.

"You have had a little siesta, yes?" he said to Tess, as the two men muscled the cart over beside them. "I hope you feel rested."

She nodded.

"And you find your quarters *cómodo*—comfortable? You have everything you need?" His eyes raked over her, and Sandoval saw him taking in her different appearance now that she had changed from her Anglo garments. If he had any thoughts about her wearing his discarded mistress's left-behind clothing, it didn't show in his opaque gaze.

"Yes, it's fine. I—I don't need anything." She darted a glance at Sandoval, and her blue eyes flashed another story. *Except my freedom*.

"*Bueno*. We will commence then," he said, as the two henchmen carried out an ornately carved ebony wood chair padded in red velvet. It was practically a throne.

Tess posed Delgado in the chair, much as she had posed Sandoval—had it only been yesterday?—and took his picture, then disappeared under the canvas to begin the development process. Sandoval saw Delgado fidget as he waited, sweating in the heavy uniform, for Tess to reappear.

"Is that something I could do for you, Miss Hennessy?" Sandoval called, stepping forward.

"I—I suppose it would make things quicker," she said. "I'll show you what to do after I take the next picture. If you came in now, the light would harm this one."

When Tess emerged, she said, "Why don't we pose you in a more active way this time? You could draw your sword, for example."

Delgado beamed. "I believe you have the soul of an artist, Señorita Hennessy." Grinning, he struck a pose, his right arm holding the sword dramatically aloft, his left hand on his hip.

As he had suggested, after Tess removed the collodion plate from this exposure, Sandoval ducked under the canvas with her. It was hard to force himself to pay attention as she showed him how to use the metal dippers to lower the plate into the developing bath, rather than to savor her nearness in the murky half light, but he didn't want to ruin her pictures.

When she was ready to take the next exposure, she suggested, "This time, Mr. Delgado, why don't you do like so…?" She lunged forward as if to parry with an imaginary rapier.

Delgado was clearly delighted at her idea and slid into the pose. "*Señorita,* you are *un genio,* a genius, truly! I already know I will be very pleased with your work, for the world will see Diego Delgado for the warrior he truly is."

Tess couldn't help but smile at his enthusiasm but laid a finger on her lips. "No talking now, Mr. Delgado, until we have made the exposure."

Sandoval could hardly hide his own amusement as he ducked under the tent to develop picture after picture. If Tess was at all intimidated by her situation, she was hiding it well, and she was demonstrating a natural flair for appealing to Delgado's vanity and sense of the dramatic. Sandoval knew Delgado saw himself not as a mere bandit leader, but something more heroic, more like Robin Hood leading his merry men, and Tess had instinctively sensed that, too.

They had taken perhaps half a dozen pictures, and Sandoval had just emerged from the tent after developing the last one, when Delgado decided he wanted to have Tess take his picture while he sat on his stallion.

Sandoval saw Tess glance skyward. "I'm afraid we are losing the light, Señor Delgado," she said, pointing to the sun, which was beginning to make its descent behind the canyon wall. "Perhaps we could do that tomorrow?"

"Ah, but tomorrow Delgado and his men ride at dawn," Delgado said, thumping his chest with one fist. "We will go on a raid, and there will be much booty! But perhaps that would be the ideal time for you to take my picture, eh? Both before, when I am ready to ride out on a victorious raid, and after, surrounded by fabulous plunder, *si?*"

Tess nodded. "I will be ready to take the picture when you depart, Mr. Delgado."

"Please, Señorita Hennessy, you must call me Diego," Delgado insisted. He came forward and took her hand, kissing it. "And you must dine with me tonight in my quarters. I usually dine with my men, but tonight we must celebrate your arrival. And you will bring me the developed pictures then, all right?"

Sandoval saw Tess dart a frightened look at him, but before he could speak up, Delgado said, "Ah, you need not worry for your virtue, *señorita,* for I will have Sandoval dine with us. And Delores will be serving the meal, so that will be chaperones enough, *si?*"

"*Sí*—that is, yes, I suppose that would be all right…
Señor Delgado—"

Delgado wagged a finger at her playfully. "Ah-ah-ah, I am *Diego* to you, at least when the other men are not present," he said.

"D-Diego, then," she stammered. "Yes, I will have dinner with you and Mr. Parrish."

"*Bueno*," he said, and turned on his heel, then halted. "Oh, and wear your hair down, eh? It is such a lovely color—I would see the full effect of its fire." It was a command, not a suggestion. He turned again and disappeared inside.

Sandoval felt his jaw clench and when he looked down, both hands had tightened into fists. He saw that Tess was staring at the bandit leader's door and gnawing her lower lip.

He stepped closer so he could speak in a lowered voice. "Don't worry, Miss Hennessy, I'll be there the entire time," he said.

"Until he orders you to leave," she fretted.

He made a dismissive gesture. "Don't worry. He likes to play at being the suave courtier, just as he reveled at posing as the master swordsman a few minutes ago," he said reassuringly, but inwardly he was not so sure. He was six kinds of a fool to have gotten Tess involved in this. He ought to have foreseen that, having banished his woman weeks ago, Delgado would find Tess's beauty tempting. He was going to have to walk a tightrope to fulfill both his promise to Pilar and to Tess.

Chapter Six

"Dinner is ready, Miss Hennessy," Sandoval called through Tess's door. "Delgado sent me to fetch you. Are you ready?"

She pulled the blanket door-covering aside, and he saw to his surprise Tess had not complied with Delgado's command—instead of wearing her glorious, red hair down, it was drawn up in an elegant chignon held in place by decorative combs. Was it meant to be a subtle bit of defiance?

Good for you, he cheered inwardly, but then he saw how the hairstyle, coupled with the simple drawstring neckline of the *camisa,* left an enticing amount of her neck and shoulders bare for a man's gaze. And perhaps she hadn't noticed the subtle hints of Alma's perfume that clung to the fabric. Sandoval smothered a groan. He was going to have his work cut out for him to protect Tess Hennessy without appearing to do so.

"The photographs are ready," she said, pointing to where they lay, pinned to a drying board on the earthen floor. "Should I bring them?"

Sandoval shook his head. "No, let's wait until after the meal," he suggested. When we might need a diversion to distract Delgado from your very lovely self, he thought.

"I can always go get them for you," he said.

"And leave me alone with him? Don't you dare."

He saw that beneath her bravado, she was nervous. "Very well," he agreed. "We can send Delores for them."

Delgado opened his door—a real door—before they even had a chance to knock. "Good evening, Miss Hennessy," he said smoothly, beckoning them inside. "And to you, too, Sandoval, of course. But you put your hair up, *señorita!*"

"I'm sorry, but my hair is just so thick and heavy, and it's so very hot. I hope you don't mind," she said.

"Mind? Of course not!" Delgado exclaimed, and Sandoval saw that he, too, was unable to take his eyes from her graceful neck and shoulders. "I want above all things that you should be comfortable here, Señorita Tess. And it happens that I have just the thing for you," he added, crossing the room to a mahogany desk and opening a drawer. When he turned around, he held out an object to her—an ivory-handled fan.

"A gift for you, Señorita Tess," Delgado murmured, watching in patent delight as she opened it and admired the hand-painted floral design revealed when she unfurled it. The breeze she created with the fan fluttered the fiery-red, curling tendrils about her forehead.

"Oh, but I could not accept such a lovely thing. I'll just use it while I am here tonight."

"Nonsense, I want you to have it," the outlaw leader insisted. "Now come, dinner awaits you. I hope it will be to your liking."

Delgado gestured toward one end of a long, rectangular table lit by long beeswax tapers flickering in a pair of silver candelabra. Three place settings of elab-

orately painted china, heavy silverware, and cut-glass
goblets stood at the ready. A nearby sideboard was
heaped with an array of savory-smelling dishes.

Delgado held a chair for Tess on his right and indicated that Sandoval was to take the seat on his left, so
that Sandoval was sitting opposite her. Delores came
forward and filled the cut-glass crystal goblets with
claret from a crystal decanter.

"I... Would it be possible for me to have water instead, please, Mr. Delgado?" Tess asked, looking uneasily at the blood-red liquid. "I... I don't drink spirits,
you see."

Delgado blinked. "You are...how do you say it? A
teetotaler? I see," he said when she nodded shyly. "Delores! *Agua para la señorita, por favor,*" he said, and
the old woman came forward with another glass and
a pitcher. "That is most commendable, *señorita.*" He
turned to Sandoval. "I think we should toast our lovely
guest, do you not? *¡Salud!*" he said, lifting his glass,
and Sandoval did likewise. "To our guest, Tess Hennessy, a long and happy life!"

Sandoval watched as a faint flush of color rose up
Tess's cheeks. "Thank you," she said, leaving her eyes
downcast. Sandoval suspected she had never been
toasted before in her life, and marveled at the blind-
ness of Anglo men.

"Delores has surpassed herself tonight," Delgado announced, indicating the dishes on the sideboard. "We
have chicken with *mole* sauce, which I warn you is
rather spicy, *carne asada, ensalada guacamole,* as well
as the usual black beans and rice."

"All of this is for the three of us?" Tess asked, her
eyes wide.

"*Sí,* to celebrate your arrival. Of course, my table

does not look like this every night, you understand," Delgado told her, obviously reveling in being the bountiful host. "On nights when we have come home late from a raid, I am lucky to get a bowl of warm soup, eh, Delores?"

The stolid-faced old woman nodded.

"Please, allow me to place a sampling of the dishes on your plate," Delgado said to Tess, "and when you have decided what you like, you must have more, eh? But save room for dessert at the end," he warned.

"Only a little, please," Tess pleaded. "At home we do not have such a big meal at night."

"Ah, but at home you do not sleep through lunch, do you?" Delgado asked with a chuckle. "Don't worry. I like a woman with a hearty appetite."

Sandoval saw Tess dart a look at Delgado that plainly said, "I don't care what kind of woman you like," but Delgado was concentrating on serving her and didn't see it. Once he had placed the plate in front of her, she hesitated, and Sandoval thought she was waiting for Delgado and himself to make their selections, too. But when they had both done so, she still did not lift her fork. Surely she wasn't refusing to eat? But then he saw her duck her head and close her eyes for a moment, and realized she was silently saying grace.

How long had it been since *he* had thanked God for what he put in his mouth? Pilar had always been the one to bless the family dinners.

He saw that Delgado had also noticed what she was doing. Then Tess raised her head, and both men picked up their knives and forks and pretended they had not been watching her.

"Tell me about yourself, *señorita,*" Delgado invited, after a moment or two. "I know little about you except that you are a lady photographer. Tell me of your family."

Tess shrugged, unconscious that the gesture called attention to her lovely shoulders. "There's not much to tell," she said, and went on to tell Delgado what Sandoval already knew of her family.

"Have you ever been away from home like this?" Delgado asked.

As Sandoval listened, Diego Delgado effortlessly drew her out. She told them about being sent away to a fancy finishing school, which purported to be all that was needed for a young lady of good family to be ready to make a brilliant marriage.

Who knew that a notorious outlaw like Diego Delgado could be such a good host, Sandoval mused. He could see Tess relaxing in the midst of Delgado's concentration on her answers and was glad for that, at least.

"But how did you develop an interest in photography?" Delgado inquired. "It is an unusual pastime for a lady, no?"

Spearing a piece of the spicy chicken and dipping it in the chocolate-based sauce, Tess told them about her uncle James, who had been a Brady photographer and had taught her all she knew, and about her goal of going to New York to work for Brady.

Sandoval pretended absorption in his beef as he fought the surprising sense of jealousy that twisted his gut. *He* should be the one plying Tess Hennessy with clever questions, drawing her out, not this scoundrel! She had been standoffish with him when they had met at Taylor's, but surely with time and charm he could have won the right to court her.

And so he might have been the one, if he hadn't decided first to use her to achieve his own goal regarding Delgado.

"Ah, you are a woman of amazing ambition," Delgado purred, after taking a long draft of his wine. "Do you not wish for a home? A husband? Babies to dandle on your knee?"

Sandoval saw two spots of color spring to Tess's cheeks and sparks flash from her eyes. "*Jefe,* I think your question may be a little too personal..." he began, but Tess found her voice before he could finish his sentence.

"I'd like to ask *you* a question or two, Diego," she said, biting out the words. "Such as, how did you develop an interest in thievery? Especially thievery on such a grand scale?"

Slowly, deliberately, Delgado laid down his knife and fork in turn. The color had fled from his face. "How did I become Delgado, scourge of the Rio Grande Valley, you mean? This land is rightfully Mexican, Tess Hennessy. So I don't really feel that I am doing anything wrong—I am merely taking back those possessions which should belong to my people."

"But people have been killed who sought to protect their property from you and your men, Señor Delgado," she protested.

Sandoval could see the nerve jumping in Delgado's temple and knew the outlaw was perilously close to losing his temper at her outspokenness.

"I kill no one who does not resist us," Delgado said.

"That is your excuse?"

Sandoval knew it was time to intervene. Delgado had been so affable a host before they got on this subject that Tess had forgotten who and what he was. Beneath the table, he very gently but firmly put his booted foot down on Tess's foot. "I think you have said enough, Miss Hennessy," he warned. "Do not forget you are a captive here, and dependent on Delgado's goodwill."

Yes, that's it, he thought, when she transferred her indignant gaze to him. Show me your anger, not Delgado. It's much safer.

He increased the pressure on her foot, hoping she'd take the hint and not insist on having the last word.

Her eyes were disks of ice as she stared at him, her mouth a thin, tight line, but she held her peace.

"I believe you will be pleased at the pictures Miss Hennessy took today, *jefe*," Sandoval said, praying Delgado was ready to let go of the conflict, too. He turned to Delores, who'd been half dozing in a corner of the room, asking the old woman to bring the photographs from Tess's hut.

Delores was back in a few moments, and Delgado was so thrilled with the results of Tess's first session that he was once again beaming at her, all his wrath forgotten.

"You are a true *artista*, Señorita Tess," Delgado enthused, kissing his fingers at her as if the past, tense moments had never happened. "A genius of daguerreotype, isn't she, Sandoval?"

"Indeed she is," Sandoval said, watching Tess warily.

"And it was masterful on your part to think of bringing her to me," Delgado went on, slapping Sandoval on the back. "Thank you, my loyal amigo!" He turned back to Tess. "And you will be ready at dawn tomorrow to take the pictures of me on horseback, just before we ride out on our raid, *si?*"

Tess nodded.

"That being the case, perhaps I should escort Miss

Hennessy back to her quarters so that she can get her rest," Sandoval said, rising.

"Oh, but we have not had our dessert," Delgado protested. "Delores makes the best *flan* in Mexico, perhaps in the world!"

Tess rose also, protesting that she couldn't eat another bite, as polite as any guest could be.

"Then go and get your beauty sleep, *señorita,*" Delgado said, bowing. "Sandoval, after you have seen her safe inside, summon my other lieutenants and come back. We need to plan our strategy, eh?"

Tess was silent until Delgado closed the door and she was alone with Parrish on the short path to her hut.

"I'm sure I can manage the rest of the way by myself," she told him, her voice burning with suppressed fury. "Go summon the rest of his lieutenants as you were told." She mimicked Delgado's accent mockingly. "You have strategy to discuss, don't you?"

"Woman, hold your tongue," Sandoval snapped, taking hold of her elbow so tightly she almost squeaked at the sudden, unexpected roughness. He yanked her along and pushed her roughly inside the hut, and to her alarm, followed her inside. The interior was dimly lit by a flickering tallow candle burning in a niche in the adobe wall above a pallet like the one Tess had slept on.

"Now, just a minute," she began, beginning to realize too late she might have pushed him too far. "I didn't invite you in—"

Chapter Seven

His dark eyes smoldered down at her, frightening her with their intensity.

"I had to come in, since apparently you have no more sense than to mock me right outside Delgado's quarters," he said in a low voice. "I don't care how you feel about me," he told her, "but don't you think he'd be listening at the window for what you might say? You can't take hints, evidently, so I came inside to tell you what you need to hear."

"Oh, and what is that, pray tell?" she retorted, with all the bravado she could muster.

"Don't think you can be insolent with Delgado, Tess. He may act the courtier at times, but don't forget he's an unprincipled bandit. You're going to have to mind that red-headed temper of yours and at least pretend to respect him and his men if you hope to get out of this situation unscathed."

"How dare you, Sandoval Parrish?" she demanded, taking a step forward and thrusting her chin out. "I wouldn't be in this *situation,* as you so charmingly put it, if it weren't for your desire to curry favor with that same unprincipled killer!" She was too angry at him to care that they were alone in this hut, and she was very much at Sandoval Parrish's mercy.

His head snapped back as if she had slapped him, and he paled. For several endless moments they stared at one another, breathing hard. Then Parrish walked past her and she thought he was leaving, but he only went to the door and stood there for a few moments, peering out into the darkness. Tess realized he was making sure no one was nearby.

He walked back to her. "You're right, you wouldn't. You have every right to think the worst of me, Tess Hennessy. And I can see why you'd think I had you kidnapped to make myself look good to Delgado—but I'm telling you that's not exactly the case. There's more to it than that, and it's up to you whether you believe me or not. The best thing you can do is trust me, and mind what I tell you. I told you I wouldn't let any harm come to you."

"But *why,* Sandoval? What do you hope to gain?" she demanded, self-control slipping, the tears of outrage and fear suddenly threatening to spill over onto her cheeks.

His gaze became more intent then, and she realized she had unconsciously called him by his first name for the first time.

"I can't tell you that, Tess," he said. "Not yet, anyway. I...you may not believe this, but I'm not a bad man."

Something about the softness of his tone and the kindness in his eyes was her undoing, and she gave in to her tears. Then suddenly he was holding her, patting her back as she wept. There was nothing disrespectful about the way he held her, but even so, Tess knew she should move out of his embrace. But it felt comforting and right, and she remained where she was until her tears stopped.

He took a step back from her then, regret that he must do so showing clearly in those dark eyes of his.

"*Buenas noches,* Tess," he whispered. "Go to bed now. Delores will be along as soon as she has cleared Delgado's table, and will sleep out here," he said, indicating the rolled-up straw pallet. "No one will bother you."

Dazed, Tess watched him turn and lift the blanket door, and then he was gone.

Leaving the candle lit in the wall niche for Delores, she walked into her bedroom area and saw that the lace-trimmed muslin nightgown she'd found in the trunk was laid out on the pallet for her. She changed quickly into it in the darkness, unpinned her hair, then lay down on the pallet, sure sleep would come with difficulty if it came at all.

Now that Parrish had held her—and she had allowed him to do so—she was more confused about who he was than ever before. What kind of a dangerous game was he playing with Delgado? She'd thought she knew why he'd kidnapped her, but he had said she was wrong, that she didn't know the real reason. Could she—*should* she believe that he was on the right side?

Yes, her heart told her. He'd had her under his power moments ago, and could have done anything he wanted to her, then fobbed Delgado off with some excuse for why it had taken him so long to return. He had only held her—but what strength and comfort she had found in his embrace. She had felt at home there. It seemed to her he had been showing her a glimpse of his heart, showing her that despite the reasons he had for thrusting her into this dangerous situation, he cared for her. Or was that only what she wanted to believe?

If he wasn't trying to get into Delgado's good graces, then what *was* his purpose?

Uncle Samuel had said Parrish was a "man to ride the river with." Was *he* merely under the spell of Sandoval's charm—and Tess had seen that charm was considerable—or did the older man have good reason to respect Sandoval Parrish?

Before she'd been kidnapped, the worst predicament she had ever been in had been at Miss Agnes's Finishing School for Christian Young Ladies, when it seemed she would fail her class in deportment, a subject that had bored her to distraction. Back then, she had solved the problem by getting on her knees, praying and then opening her Bible at random.

She still remembered the verse on which her finger had fallen—Philippians 4:13—"I can do all things through Christ which strengtheneth me." And it had proven true—she had achieved the third highest mark in the class, though studying after she had prayed probably hadn't hurt.

Now she was in genuine peril, and she knew Parrish had been right about not provoking Delgado too far. He had promised to keep her safe, but what if something happened to Parrish in this nest of cutthroats? Delgado's moods could be capricious—she had seen that for herself tonight.

What she wouldn't give for her Bible right now, to be able to open it up and find a verse that would comfort her! But, of course, her Bible was safely at home on her nightstand, likely covered with at least a week's dust. Tess realized with a guilty start she'd rarely touched it lately except to carry it to church. *Why* hadn't she been more diligent about memorizing Scripture?

She hadn't prayed in ages, either. She'd been so consumed with her photography she'd hardly given a thought to God except during Sunday-morning services—and sometimes not even then, for it was far too easy to slip into daydreams about working for Mathew Brady in faraway New York City.

Had the Lord allowed her to be kidnapped to punish her for neglecting Him?

Her soul instinctively rebelled at that idea. She'd given Him her heart at an early age, and had always known He was a God of love. But perhaps He was allowing this circumstance in her life to draw her back to Him.

Tess got to her knees. *I'm sorry, Lord,* she prayed. *Please forgive me for finding photography or anything more important than You. Please teach me what You want me to learn through this experience, and bring me safely back home as soon as possible. And please help Papa and Mama not to worry!*

A sense of peace washed over her—a trickle first, and then an ever-increasing stream as the words of a Psalm came to her from some distant part of her memory—"God is our refuge and strength, a very present help in trouble. Therefore will not we fear..."

Night sounds floated in through the window—the distant sound of someone strumming a guitar and singing, the hoot of an owl, the lowing of cattle. She smelled the smoke coming from one of the campfires beyond the stream.

She heard Delores come in then. The old woman shuffled around the outer room for a few minutes, then blew the candle out. The hut was swallowed in darkness.

There was a rustling as the old woman settled herself on the straw pallet with a grunt. Within minutes, soft snores emanated from the outer room.

At last, lulled by the regular rhythm of the sound, Tess slept, too.

In his own adobe, sleep eluded Sandoval. He couldn't stop reliving the pleasure of holding Tess, of savoring her trust—at least, her trust at that moment that he would not take advantage of her nearness, and that he intended to protect her from the danger posed by Delgado and his men. He wanted her to feel secure during the time she was with the outlaws. When she'd been tense and apprehensive, it had felt like a dagger in his heart. What more could he do to assure her of her safety?

Should he confess the truth, that he was a Texas Ranger on a mission to bring Delgado down? Or might that knowledge be too dangerous if Delgado suddenly had some reason to suspect him, and put the question to her? She couldn't tell what she didn't know.

It seemed as if she had only shut her eyes moments ago when she was being shaken awake.

"*Señorita, señorita,* it is time to get up. Wake up, *por favor.*"

Tess opened her eyes with reluctance and saw that Delores was bent over her. Once she saw that Tess was awake, she straightened and left.

Soft light filtered in through the makeshift curtain. Beyond it, Tess could hear the camp waking up. Horses whinnied. Men called to one another. Chickens clucked nearby, and a rooster crowed from somewhere above her, perhaps perched on the straw thatch roof. The smells of coffee and cooking bacon wafted to her on the breeze, causing an answering rumble in her stomach.

Tess dressed quickly, braided her hair and splashed some water on her face from the pitcher Delores had apparently left on her trunk.

Still sleepy, she hoped she would be able to get a cup of coffee before she began photographing, but a shout went up from the direction of Delgado's quarters as soon as she stuck her head outside. Tess saw that Esteban was holding the rangy black stallion that had given her mule such a rude welcome yesterday. The beast was saddled, bridled and obviously ready to go. Her wagon with its photographic supplies still stood next to the adobe.

"Buenos días, señorita," Esteban said, his eyes clearly approving of her Mexican garb.

Beyond the stream, Tess saw that the members of the bandit band were saddling and bridling their horses, some already mounting them. Where was Parrish?

As she returned his greeting, Delgado stepped outside. Gone was the suave courtier of last evening. Here was a man ready for a raid, dressed in rough trousers, a dark shirt and boots, with two bullet-studded bandoliers crisscrossed over his chest and a gun belt with two pistols slung over his hips.

Behind him, Parrish exited Delgado's quarters, and Tess saw with a shiver that he was dressed similarly. His gaze raked over her, nothing in it betraying that he was anything more to her than another of her captors. There was something lean and wolfish about his angular features, the way his eyes narrowed against the morning sunlight, and the tight line of his mouth. Had Tess only dreamed of his tender embrace the night before?

"Ah, I see you are ready," Delgado said to Tess, all business. "That is good. Let us get on with it, for we must be off soon, eh, Sandoval?"

"*Sí, mi jefe*. Señorita Hennessy, I will lift the camera down from your wagon before going to get my horse ready."

Delgado mounted his horse. The big black pawed the ground as his rider took up the reins, clearly eager for a gallop beyond the canyon walls. As soon as Delgado settled himself in the saddle, the black curvetted in the dust, arching his proud neck. It was going to be diffi-cult to get the beast to hold still long enough to take Delgado's picture, Tess thought.

"*Cálmense, mi amigo,*" Delgado said, holding him with some difficulty, but he seemed to share the horse's eagerness and impatience to be off.

Now, if she could just capture that emotion on one of her photographic plates, it would be quite a picture!

Tess worked as quickly as she could, knowing Del-gado would not be endlessly patient, and had made half a dozen exposures when the outlaw leader raised his hand and pronounced, "Enough!"

Just then Parrish returned, leading his mount, a striking black-and-white pinto. Tess watched as Par-rish mounted.

"Miss Hennessy," he said, once in the saddle, "De-lores will see to your needs while we are gone. You have but to ask her." His eyes were impersonal—was it because Delgado was present? Or had he thought about her weeping last night, and decided she was but a silly crybaby?

"But do not seek to escape," Delgado said, wagging a finger at her. "It is impossible."

"I wouldn't think of it," she said coolly, and met

Delgado's black stare without blinking, until at last he
and Parrish wheeled their horses and splashed through
the shallow stream to join the rest of the band, already
mounted and waiting.

"¡Vayan, muchachos! ¡Rápido!" Delgado cried, and
then the band was galloping out of the canyon's mouth.
She thought she saw Parrish look back at her before the
horses' hooves churned up a cloud of dust that soon hid
them from sight.

Tess wondered where they were going to raid today,
then realized with a stab of anxiety that not only were
they going to cause danger to others, but what they were
about to do would expose them to danger, too.

She didn't care so much about the other banditos,
except in the way she would care about the fate of any
human being. But, *dear Jesus, please don't let anything
happen to Sandoval Parrish! Don't let him be wounded
or captured.* He might not truly be an outlaw—as yet
she didn't know what he truly was, but if he were taken
by the Texans, they might not allow him time before
stringing him up to explain what he had been doing
raiding with Delgado.

And then she had to smile at the irony of it all. Here
she was, having photographed an outlaw in his lair
today, and she had just thought of the Texans, *her own
people,* as "them." And she had prayed specifically for
the safety of one of those riding out on the raid, even
though Parrish might be nothing but an outlaw himself.

Chapter Eight

With the outlaw band gone and the new exposures drying underneath the canvas hood, Tess was finally free to break her fast, and crossed the little bridge to the campfire. Delores, wrapped in a black rebozo against the early morning chill, was already there, stirring something in a skillet. At Tess's approach, she poured steaming coffee into a tin cup and handed it to her.

Tess sank onto a log nearby and drank gratefully. Moments later she was devouring not only eggs but the remains of a loaf of bread that tasted freshly baked. How early had this woman arisen, to have baked bread already? The sun was only now rising over the canyon wall.

"This is really good, *señora*," Tess praised, realizing she had never enjoyed breakfast so much at home. She gestured at the last hunk of bread in her hand. "How on earth do you manage to bake bread in a place like this?"

Delores beamed. "In that *horno*," Delores said, pointing to a rounded-edged, shoulder-high earthen mass that Tess hadn't noticed before. "The Indians taught our Spanish ancestors to use them."

It was a good thing she'd learned to speak fluent

Spanish from the servants at Hennessy Hall, Tess thought. Her mother knew only enough to give directions to Rosa, the cook, and Flora, the housemaid, and would have been helpless to carry on a conversation like this. Maybe Tess could learn something from Delores that would help her to find her way out of this predicament.

Delores rose, and gathering up the stack of dirty plates the men had left scattered about on the other side of the campfire, ambled in the direction of the stream.

"Let me help you carry those," Tess said, taking the stack from her. Delores nodded, picking up a nearby bucket and a cake of soap instead. Together they walked to the water and, kneeling, washed the plates, cups and forks with a couple of rags Delores produced from a pocket in her threadbare skirt.

"Have you been among the bandits long, *señora?*" Tess inquired.

The woman seemed surprised at her curiosity. "Yes, for about two years."

"Why did you come?" Tess was careful to keep her tone nonjudgmental, but surely there had to be something more for a woman up in years to be doing than cooking for outlaws.

Delores shrugged. "I am a widow. My son Esteban, who is my youngest child, chose to ride with Delgado. I had nothing else to do. If I came along, I could make sure he got enough decent food to eat, at least when they are in the canyon."

So the mustachioed young man who had led the kidnapping and initially taken Tess's money was Delores's son. And he was a youngest child, too. Delores was certainly pragmatic about her son joining the outlaws, even coming along herself to look after him, more than Tess's mother would have been!

The day was rapidly growing warm. Tess had removed her boots and stockings and was enjoying the cool play of the water over her feet. Delores had shed her rebozo long ago. Now, with the dish washing done, she yawned widely, then rose to her feet and told Tess she was going to take a siesta in the shade and that Tess should, too.

Here was Tess's chance to explore. She didn't know if they had posted a guard or were counting on her, a foreigner far from home, being too intimidated to try to escape, but she didn't believe Delgado's assertion that escape was impossible. She hadn't seen the opening of the canyon when she had arrived yesterday, but all she had to do was walk in the same direction where they had ridden off.

After putting her stockings and boots back on, Tess waited until the old woman had lain unmoving in the shade for several minutes before getting up and looking around. The camp was eerily quiet except for the buzz of insects and the occasional stamping of her mule. The fact that she couldn't see anyone as she peered around the camp didn't mean one of the men wasn't watching them from some vantage point right this very minute! But if she didn't spot a guard, she was determined to try to escape. She could always ride Ben out of the canyon bareback, if need be.

Tess walked quietly up the stream past the sleeping woman until a bend in the canyon wall hid her from sight.

She walked about a hundred yards down the rocky, curving mouth of the gorge and encountered no one. She could see ahead of her where the canyon opened.

Could it really be this easy to get away? A rising sense of hope surged within her.

"Buenas tardes, señorita," a voice said.

Tess gave a stifled squeak of alarm, nearly jumping out of her skin. A figure of a man, clad in the usual un-bleached cotton garments of a Mexican peon, separated itself from a rocky boulder on which he had been leaning, holding a rifle with casual negligence and grinning at her.

It was the rude, aggressive man from the night of her kidnapping—Tess had heard him called Jaime Dominguez.

"Going somewhere, *señorita?* Or perhaps you came to chat with me, eh?" His knowing eyes indicated he knew exactly what she was up to.

Tess bit back a thoroughly impolite reply. It wouldn't be wise to trade barbs with this one while he was the only man left at the hideout.

"No, I was just taking a walk," she said. "I—I'll just be going back to Delores now…." Tess reversed her position, walking for a few paces, then breaking into a run back into the canyon. The man's scornful laughter echoed off the canyon walls.

Tess didn't stop running until after she reached the sanctuary of her hut. Evidently she wasn't meant to escape—at least not yet—so she must look for the good in the situation. And as she sat in the shade of a clump of mesquite that afternoon, sketching with a bit of charcoal on a piece of paper Delores had found for her, it came to her what the "good" might be.

She had been looking for some way to distinguish her work so Mathew Brady wouldn't be able to resist hiring her when she arrived in New York City. There had never seemed to be any way to achieve that, living in the sleepy Rio Grande Valley where nothing ever happened. Brady would not be impressed by her portfolio of stiff portraits of local residents. Now, it seemed, being kidnapped had dropped an amazing opportunity into her lap.

By saving the negatives of her photographs of Delgado and his bandits, Tess could put together a photographic essay of life among the *bandoleros*. The fact that the photographer was a woman would only add to the collection's appeal, and she would have proved she was a woman who could seize the initiative. He would beg her to work for him!

There was no sign of the outlaws until sundown. Tess tried not to fret as the endless hours crawled by, but Delores went about her tasks unperturbed. Finally Tess decided to pass the time by taking photographs of the older woman and her typical activities—grinding corn for tortillas, shelling beans, mending a rent in one of her voluminous skirts. Delores seemed bemused to find herself the subject of Tess's lens, but when she showed the old woman the photographs, Delores's mouth gaped in amazement. She had probably never expected to see a photograph of herself, let alone several.

The first sign of Delgado and his men returning was a steady thunder, distant at first, gradually building until Tess looked upward to see if rain clouds had stolen over the evening sky. Then she heard the bawling of cattle and, over that, the occasional yips of the men as they drove along the stolen herd.

A rising cloud of dust heralded their imminent arrival into the canyon. Delores yanked Tess's sleeve, gesturing for Tess to follow her, and hastened across the bridge and into the hut. They watched from the window as the bellowing cattle, a mixture of rangy longhorns and fat Herefords, pounded into the camp. Scenting water, most of the cattle headed straight for the stream, stopping there and lowering their heads to drink, though some ran straight through the water and past the hut, looking for the way out. As soon as a few of the beasts finished drinking and lurched away from the stream, others took their place, and the banditos funneled the satisfied cattle into the empty one of the two corrals.

Peering through the gathering gloom, Tess looked for Parrish, but without success. She saw that Delores also appeared to be watching for someone—her son? She saw Delgado ride past on his black stallion. The horse's earlier fire was gone now, his flanks lathered, his head hung low. Jumping off his mount and handing his reins to one of his men, Delgado headed for his quarters without acknowledging her.

And then she saw the pinto—his bold white patches standing out in the shadows. His pace was slow because Parrish cradled someone else ahead of him on the saddle, someone whose light cotton shirt was splotched with dark patches of dried blood.

Beside her, Delores shrieked, *"¡Esteban! ¡Mi hijo!"* The old woman was running out of the hut, faster than Tess had imagined she could possibly move, wailing and skirting the milling cattle, heading toward Parrish and the wounded man he carried.

Tess followed, and was in time to help Sandoval lower the unconscious young man into Delores's waiting arms. The old woman sank down onto the dirt with him, moaning and murmuring while she frantically searched him for wounds.

Parrish dismounted, then spoke to Delores, his tone calm and reassuring, but Delores was far too upset to be comforted while Esteban lay insensible and pale in her lap. Parrish turned to Tess, his face coated with dust, his eyes unspeakably weary. "His only wound is in the shoulder, but he's lost a lot of blood, and we're going to have to dig the bullet out if he's not to die of blood poisoning."

"But...but he needs a doctor," Tess protested. "Why didn't you find him a doctor?"

His dark eyes raked her, their depths lit with impatience. "You think we should have stopped the herd on the Texas side of the river and taken Esteban to some Anglo sawbones? The rancher we stole that herd from and the Rangers pursuing us would have appreciated it, I'm sure."

"Of course I don't mean that! I meant once you were safely across the Rio Grande," she retorted.

"Just how many competent *médicos* do you think there are between here and Mexico City?" he asked, his tone bordering on contemptuous. "Even supposing the *Rinches* hadn't pursued us across the river, which they did! They shot Pedro Sanchez right off his horse just before we reached the other bank. He was dead before he hit the water, I think. We had to ride hard until they finally gave up a few miles ago and turned back—didn't want to battle us in the dark in unfamiliar country, I guess."

Tess wasn't sure which of the outlaws Sanchez had been, but she saw the grim set of Parrish's mouth and bit back what she had been about to say. "I... I'll help however I can," she said.

"I've got a bottle of tequila in my quarters, hidden under my bedroll. Would you please fetch it? I'll be by the campfire—I'm going to need the light, as well as a place to clean my knife blade before I go digging for that bullet." Tess realized he meant to pour the liquor over the wound, not drink it. But what made Parrish think he could remove a bullet? He wasn't a doctor.

Because someone had to do it. There was no one else capable.

Over her shoulder, she heard Parrish call out to one of the banditos thronging around them to help him carry Esteban over beside the fire. Delores ran alongside, still moaning and muttering frantic prayers, until at last they could lay him down near the campfire.

Parrish's quarters were spartan and orderly—just a bedroll and a small trunk like the one in her hut.

When Tess returned, she found Esteban lying with his head pillowed in his mother's lap while Parrish cut away the bloodstained shirt with a bowie knife. She held out the bottle. Without thanking her, Parrish took it, uncorked it and poured tequila over the exposed, sinister-looking hole in the front of Esteban's right shoulder.

Esteban uttered a sharp, incoherent cry, rising up and swinging at Parrish with his other arm, then sank back into insensibility. The other men milled around the edge of the firelight, passing a couple of bottles around, watching.

"I hope he'll stay unconscious," Sandoval muttered. "Sit down here and be ready to help Delores hold him. He'll fight me—he won't know what he's doing, or that I'm trying to help him, only that he hurts like h—like blazes," he amended with a wry twist of his mouth. Tess obediently knelt down beside the wounded man. While Delores murmured in Spanish into her son's ear, Parrish held the blade of his knife in the midst of the flames for a moment, then bent to his task.

Esteban went rigid, screamed, then bucked and struggled against the restraining hands. It took all of Tess's strength to help Delores hold him down. One of the other banditos threw himself over Esteban's legs, preventing him from kicking at Parrish, until at last the bullet he'd been digging for fell out into the dust with a soft *plop*. Esteban sank back, completely unaware that Parrish was once again pouring fiery alcohol over the bloody wound. Tess looked away, feeling sick as the world spun around her.

She was vaguely aware of Delgado having returned, standing among his men, watching Sandoval and her with hooded eyes.

Delores, still crooning to her son, reached into one of her capacious pockets and produced clean, folded rags to use as bandages. Tess realized she had placed them there to be ready for the men's return, little realizing her own son would be the one who needed them.

"I need to have him taken to your quarters," Parrish told her.

"I can sleep outside," Tess agreed.

Parrish shook his head. "It wouldn't be safe." He nodded toward the door. "I meant Delores can watch over him in the outer area, while you sleep on your pallet." He spoke to the surrounding men, and several of them bent to the task of carrying Esteban into her hut. Delgado followed.

His eyes on the procession, Parrish let out his breath, almost as if he had been holding it the entire time. She saw his shoulders sag with weariness. She wanted to go to him, put a hand on his arm and tell him how brave he had been to take on such a hazardous task.

Then he turned back to Tess, and to her surprise, his eyes were warm with approval. "You did well," he told her.

Chapter Nine

Her eyes—those impossibly deep blue eyes—widened as if she couldn't believe what she had just heard. "I—*I* did well? But I didn't do anything. *You* dug the bullet out, not me."

He could tell by the way Tess paled she was remembering the way the crimson rivulet had flowed past his knife, and the heavy, coppery smell of the blood. Possibly she had never been exposed to such a sight before. Delicately reared young ladies were usually sheltered from such things.

"But you didn't cry or faint at the sight of all that blood," he told her. "You didn't make a nuisance of yourself—you made yourself useful. Thank you."

She raised her eyes to his, blinking as if trying to hold back tears. "Y-you're welcome."

Had she never been praised for bravery before?

Now Sandoval could see weariness taking over her features like a veil swirling between them.

"You'd best get some sleep," he told her. "Come on, I'll walk with you."

"Will he…will he recover?" she asked.

"Esteban? I think so, with a little luck, if no infection sets in. Delores has nursed wounded men before."

"Is there anything else I can do?" she asked, pausing just outside her hut. "Maybe I could offer to take over for Delores when she gets too weary."

He stared down at her in the darkness. Someone had built another campfire just beside the hut so Delores wouldn't have to go far from her son. The light of the campfire cast flickering shadows on Tess's earnest, upturned face.

"She'll let you know if she needs something," Sandoval told her. He wanted so much to kiss her, to caress her, to promise her everything would turn out all right.

"I'll pray for him."

Sandoval felt a tightening in his throat at her offer. She was a captive, but she was offering to pray for the recovery of one of the very men who had taken her prisoner on the road to her home. What kind of a woman was this? He wanted to say, Pray for me, too, while you're at it. But he didn't want to answer the questions such a request might raise. "Get some sleep, Tess," he said again, and walked away from her toward his own hut.

A moan from beyond the curtain wakened Tess just as dawn began to break. Was Esteban worse? Wrapping the sheet around her like a shawl, Tess pushed the blanket aside and went to where Delores knelt by her son's side.

Esteban's eyes were still tightly shut, his brown forehead pearled with sweat. Strands of black hair were pasted damply to his temples. His bare chest rose and fell rapidly under the light bleached-muslin sheet.

Delores murmured something to him, pouring a

spoonful of dark liquid from a brown glass bottle and holding it to his lips. His mouth slackened, accepting the liquid, but he made a face as it trickled into his mouth.

"Is he feverish?" Tess asked, kneeling down on the other side of the man lying on the striped blanket.

"*Sí.* It is expected," Delores told her matter-of-factly. "The body protests both the invasion of the bullet and the knife that dug it out."

Tess reached out a hand to touch his forehead. Esteban's skin felt moistly hot, and her eyes went to Delores with alarm.

The older woman, her face concerned but not fearful, pointed to the brown glass bottle on the dirt floor beside her. "This will help."

Esteban passed once again into deep sleep, and Delores settled back against the adobe wall with a sigh. Had she been awake all night?

"I could stay with him while you sleep."

Delores smiled but shook her head, then pointed at the growing light stealing under the blanket door. "It is time for me to cook the men's breakfast."

Of course. Her son might be wounded, but Delores still had a camp full of hungry men who would expect to be fed.

"I'll sit with Esteban while you cook," Tess said. She wished she could offer to do the cooking, but though she'd learned a few basics at the finishing school, cooking was strictly the job of Señora Rosa at home. Her mother had made vague remarks about Tess needing to learn the skill "someday," but someday had never arrived. Perhaps that was something else she could learn a bit while she was here.

Delores smiled, her eyes tired, and rose stiffly to her feet. *"Gracias,"* she said, and went outside.

Time passed, and with nothing to do but watch the sleeping man, Tess had too much time to worry over her situation. How would she get free? What if something happened to Parrish, and she was left alone with the outlaws? Was there a posse searching for her, even now? What if they were killed trying to save her?

But once she had prayed for deliverance, what could she do but fret some more?

Finally she reprimanded herself. She might not be a competent cook, but she could pray for Esteban as she'd promised, at least. She knelt.

"Lord, please help Esteban to heal. Keep his fever down and please keep infection from the wound. He seems like a good man, even though he's an outlaw, and Delores loves him, Lord—"

Suddenly the blanket over the door was pulled open and a tall shadow blocked the doorway and the sunlight.

It was too tall to be Delores but, thinking it was Parrish, Tess's features had begun to relax when the figure spoke. "Ah, the angel of mercy, interceding with Heaven for a sinner. What an inspiring picture, to be sure. *Señorita,* it is a pity you cannot take your own picture."

Delgado. There was something about his voice that reminded her of a snake—the original snake in the Garden of Eden, beguiling with its lovely words, but the voice came from the same part of its body as the fangs.

"You give me too much credit, Mr. Delgado," she said crisply. "I merely agreed to stay with Esteban so Delores could perform her other duties." She wished Parrish would come, or Esteban would wake up, so she would not have to be alone with this man. His eyes were too intense as they roamed over her, missing nothing.

"Not at all," Delgado said, coming forward to where she sat. "I realized while you watch over my injured compadre, you are not breaking your own fast. So I came to bring you some food." He lifted the blanket again, leaned over and reached outside on the ground, and brought in a tin plate heaped with tortillas, eggs and bacon and a mugful of steaming coffee, which he set down by her.

"Thank you."

Tess's hopes that Delgado would go after performing this service were dashed immediately when he lowered himself to the ground and sat across from her with Esteban between them.

"And how does the patient this morning, eh?"

Tess reached out a hand to test Esteban's forehead, and found it already cooler. "Better," she said. "He had a fever when I awoke, but Delores gave him something, and it seems to have broken."

"Ah, Delores is a wise woman, no? But it is also good of you to tend him."

Just then Esteban began to stir, saving her the necessity of a modest demur. As both of them watched, the wounded man opened one eye, blinking up at Tess, and then opened both eyes, his gaze shifting to Delgado. He smiled weakly.

"*¡Hola, Esteban, mi amigo!* How goes it, my brave man? Esteban's bullet was meant for me, did you know that, Señorita Tess?"

Tess shook her head.

"Esteban is a tough man. It takes more than an Anglo bullet to kill him, eh?"

Esteban grinned and weakly thumped his chest.

Tess nodded. "I hear one of your other men was not so lucky."

Delgado's mouth tightened. "Yes, we lost Pedro, gunned down by a cowardly Anglo dog."

Who was probably just trying to protect his property—Tess bit back the retort, aware Delgado was baiting her. Parrish had advised her not to argue with Delgado, and in any case she would not do so in front of a sick man.

"We could not even bring back his body without risking the loss of other men," Delgado told her, eyes hot with anger, as if she were somehow responsible merely by being a Texan. He pointed to Esteban. "You will take a picture of this victim of the *Norteamericanos*."

He waited, but when she did not respond to his taunts, Delgado got to his feet and headed for the door. "We will rest today and recover from our exertions. I will tell Delores her son has awakened, so she can bring him something to eat. Then you must come see the spoils from our raid, and make a picture of it all, eh? I have kept the men from taking their shares until you do this."

Later, when Tess emerged from the adobe, she found Parrish, Delgado and several others drinking coffee and standing around a blanket piled high with objects. Parrish watched her approach, his eyes guarded.

As she drew nearer, items distinguished themselves—jewelry, including a brooch, a pair of onyx earbobs and a string of pearls, a man's pocket watch, a pair of fancy tooled-leather boots, an ornate silver-studded saddle, an ormolu clock, a large gilt-framed landscape painting.

"Quite a successful raid, I see," she commented, wondering if all these items had come from one home or if they had struck several ranches. Esteban had been wounded, and another of the banditos had died for these things. Had anyone been wounded or killed, trying to protect their property? The idea sickened her.

"Yes. I have decided we will have a celebration tomorrow," Delgado told her. "We will enjoy some of that good beef over there," he added, pointing to the corral where the stolen cattle stood, some of them grazing, others standing idly, swatting flies with their tails. "We will ride into Santa Elena and invite everyone to come and feast with us—very enjoyable, no?"

She stared at him. There was a *town* nearby? A town where people knew of the hideout, but did nothing to bring the outlaws to justice? Were they afraid of Delgado and his men? Or perhaps they were indifferent to the idea of Anglos being raided. Most Mexicans regarded all of Texas as land that had been stolen from *them,* after all. Maybe they benefited from the goods Delgado stole, too. But if she could find *someone* among those who came to celebrate who would be sympathetic to her desire to escape...

"And I have something especially for you, something you will like," Delgado said, reaching into the pocket of his trousers and bringing out a gleaming gold necklace with an ornate cross pendant studded with sapphires— a necklace Tess had last seen around the plump neck of Mrs. Dupree at Uncle Samuel's barbecue. The fact that Delgado had it meant that the raiders had struck near Hennessy Hall.

"You didn't kill the lady this belongs to, did you?" she demanded, glaring at Delgado.

He chuckled and grinned at her. "No, do not fear. She was very willing to give it up when I explained the alternative to her. Here, let me fasten it on your lovely neck," he said, holding up the necklace and gesturing for her to turn around. "I thought of you immediately when I saw it—it matches your eyes."

Tess took a step back. "No, thank you. I already have one." She pulled out the plain, small gold cross that hung from a thin chain around her neck, the same one she had been given when she went away to finishing school.

"Oh, but this one is much more beautiful," Delgado said, dangling the sapphire cross in front of her as if he thought it might tempt her.

"This one is all I need."

Delgado shrugged, amused. "Then perhaps what Sandoval obtained for you will be more to your taste."

Tess's gaze flew to Parrish, and he reached inside his vest and brought out a small, black leather-bound book she recognized—*her own Bible.*

"How did you get that?" she cried, grabbing it. "Did you raid Hennessy Hall? Did you hurt my father or my mother?"

He held up a reassuring hand. "Your parents never knew I was on the property. Only one of the housemaids, who was very willing to get it for you without telling anyone I was there."

Tears stinging her eyes, Tess clutched the familiar book to her, suddenly very homesick. And touched that Parrish had thought to obtain the one thing that would bring her a measure of real comfort. Why had he done such a thing?

"You took a chance," she told him. "My father would have had you horsewhipped at the very least if he'd caught you."

Sandoval's eyes danced with mischief. "And the neighbors would have held a lynching," he agreed. "But he didn't catch me. And I also had the housemaid leave a note on your bed that you were alive and well and would return soon."

"Did he know it was from you?"

Parrish shook his head. "I signed it 'A Friend.'"

All at once she was conscious of Delgado watching them.

"As soon as the *señorita* takes a picture or two, let's ride to town and issue our invitation," Delgado said to Parrish. "I know Lupe, especially, will be happy to see you."

Lupe? Who was that? Some Mexican sweetheart of Parrish's?

His expression gave her no clue, but she shouldn't have found it surprising that a man as handsome as Sandoval Parrish had a girl nearby. He probably had one in each town on both sides of the river. She had no reason, she reminded herself sternly, to care.

But against all reason and common sense, she *did* care. She had thought he cared—there had been something in the air between them, she thought. But she must have been wrong about how he felt about her. The idea of Sandoval's sweetheart joining him in camp made her sick with jealousy.

Chapter Ten

The canyon hummed with the afternoon drone of insects. Everyone else in camp seemed to be enjoying siesta, though Tess had no doubt someone was on guard duty at the mouth of the canyon. Ignoring the trickle of perspiration down her neck, she labored to develop the pictures of the booty—and of Esteban, who had been assisted out in front of the adobe for the photograph. Afterward, she made up some new collodion plates, using the chemicals from her wagon.

Her photographic duties done for the moment, Tess retreated to her hut. Esteban had been assisted to join the other men, who had gathered in the shade. She could see Delores napping again under the shade of the biggest cottonwood by the stream.

Her Bible lay waiting for her on her pillow in the shadowy coolness inside the adobe. *God, please encourage me.* The Psalms were usually good for that, weren't they? Flipping through the gilt-edged pages, she paused at Psalm 62—"He only is my rock and my salvation; he is my defense; I shall not be greatly moved."

Thank You, Lord, for reminding me of that. Tess had intended to spend the rest of the afternoon reading, but lulled by the heat and shadowy stillness inside her hut, her eyelids drooped....

It was nearly dusk when she awoke to sounds drifting in through her window—men laughing and talking, the whinnies of horses, the clang of metal against metal. Had Parrish and Delgado returned?

She paused in the doorway, her eyes taking in the sight of several of the outlaws standing waist deep in a hole, throwing red dirt from their shovels. Evidently this was to be the barbecue pit tomorrow. Bawling as if they suspected their fate, half a dozen steers were even now being funneled into a smaller holding pen nearby.

Delgado came out of his quarters just then, flanked by a slender whip of a woman taller than he. She wore a silver-studded black riding outfit with a divided skirt and a short jacket that showed off an enviably narrow waist. Possessed of the same dark, sinister beauty as Delgado, the same sinuous grace, the same glittering obsidian eyes, she had to be his sister.

"Ah, Tess, there you are. Come meet Lupe." He turned and said something to the woman.

Lupe. It was a common enough Mexican name. Could it be the same Lupe who Delgado had said would be happy to see Parrish? But of course it was, Tess realized, when Parrish, ducking his head so as not to hit the lintel, followed her from the outlaw leader's adobe. So Sandoval had yet another way to earn favor with Delgado, by romancing his sister.

"Lupe María Consuela Delgado y Peña, I am honored to present Señorita Tess Hennessy, who has so kindly consented to immortalize our exploits in photographs," Delgado said, as ceremonially as if he were presenting Tess to a queen.

And Lupe considered herself a queen, Tess realized,

watching as the outlaw's sister inclined her head regally, then inspected Tess from head to toe, eyes narrowed as if she were searching for minute stains on her clothing. Tess almost expected her to extend a hand to be kissed in obeisance.

"Buenos días," Tess said at last, when the other woman said nothing. Perhaps she spoke no English.

"So, you are the little...what is the word?—*photographer* my brother has hired?" Lupe purred, her voice unexpectedly deep and amused.

Little? Tess found herself bristling at the condescension in the woman's tone. She was shorter than Lupe-whatever-Delgado, but so what? "I am the photographer, yes, but I wouldn't say I was *hired,* precisely. Kidnapped, I would call it." She shot a look over Lupe's shoulder at Parrish.

Lupe allowed herself a husky, entrancing laugh, half turning to Parrish. "Ah, she is a fiery one, no? It goes with her hair. You did not get burned when you tied her up, did you, Sandoval, *querido?"* She laid a caressing hand on his cheek, gazing up at him through dark, thick lashes for a moment, then over her shoulder at Tess.

It was an unmistakable gesture of possession. Involuntarily stiffening, Tess studied Parrish's reaction.

His eyes gave away nothing. He did not seem to move so much as a muscle away from the caress, but he didn't lean into it, either. Was he merely too polite to display his feelings for the woman in front of Tess?

"Actually, I wasn't even there," he told Lupe. "I merely let them know where and when they could find her alone, and rode on ahead."

Unwilling to watch Lupe touching Sandoval any longer, Tess swung her gaze to Delgado, and found him studying her speculatively.

"H-how pleasant that your sister could come for a visit," she managed to say.

"Yes, she loves to come and visit her brother the famous *bandolero* from time to time, when living in Santa Elena grows tedious. She will come along with us on our next raid, when we will be gone for several nights."

"She...she goes raiding with you?" Tess repeated, incredulous.

"You find that remarkable for a woman, when you yourself are a photographer? Lupe rides like she was born on a galloping horse and is utterly ruthless, not to mention deadly accurate with a pistol. A most formidable opponent, as many Anglos have discovered to their sorrow. You might not know that her name means *wolf*."

"How very apt," Tess murmured, well able to imagine Lupe as a female version of her outlaw brother. So the outlaws would be away for a while—might she have the opportunity to escape while they were gone?

"And since Lupe will be with us, she can serve as a chaperone so you can come, too."

Tess's mouth dropped open. "*Me?* Come along on a raid? No, I don't think so! I'll stay back here in the canyon." Or at least I'll let you believe I'm content to do that, she thought.

"Come now, *señorita,* you can hardly expect me to leave you here with only a wounded man and an old woman to guard you," Delgado told her.

"But I could hardly hope to keep up with you, driving my cart full of heavy equipment," Tess pointed out. "Aren't you afraid I'll slow you down, cause you to risk capture or worse?"

Delgado shook his head. "On this expedition you will not bring your big camera and mule cart, only drawing paper. Delores showed me some of the sketches you did yesterday while we were gone. Your gift for drawing is nearly the equal of your talent behind the camera lens. No, for the raids, we will mount you on a swift horse—perhaps that sorrel in the corral over there."

"But…aren't you afraid I will escape?" Tess asked. Out of the corner of her eye, she saw that Lupe had stopped batting her eyelashes at Parrish and was taking in every word.

Delgado chuckled. "No, *señorita*. I have told you my sister is a crack shot, and utterly ruthless. She would not hesitate to shoot your horse out from under you, if you were to try such a thing."

"Why waste a good horse, *hermano?*" Lupe inquired, her eyes narrowed at Tess. "If it comes to that, perhaps I will just shoot the *gringa* herself. From what you have told me, she has already taken enough pictures."

Tess felt a chill entirely at odds with the July heat gripping her heart like a squeezing fist. Looking into the flat, soulless, dark eyes of Lupe Delgado, she did not doubt the woman would do exactly what she threatened without a qualm.

Delgado's hand snaked out and seized his sister's wrist, and he uttered a spate of low, hissing Spanish at her. Tess could only wonder what he said, but she saw Lupe's eyes flash angrily up at her brother before they turned with hot resentment on Tess.

Lupe snarled something at Delgado. Then she yanked her arm out of her brother's grasp and flounced back inside the adobe.

"Do not worry, *señorita,*" Delgado murmured. "My sister now understands that you are under my protection, and any harm to you would touch upon my honor."

Tess could only stare in Lupe's wake. Despite Delgado's assurances, if looks could kill, Tess would be dead.

"Go smooth her feathers, Sandoval," Delgado urged. "You seem to have a way with my sister."

Parrish shot a look at Tess she couldn't interpret, then ducked his head to reenter the adobe. Tess didn't see him alone again for the rest of the day—only later, at a distance, walking with Lupe down by the stream.

The townspeople of Santa Elena began arriving in late afternoon the next day, on foot, on donkey or horseback, and by oxcart. Everyone from the oldest graybeard to the youngest child able to toddle was dressed in their festive best. They treated Delgado with the respect due a *patrón* opening up the grounds of his spacious estate rather than a local bandit inviting the peons to a party in a dusty canyon.

Many greeted brothers or sons or cousins among the outlaws. Several men arrived with guitars strapped to their backs, and soon the air was filled with lively strumming as well as the savory aroma of roasting beef. The women had brought platters of sliced mangos, oranges and bananas, bowls of salsas and sauces, as well as mounds of freshly baked red-and-green striped cookies, and laid them out on a makeshift table of planks and sawhorses. Fat-cheeked, black-eyed children ran everywhere, shrieking merrily or staring at Tess as she indicated to a trio of banditos where to place her photography wagon.

At first she and the wood box she set up on its tripod were the subjects of much staring, pointing and whispered commentary, but all at once, Parrish materialized at her side.

"This is Señorita Hennessy," he announced, after clapping his hands to obtain silence. "She is a friend of Señor Delgado. She's here to take pictures with her camera."

Suddenly everyone was crowding around Tess, all

smiling and talking at once. The children, even less inhibited, began jumping up and down and pulling at her sleeves. Only a few of the older women backed away, muttering and making odd gestures in Tess's direction.

"Some of those older women think your camera is the evil eye, out to capture and imprison their souls," Parrish explained. "But the rest of them all want their pictures taken."

"But I don't have enough chemicals and paper for all of them," Tess said, eyeing the growing throng with dismay. She didn't want to disappoint anyone, especially the laughing, excited children. "I wouldn't be able to take any more of Delgado, and he still seems to want more."

"Maybe you could arrange them in a group—the tallest men standing in the back, the women kneeling in front of them, the children sitting in front of the women?" Parrish suggested. "Then you could make just one photograph of all of them. It would probably hold the place of honor in the local cantina for the next hundred years."

Tess chuckled, imagining it. "That might work," she agreed. "You'll have to explain the necessity of remaining very, very still once I give the word. I'm not sure those children can do it. They all seem to be part grasshopper."

Sandoval grinned, then called out instructions. In a couple of minutes, most of the townspeople of Santa Elena had arranged themselves in orderly rows. Even the children froze in their places, staring into Tess's lens with all the solemnity of statesmen. A couple of minutes later, Tess emerged from under her canvas and told Parrish the photograph had been a success.

"How did you manage to get the children to hold so

still? They were better behaved than the Dupree girls
at Uncle Samuel's party!" Tess praised him.

He smiled down at her. "There is a very badly chiseled
stone statue of Santa Anna that stands in front of the cantina in the village. I told them to pretend to be that statue."

"I'll have to remember that ploy," she told him. When
he smiled at her like that she could almost forget what
was happening—forget that he was the very man who
had arranged her kidnapping, forget that he had brought
his *inamorata* to camp, forget that thanks to Parrish,
she was utterly at the mercy of an outlaw leader whose
moods were as changeable as the wind.

"I am ready for you to take *my* picture now, *gringa*,"
Lupe announced from behind her.

Tess nearly jumped out of her skin. How did the
woman move so silently, especially dressed as she was?
Lupe was clad in an elaborately frilled gown of low-cut
black satin which clung lovingly to her impossibly narrow
waist. The hem was shorter in the front to show off lacy,
white-ruffled petticoats. She carried a pair of castanets.

"And unlike these peons, I have been photographed
before," she hissed. "So make it the best picture you
have ever done, *gringa*."

Or what? Tess wanted to ask, guessing Lupe had
seen Parrish smiling at her and hadn't liked it one bit.
"I have always tried to make each exposure better than
the one before," she said, her voice calm. "How would
you like to pose?"

Lupe narrowed her eyes suspiciously at the mild
reply, then stood a few feet away and struck a dramatic
attitude, her arms gracefully raised with the castanets
held in her fingers, her face in profile, gazing upward.

"Sandoval, remember when we danced the flamenco
together? We were like twin flames, eh?" Lupe said,

slanting her eye at him. "Come and pose with me as if we're dancing again," Lupe invited, running her tongue over her lush, full lower lip. Tess saw the woman dart a glance at her as if to see if she had caught the implications of her silky words.

Parrish shook his head, indicating his dusty trousers and shirt. "I'm not dressed for it, Lupe. I'd detract from your picture."

"Nonsense," Lupe said, pouting. "Come, *querido,* I want you to be in the picture."

But Parrish stood firm in his refusal. "No, you go ahead. I've already posed for Miss Hennessey."

Lupe stuck her lower lip out farther. "Very well, *querido,* but stay right there where I may see you for inspiration."

Tess had to duck hurriedly under the canvas so Lupe would not see her rolling her eyes. How could Parrish stand there with a straight face? But perhaps he enjoyed such antics from this woman.

Lupe pronounced herself displeased with Tess's first, second and third photographs, threatening to seize them and rip them up. "I don't know how you did it, *gringa,*" she snarled. "But do not make me look fat or stupid again or you will regret it."

Only Parrish's wink behind Lupe's back kept Tess's temper in check. Perspiration had begun to run down her back in rivulets and her hair clung to her damp neck.

Finally, on the fourth attempt, when Lupe saw that everyone else was sitting down to eat, she declared herself satisfied.

Chapter Eleven

Patrick Hennessy's shoulders slumped in discouragement as he rode up to the house. He and Samuel Taylor had ridden all the way to the closest Ranger headquarters, which was at Brownsville, only to be told by the captain there that Governor Roberts, who was trying to get along with the government in Mexico City, wouldn't authorize him to send a search party across the Rio Grande.

"But that's my *daughter* he's taken, man," Hennessy had protested. "Are you a father? If you are, surely you'll understand how distraught her mother and I are! How am I to go back there and tell her you won't even look?"

"That's not the way we used to do it in McNelly's day," Taylor had growled by his side.

"It'd be different if we knew exactly where to find her," the captain had said. "Then we could notify the Mexican officials we were coming, and secure their cooperation."

"I doubt very much they know the meaning of the word," Taylor snapped. "They've been turning a blind eye to Delgado's raids on Texas soil as long as he's been making them."

"Yes," the captain was forced to agree. "But if I know Delgado, he won't be able to resist raiding again, and soon. And if we can catch him in the act on Texas soil, we're within our rights to pursue him across the river."

"*If* you catch him! The man strikes like lightning and is gone that fast, too!" Hennessy retorted, despair nearly robbing him of reason. "And he might not have Tess with him! She's a beautiful girl—he might have sold her to someone, can't you see that?" Imagining his precious daughter in the hands of evil men, Patrick sank down on a nearby chair, his head in his hands.

"We have...*ahem!* Shall we say, *sources of intelligence* in Mexico? Perhaps someone will spot her. The way you described her—red hair and blue eyes—she won't blend in, Mr. Hennessy. Don't give up."

But now, as Patrick Hennessy dismounted in front of his home, giving the reins of his lathered horse to Mateo, he saw Amelia running down the steps, and his heart sank.

"Is there any word of her? Are they going after Tess?"

Putting his arms around his wife, Patrick told her what the Ranger captain had said, and let her weep in his arms. Then when he thought she had cried herself out, she lifted her head and told him what had happened while he and Taylor were gone. Delgado's men had struck the Duprees, who lived about five miles away. One of the bandits had been killed, another wounded, but after taking all they'd wanted, they'd ridden off as fast as they had come. And after they had gone, the maid had brought Amelia the note about Tess.

Sandoval wondered, as the day of the fiesta went on, what Tess must be thinking. At times, she appeared to be taking pleasure in the moment, and there was much about the day to find pleasurable—the simple joy of the children and the smiles of the adult villagers at this unexpected party, the delicious food, the lively music. Maybe she appreciated the opportunity to forget that she was a prisoner. But Lupe stuck to his side like a burr to a blanket and he had no opportunity to speak to Tess. Once, he saw her looking at Lupe and him with a strange expression on her face. Did Tess think he found the constant attention of Delgado's sister appealing?

He'd met Lupe only once before, when he'd first become allied with Delgado and his band, and even at that first meeting she'd made it very obvious she found Sandoval attractive. He hadn't felt the same about her, but he'd been able to pretend he didn't notice the seductive signals she'd sent him with her glances and seemingly accidental touches.

Now Delgado had invited her to stay with them for a prolonged visit, and because of it, Sandoval would have to walk a tightrope, appearing to find Lupe's lures irresistible without actually giving in to them. In time Lupe might be able to accept Sandoval's lack of interest—especially if others in the band were panting after her—but if she ever suspected Sandoval's growing feelings for Tess Hennessy, she would react with all the fury of a woman scorned, and it would be Tess who would suffer.

Dusk now deepened into dark in the canyon, and the ground was littered with empty whiskey, beer and tequila bottles. Sandoval spied Tess sitting at the edge of the firelight, looking weary and a little uneasy as the music got louder and the songs more raucous. At last, Delgado, who had been standing next to Sandoval and Lupe, leaned over and murmured, "Lupe, why not dance for us now?"

Preening, Lupe feigned reluctance to leave Sandoval's side. Sandoval knew what she wanted, and he gave it to her. "Please, Lupe, I'm sure everyone would enjoy seeing you dance."

"Even *you, querido?*" she murmured, looking sidelong at Sandoval.

"Oh, especially me, Lupe."

"Very well, then…"

"Sanchez!" Delgado shouted to the guitar player. "Play some flamenco for my sister to dance to, eh?"

Obligingly, the guitar player switched to a more lively tune and the audience began to clap in time.

As if she were mounting a stage, Lupe pranced into the center of the circle with a swishing of skirts. She struck a pose, head up, throat exposed, and began to move, twirling around and clicking her castanets in time to their clapping. She whirled this way and that, dipping low to entice the men, then flipping up her petticoats and dancing away as if taunting them. The emphatic stamping of the dancer's feet, so much a part of traditional flamenco, was somewhat muffled on the hard dirt beneath her, but the enthusiastic, rhythmic clapping of her audience more than made up for it.

Knowing what was required of him, Sandoval stared at Lupe and waited, hoping Lupe would get so caught up in her dancing she'd forget about any individual man watching. In time she did just that, closing her eyes and swaying as if her life began and ended with the rhythm of her stamping and the villagers' clapping.

Moving gradually, he stepped behind Delgado and moved to where Delores was sitting with her son. Leaning down, he used the music to cover his voice, and said,

"*Señora,* please tell Tess this would be a good time for her to retire to her hut. These men are only going to grow drunker, and we would not want her to have to discourage any unwelcome attentions, would we?" He winked at her. "Once she's in there, I'd appreciate it if you stayed with her and moved your pallet in front of the door."

Delores winked back. "I will be happy to do that for you, Sandoval."

The old woman read him too well. It was fortunate he could trust her. If only Delores could discourage Lupe from bothering him, also. After her dance, Lupe would seek him out, expecting him to feel amorous. He was going to have to feign a drunken slumber at the campfire.

It was a long time before the music and the hooting and laughter of the celebrants died down enough for Tess to fall asleep. She thought she had only just nodded off when Delores gently shook her awake. She saw from the light behind the towel-curtain that it was morning.

Delores held out a folded garment to Tess, mumbling something about Lupe. Apparently the skirt belonged to Delgado's sister, but Tess was to don it. Once dressed, she saw the breakfast of tortilla-wrapped strips of beef Delores had left on her trunk.

Now, as she stepped from the hut, bringing her sketching pad as ordered, the rising sun illuminated the forms of rebozo and horse-blanket-wrapped villagers sleeping everywhere on the ground.

Delgado, standing next to Esteban, who held his black stallion, grinned approvingly at her skirt. "*Buenos días.* I hope you slept well and are ready for a long ride, Señorita Tess. Sandoval is saddling your horse. We will soon be on our way."

His high-handed, authoritative tone sparked Tess's temper.

"Señor Delgado, you had me brought here to take your picture. I've done that. Several times. Why can't I just go home now?" She knew it was futile to ask, but she didn't want him to be in any doubt about her unwillingness.

"Because I want you with me, *señorita,*" he said, and the gleam in his eyes when he said it sent a chill of foreboding spearing through her.

"But…what about them?" she said, indicating the sleeping villagers.

Delgado shrugged. "Many will wake up with sore heads, but Delores will feed them and send them on their way to Santa Elena. They will talk of this fiesta for weeks. No more arguing, *señorita.*"

Parrish returned, leading his pinto and a sorrel mare. Lupe followed, holding the reins of a prancing white gelding. Lupe scowled as she saw Tess standing by her brother.

"I hope you can ride, *gringa.* This will not be a gentle outing in a park."

"I have ridden since I was old enough to walk," Tess told her, striving to keep her tone neutral. "My father taught me. Thank you for loaning me this riding skirt," she added politely.

Lupe's full lips twisted into a sneer. "It was one I had grown tired of," she proclaimed. "So don't think I will hesitate to shoot you out of the saddle if we're pursued and I think you lag behind on purpose."

"Lupe! Remember your manners!" Delgado snapped.

Over Lupe's shoulder, Sandoval caught Tess's eye,

his look warning but full of sympathy. It heartened her and gave her the will to hold her tongue and nod meekly, as if Lupe had succeeded in intimidating the *gringa*. She saw Parrish's shoulders relax.

The mare, which Parrish called Dulce, nuzzled Tess in a friendly fashion. Tess soon found that Parrish had chosen her mount well. Dulce's trot as she rode out of the canyon was easy to sit, and when they accelerated, Dulce's canter was as smooth as a rocking horse's. If only this were a pleasure ride! One glance at the bandits riding on all sides of her, however—a crisscrossed bandolier full of cartridges decorating each chest, pistols in holsters and rifles strapped to their saddles—made that pretense impossible.

They headed northeast, crossing the Rio Grande at a shallow point where the muddy water reached only as high as the stirrups. Tess was relieved—she knew if the horses had had to swim, her wet thighs would chafe, slapping against the soaked leather of the saddle.

Once across, Tess looked around her. She was once again on Texas soil. If only she knew exactly where she was—how close to any town! The scrubland on the northern side of the river, however, looked much the same as it did in Mexico. They rode on, occasionally passing isolated shacks, some with a bony horse or two standing in a small, weathered corral, but they kept going. Evidently the pickings weren't rich enough to tempt Delgado.

The sun was directly overhead when they spied a ranch in the distance with a pasture full of fat cattle and horses. The ranch house, built of fieldstone, was large and sprawling. On either side sat an outbuilding; one of them like a smaller version of the house, the other, more crudely built, looked like a bunkhouse. Behind them stood a large barn.

"Ah, there is a worthy target, eh?" Delgado said to Parrish.

Parrish shrugged. "I don't know...maybe we ought to ride farther north, hit a small town—concentrate on money and jewelry, things we can carry. Once we're driving horses and cattle, though, we have to hurry back across the river to one of your hideouts before they can put together a posse or summon the Rangers. Why not hit this place on the way back?"

Parrish wanted to penetrate farther into the interior of the Rio Grande Valley? Why? Tess wondered. If they did that, there was a risk of the bandits being cut off and taken. She sought his gaze, seeking a clue. Did he want to give her the chance to escape? But Lupe was studying him with narrowed eyes, and Parrish didn't look Tess's way.

"No, we strike here. Now," Delgado pronounced, his jaw set. "Look how easy they make it—they haven't even posted a lookout."

Parrish shrugged again. "A bird in the hand..."

Lupe reined her mare next to Tess. "You stay with me, do you hear, *gringa?* We will hang back until the gringos are subdued." Her scornful eyes made it very clear she begrudged the fact that she had to guard Tess instead of being in the thick of things with her brother.

Tess nodded, apprehension crawling up her spine like an icy spider. *Please, Lord, don't let the outlaws kill anyone. Protect Sandoval, please.*

Delgado looked over his shoulder at his men. "Ready, *muchachos?*"

"*¡Sí!*" they chorused, pulling pistols out of holsters

and rifles from their bindings behind their saddles.
Lupe gave Tess a dark, threatening glare.

Just then a cowboy ambled out of the barn carrying a
pitchfork, and stopped stock-still, staring. Dropping the
pitchfork, he let out a shout and ran for the bunkhouse.

"Curse him, he'll alert the others," growled Delgado.
"But no matter!" He uttered a hoarse cry and threw his
arm forward. As one man, the outlaws charged, the air
ringing with the ear-splitting report of their rifles.

Shutters slammed back from windows on either side
of the bunkhouse door, and puffs of smoke erupted from
rifles firing at them. Through the haze of gunfire, Tess
saw a window thrown open in the house, too, and red
flashes as a rifle began to spit bullets from there, too,
even as a bandit on the left flank fell limply from his
saddle. She lost track of Parrish.

Undeterred, the bandits kept going. As they closed
on the house and bunkhouse, a cowboy was unwise
enough to poke his head above the windowsill, and one
of the outlaws took aim and fired. Tess heard a scream
and the cowboy disappeared. A pair of bandits split off
from those riding toward the house, and hanging low
over the far side of their mounts like Comanches, using
their horses as shields, they shot directly into the bunkhouse windows. All return fire ceased.

Within the main house, Tess could hear women
shrieking and a man trying to shout over them, though
she couldn't make out the words. She felt tears streaming down her cheeks.

"Come out with your hands up and no one else will
be shot!" Delgado shouted at the house, while the outlaws who had shot at the bunkhouse dismounted and
yanked the bunkhouse door open. Seconds later two
cowboys emerged, pale-faced and trembling, their

hands raised high. One of them wore only pants held up by suspenders over his bare chest.

Parrish reappeared out of the floating smoke. Lupe grabbed a rein of Tess's mount and rode forward, her eyes gleaming in avid triumph.

A trio of trembling women emerged from the ranch house, one of them gray-haired, another younger, the third probably the cook, judging by the apron she wore around her rotund waist. All of them held their hands high; the younger woman wept.

"Don't hurt us," the older woman begged, clutching a shawl around herself. "Please. You can take what we have."

"Yes, I can, *señora*," Delgado agreed, smiling broadly, "Who was firing at us from that window in the house?"

The older woman straightened. "I was," she said, staring stonily at Delgado.

"Sandoval, go in and see if she tells the truth," Delgado ordered.

Tess watched as Parrish dismounted and complied, his pistol at the ready. A minute or so later he reemerged, using his pistol to push a shambling, balding man with his hands raised high. In his other hand Sandoval held a rifle. She saw Parrish saying something into the man's ear.

"I thought there was no one else, *señora*? He was the one firing, wasn't he?" Delgado taunted.

Parrish threw the rifle down on the ground. "It's empty," he said. "That's what he was firing with."

Both women fell down on their knees, shaking, tear-drenched eyes darting between the outlaw leader and Parrish's captive. "Please, don't kill him! He's all we have."

Delgado stilled, staring at the man, and raised his pistol.

The man in front of Parrish trembled, too, his eyes bulging in terror. Seconds ticked by, but they seemed like an eternity to Tess.

Suddenly the man's eyes rolled back in his head and he collapsed in the dirt. The women shrieked.

Parrish bent over him, then straightened and spoke to the women. "He's fainted."

Delgado's laugh dripped with scorn. "What a brave man! He'd rather pass out like a girl than fight to his last breath to save his women. Mendoza, Jimenez, tie up those cowboys, the women and that pitiful excuse of a man. Guard them while we do a little exploring inside," he said, pointing at the house.

Tess watched, agonized that she couldn't help the two women, while the two banditos did as Delgado had instructed them, and a handful of the other bandits disappeared inside the house. Parrish, however, remounted his horse.

"Watch her, *querido*," Lupe told him, jerking her head toward Tess. "I believe one of the ranch women is hiding something I might want."

Parrish did as she said, his face a mask, while Lupe slipped off her mare, lithe as a cat, and stalked up to the younger woman, who had struggled to her feet.

"Very pretty," she murmured, using the long muzzle of her pistol to caress the woman's neck, then to pick up a gold chain at her throat. As she lifted the muzzle, the chain pulled out an oval ruby pendant set in gold filigree from within the woman's bodice. "Ah, I thought so," Lupe said. "Take it off."

The young woman set her jaw and did so, staring

fixedly at a point in the distance. Then she deliberately dropped the necklace into the dust at her feet.

"Pick it up, *gringa,* or I'll make you very, very sorry."

The younger woman hesitated, then complied, her eyes stony.

Now the old woman seemed to see Tess for the first time. "You're not one of them, are you? How can you just sit there and watch?"

Chapter Twelve

Sandoval saw Tess pale and flinch as if the woman had slapped her.

"I… I'm not here by choice," she said, her voice barely above a whisper.

The woman looked unconvinced. "What's your name?"

"Tess Hennessy…of Hennessy Hall, near Chapin. Could you please send word to my parents that you've seen me? That I'm all right?"

"Liar! She's my brother's mistress," Lupe snapped. "I'll have those earrings, too." She pointed at the garnet pair dangling from the old woman's lobes, and held out her hand until the woman removed them and gave them to her, transferring her glare to the insolently smirking Lupe, who was not troubled by it in the least.

The bandits emerged a few minutes later, laden with booty—a brass candelabra, a pair of Colts with inlaid ivory handles, a gold pocket watch, a silver platter.

"Be thankful I left you the boxful of silverware," Delgado told the angry women. "A service for twelve, no? A pity it is so heavy, but we must ride fast. Be thankful. *Muchachos,* it's time we were on our way.

Drive the cattle and horses out of their pastures and let's get going."

"But you can't leave us tied up like this!" the younger woman protested.

"I say we herd these fools inside and fire the house," Lupe suggested to her brother, deliberately using English, Sandoval knew, so she could enjoy the horrified reaction on the captives' faces. "In revenge for Pablo, over there." She pointed to where one of the men was tying Pablo's body onto his horse.

"As much as I like revenge, Lupe, that would not be nice for our guest, would it?" Delgado asked, nodding toward Tess. "Don't be so bloodthirsty."

Lupe pouted.

"I left your knots a little loose," Sandoval told the woman, his voice curt and impersonal. "If you work at it awhile, you ought to be able to free yourself, and then the others."

"Of course, by that time we'll be safely back in Mexico," Delgado added. *"¡Adios!"*

They wasted no time reaching the river again, driving the stolen cattle and horses ahead of them as fast as they could go. At this crossing, the Rio Grande was so deep the animals had to swim. Once across, they didn't linger. It wasn't safe to dally on the other side—they had to put some distance between themselves and any pursuers. Rangers and posses of vengeful civilians had crossed the river before.

By late afternoon they reached one of the small, hidden valleys Delgado had used before on his forays away from his main camp in the canyon. Everyone was exhausted from the hard ride. No one spoke while several of them dug a grave for their fallen compadre, and no one wept. Dying was a known hazard in the life of a bandito. Sandoval saw Tess sketching the burial scene from the fireside, where she was tending a pot of cooking beans, and wondered what she was thinking.

After supper, night watches over the stolen livestock were assigned, and the men who did not have the first watch rolled up in their serapes and were soon snoring by the fire. At last only four remained sitting near the campfire and watching the sparks fly upward from its flickering blue-and-orange depths—Sandoval, Delgado, Lupe and Tess.

Tess looked strained, Sandoval thought. She stared with unfocused eyes into the fire, as if haunted by what had happened today. He willed her to announce she was going to her quarters. Then he could walk with her without being too obvious and speak to her alone, at least for a few moments. He clenched and unclenched a fist. Blast it, there was never a chance to tell her what he was thinking, to begin to tell her what was in his heart. Always, Delgado was around, or Lupe, or one of the men—and most of them, he thought, jealous of Sandoval's position as Delgado's right-hand man, would gladly do what they could to discredit him. Telling the outlaw leader that his lieutenant was paying too much attention to the pretty lady photographer that Delgado fancied would certainly accomplish that.

Tess remained where she was, perhaps hypnotized by the flames, perhaps too deep in her thoughts.

Delgado seemed determined to stay out here with Tess, too, so Sandoval continued to wait. He didn't want to leave Delgado with Tess—nor did he want to give Lupe an opportunity to seek *him* out alone.

"Where do we go tomorrow, *hermano?*" Lupe asked at last, breaking the silence. "Into Ciudad Rio Bravo to sell the booty?"

Delgado took a puff of his cigarillo, shaking his head. "No, it's a poor town. I doubt even the *alcalde* has the price of that watch or the silver platter, much less the cattle. What would you think of riding up to Rancho Cordoba and spending a day there? I'm sure Andrés Cordoba would be delighted to buy the cattle and horses we took today."

"Diego! You are the best of brothers," Lupe exclaimed, throwing her arms around him and kissing him on the cheek. "I'm sure he will invite us to dine with him! Perhaps we could prevail on him to invite Sandoval, too?" She fluttered her lashes at Sandoval.

Across the fire, Sandoval saw Tess watching the brother and sister. He could practically see her mind working, and knew she was hoping that if the Delgados were going visiting, she would get her chance to escape.

Delgado chuckled. "Are you trying to make Cordoba jealous, *hermana?* He's never made any secret of his affection for you—maybe you ought to encourage him. You could become a lady of leisure, you know."

"Perhaps I will…." She shot another look at Sandoval, as if daring him to object; then, when he didn't rise to the bait, she said, "I don't know…perhaps I would be bored, not being free to go raiding with my brother the bandit, and his handsome lieutenant…."

"And we could not very well invite Sandoval without Señorita Tess, eh? I would be a very bad host if I left Tess behind while you and Sandoval and I dined with Cordoba."

Across the fire, Sandoval saw Tess's mouth tighten in frustration.

"I think you're more concerned I'll escape if you leave me here," she said. "But aren't you afraid I'll tell this rancher that I'm your captive, and he'll demand you free me?"

Delgado threw back his head and laughed. "Hardly! Cordoba's father was killed by the *Norteamericanos* at Veracruz. He wouldn't lift a finger to help a Texan, even such a lovely one as you." He reached out a finger and casually chucked her under the chin.

Sandoval had to look away so Delgado and Lupe wouldn't notice his clenched jaw. Tess looked as if she wanted to slap the outlaw leader.

"I imagine he would find it fascinating to meet you, though, *señorita*," Delgado continued. "It's too bad you don't have your photographic equipment with you, but perhaps you could offer to draw him, eh? Very well, tomorrow we visit Rancho Cordoba, so you ladies had better get your rest. The more beautiful you both are, the more Cordoba will be dazzled and pay me what I want for the livestock."

As if in mutual consent, the Delgados and Tess rose and started for their respective quarters. Sandoval trailed behind, watching sister and brother enter Delgado's quarters and Tess hers. He knew Delores was already inside.

Sandoval was well satisfied with the plan for tomorrow. If they spent the day at Rancho Cordoba, that was one day Tess would not be exposed to the dangers of raiding. And if Cordoba kept Delgado busy dickering over the price of the livestock, and distracted Lupe with flirtation, surely he could find some time to speak to Tess alone....

"You drive a hard bargain, Delgado," said Andrés Cordoba, a tall, urbane man whose proud, erect carriage hinted at his descent from Spanish grandees. They stood in front of the corral where the stolen cattle and horses had been driven for his inspection. "But I find it hard to haggle anymore in this hot sun if it means keeping your beautiful sister—" he winked at Lupe "—and the charming Señorita Hennessy from refreshing themselves in their guest chamber. A good siesta, and then later we will dine. I think you will find my cook has outdone herself in your honor," he said, bowing low and raising Lupe's hand to his lips.

Lupe giggled and fluttered her thick lashes at Cordoba; then, when the rancher turned his attention back to Delgado, shaking his hand to seal the deal, Sandoval saw Lupe aim a challenging look at him. But he shook his head subtly, as if hinting he couldn't show his feelings, and kept his features impassive.

"Very well then, we will see you later, *mi amigo*. It's a pleasure doing business with you," Delgado said. "Sandoval, you will station yourself in front of the chamber Lupe and Tess share, eh?"

Cordoba pursed his lips. "But I assure you, no one would dare bother a guest in my house. I'm sure that's not necessary."

Sandoval saw how he could use the rancher's interest in Lupe.

"But remember I have told you I am still trying to persuade Señorita Tess to remain with us," Delgado said, winking at Cordoba, as if entrusting the silver-haired rancher with his roguish secret.

"Yes, yes, of course," said Cordoba, glancing up and down at Tess, then winking back. "Very well then, until later…"

While Delgado, Lupe and Tess began walking toward the imposing house, Sandoval deliberately caught

Cordoba's eye, jerking his head as if to indicate that he wanted the rancher to lag behind.

Fortunately, Andrés Cordoba guessed his meaning. "There was something you wished to talk to me about, Sandoval?"

Sandoval nodded. "I must tell you something, but first I want to assure you that while I am in her confidence, Señorita Lupe and I are merely friends. I am like a brother to her—except that she can confide in me more freely than she can to her real brother."

Cordoba waited, one eyebrow raised.

"The *señorita* is a woman of great passion," Sandoval said. "And I believe the object of that passion is *you*, Señor Cordoba. She begged her brother to bring her back here to visit you. The cattle were only an excuse."

Cordoba blinked. "Can that be true? She said so?"

Sandoval gave an elaborate shrug. "Not in so many words… But I believe if you were to press your suit while she is here, you would find the results very…rewarding." Sandoval glanced meaningfully in the direction of Lupe's gracefully swaying figure.

Cordoba's eyes widened. "You do not jest with me? You are serious?"

By this time the others had reached the wrought-iron gate to the courtyard and didn't seem to notice that the rancher hadn't kept pace with them. Sandoval stopped stock-still, forcing Cordoba to stop, too.

"Couldn't you tell by her flushed features, the light in her eyes, when she saw you?" Sandoval said.

Cordoba clapped his hand on Sandoval's shoulder, grinning. "Ah, Sandoval, that is good news! Being around Lupe makes me feel like a young man again. I thought I would never fall in love a second time, after my late wife died so tragically. She was never able to give me children, the poor woman...."

Sandoval grinned back. "I think that would not be a problem with the *señorita* in question, *señor.* Just look at her."

Cordoba did so, licking his lips. "So what would you suggest I do, Sandoval? Ask Delgado for the beauteous Lupe's hand in marriage after dinner tonight?"

Sandoval allowed his features to become grave. "I think the lady would like you to woo her first. You know how women are. They don't want to be handed over like a sack of cornmeal! Perhaps you should find a way to be alone with her this afternoon...."

"And how would I do that, Sandoval? She will be very effectively guarded by you, and chaperoned by the presence of that pretty redheaded Texan, *si?* Speaking of her, I must admit that if it were not for my love of Lupe, I would beg Delgado to leave that little morsel with me!"

Sandoval forced himself to chuckle. "No, you have chosen the right one. You wouldn't suspect it to look at her, but that red-haired Texan has the very devil of a temper. I would suggest you come to their chamber in a little while and tell her that you crave a few precious minutes to speak to her." He waggled his eyebrows.

"But what of Señorita Hennessy?"

"She's guessed Lupe's feelings and is sympathetic. She won't tell Delgado you were there."

"Amigo, I am in your debt," the other man said, beaming.

"And I will be happy to dance at your wedding," Sandoval replied, praying his ruse would work. He *had* to find a time to speak to Tess, to let her know what he was planning. "Oh, and one more suggestion..."

"Yes?"

"I wouldn't mention to the lady that I told you all this. Ladies like to think their suitors' actions are spontaneous, you know what I mean?"

"Of course…" Cordoba pumped his hand.

The clean, smooth sheets and the luxuriously appointed room reminded Tess of her room back at Hennessy Hall, sending a wave of homesickness over her as she sat sketching at the table, while Lupe lay on the big bed. If she ever reached home again, Tess was sure it would be very hard to leave it, even if Mathew Brady himself issued her an invitation to come to New York!

"Stop rattling the paper, *gringa!*" hissed Lupe, turning from where she had been lying with her back turned to Tess. "The flickering candlelight is bad enough. How am I supposed to fall asleep?"

"I… I'm sorry, Lupe," Tess said. "Perhaps I should blow out the candle and lie down, though I don't feel very sleepy—"

"So I can feel you tossing and turning? Stay where you are!"

"All ri—"

Suddenly both women stilled as they heard a soft knock at the door.

"Who is that? Sandoval? What do you want?"

"No, it's I, Andrés," came the soft, cultured voice. "I must talk to you, Lupe!"

Lupe sat up, staring first at the door, as if she didn't believe who had come, then at Tess.

"I—I'm not alone, Andrés! That…that *gringa* is with me, you remember?" She glared at Tess as if she expected her to disappear if she looked hard enough.

"I know, my sweet," he called softly through the

door, "but Sandoval has volunteered to take her else-where so that we may be alone for a while...."

"But, *señor*..." Lupe gave a girlish giggle. "I'm not sure it's entirely proper for me to be alone with you here...perhaps Tess should remain as my duenna?"

Tess heard Cordoba groan against the door.

"I swear you have nothing to fear from me, Lupita, *mi corazón*," he declared. "My intentions are entirely honorable. We can go down to my chapel if you like. But I cannot speak freely in front of another..."

Lupe smiled, smug as a cat that had just captured a particularly choice mouse.

"No, I trust you, Andrés. I'll be ready in a minute, then..." Lupe called, then grabbed at the blouse and skirt she'd thrown over a chair. "*¡Gringa!* Help me get dressed and comb my hair!"

It was fortunate Tess had remained fully clothed, for Lupe threw the door open as soon as Tess finished combing Lupe's thick, ebony hair. Cordoba stepped inside. Tess caught a glimpse of Parrish standing just behind him, his expression hotly sulky as he watched the rancher bend to embrace Lupe.

He's jealous, Tess realized with a stab of pain. Lupe had monopolized Sandoval's time the first day she had come to camp, but since then, Tess had seen no more evidence that Sandoval returned Lupe's interest, and she'd begun to think Sandoval had only been polite to Lupe. But here was unmistakable evidence she had been wrong.

He does want Lupe Delgado for himself, she thought. How could he be so foolish as to care about Delgado's sister, with her bold eyes and loose ways? She doesn't care about Cordoba for himself—she just wants to make Parrish want her more!

For a moment she thought past the blinding pain and felt sorry for the older rancher. If he sincerely loved Lupe Delgado, he was going to hurt one day, too.

"We'll go for a walk," Parrish announced, pulling Tess outside. He called over her head to the other two, who were still clasped in an oblivious embrace, "If we return to find the door ajar, *señor,* we'll know you've left."

Cordoba kicked the door closed without answering.

Parrish took Tess by the elbow and marched her down the outdoor corridor that overlooked the inner courtyard.

Tess waited until they had descended the shadowy steps to the flagstone courtyard. "Take your hands off me!" She yanked her arm from his grasp. "Where are we going?" she demanded, when he kept striding on, not looking at her.

"To Cordoba's chapel," he said in a low voice. "That's the one place I'm sure no one will bother us. Even if they leave the room, Lupe won't want to go there."

The rancher's small, private chapel lay diagonally across from the chamber they had just left, but rather than cutting across the square inner courtyard, Parrish kept to the shadows beneath the overhanging balconies of the upper rooms.

He turned to see if anyone was watching, then pulled open the door and gestured her inside. He had thought it would be safer for her not to know everything, but he could no longer bear for her not to know the truth.

Chapter Thirteen

The chapel was small and dimly lit only by the sun penetrating one brilliant stained glass window in a corner and a candle burning on the altar beneath it. Tess stared up at Parrish's earnest, shadowed face.

"There's no need to be angry," he said.

That was the last thing she had expected to hear. "*Me? Angry?* I would have said it was *you* who was angry—at Cordoba, for desiring Lupe, too."

To her annoyance, he laughed. "'Too?' *I* don't want her."

She blinked up at him. "Y-you *don't?* B-but I thought you did, that you found her…" Her voice trailed off. She didn't want to say *entrancing, irresistible* aloud, for fear he'd change his mind.

"If that's the way I made it look, I was successful," he told her. "I wanted her to think I felt that way about her because it's what she expects from a man. It'd be hazardous for me to show her otherwise, particularly since she's Delgado's sister. And more dangerous still for you, if she guessed it's *you* I care about."

Her jaw fell open. "Y-you *do?*"

Sandoval nodded solemnly, his dark eyes black as night in the shadowy chapel. "It's not what I intended when I set this whole plan in motion," he admitted, "and I've been fighting it from the first moment I met you at Sam Taylor's barbecue, but I'm not winning that struggle. Something was telling me not to go through with this kidnapping scheme, but fool that I was, I went ahead. Now, of course, I wish I hadn't, but it doesn't do any good. We're in the thick of things and I have to keep you safe till I can get you out of it."

"I… I see," she breathed.

He turned and paced toward the altar, then back to her.

"Lupe isn't content with mere adoration, of course, so I needed to do something to distract her from me. Delgado mentioned that the last time Lupe went raiding with him, he could see Cordoba fancied her, so I only had to hint to Cordoba that this time she might accept him. If he can woo her into staying here and marrying him, we'll only have her brother to worry about."

Tess nodded, considering. It was a lot to take in. He cared for her. What did that mean, exactly? And why had he made this plan to get her into Delgado's hands in the first place?

"I…don't blame you for being angry at me," he said. "I was wrong to do what I did, bringing you into his camp, involving you."

"I'm not angry. I… I was," she confessed, "at first."

"So…you don't hate me?" he asked, behind her.

"Hate you?" she repeated, turning back around. "No, I don't hate you, I—" She stopped short. Had she really been about to say she loved him? She did, but it made no sense. There was no future in loving Sandoval Parrish, a man whose loyalty lay with Mexico—a man whom she could never imagine wanting to settle down and be law-abiding, on either side of the Rio Grande, let alone raise babies with her!

"No, I don't hate you," she said again. "But I still don't know why you've made this choice to ride with Delgado, yet you like hobnobbing with Texas planters and ranchers as one of them, too. Aren't you afraid someone will recognize you when you go raiding?"

"I wear a bandanna over my face where I might be known. And no, I didn't choose what I'm doing. It's a matter of retribution."

Retribution. It was a chilling word, a word that echoed in the quiet stillness of the chapel. A word that seemed to have been ripped from the recesses of his heart. Parrish's features were suddenly wintry and hard.

"Retribution? Against Anglos? Are you one of those Mexicans still angry that Texas is no longer part of Mexico?"

He shook his head. "Not against Anglos. Against Delgado."

"But why?"

"That's what I brought you here to tell you. I've wanted to tell you for a few days now, but there's never been a safe place to talk to you, a place where we couldn't be overheard."

Parrish held up his hand as if to indicate that he would speak again in a moment, then walked stealthily to the door and threw it open. She saw him look up and down the shadowed, cloisterlike walkway. The abrupt gust of indrawn air made the candle flame dance wildly on the altar. Then he shut the door again and returned to her, taking a deep breath.

"No one is around," he said. "Tonight at dinner, I believe Cordoba will ask Delgado for Lupe's hand, if he's been successful in his courting," he said, nodding in the direction of the room across the courtyard and up the stairs. "That means Lupe will stay with him."

It would be wonderful to be free of the woman's hostile, sarcastic, ever-watchful presence, Tess thought—and to not have to watch her staring at Parrish with those avid eyes.

"We'll remain with Delgado," he went on, "till we return to the canyon camp. Then we'll escape."

"Wouldn't it be easier to make a run for it while we're across the river on a raid?"

"Yes, but there's something back at camp I need to get."

Tess let her eyes ask the question. Tess couldn't imagine what he could be referring to. Surely if either of them had something in camp to return for, it was she. But she could not imagine how they could flee with Ben and the heavy, slow wagon full of photographic equipment. As fond as she was of the old mule, he wasn't capable of speed. She hated the idea of leaving him and her precious camera behind, but she'd do what she had to, of course, to make it to safety and hope she could somehow get them back.

"You have negatives of the pictures you took of Delgado, correct?"

Tess nodded.

"I want a couple of those. One full-face, one profile. Maybe one of the developed pictures, too."

She waited, twisting a fold of her skirt in her hand.

"I want to be able to reproduce his image all over the Rio Grande Valley—farther, if need be—on Wanted posters, so Delgado can be captured. The problem has been that when the government has sent army detachments to capture him, he goes to ground, blends in with the peons. And when Delgado's not wearing that fancy stolen uniform, he's ordinary looking, isn't he?"

She nodded, realizing it was true. Take away his

swagger and arrogant confidence, and Delgado *was* ordinary—totally unlike Sandoval Parrish.

"But why are *you* the one doing this?"

He sighed, and drew her to the only place to sit in the chapel, a wooden bench in the back.

"I'm not an outlaw, Tess. I'm a Texas Ranger."

She stared at him. So much made sense now—especially Uncle Samuel's trust of him, when so many of the planters in the Rio Grande Valley were suspicious of Parrish. Sam Taylor was a retired Ranger. And now she knew why Parrish had had her kidnapped. As she had known, it was to take pictures of Delgado, but not because he wanted to pander to Delgado's ego.

"But don't Rangers usually work with other Rangers?"

"Usually, yes, but a whole company of Anglo-looking Texas Rangers can't infiltrate a pack of banditos."

No, they couldn't. But Sandoval Parrish, with his Hispanic heritage, dark eyes and hair, who'd grown up speaking Spanish as well as English, could.

The peril of his task unnerved her. Hardly aware of what she was doing, she grasped his wrist with urgent fingers. "You're playing a dangerous game, Sandoval. If they find out, they'll kill you."

"Yes," he admitted, looking down at her hand, then covering it with his own. "Probably slowly and painfully."

"Then why take the risk? Why does it have to be *you*, Sandoval? Why do you need retribution?"

Tess could see from the way his eyes changed that what he said next would transform everything.

Parrish took a deep breath and stared at the altar. "Because of what he did to Pilar."

"Pilar?" she echoed. "Was she…was she your wife?"

"My sister." He closed his eyes as if fearing she would read the pain in them.

"Tell me," Tess urged quietly.

"Pilar was older than me by five years, the sweetest, most beautiful girl in Montemorelos, maybe all of Mexico. Delgado had already begun the life of an outlaw, and was riding all over northern Mexico recruiting young men to join him. He'd swagger into a village and promise them booty and women and fame, and many believed what he promised."

"But not you."

"Not me," he agreed. "I wanted to be a ranchero like my father, and carry on what he'd begun when he met my mother and settled down near Montemorelos. Delgado kept coming around, trying to persuade me, and then he saw my sister coming out of the church in town. He lost all interest in me, of course. He decided he had to have her."

She waited.

"Papa tried to run him off. Pilar was the apple of his eye, and he wasn't about to let a man like Delgado close to his angel. One day when I was away from the ranch, Delgado rode in and asked our father for Pilar's hand in marriage. My father refused, naturally. Delgado didn't settle for that—he seduced my sister instead. One morning we found her bed empty—she had left with him in the night. We never saw her again, and Papa died of a broken heart."

"You...you don't know what happened to her? Whether she died, or..."

He shook his head. "She must be dead," he said bleakly. "It's been five years. Why wouldn't she have come back if she was alive? No, he must have killed her. And now you know why I'm with Delgado. I'm going to destroy him. For Pilar. But I'm going to do it legally. I've had any number of chances to shoot him in cold blood—but that would make me the same as him."

"But…he doesn't recognize you? Or your name?"

Sandoval shook his head. "I was a skinny, half-grown boy whose voice still cracked. I'd hardly begun to grow a beard," he said, rubbing his cheeks and chin with a thumb and forefinger. "My parents always called me by my baptismal name, Juan, and in order to qualify for a land grant, my father had taken my mother's surname, Morelos—though everyone in the village knew his last name was Parrish. Delgado never knew it, though."

"Oh, Sandoval," was all Tess could say.

"I only hope she didn't suffer too much," he said, and though he looked in Tess's direction, his gaze was unfocused—a thousand miles, or ten years, away.

"But you have to find out what happened to her," she told him.

"I told you, she's dead. She must be," he insisted, turning his head away from Tess.

"You don't *know* that," she argued. "And you can't let him go to his grave carrying that secret. You'd always wonder."

"Tess, what am I supposed to do? Tell him I'm that skinny boy from Montemorelos, the one with the beautiful, innocent sister he despoiled, and I'd like to know where he left her? Mexico is probably full of women with the same story." Parrish turned back to her, his eyes full of a frustrated anger. "Even if I had him tied up and put a pistol to his head, he'd just laugh at me like the demon he is. No, I'll have to be content with seeing him pay for his crimes."

"Maybe *I* can find out," she said.

Chapter Fourteen

"You? How in—how do you propose to find out something like that?" he demanded, hands outspread. "Even if you could get him talking, he probably doesn't even *remember* what he did with her when he was tired of her."

"He might not," Tess admitted. "But then again, he might. All I can do is try. After we leave here it'll be a while before we return to the canyon camp, right?" Tess said. "That should furnish plenty of evenings to get him talking—you know he loves to brag of his exploits, especially when he's drinking. I'll pretend to be fascinated with his stories, and after a while I'll ask him about the early days."

Sandoval pictured what Tess was saying, of her leaning toward him, murmuring words like, "Really? Go on…tell me more…" while Delgado sank deeper and deeper into his bottle of tequila. And he realized how even a drunken Delgado would react to her rapt interest. It might well go far beyond talking.

"*No!*" he cried suddenly, making Tess jump with his vehemence. "You'd be playing with fire, Tess! You don't know what he's capable of."

"I think I do," she argued. "I've seen some of it, and you've just told me a good deal more. We *must* find out if Pilar's alive, Sandoval, if it's possible."

She thought he meant Delgado's anger, Sandoval realized. He had to be plainer. "Don't you see, Tess, I don't want what happened to Pilar to happen to *you*," he said, desperate to convince her.

"It won't. *You'll* be there," she told him, her eyes shining with confidence in him. A confidence he didn't deserve. "And we'll pray about it and ask the Lord to help us—"

He ignored her last words. "And what if Delgado shoots me, or stabs me when I step in to save you from his...*attentions,* shall we say? Then what? I don't care about me," he declared hotly, jumping up to stand in front of her. "I've long thought I deserved to die after failing to protect my own sister from that monster. But what would *you* do then? No, let Pilar rest in peace, Tess. Leave it alone. It's my responsibility to get you to safety and achieve justice for her."

"No."

"No?" He couldn't believe his ears.

She stared up at him, her eyes enormous in her pale face, but her gaze was steadfast and determined. "No," she repeated. "You've been with Delgado how long? And he hasn't happened to mention your sister, has he?"

"About a year," he admitted grudgingly. "Before that, I was learning the ropes as a Ranger, and showing them they could trust me, a man of mixed heritage, to be fully Texan in my loyalty. But I wasn't expecting Delgado to just blurt out Pilar's fate—I was hoping to set up an ambush so he and his men could be captured. But I haven't been able to, since he never picks his targets far enough in advance, or at least, announces his choices.

Then I decided if we could publish his picture all over the Southwest, he could be captured when he tries to go to ground in Texas, as he's had to before. That's why you're with us, to help me do that."

"I've taken the photographs, so that's done," she said. "And now I'm going to help you find out about your sister."

Sandoval crossed his arms. "Forget it, Tess. I forbid it," he told her.

It was the wrong thing to say. He saw frustration kindle her temper, and in a heartbeat she had jumped up, too, her chin jutting out as she glared up at him. "Who are *you* to forbid me anything? What right do you have to talk to me that way?"

"No right." He threw the admission at her, his own anger sparked now. "But I love you, and I won't let you put yourself under the cat's paw like that."

His declaration in the midst of their mutual anger had shaken her to the core—he saw that. Tess grew paler still, and she blinked—once, twice, three times.

"You love me," she repeated.

"Yes. I can't imagine why. You're stubborn and full of Irish temper as fiery as your hair," he said, reaching out and lifting the thick red braid that lay over her shoulder, then dropping it as if it burned him. "And set on having your own way, even if it destroys you, woman," he shot back. "I'm not worthy of you, I know. But I love you, Tess Hennessy, and I would die for you. That's why you must listen to me."

If he thought his words would render her submissive to his will, he was doomed to disappointment.

"I love you, too, Sandoval Parrish," she said, her eyes still blazing. "And if your Latin blood convinces you to think you have only to raise your voice to get your way, then maybe you'd better think twice about loving me, because I'm not a silly little mouse who will tremble if you yell."

No, she was no mouse. She was Tess, *his* Tess, and she was magnificent, even when she defied him and her rash ideas made him fear for her.

For a moment they just stared at each other, their faces inches apart, and then he was kissing her, pouring his soul into her, holding her so tightly that he could feel her heart race with his.

"Sandoval—"

"Tess—"

He was about to beg her to listen to him, not to try to trick Delgado for information, if only because she loved him. Just then, however, they heard approaching booted footsteps, accompanied by the characteristic clinking sound that spurs make against stone.

They had only a second or two to spring apart—she to throw herself down on her knees before the altar as if she had been praying, he to stride quickly and noiselessly toward the back of the chapel, and then Delgado came in, carrying something over his arm. Sandoval hoped the shadowy dimness of the chapel would hide Tess's flushed cheeks.

"Ah, I thought I might find our devout little lady photographer here," he said. "Are you praying for my soul, *señorita?*"

"Oh, did you feel in need of that?" she asked.

Sandoval saw Delgado search her face for mockery, but it seemed he found none. "Certainly. Prayer for oneself is always appreciated."

The hypocrite, she thought. He sounded pious as a Franciscan monk.

"Perhaps I was only praying for *my* safety until I'm able to return home, *señor*," she told him frankly.

"Only yours?" Delgado *tsk-tsked*. "How disappointing." He shrugged. "I came to bring you and Lupe dresses that belonged to Cordoba's late wife. He thought you might want to dress for dinner. I knocked at the door of your and Lupe's room, but no one answered. I suppose Lupe was sleeping soundly, eh?"

Sandoval saw Tess quickly look away from Delgado, but too late. He'd seen some hint in her expression that whatever his sister was doing, it probably was *not* sleeping.

"*¿Señorita?* Are you trying to hide something from me?"

Sandoval spoke up. "Cordoba came courting, Diego. Your sister and he are probably strolling the grounds somewhere."

"Ah, I see." Delgado's lips formed a smirk of satisfaction. "*¡Bueno!* I told Lupe she should latch onto him if he was still interested. She could do much worse than to marry a rich, old fool who would die soon and leave her a wealthy landowner, eh?"

He didn't wait to see if they agreed, but laid one of the garments, of a purple so dark it was nearly black, on the bench, saying, "That one is for Lupe." He held out the other, a rich, deep blue, to Tess. "I think this will look very well on you, *señorita*. I look forward to seeing you in it."

Tess took it and the other, nodding. "It'll be nice to wear something else for a change," she said, indicating her drawstring blouse and split skirt as if she had nothing more weighty on her mind than what she wore, and had not noticed the subtle tensing of Sandoval's muscles.

"We dine at eight," Delgado said, turning on his heel

to go, then back again. "Oh—I almost forgot—as I left the upper floor, servants were bringing up buckets of hot water and a couple of hip baths, so you ladies can bathe the dust of the trail away. If Lupe lingers too long under the grape arbor kissing Cordoba, her water will be cold, eh? Just the thing to cool her hot blood," Delgado joked.

His eyes met Sandoval's across the room, and there was finally sympathy in them, sympathy that Sandoval, despite his handsomeness, could not compete with Cordoba's wealth for Lupe. Sandoval's expression was convincingly aggrieved.

"Welcome, ladies, you grace my humble table," Cordoba said, rising along with Delgado and Parrish as Tess followed Lupe into the dining room. With a gallant flourish, Cordoba pulled out Lupe's chair. Parrish took a step forward, but Tess quickly fired a warning look at him, for Delgado was already moving to put his hands on the elaborately carved back of Tess's chair. Parrish sank darkly into his seat on the other side of Lupe, which placed him diagonally across from Tess. Cordoba sat at the head of the table with Lupe on his right and Tess on his left.

After he had assisted Tess into her seat, Delgado bent low, murmuring into her ear, "You look truly lovely this evening, *señorita*." He probably would have kissed her cheek if Tess hadn't said quickly, "Thank you, *señor*," before turning brightly to Cordoba and saying, "Thank you for the loan of this dress, Señor Cordoba. It was very kind of you. And how lovely your table looks."

"Nonsense, my dear lady," Cordoba said, but his face beamed at her praise. "It gives me pleasure to have lovely ladies at my table again. And it is but a simple supper." He wore a dark frock coat with a gold brocade waistcoat over an immaculate white shirt and looked immensely dignified.

"You are too modest, *querido*," Lupe purred, her slender fingers caressing the older man's wrist. "This is truly a magnificent feast."

For once, Lupe spoke the truth. The linen-covered table fairly groaned with silver platters and gold-rimmed, fine-china bowls full of roast beef, chicken, sliced pork in an aromatic sauce, spicy-smelling rice dishes, salads, bread. The gilt-edged plates were embellished with the Cordoba crest in the middle. The gold-rimmed crystal goblets sparkled; the silverware was heavy and ornate. Tess could faintly hear the buzz of conversation outside in the courtyard where Delgado's men were feasting, too, though she guessed their menu was much less sumptuous.

Tess sighed with pleasure at the idea of eating a meal that didn't include beans and tortillas, even as she remembered to bow her head and give thanks. *Thou preparest a table before me in the midst of mine enemies.*

Dishes were passed and for a few minutes there was nothing but the clinking of silverware against fine china and appreciative remarks about the deliciousness of the food.

Tess wished she could gaze openly at Parrish. Like Delgado, he had no fancy clothes, but he'd clearly bathed, shaved, and changed his shirt. He outshone any man she'd ever known. When Delgado turned to him to corroborate a story about one of their raids, she took advantage of the time to drink in the sight of him.

Despite his obvious reluctance to take his eyes off Lupe, Cordoba was the consummate host, making sure everyone's plates were heaped with food and their goblets never empty. Tess was relieved to see her glass had been filled with water rather than wine.

She could almost have enjoyed herself if it hadn't been for Delgado's closeness and his wandering eyes—the neckline of her borrowed dress was too low for her comfort. Tess grabbed the lacy shawl she had draped over the back of her chair and wrapped it around her shoulders, acting as if she felt a draft.

"Diego tells me you are a photographer, Señorita Hennessy, and that you have been taking pictures of him," Andrés Cordoba said. "What a surprising pastime for a young lady, to be sure."

Tess sensed Delgado holding his breath, probably wondering if she would embarrass him in front of their host by telling him the full story of how she had been brought to the outlaw against her will. Little did Delgado know how safe he was from that, now that she was determined to delve into his memories of Parrish's sister.

"It's my profession, sir, rather than a pastime," Tess corrected Cordoba, though she smiled to soften it. Out of the corner of her eye, she saw Delgado relax a little. "As soon as my work with Señor Delgado is done, I hope to go to New York to work for the famous Mathew Brady."

"I am hoping to talk her out of leaving, however," Delgado told him. "I had wanted my picture taken, yes, but once I beheld this charming lady, I was captivated—by her beauty, her fire."

"Ah…" Cordoba said. "I wish you luck, my good friend."

Tess felt distinctly uneasy as Delgado placed an arm casually but possessively around her shoulder. She did not dare look at Sandoval. She could not indignantly

remove Delgado's arm if she hoped to pump him later
for information.

Cordoba stood again and lifted his goblet. "I would
like to propose a toast," he proclaimed, "to Diego Delgado, a friend and business partner who is about to become a relative, and to his lovely sister, Lupe."

Delgado, on Tess's left, pretended—not very convincingly—to be mystified. "My good friend, whatever do you mean?"

Cordoba smiled broadly, and it made him look ten
years younger. "Perhaps I should have asked you for
your permission before I approached the lady, but I hope
you will forgive me, Diego. Your lovely sister has consented to become my bride—but only with your permission, of course."

At his side, Lupe preened and even managed a maid-
enly blush. Tess wondered how she did it.

"But this is wonderful news!" Delgado cried, jumping up and coming around behind Tess to embrace Cordoba and his sister in turn. "But of course I consent and
give you my heartiest blessing!"

Since Delgado, his sister and Cordoba were all
wrapped up in the moment, Tess felt it safe to exchange
a triumphant look across the table with Sandoval. The
remainder of her captivity would go so much more easily if she didn't have to cope with Lupe's ever-watchful
eyes, her scorn for Tess and her attempts to get Parrish alone.

"In that case," Cordoba said, reaching inside his
waistcoat, and taking Lupe's hand with his other hand
as he sat back down next to Lupe, "I would be honored,
my dearest, sweet Lupe, if you would wear this betrothal
ring as a symbol of our love."

The ring was a large emerald cabochon set in gold.

"Oh, Andrés, it's lovely," cooed Lupe, smothering a wince as Cordoba pushed the slightly-too-small ring onto her finger. Tess wondered if the ring had been Cordoba's late wife's; if so, her fingers had been more slender.

"And when is the wedding to be, since you have already settled everything else without asking the consent of her brother and head of the family?" Delgado demanded with mock severity. "I would assume you will need a little time to prepare, but that my sister will be unwilling to leave your side in the meantime, eh?"

Cordoba's smile dimmed a little. "Ah, that is the only, slight flaw in my happiness," he admitted. "I have asked Lupe to remain with me until the wedding, even promising her a trip to Mexico City to commission a wedding gown fit for a queen, but she insists on departing with you on the morrow so that she can have her seamstress in Santa Elena sew her a dress. She says you and she will return in a month for the wedding."

Tess could hardly hide her dismay as Lupe, confident that her new fiancé was looking at Delgado, winked at Parrish across the table and then smirked at her. So they were not to be free of Lupe's presence, after all! What was Lupe hoping to accomplish? Tess didn't believe Lupe's excuse for leaving tomorrow in the least.

This time Delgado was genuinely surprised. "But, Lupe, are you sure that's what you want to do? Surely the seamstress in Santa Elena is not the equal of a dressmaker in Mexico City...."

"Oh, but I promised Señora...ah, Gutierrez she could make my wedding dress someday," Lupe said with sighing regret.

"I am willing to grant my beautiful *novia* her slightest wish," Cordoba said, kissing Lupe's cheek, "no matter how I will miss her until her return. But it is too bad that circumstances did not permit you, Señorita Hennessy, to bring your camera. I would love having a photograph of my beloved, above all things, to comfort me while we are apart."

"Perhaps I could return for the wedding," Tess offered, hoping she would be long gone from the outlaw band by then.

"Oh, but she is quite talented at drawing, too, Andrés," Lupe said. "Perhaps she could do a sketch of me after dinner so you would have that, at least. You would do that for us, wouldn't you, *mi amiga* Tess?" she coaxed, as if she and Tess had become fast friends. "And perhaps you could draw a picture of my dear Andrés for me, too. I would carry it next to my heart," she declared, dramatically pressing her outspread fingers over that organ.

Tess stifled a desire to roll her eyes. If only she could draw Lupe as she saw her true personality—greedy, grasping, faithless—to warn the old man.

Cordoba took Tess's agreement as a matter of course. "Ah, that would be wonderful. No wonder you've become fond of this talented lady, Diego."

Chapter Fifteen

❧

They left the next morning at dawn. The bandits were in good spirits, after a night spent feasting and not having to sleep in the open, and Delgado's mood was buoyant, too, since he had pocketed a handsome sum from Cordoba for the stolen livestock and the other plunder. Lupe seemed equally glad to be back on the trail, after kissing Cordoba goodbye and giving him a merry wave as she rode away.

"I'm surprised you can leave him so easily," Tess said, after they'd ridden out of sight. "He seems a kind man."

Lupe eyed her suspiciously. "Cordoba? Bah! He's nice enough, all right, but he's a dried-up old stick next to an hombre full of *brío* like Sandoval, here," Lupe said, winking at Parrish, who was riding on Lupe's other side. "I'll settle down into the lap of luxury as Cordoba's wife soon enough, but there's no sense depriving myself of a stallion before I have to settle for an old gelding. We have some unfinished business, do we not, *querido?*" she said, fluttering her thick, black lashes at Parrish.

Parrish stared pointedly at Lupe's heavy betrothal

ring, winking in the light of the rising sun, then kneed his pinto forward until he was riding next to Delgado.

Lupe wasn't the least abashed. "Men!" she said with a husky chuckle. "They get so jealous. But I'll make it up to him," she added, with a secretive smile.

Lupe thought that Sandoval was jealous, instead of disgusted at her? Tess was glad that she knew the truth about Sandoval's feelings, and marveled that Lupe could deceive herself as well as she could Cordoba.

"In any case, Tess," Lupe went on, "how could I tamely stay with Cordoba when I have a job to do? I'm here to chaperone you amid all these wild men." She chuckled, then lowered her voice. "I'm also here to make sure you don't try anything foolish, like escaping. Diego wants you, *gringa,* and what my brother wants, I'm going to see that he gets."

Delgado, perhaps hearing his name mentioned, turned to look over his shoulder, and all the menace faded from Lupe's sharp features. "And besides," she went on, her tone merry again, "I haven't had the chance to shoot anyone yet. That's always the high point of going raiding for me."

Lupe was baiting her, Tess knew, and struggled not to tighten her hands on the reins. "What will your betrothed say when you return to him without a wedding dress?" she asked. "There's no seamstress in Santa Elena, is there?"

Lupe laughed again. "Of course not! But who says I'll return without a wedding dress? Perhaps I'll find one to steal."

More than ever before, Tess understood why Parrish and the Rangers were determined to put an end to raiders like the Delgados—both of them. The cause had become hers, too.

Delgado decided to strike a little settlement just across the river from Reynosa that day, a place so small that it could hardly be called a town as yet, but big enough to boast a post office, a small general store, a cantina and a church. They paused just after crossing the river, studying the town, while Delgado announced his plan.

"We'll take the post office," Delgado said, indicating himself and two men. "They should have a little cash, and then we'll pay a visit to the cantina. I'm sure they're overstocked, and would be glad to donate their excess to us, eh? Sandoval, you guard Lupe and Tess, and take Elizonda and Aguilar, and see what the general store has to offer, eh? Maybe they'll have some pretty cloth for your wedding dress, sister."

Tess tensed, wondering if this was the time she'd be caught in the crossfire and killed—or Sandoval would be.

Sandoval shot Tess a look, his eyes eloquent with regret and an unspoken promise to protect her, even if it cost him his life. Tess lifted her chin and tried to smile back at him, so he wouldn't worry, but she knew it was unconvincing.

Lupe turned around in her saddle. "Don't even think of trying to escape, *gringa*—"

A bell began to peal in the steeple of the small church just then, interrupting her.

"What's that? Is it a signal?" Delgado hissed, starting to wheel his horse around. "Let's get out of here!"

"No, wait, brother," Lupe pleaded, catching hold of her brother's arm. "Look—we could not have planned it better!"

The church door had opened, and as they watched, a throng of people spilled out on the lawn. As they watched, a man and woman walked out, arm in arm, the woman dressed in white. A bride.

"Lupe, no, please!" Tess pleaded, guessing what the woman had in mind. "Have a heart!"

Lupe flashed her a look of withering scorn. "A wedding party!" she crowed. "What luck. Rich pickings there, brother. There will be jewelry at the very least, and from here, it looks like that wedding dress would fit me just fine...."

"Lupe, please don't spoil her wedding day," Tess said again. "I'm begging you."

"Don't be silly, *gringa*," Lupe said with a derisive laugh. "As you pointed out, I need a bridal gown."

"Lupe, perhaps we ought to leave the wedding party alone," Sandoval said. "Just think how much easier it will be to rob the businesses in town—probably most of the people are at this wedding."

It had been daring of him to speak up, Tess thought. But Sandoval's effort to appeal to Lupe's logic failed simply because it ran counter to what Lupe wanted to do—and possibly because he'd failed to return her blatant overtures.

"We? The last I knew of it, Sandoval, my sweet, you were merely my brother's lieutenant. Do not presume to advise me," she snarled. "Diego, what do you say? Am I to have this wedding dress I want, or will you listen to the whining of the *gringa*?"

Diego, who had been watching this byplay, shrugged. "Señorita Tess, I'm sorry, but we are outlaws, after all. What could be easier than robbing that flock of pigeons, and then the stores they have left unguarded?"

He started to gesture them forward, but his arm froze in midair as another sound intruded on their ears: the clatter of horses' hooves, the creak of leather and the jingling of bits. As one, they whirled in their saddles.

A mounted patrol of blue-coated soldiers was approaching, a score of them, Tess saw at a glance. All of them had pistols in holsters, and carbines strapped to their saddles.

"The cavalry!" Delgado cried. Beside him, Lupe swore viciously, even as her brother called, "Scatter, *muchachos!* Rendezvous at the hideout beyond Reynosa!"

Even as the bandits began to wheel their horses in different directions, the officer at the head of the patrol shouted, "Halt! I'm Captain McCoy of the U.S. Army and I am ordered to detain any suspicious parties of Mexicans. Halt or we'll shoot!"

Sandoval had used Delgado's distraction to maneuver his horse close to Tess's. "Tess, *go to them,*" Sandoval whispered urgently. "Ride toward them with your hands up. You'll be safe! You could go *home!*"

Before she could refuse, however, and whisper back that she wasn't leaving till she found out about Sandoval's sister, the first volley of bullets buzzed past like angry wasps. One of the bandits—the one called Mérida, Tess thought—screamed and fell out of his saddle.

Lupe grabbed the reins of Tess's horse. "You're not getting away so easily, you fool!" and spurred her own horse toward the river. Tess grabbed her saddle horn as Dulce followed willy-nilly, and held on for dear life, while Sandoval brought up the rear, firing behind them to cover their escape.

They rode hard for miles south along the Rio Grande before Lupe, Tess and Sandoval shook their pursuers and felt safe to swim across. It was hours before they were able to make their way to yet another of Delgado's hideouts on a *riachuelo* feeding into the Rio Grande on the Mexican side. Delgado and several of the other outlaws were already there, and others trickled in afterward.

Tess, exhausted, unsaddled her lathered mare, rubbed her down, then lay down with her head against her saddle. Lupe was at her quarrelsome worst, now that she had been deprived of her prize and her joy in bringing misery to an innocent crowd of wedding guests, and she had been trying to pick a fight with anyone who came near her. Tess planned to feign sleep to get away from her, but the next thing she knew, it was evening.

It wasn't long after the usual supper of beans and tortillas that the men started passing around the bottles. Tess made herself comfortable by the fire with her sketching pad and a bit of charcoal. She'd seen Parrish walk away from the camp shortly after he'd finished his meal, and it wasn't long before Lupe got up and followed him.

Tess wondered if Lupe had heard Sandoval's whispered suggestion that she should seek refuge with the cavalry, and was going to vent her displeasure about it. But given her treacherous nature, it seemed more her style to denounce Sandoval to her brother. No, she was probably attempting yet again to snare Sandoval with her wiles. If so, the woman was unbelievably persistent.

Dear God, help Sandoval walk the tightrope between revealing his true dislike of Lupe Delgado and being forced to pretend desire for her.

"Ah, you've been drawing again, I see," Delgado said, folding his legs and sitting down beside her. The outlaw leader carried a bottle of brandy, which must have been a gift from Cordoba, and his first exhalation informed Tess that he'd already imbibed some. Tess wanted to find some reason to excuse herself, but this was her chance to draw him out, and she must take it.

"Yes," she said, looking down as he did at her rough sketch of how she imagined the raid this morning if the cavalry had not come along—the bride and groom and their guests, all with their hands up, the bride with tear-drenched cheeks as Lupe, cruelly smiling, held a gun on her. Behind her, an amused Delgado sat on his horse, watching.

The outlaw leader picked up the pad, studying the drawing more closely. "You draw with painful honesty, *señorita*," Delgado observed ruefully. "Perhaps we will not show this one to Lupe, eh? You feel sorry for the subjects of our raids?"

"Oh? I thought she'd enjoy it, since this was how she wanted things to go," Tess told him. "And yes, I do feel bad for them. They're only trying to make a living and have an occasional celebration." Being bluntly critical was no way to coax this man into bragging about himself, yet she had to answer honestly, didn't she?

"As am I and my men," Delgado countered, "though not an honest living, I'm sure you would say."

"No."

"I must commend you for trying to stop my sister from robbing the wedding this afternoon, even though you knew it had little chance of succeeding. It was only chance that the bluecoats came by when they did. You knew your protest would draw her wrath to you, yet you did it anyway. You have the heart of a lion, *señorita*."

"You give me too much credit," Tess said, waving the idea away. How was she to work this conversation around to Delgado's past? "A bride shouldn't have to face robbery on her wedding day, of all days. I'd think that since Lupe was about to be a bride herself, she could have a little compassion for a woman on her wedding day."

"Lupe is a hard woman," Delgado admitted. "Life has made her so. Perhaps she should have been born a man—even a general, eh? She would have made a ruthless soldier."

"All men are not ruthless and bloodthirsty—even soldiers."

Delgado shrugged. "Don't worry about Lupe. I won't let her harm you. Though heaven knows, it's hard to control her tongue."

"I'd rather you kept her from harming the people you steal from," she said.

Delgado said nothing. Night sounds surrounded them—the crackling of the fire, a bawdy song some of the men were singing, the screech of an owl in a tree nearby, the call of a distant coyote summoning his mate.

"You don't like being with us, do you, Tess Hennessy?"

"I would rather be at home, with my family, naturally. They're probably worried sick."

"I had hoped you would have learned to appreciate the outlaw life a little by now, if not Delgado. Do you hate me, Tess?"

Appreciate the outlaw life? Did he seriously think—

"No, I don't hate you," she said. She couldn't help being a little amused that he'd referred to himself in the third person.

"Because your faith forbids you to hate, eh?"

"I dislike what you've done in having me kidnapped, of course. But you haven't harmed me." Tess watched him warily. Just as Parrish must take care with Lupe, so must she walk a fine line with Delgado. Swallowing hard, she said, "I can see that you have a lot of ambition and energy in getting what you want. But I don't really know you, Señor Delgado."

"Diego, please."

He leaned closer to her, and Tess had to stifle the urge to scoot away from him. *Lord, please give me the right words to say.*

Chapter Sixteen

"**Y**ou say you don't really know me, Tess," Delgado said. He spread his hands wide. "Here I am, an open book. Ask me what you will. I would like you to know me very well, eh?"

Again Tess felt that warning tickle of ice on her spine that warned her to proceed carefully. Very, very carefully. She drew in a breath, wanting to draw back, to increase the distance between them, but that would telegraph the discrepancy between her words and her feelings, so she forced herself to remain still. "I... I tried to ask you about something, if you will recall, that first night in camp. But I'm afraid my approach was a little... um, *confrontational.* I've often been sorry for that." Tess fluttered her lashes at him as she had seen Lupe do to Cordoba, praying it didn't look like she had just gotten dust in her eyes instead.

It worked better than a proverbial charm. Delgado smiled sympathetically. "Ah, Tess, there is no need to berate yourself about that night. I understood. You had just been captured, and you did not know what to expect. And you have *this* that influences your temperament, eh?" He caressed the hair on the side of her head. "I like a woman of fire, Tess. So ask, and do not be afraid."

She had to school herself not to shrink away from his touch, even while praying it did not go further.

All right, what did you do with Pilar Morelos?

If only it were that simple.

"Very well," she said, making her tone brisk. "At dinner that night, I asked you to tell me about your early days, when you first turned to the outlaw life. I'd still like to hear about that time. What was it like?" Tess knew she had to make her questions general at first, and gradually lead into specifics, or he would become suspicious.

Delgado smiled in remembrance, his eyes losing focus. To her relief, he leaned back, away from her. "Ah, those were the days, *señorita*. I would ride into a town, sit in the cantina and spin my tales of how the devil Texans had killed my family, and tell how I planned to wreak vengeance on their behalf and for all Mexicans who had suffered at the Texans' hands. I was raising an army, I declared, of brave, like-minded men. Everyone would buy me tequila and clap me on the back and tell me what a fine fellow I was." He took another long draft on his bottle of brandy.

"Young men flocked into the cantinas to join up. I made them sign—or make their mark—on a pledge of loyalty in their own blood. That paper gave me the right to cut the throat of any man who betrayed me. Not that most of us could read, mind you, but knowing the consequences of betrayal impressed on them that Diego Delgado was serious.

"When I had enlisted everyone who was interested," Delgado went on, arms around his drawn-up knees, "we would go on to the next village. Our army swelled with each town we visited."

"I imagine the ladies found you fascinating," Tess dared to say.

Delgado grinned, too lost in his memories to be modest. "*Sí.* I had women cooking my meals, washing my clothes, volunteering to ride along, not to be outlaws, you understand, but to be close to me. But I refused, wanting to keep my band quick and fast. And besides, there were always more women in the next town for Delgado—and the ones I didn't want, I let my men have."

There was no end to this man's ego, Tess marveled, striving to keep her distaste from showing on her face. He'd apparently forgotten he was trying to woo the very woman to whom he was bragging of his conquests.

"I notice you said *women,*" Tess murmured. "You liked them older? Not…girls?"

He blinked at the question, and Tess hoped she hadn't gone too far in her haste to get the information Parrish needed.

"I suppose you *could* say that, yes… In those days I liked my lady friends…ah, shall we say *experienced?* They didn't expect impossible things of a man always on the move. They didn't weep—much, anyway—when it was time for Delgado to leave. Ah, but there was a girl once…"

Did he mean Pilar?

"Tell me about her," she encouraged, leaning forward.

Delgado inclined himself toward her. "This girl, she lived in—"

"Diego, what are we doing tomorrow?" Lupe said, bursting into the circle of firelight and shattering the moment. Tess wanted to gnash her teeth in vexation.

Even in the flickering firelight, Tess could see the bright patches of scarlet flushing Lupe's cheeks and the angry glint in her eyes. She reminded Tess of a cat whose tail had been caught under a rocking chair.

So Lupe's little tête-à-tête with Sandoval hadn't gone as she had hoped. Tess found that immensely cheering in the midst of her own frustration.

"Sorry—was I interrupting something?" The look Lupe threw at Tess was anything but apologetic.

Delgado frowned at her, shaking his head as if to clear it. "What do you mean, what are we doing tomorrow?"

Lupe gave an elaborate shrug. "Where do we raid?"

"I haven't decided yet," Delgado growled. "Why must we discuss it this minute?"

Lupe ignored his question. "Let's rob a bank, brother. What do you say? We haven't done that in a while."

"Why do you want to do that? It's more hazardous, and dollars must be converted to pesos."

Lupe shrugged. "It's more of a challenge than stealing from gringo ranches. And I don't imagine Cordoba would mind exchanging them for you. Or it could be my dowry—a dowry of dollars."

Delgado shot a considering look at Tess. "I don't know, Lupe. Banks are more dangerous. I wouldn't want Tess to get hurt. She is our guest, after all."

Lupe's face hardened, and she leaned down to her brother. "Oh, well, if you're going to let a *gringa* rule your choices, then you will no longer be the Scourge of the Border. Bah! Next you'll be saying you want to buy a *rancho* and settle down."

Delgado was instantly on his feet, his fist cocked. "Shut your mouth, woman! You do not tell me what to do!"

It was a mistake, Tess thought, for Lupe to mock her brother in front of anyone, let alone her, since Delgado was trying to impress her. Delgado always had to be master of any situation.

Lupe recoiled, her expression transfiguring from scornful and mocking to that of a hurt child. Tess watched in amazement as Lupe's lip quivered and tears welled up and spilled from her eyes.

Even more astonishing was the change in Delgado. His angry, tense features immediately softened, and he gathered his sister into his arms. "I'm so sorry, little one, I did not mean to yell," he soothed her. "Forgive your cross brother, eh? We will do anything you want tomorrow, anything."

Couldn't Delgado see through his sister, see how she was playing him?

Lupe knuckled the tears from her eyes and gave Delgado a tremulous smile. "*Really,* Diego? Do you mean it?"

"Of course," Delgado said, just as Parrish entered the circle of light. "Sandoval, tell the men. We're robbing a bank tomorrow."

Parrish's face was impassive. "Tomorrow? It's Sunday. The bank will be closed."

All of them stared at him in surprise, Tess included. She had completely lost track of time.

Lupe swore under her breath. Delgado gave her a one-armed hug. "Ah, don't fret, *hermana.* We'll do it the next day. I'll take you to church tomorrow instead, and Tess, too. That will be nice, eh? And our bank robbery will go that much better for having an extra day to plan it."

The town of Mission came into sight about five miles after they'd crossed the river. Lupe grinned at Sandoval, clearly exultant that they were about to unleash terror on the unsuspecting townspeople of Mission and rob many of them of their life savings—and that she would be in the thick of it.

Parrish didn't acknowledge her look. Apprehension tightened his spine as if he were stretched out on a rack. He hoped desperately that no innocent citizens would be harmed today. He had to find a way to bring this charade of his to a close, with the Delgados both captured. Or killed. It didn't matter much to him which way they paid the penalty for their crimes.

He risked a glance at Tess, sitting rigid in her saddle, her freckles standing out against her pale skin. She stared straight ahead at the town. He thought he saw her lips moving—in prayer?

He and Tess should be anywhere but here. At that moment Sandoval would have given anything, even his soul, to be calling on her at Hennessy Hall, taking her to barbecues, riding, picnics, to church on Sundays.... He'd been completely stupid to involve her in his convoluted scheme to bring Delgado to justice. He'd never foreseen that the outlaw leader would do anything more than have Tess take a few pictures, then let her go. But you could never quite predict what a snake would do, so he had no excuse.

"Let's *stage* a robbery at the bank in Santa Elena," Sandoval had suggested last night at the campfire. "Those townspeople would be happy to pose for you, knowing it wasn't real, and no one would get hurt. Tess could even use her camera then."

Sandoval had felt a flash of hope when he saw Delgado rub his chin thoughtfully. He was considering it.

"And the camera would show that the bank teller and customers were as Mexican as we are, not lily-white

Americanos," Lupe had snapped scornfully. "Anyone would know it was faked."

Her remark convinced her brother, of course.

Now Sandoval was in the ridiculous position of being a Texas Ranger about to help rob a Texas bank. Now he'd have to not only get Tess to safety, and find Pilar— he'd also have to find a way to take the money back from Delgado when they escaped, or he'd never be welcome on either side of the border.

At that moment he hated Delgado more than he ever had. Delgado had led them all to church yesterday, the hypocrite, and today he was leading them in a bank robbery.

"Sandoval, I want you to stage a diversion at the north end of the town," Delgado ordered. "That will draw the sheriff and deputies, if he has any, away from the bank. Maybe you can even get them to chase you out of town, then lose them and double back to the border. Garza and Rivera, stand as lookouts on either end to the street. Prieto, Aguilar, take the rear exit of the bank into the alleyway. Don't let anyone in or out. Elizonda, watch for snipers from the right side of the street, Barriga, the left. Zavala, Dominguez, Lupe, you're with me in the bank."

"What about Tess, *jefe?*" Sandoval asked. "Why don't we leave a man guarding her here, so she can watch, but she's not in danger?"

Leave me with her, he wanted to say. Let someone else divert the sheriff.

He'd try his best to talk Tess into fleeing toward Chapin, given the chance. He knew, though, there was no chance Delgado would agree.

Lupe's narrowed eyes were hard as obsidian. "You're very solicitous of her all of a sudden, Sandoval. Should we worry about that, brother? Perhaps, Sandoval, the gringo blood is singing more loudly in your veins today than the Mexican?"

"Not at all," he said, with a calmness he didn't feel, keeping his eyes from Tess. "I'm sure Diego wouldn't want Tess caught in the crossfire, as she would be if the citizens put up a fight. Why not let her come with me, *jefe?* Then she would see some action, but not be in so much danger."

And I could at least watch out for her, he thought.

Lupe glared at him.

Delgado straightened in the saddle. "Tess will come in the bank with us, of course. How would she be able to make one of her excellent drawings of my exploits if she doesn't experience a real bank robbery? She will soon have enough material to write an entire book about me, eh? Dominguez will guard her. They'll stay near the door, out of the way, and be the first out when we make our getaway."

The rack of apprehension along Sandoval's spine tightened to the point of agony. Dominguez, the very bandito Tess disliked the most, the one Tess had told him she'd struggled with during her kidnapping and had kneed in the groin. The man still ogled her whenever Delgado wasn't looking. Dominguez would care less than nothing if Tess came to harm.

"Diego, let *me* come inside. Dominguez can stage the diversion," Parrish said.

"Sandoval, you're sounding like my old maid aunt. No more arguing," Delgado snarled. "Do as I told you."

Delgado had assigned Parrish where he couldn't see what was happening to Tess, couldn't protect her. *Lord, it's up to You to keep her safe. Please, if You never answer any prayer of mine again, shield her.*

He shot a cold warning look at Dominguez—Don't let anything happen to her, if you value your life, hombre.

Dominguez smirked.

"Let's go," Delgado said, and brought his arm forward. They walked their horses toward Mission, in no apparent hurry, doing nothing to draw any watcher's attention to the fact that disaster was fast approaching.

Chapter Seventeen

Tess locked eyes with Parrish one last time before, grim-faced and silent, he reined his horse away from the rest of them to skirt the town. What kind of diversion would he mount? Would he be successful in drawing the sheriff's attention away from the bank? And then, would he be able to escape? Would she ever see him again, or would one or both of them be killed today? *Please, Lord, protect us!*

They entered the town, silent and unobtrusive as a breeze, and fanned out as Delgado had specified. She saw no one on the street except for an old codger whittling in front of what looked like a saloon next to the bank. Delgado, Lupe, Zavala, Dominguez and Tess dismounted in front of it, tied their horses to a hitching post and climbed up onto the boardwalk. Tess's legs felt like pudding.

Dominguez grinned nastily at her. "Afraid, *gringa?*"

She ignored him.

Just before Delgado reached for the door, they all paused to pull bandannas over their faces. The bandanna Tess wore was a spare one of Dominguez's, and it stank of stale sweat. Surely she was in the middle of a nightmare, and any moment she would wake up in her bed at Hennessy Hall and find that her time among Delgado's banditos had all been a bizarre dream. Only Dominguez's iron grip on her shoulder with his left hand, and her sidelong view of his long-muzzle pistol held in his right as he pushed her through the door convinced her that it was all too horribly real.

"Hands in the air, everyone!" shouted Delgado, and everyone whirled around.

"It's *Delgado,*" the teller quavered. The bank president and three of the four customers raised their arms obediently. The fourth, a woman who had been standing in front of the teller's window, swooned, collapsing like a suddenly empty sack. Tess envied her. If only she were that delicate sort of female! Then she wouldn't have to endure the next few minutes. In fact, copying that woman's action might be the very smartest thing she could do. The outlaws would have to leave her behind!

Tess let herself waver as if she were about to lose consciousness.

Dominguez's fingers on her shoulder clamped down like talons. "Don't pretend to faint, *gringa,*" he whispered in her ear. "I'd take pleasure in shooting you."

Tess went rigid.

"Yes, it is Delgado himself, and a few of his amigos," Delgado agreed with a beatific smile, as if he had been announced as the guest of honor at a party, "come to relieve you, the good citizens of Mission, of your excess *dinero.* Be wise and hand the money over without any problems, and all of you will live to appreciate the virtue of poverty, yes? Give us any trouble, however, and you will be sorry—the very last feeling you ever have," he added, brandishing his pistol. All geniality had vanished.

"Is anyone back there?" Delgado asked the short,

gray-haired bank president, motioning to a door to the right of his desk.

"No, no," the man said, nodding his head so violently that his jowls wobbled like a turkey's wattle. "That's my private office...for meetings..."

Tess heard the sound of gunfire then, coming from the north end of town. Parrish had begun his diversion. Everyone tensed, a couple of them uttered cries of alarm, but no one took his eyes off Delgado and his pistol.

Except for Tess, who couldn't help looking over her shoulder out a window behind her at the jail across the street. No one tried to run out the door. No one appeared at its window.

Lupe held out the large gunnysack she had been carrying folded up under her arm, and motioned to the teller with her pistol. "Fill it up with the money—all of it. And the rest of you start removing your jewelry and pocket watches," she ordered, jerking her head at the paralyzed customers. "Don't try to hold anything back, or it will go worse for you."

Just then the door to the right of the desk banged open and three men burst out, the one in front yelling, "Drop your guns, Delgado, you and your men!"

Chaos erupted. Customers screamed and dropped to the floor. Lupe let go of her sack and fired in the sheriff's direction, while Delgado aimed at one of the deputies behind him, collapsing him with a wound in his chest that blossomed into an obscene crimson flower. The wounded man managed to fire once more, but the bullet went wide, missing Delgado and embedding itself in a wall, sending plaster flakes flying. Dominguez shot at the other deputy, but he threw himself behind the desk, firing around it a second later. Zavala went down, moaning. Then the sheriff fired at Dominguez, but he ducked behind Tess. She threw her hands up in the air, had time to think, *Lord, help—!*

A flash of fire scorched the side of her head. Everything went black.

No one had come running out of the jail after his first shots into the air. Garza, the only bandito positioned where Sandoval could see him, shrugged and went back to staring at the bank.

Sandoval fired into the air again. All at once the window of the nearest house was thrown open. The long muzzle of a rifle poked out and immediately spat bullets in his direction, kicking up the dust around his horse's hooves, causing the pinto to dance and whinny.

He fired at the window, shattering the glass. Then, from the other end of town, a rider came galloping toward him, shooting as he came.

Finally, some response! Sandoval kicked the horse in the ribs. *"Hyaah!"*

The pinto needed no encouragement to take off.

Once he'd left his pursuer far enough behind, Sandoval galloped in a wide arc for an hour before heading for the river. By now, God willing, Tess would be safely across the Rio Grande with the others and waiting at the agreed-upon rendezvous in one of Delgado's hideaway valleys. He wondered if all of the bandits had made it out of the town, and if the man who'd ridden after him had been the sheriff.

The pinto was lathered and blowing by the time Sandoval arrived at the valley. He knew he should have slowed the horse, sparing him, when no one had chased him to his crossing point, but he was driven by anxiety for Tess. Nothing else mattered till he knew she was all right.

The drawn, haggard expressions on the faces of Garza and Aguilar, posted at the entrance of the valley, did nothing to reassure him. They looked up when he trotted past, but he saw none of the usual exhilaration that followed a successful raid. He rode on until he spotted two horse-blanket-covered forms on the ground.

Jumping off the paint, Sandoval ran to the blankets. *Please, God...don't let one of them be Tess....*

He yanked the blanket back and saw with unspeakable relief that both corpses were men—Zavala and Dominguez.

But Dominguez was supposed to have been assigned to Tess. Where was she?

He turned on his heel, his eyes seeking Delgado among the banditos until he spotted him kneeling in the shade of a cedar elm by a supine, skirted figure. *Tess?* He ran toward them.

It was Lupe, her head pillowed by folded horse blankets. She and Delgado looked up as he broke into the circle.

"Where's Tess?" Sandoval demanded without preliminaries. "What happened?"

"*Muchas gracias* for your solicitude on *my* behalf," Lupe whimpered. "I'm wounded! See?" She pulled part of her riding skirt up to show a thick bandage around her calf. A spot of blood the size of a *centavo* showed through.

"The bullet went on through," Delgado said. "She'll be all right, thankfully." But his eyes were troubled. "Sandoval—"

"It *hurts*," moaned Lupe, interrupting. "Will you sit with me, Sandoval?"

Sandoval ignored her. *"Where is Tess?"*

Delgado got to his feet. "Sandoval, I'm afraid I have some bad news. Tragic news…"

Now Sandoval saw the pallor underlying the bandit leader's bronzed cheeks, and he froze for a moment, then lurched forward unsteadily, grabbing Delgado by the shoulders. "What are you saying? What happened?"

"Amigo, they were waiting for us inside the bank. It was an ambush."

"Who was waiting?"

"The sheriff," Delgado said dolefully, "and two other men. They jumped out of a side office in the bank and shot at us. I killed one of them, I think, but Zavala was badly wounded and died on the way here, God rest his soul…."

"What about Tess?" Sandoval couldn't care less about Zavala at the moment, didn't care that he was shouting now at the most feared outlaw in the Rio Grande Valley.

"When they started firing, Dominguez ducked behind Tess, the cursed *cobarde!* Tess—oh, amigo, I don't know how to tell you this—I saw them shoot Tess. She fell down, her face all bloody…she must be dead. When we reached this valley I shot Dominguez myself for his cowardice. He got the *señorita* killed! I should have listened to you, should have let you stay with her…."

Sandoval felt as if his blood had frozen. *Tess, dead?* Then what Delgado had said repeated itself in his brain. "You said she *must* be dead. You don't *know?* Why didn't you bring her with you?"

Delgado's eyes were haunted with pain. "Sandoval… my sister and Zavala were both wounded. Tess wasn't moving…there was so much blood… I was sure she was gone. Everyone was shouting and screaming…."

Sandoval felt his hands clench into fists. He wanted to pummel Delgado into the earth, then choke him. "I'm going to get her," he said. "Dead or alive, I have to *know*." Lord in heaven, how was he going to face her parents and Sam Taylor, if Tess was dead?

Delgado stared at him. "Don't be loco, hombre. If she wasn't dead then, she is by now. My heart is full of pain to think this, my friend, but we must face it. Don't stick your neck in a noose for nothing!"

"I'll need a fresh horse," Sandoval said, as if Delgado hadn't spoken. "Fresher than mine, anyway."

Delgado's shoulders sagged. "Take my black," he said. "But you're going to your death, amigo. Those gringos will be out for blood, and any Mexicans will do."

"Bah! He's only part Mexican," Lupe's voice mocked from the ground a few feet away.

"Shut up, Lupe," snapped Delgado, surprising Sandoval with the fury in his tone. "If he can use his Anglo blood to bring my Tess back, alive or dead…" His voice broke and he turned away.

Someone was sponging her forehead, and every stroke shot fresh waves of burning pain spearing deep into her skull. Tentatively, Tess opened one eye, and when she was able to focus, she beheld an elderly, bespectacled man sitting by the cot on which she lay. Looking behind him, she saw floor-to-ceiling bars. She was in a jail cell?

Then she remembered Dominguez shoving her in front of him, the flash of fire coming straight at her head, the sudden, overwhelming pain before everything faded away.…

"You're awake," the man said. "You speak any English?"

"Of course I do," Tess said. "I'm American. I—"

"Take it easy, missy. I'm Doc Waters, and you got yourself creased by a bullet. Lucky you weren't killed," he murmured. "Or maybe not so lucky," he said, with a meaningful look at the bars. Outside she heard a rumble of voices, but she couldn't make out what they said.

"Wh-what do you mean?"

"Your amigos killed a deputy. Or maybe it was you who shot him—I dunno, I wasn't in the bank, but they said they found a pistol near where you fell."

"It wasn't mine! I wasn't even armed," Tess cried, but her indignation only made her pounding headache worse. She put a shaky hand up to her forehead and felt something sticky. When she looked at her fingers, they were streaked with blood.

"Yep, scalp wounds bleed a lot," the doctor said. "The blood had clotted, but when I started cleaning the wound it commenced t' bleed again."

Tess didn't care about that. "What am I doing in jail? I didn't want to be in that bank with Delgado any more than any of the customers—"

"So it *was* Delgado," interrupted another man, who had appeared beyond the bars. "Thought so, but I wasn't sure."

"Who are you?"

"Sheriff Mason," the grizzled, stocky man said as he let himself into her cell with a ring of keys. "And I'll ask you the same question. What's an American girl doing ridin' with Mexican bandits, robbin' banks?"

"I'm not a bandit," she protested. "I'm Tess Hennessy, and I was kidnapped by Delgado's men—"

"Sure," he retorted. "Mighty convenient t' claim that, now that you're sittin' in my jail, girl."

Tess pushed herself up on her elbows. "You can't possibly believe I wanted to rob that bank!"

He stooped over her. "Don't you tell me what I cain't believe!" he cried, wagging a thick finger at her. "All I know is a good man was killed by you an' your Mex friends t'day."

"*I* didn't kill him," she cried. "I'm a photographer, and Delgado had me abducted because he wanted his picture taken, and—"

"A woman photographer?" he retorted skeptically. "So where's your camera box? I didn't see anything of the sort! You think you can spin some yarn, and I'm gonna buy it? You'll have to do better than that, Miss Hennessy."

"I can draw as well as photograph, and Delgado wanted a sketch of the bank robbery done later. I'm telling the *truth*," she protested, when his expression remained skeptical. "I live at Hennessy Hall, near Chapin, and my parents are Patrick and Amelia Hennessy. You could contact them—does Mission have a telegraph? They'll tell you what I'm saying is true." She closed her eyes, not wanting this man to see her pain at the thought of her parents being informed their daughter was in jail, charged with attempted bank robbery.

"Mebbe you're tellin' the truth and mebbe you ain't," the sheriff said. "An' no, this town don't have no telegraph office. You kin tell your story to th' judge tomorrow morning—*if* you're still around, that is."

"If I'm still around?" she echoed. "Where would I be?"

He pointed at her window, where the rumble of voices had grown to an angry buzz, like a swarm of wasps confined to a tiny bottle. "Hear that? Remember I said a deputy was killed? Well, his older brother is the biggest rancher in this area, and he wants someone t' pay fer his brother's death. He organized a posse to catch them murderin' bandits, but by th' time they was all mounted up, the bandits had scattered. He's wantin' t' lynch someone, an' he's too mad to care if it's a woman."

Tess stared at him, feeling the rough scrape of hemp tightening around her neck, choking off her air.... "But I'm innocent! You can't let that happen, Sheriff. Not without a trial—"

"I'll be here all night, doin' what I kin t' save your skin," he said grudgingly. "But you hear 'em out there," he repeated, jerking his head toward the sound. "He's mad as a teased snake and he's gettin' the rest of 'em all riled up. I ain't about t' get hurt protectin' some girl who thought it'd be a lark to ride with outlaws."

Chapter Eighteen

Yes, she heard them out there, all right. There had been individual voices muttering threats and ideas about what should be done with her, but just then they united to chant, "Lynch the redhead! Hang 'er high! String 'er up!"

The doctor, having rolled a wide strip of clean linen around her head, got to his feet. "Well… I've done all I can…perhaps I'd better be going…." He shook his head uneasily. "Mason, don't you let them take this young woman. Whatever she did, she's at least entitled to a trial," he added as he motioned for the sheriff to let him out of the cell.

"Whatever she did?" Even the doctor thought she was guilty?

"Doctor Waters, on your way out, would you ask the brother of the deputy who died to come in here? I want to talk to him," Tess called to the physician.

Waters turned around in the doorway between the jail's two cells and the sheriff's office, blinking in surprise. "Miss Hennessy, are you sure that's wise?"

It had been an impulsive act on Tess's part, and she wasn't sure at all, but she nodded. "It's certainly better than sitting here listening to them planning what tree to throw the rope over," she said. Surely, if she talked to the grieving man, she could make him see that she was innocent.

Waters looked to Mason for permission, and at last the sheriff nodded. "I don't think it'll do any good, but you can try, Miss Hennessy. Doc, you tell Amory I'm only lettin' him in, no one else."

A minute later, Tess heard heavy footsteps approaching the cell, and looked up.

Backlit by the sunshiny office behind him, Amory at first appeared only as a dark, hulking shape against the bars of her cell, but even from this distance the reek of stale whiskey reached her nose.

"You th' red-headed witch—" it came out *wissch* "—who kilt my brother Bill t'day?"

"My name is Tess—Teresa, that is—Hennessy," she said with a calmness she was far from feeling. "And I didn't kill your brother. I've never fired a gun at anyone. I was with Delgado and his outlaws not of my own free will, but because—"

"*Shuddup!* You jus' shuddup, y-ya hear? I don' wanna lissen t' yore lies!" the man shouted at her, rattling the bars in his fury, his red-rimmed eyes glaring at her. "You can't trust nothin' no red-haired wumman says— an' I oughta know, 'cuz my no-good wife was one! You jes' enjoy the air yore breathin' right now, mishy, 'cuz purty soon it's gonna be choked right outta ya!" With that parting shot, he turned on his heel and lumbered unsteadily out of the jail, slamming the door behind him.

The hum had quieted while Amory had been inside, no doubt so the men could hope to overhear what was being said. Now it rose to a buzz again.

Sheriff Mason shot her an "I told you so" look. "If you

got any other good ideas, I'll be out there at my desk."
He let himself out, then locked the cell behind him.

Where was Sandoval? Had he been killed during
his attempt to stage a diversion? He couldn't have been
captured, or he'd be in the other cell.

"Sheriff Mason, were there…that is, I don't remember…were any of the outlaws killed?" she asked as he
reached the doorway.

He turned around. "I wounded the Mex woman—in
the leg, I think—and Edgerton, the other deputy, wounded
the one that wasn't standing next to you. Gut-shot, he was,
so I don't reckon he'll live, but Delgado drug him onto a
horse and rode outta Mission holdin' onto him."

"No one else?"

Mason studied her. "One of the men told me some
fella was shootin' his pistol in the air down t' other end
of the street. He chased after him, but he lost him. Why?
You got a sweetheart among them banditos, even if it
ain't Delgado?"

She shook her head quickly. "No, I was just wondering."

So Zavala was probably dying, if not already dead,
and Lupe had been wounded. For a moment, Tess wished
fiercely that it had been Lupe who had been more gravely
hit. The whole idea of robbing the bank had been hers,
and the responsibility for the deaths of the deputy and
Zavala could be laid squarely at her door—and at her
brother's, too, for agreeing to it.

Delgado would have told Sandoval he'd seen her go
down, shot in the head. Sandoval must think she was
dead, too. Was he even now mourning her, holed up in
some hidden valley with the other outlaws, not knowing she was still now in as much danger as she had

been during the bank robbery? If so, she was truly on her own.

"My sister'll be bringin' us some supper in a while. Mebbe you oughta get some rest till then."

Rest? Tess fought an urge to laugh hysterically, knowing it would only make her headache worse. Would this supper be her last meal? *Lord, help me!*

Sandoval waited in the darkness, watching as the mob outside the jail trudged en masse down to the saloon. They were going to use whiskey to shore up their determination to storm the jail. One of them had knotted a rope into a hangman's noose. He'd seen the fellow twirling it around all through the evening while the men talked about the killing of the deputy. A few had been uneasy lynching her since she was a woman, but they were shouted down by their fellows who said they had to make that redhead pay since she was the only one captured. She must be a bad woman, to be riding with outlaws, anyway.

As soon as they were gone, Sandoval led the two horses—he'd declined Delgado's black in favor of a less flashy, brown horse, and Tess's sorrel—to a hitching post in front of the jail. He climbed up onto the boardwalk and peered through a curtain. A kerosene lamp inside revealed the sheriff sitting with his feet propped up on the desk, his eyes closed.

Parrish knocked at the door as if he had every right to be there.

Within, he heard a thump as if chair legs had just hit the floor, and a second later the sheriff was pulling back the curtains and opening the window a crack.

"Who're you? I kin tell ya right now, ain't no one visitin' my prisoner for any reason."

Sandoval flashed the badge he'd brought out of the hidden pocket in his pants.

"Texas Ranger, huh? C'mon in, then. I'm Sheriff Mason," he said, offering his hand. "What kin I do for you?"

"I'm Sandoval Parrish," he said after the sheriff shut the door behind him, "and I understand you're holding Tess Hennessy here."

The older man nodded. "She helped rob a bank today. One a' my deputies was killed."

"So I hear," Sandoval said with a somber nod. "Well, she's been riding with the Delgado gang for a while now, so she's wanted for several crimes. I'm here to take her to Brownsville for trial."

The man's relief was palpable. "Thank God. Sounds like she'll pay for her crimes, then, but at least no one can say vigilantes took her from *my* jail. Them fellas was about ready t' lynch her. C'mon back here," he said, beckoning for Sandoval to follow him into the cell area. "If yore quick y' kin be gone afore they're done drinkin'."

Sandoval hid a smile, realizing Sheriff Mason hadn't thought to ask him how he knew Tess was in a jail cell in Mission.

The jangling of the ring of keys jerked Tess awake in her dark cell. She blinked at the flickering light of the lantern. Then she shrieked, seeing only a dark form standing behind the sheriff as he opened her cell door.

Had Amory come back to drag her outside?

"Calm down, Miss Hennessy, it ain't those boys who been loiterin' around beneath your window, don't worry. This here's a Texas Ranger, come for you. Says you're already wanted in other robberies with them greasers, so I reckon you'll get your fair trial afore th' rope, at least."

She saw now that it was Parrish who stood behind the sheriff, and relief flooded over her. Tess saw him shake his head in warning, and she turned back to the sheriff. "But what about…what about the mob out there? Won't they try to—"

"You don't hear 'em, do you? That's cuz they're all down at the saloon gettin' likkered up. Mr. Parrish and me figgered it was a good time to take you away, 'specially as they're probably tryin' to get drunk enough t' come force their way inta th' jail."

She looked over Mason's shoulder into Sandoval's face, but nothing in those dark eyes gave him away. He appeared stern and even contemptuous as he stared back at her, exactly as a Ranger should look when he was about to take custody of a notorious female criminal. She saw his eyes rake over the angry furrow on the side of her forehead where the bullet had scraped her scalp.

"You wanna borrow my handcuffs?" Mason offered, reaching for a pair of metal restraints that hung from a hook on the wall outside the cell. He was only too ready to give any assistance to this Ranger who was going to take the source of his trouble off his hands.

Sandoval shook his head. "Thanks, but this'll work, I reckon," he said, pulling a length of braided rawhide cord from his pocket. He made an abrupt gesture at Tess. "Hands out in front, miss."

Tess watched as he bound her hands, keeping her face poker-straight with an effort. It would make Mason suspicious indeed if she grinned at the Ranger who was supposedly taking her to justice!

"We'll be going now," Sandoval said as he took hold of the cord between her hands. "There's a lot of riding between here and Brownsville. I want to get far away from here before I make camp, so if Delgado comes looking and finds she's not in Mission, he won't ride on and find us."

Mason's brow furrowed as if he hadn't even considered such a possibility. "You don't think he'd dare come *here*?"

Sandoval gave a whistle and shook his head. "I wouldn't put it past him. Miss Tess here was his *amante,* his sweetheart. If I were you I'd keep a sharp eye out tonight."

"Sweetheart, huh?" Mason gave a disgusted snort. "She tried to tell me she was only with him to take pictures. I knew she was lyin'!"

Tess glared at both of them.

Sandoval didn't rein in until they were at least five miles out of town on the Brownsville Road.

"Oh, Sandoval, I've never been one-hundredth so glad to see *anyone* in my entire life!" she began, only to have him hold up a warning hand.

Positioning his horse next to hers, he listened in silence for a minute or two, but no sound rode on the breeze that tickled the palms and wild olive trees except the hoot of a sleepy owl. Then he grabbed her into his arms and kissed her, and they were laughing and she was crying, too, as he undid the cord that bound her wrists.

"Sandoval, they were going to *lynch* me!" Her voice quavered as she said the words. "Without a trial! They didn't even care that I might be innocent—they just wanted someone to pay for the death of that poor deputy...." She wept in earnest now as he held her, all her pent-up fear flowing out of her with her tears.

"Hush now, you're safe, love. Thank God that bullet only grazed you," Sandoval murmured, caressing her head near the wound. "Delgado thought you were dead...."

"But you came anyway...."

"I had to *know*," he told her, and she saw in his eyes that the possibility that she might be dead had shaken him to the core. "I wasn't about to leave you in that town, alive or dead. I'm taking you home."

She drew back in surprise. "*Home?* I can't go home yet! We're not done—I haven't found out about your sister yet."

"Tess, we're only about fifteen miles from Chapin. You could be back at Hennessy Hall by dawn. I can't take you back to Delgado, back to danger, when you're so close to home!"

She stared at him, tempted. How wonderful it would be to ride down the palm-lined lane to the Spanish mission-style house that had been home to her all her life, to be embraced by her mother and father, to sleep in her own soft bed and not the hard ground...but if she gave in, Sandoval would never know if Pilar was dead or alive, for he'd already given up hope for his sister. It was likely that Sandoval wouldn't even be able to return to Delgado, for the outlaw leader might learn that Tess had not died, but had been taken by a Texas Ranger whose description fit Sandoval Parrish. Then he'd never be able to accomplish *his* goal of publishing Delgado's picture far and wide so the outlaw could be captured.

"I won't go home," she repeated. She looked away from his expression of incredulity and gazed instead at the river they had been riding alongside. "Can we cross here?"

Chapter Nineteen

"Tess! You are alive! *¡Gracias a Dios!*" exclaimed Delgado, pulling Tess into his arms as soon as he helped her down from her horse. Tess flashed a startled, alarmed look at Sandoval as Delgado embraced her and kissed her on both cheeks. "But how on earth did you rescue her, amigo?" he asked, turning to Sandoval. "Did you storm into the jail, guns blazing, or did you sneak in and knock the sheriff in the head with your pistol? You are a miracle worker. I am indebted to you forever!" He released Tess and embraced Sandoval.

Sandoval shrugged. "I used my Anglo blood, as you suggested," he said. "I told them I was a Texas Ranger, and had heard one of the Delgado gang had been captured, and that I was taking her to trial in Brownsville on an earlier charge. Good thing I arrived when I did—the brother of the dead deputy was inciting the men of the town to lynch her."

"Thank God you were in time," breathed Delgado. "If they had harmed Tess, I would have slaughtered every man, woman and child in Mission—this I swear!"

Sandoval relaxed a bit, seeing his last dramatic statement had distracted the outlaw from questioning him further about his ruse.

But Lupe was not so easily diverted—probably because she would not have cared if Tess had been hanged. "You just walked into the jail and told them you were a Ranger, and they believed you, without any proof?" she challenged from her nearby nest of blankets under a tree. "Even an Anglo is not so gullible, I think."

"Of course not," Sandoval said shortly over his shoulder at her. "I had proof. Remember that time we were ambushed by that contingent of Rangers just as we were about to cross the river down by Matamoros, Diego?" Sandoval had set up the ambush with his fellow Rangers in an attempt to kill or capture Delgado, only to watch as Delgado and his men fought their way out of it. One of the Rangers had been killed in the action, as well as two of Delgado's men, and there had been several wounded on both sides.

Delgado nodded.

"Well, while Dominguez searched the dead Ranger's pockets and Zavala took his boots, I pocketed this." He held out his badge, hoping Delgado would believe his tale.

Delgado did. "You are one clever fellow!" he cried, clapping Sandoval on the back. "I am proud to ride with you, amigo! Hombres, let's give a cheer for Sandoval!"

Everyone cheered but Lupe. No doubt she would have preferred that Sandoval had brought back Tess's lifeless body, if he returned with her at all, Sandoval thought. He could tell Delgado's sister was still suspicious of him. He and Tess would have to be extra careful of Lupe from now on until they escaped—which was going to be as soon as possible, Sandoval vowed—even if he had to kidnap Tess again.

Lupe made an elaborate show of struggling to her feet. Delgado was instantly at her side, murmuring worriedly, putting her arm about his shoulder and helping her. She grimaced as she limped over to them, her upper teeth clamped over her lower her lip as if to smother an outcry of pain.

She stopped in front of Tess. She reached out a hand to touch the red furrow on the side of Tess's head. "Ah, *señorita,* you will have a scar there. What a pity," she said, oozing false sympathy.

Tess tensed. Sandoval imagined she was probably fighting the urge to slap Lupe's hand away, but she only shrugged and said, "No matter. My hair will cover it. I am lucky to be alive. But you were wounded, too, I hear? I don't remember—the bullet knocked me out."

"It is nothing," Lupe said heroically. "A mere scratch. But I'll make those Anglos pay for what they did! Zavala died, you know. And Dominguez." She affected a mournful face.

Sandoval noted that Lupe didn't mention that Dominguez had been executed for his cowardice in not protecting Tess.

"Yes, Sandoval told me on the ride back here."

"We buried them before you arrived. Tomorrow we will return to the canyon," Delgado said.

"Return to the canyon camp?" Lupe protested. "But I don't want to! I want to rob another bank, and this time succeed."

"Be realistic, Lupe!" Delgado snapped. "We've lost two men, Tess nearly died and you've been wounded yourself. We're going back to the canyon hideout for a while, and that's the end of it."

Lupe stuck out her lower lip at the rebuke, then glared at Tess.

Delgado's tone was softer when he spoke again. "For tonight, all is well. We have Tess back with us, safe and sound, thanks to Sandoval! We rest now, eh?"

They reached the camp in the canyon at dusk the next day, after riding all day. Fernando Aguilar had scouted ahead; Sandoval had guarded the rear in case of pursuit. They arrived without encountering any problems, however—unless one considered Lupe's constant complaining about the pain of her wound.

"Welcome back, *señorita*," Esteban said, smiling a shy welcome while he assisted Tess to dismount with one hand, his other still resting in a sling.

"Thank you, Esteban. How is your shoulder?" Tess asked, while Sandoval led their horses to the corral.

"It still aches and it is numb at the same time," he admitted. "It is kind of you to ask, Señorita Tess. I see you were wounded, too." He pointed to the makeshift bandage tied about her head.

"God was watching out for me—it could have been worse." Tess smiled at him, wishing this nice man could find some honest way to make his living so he wasn't in danger of being shot ever again.

"And how is my mule?" Tess asked. She had seen the beast prick up his long ears and bray at her from the corral. "I hope Ben hasn't given you any trouble while we were gone."

Esteban grinned. "That *mulo,* he is a stubborn fellow. On some things, we have agreed to disagree. But inside, I know he has a good heart."

"Come over and get your supper, Señorita Tess," Delores called, beckoning. Since Aguilar, the scout, had arrived ahead of the rest, she had been able to ready a hot supper for their arrival.

Gratefully, Tess accepted.

"And what is this Fernando tells me about Tess being captured by the Anglos, and nearly hanged, and Zavala and Dominguez killed?" Delores said, casting a baleful glance at Delgado. "Shame on you, Diego, for exposing Señorita Tess to such danger! Your desire to show off cost the lives of two men, and nearly hers as well."

Tess's jaw dropped, amazed at the frankness of the old woman's condemnation. She tensed, expecting a wrathful reply from Delgado, but to Tess's surprise, the outlaw leader merely hung his head, chastened as a schoolboy.

"*Sí.* I realize now it was foolish of me," Delgado admitted. "Fortunately, Sandoval was able to snatch her from the jaws of death through a clever ruse." He recited the whole saga for the benefit of Delores and Esteban, who listened raptly.

"May all the saints bless you, brave man!" Delores exclaimed to Sandoval, when the tale was fully told. She rose heavily to her feet and planted a kiss on both his cheeks. Everyone laughed as Sandoval tried to duck and insist it was nothing.

Lupe had been glowering sullenly from her seat by the fire during the entire recital. "Delores, did Fernando tell you *I* was wounded, *too?*" Dramatically Lupe flung back a length of her skirt to expose the small hole in the fleshy part of her calf with its surrounding swelling and redness. "I might have lost my leg, Delores!"

The old woman nodded placidly. "But you did not, just as my Esteban might have died of his wound, but he did not," she said, nodding in the direction of her son, who was passing out second helpings of tamales.

Lupe frowned for a moment, then tried again to capture the conversational spotlight. "Esteban, did Fer-

nando tell you I am betrothed to the rancher Andrés
Cordoba? He is old, but very wealthy. I imagine, like
all the other men, you will miss me, no? I am to return
for the wedding in a month."

"To the contrary, I rejoice in your good fortune!" Esteban exclaimed. "Why didn't you just stay with him?
Does he have a sister who needs a husband? I could go
back with you."

His fellows howled with laughter, and even Delgado
chuckled.

"Diego, I think it's time I returned to Santa Elena. I'll
leave in the morning. For now, I'm going to bed," she
added. "I've had enough of these louts." With an exaggerated limp, she headed toward her brother's quarters.

"Good night, sister, pleasant dreams," Diego called
after her. "She's overtired," he added a moment later, to
no one in particular. He stood up. "As I am also. Señorita
Tess, *buenas noches.* I hope you sleep well, too. You have
been a very valiant campaigner, never complaining. I am
much impressed."

Tess watched him go, then flashed a dismayed look at
Sandoval. She had hoped to get Delgado talking again,
especially when Lupe had flounced off.

After Delores politely refused her assistance with
the dishes, Tess strolled over to the corral to greet her
mule. She spent several minutes scratching Ben's ears.
The mule's blissful snorts lightened her heart, but she
still felt restless, so using the light from the campfire to
light her way, she wandered down to the creek.

She found a comfortable seat on a flat rock, and had
just bowed her head in prayer when a voice behind her
said, "Tess, I'll give you through tomorrow evening to
talk to Delgado. After everyone goes to bed I'll ready

the horses. We're leaving in the dead of night whether you've gotten the information out of him or not."

Tess whirled in dismay. How had Parrish crept up on her like that, in boots, over uneven, rocky ground? "But, Sandoval," she began, "if I haven't learned where he took her—"

"If you haven't found out anything, I'm taking you *home,* Tess. I love you, and I won't take another chance of losing you, don't you understand?"

"So you'd chance losing your sister forever instead?"

He was silent for a long moment, his face in shadows. "You're the only one who thinks there's any reason to hope," he responded, his voice flat, his eyes bleak. "I probably lost her years ago, soon after he took her away. Pilar wasn't strong like you, Tess. You're so brave, even after what happened to you yesterday, but I wish you wouldn't even risk trying. What good will it do if you find out she's lying in some unmarked grave?"

Strong like you. Brave. Tess felt anything but strong or brave. She was full of apprehension that Delgado would suspect her motive, or would try to force his attentions on her. But if Sandoval thought of her as strong, and with God's help, she could do anything.

"I love you, too, Sandoval," she said, reaching a hand up and feeling the roughness of his unshaven cheek. "And because I do, I have to find out what happened to your sister. She might be alive."

When their lips met, the taste was bittersweet.

Chapter Twenty

Delgado set down a bottle of tequila the next evening after supper when Tess entered his quarters, carrying the dried and mounted photographs she had taken that day.

"This is quite a nice collection of pictures you have put together, Señorita Tess," Delgado praised.

She looked at the walls around her. Four of the photographs she had taken when she'd first arrived in the camp had already been mounted and hung in ornate frames that had been among the booty. Three of them were of Delgado, the other of Lupe. The paintings and photographs that had formerly been framed in them, precious to those from whom they had been stolen, no doubt lay in the pile of trash to be burned.

"Thank you. I think I have enough pictures for the book I will write about you," she told him.

He looked inordinately pleased. "You are making it more than a collection of pictures? A full biography of the daring Diego Delgado and his *bandoleros?* Ah, that will be very fine. Everyone will want a copy."

Then she saw alarm flash across his hawkish features. "You propose to take all the pictures away from me to make your book?" he asked, waving at the stack of matted pictures to which she had just added.

"No, no, don't worry," Tess assured him, "I have negatives of all of the pictures I have made. I can make copies from them, and leave the originals with you."

It would never happen, of course. The only negatives she would be taking with her were the two portraits she had made of him, full-face and profile, that were even now secreted in Sandoval's saddlebags. All the rest of the negatives and her photography equipment, and Ben, she would have to leave here—at least for now. She hoped Esteban would continue to care for the old mule.

"But that implies *you* will be leaving, *señorita*," Delgado said.

She shrugged. "I'll have to leave eventually," she told him, hoping she had not tipped her hand too much. "For one thing—"

Delgado moved closer. "But why, Tess?" he interrupted. "I want you to stay here with me, ride at my side. It will be very lonely here when Lupe goes to be Cordoba's wife."

If she goes through with it, Tess thought cynically. Lupe had not left for Santa Elena this morning as she had threatened last night when Esteban had refused to be jealous. Delgado's sister had been flirting with Esteban today as if her life depended on his responding to her wiles. Just before Tess had entered Delgado's quarters she had seen Lupe sashay up to the young Mexican, hips swaying.

Just then Delores came in, looked at his near-empty bottle of tequila, and without a word brought another down from the shelf, setting it by him, along with a glass that she set on the desk near Tess.

"Will you have some tequila, *señorita,* or is it still

only water for you?" Delgado asked, his hands poised on the bottle.

"Nothing, thanks."

He topped off his own glass. "That will be all, Delores. *Gracias.*"

The old woman nodded and shuffled silently out.

"And Lupe is counting on you to take her wedding photograph," Delgado went on.

"That's just it," Tess said, "I will need to go home between now and the wedding to replenish my supplies. After the photographs I processed today, I'm afraid I'm out of chemicals to develop any more," she explained. "I could come back as soon as I have done that."

Please believe me, she pleaded silently. Don't make me swear to a lie.

Delgado, much too close now for her comfort, laid a hand caressingly on her cheek. It took all her will not to let herself shudder.

"You are so sweet to offer that," he purred, "but I am sure your dear mama and papa would not let you out of their sight once you return, especially since they know who you have been with, the notorious outlaw Delgado. You could not help being kidnapped, but it is another thing to return of your own will, eh?"

Tess feigned a rebellious pout that would have done Lupe credit. "I'm a grown woman," she said, "I'm not about to let them tell me what I can and cannot do anymore."

"Yes, you are, aren't you?" he said, staring boldly at her in a way that made her distinctly uncomfortable. "I love your spirit, *querida.* But there is no need for you to go home, Tess. We can purchase your chemicals in Mexico City, after all."

"But that's so far away," she protested. "I wouldn't want to put anyone to the trouble of—"

"You make it sound as far as the moon, Tess. I would find it very pleasurable to journey there with you to buy your chemicals."

"I—I'll think about it," she said, knowing that if all went as planned, she would never travel anywhere with Delgado ever again. She needed to change the subject, if she was ever to get the information she must have before the end of this night. "About my book, Señor Delgado—"

"Diego," he corrected her. His warm breath, laden with tequila, fluttered a curl at her forehead. "I would think after all we have been through these past days, you could call me by my given name, as I am doing, *Tess*."

"Diego, then," she agreed, pretending to ignore the intimate tone of his voice and his alarming closeness. "Diego, if I am to write a book about you there must be words as well as pictures, you know."

He nodded. "Yes... I will be most happy to render you any assistance you may need with this project, Tess, of course."

"Well..." Tess pretended to hesitate. "Do you have time to talk now for a while?" she said, indicating the table and chairs behind him.

His black eyes gleamed, and then he turned a pair of adjacent chairs around so they faced each other, and indicated that she should sit in the one on the right. "I am at your disposal, Tess. My time is yours."

Gingerly she sat down, wishing he hadn't put the chairs so close together that their knees could almost touch, wishing she dared to push it back, wishing that she was wearing her sturdy, long-sleeved shirt instead of this thin drawstring blouse. She wished Sandoval or even Lupe were present, too. But she had deliberately sought him out when he was alone, because Delgado might not be so frank if another person were present to dampen the atmosphere of intimacy. It was up to her. And the Lord would protect her, wouldn't He?

Please, Jesus, be with me. Keep me safe. And let me discover what I need to know.

She took a deep breath. "Well…we were talking the other night about your early days as an outlaw, when you were first gathering your band of men. You had just begun to speak of a girl you knew once."

He blinked in confusion. "A girl? I think I told you, Tess, there were many girls—many women. To my regret," he said, his face full of a sadness that, she was sure, was pure pretense. "If I had only met you sooner…" He leaned toward her—again, too close.

She sat back in her chair, as far as she could without being too obvious. "But it sounded as if this girl was different. The others were experienced, you said. Women of the world. They enjoyed your attentions, but understood it was temporary. But this girl…" she prompted.

Recognition flashed in his eyes. "Oh, yes, I know who you mean now. I must have been speaking of that girl from Montemorelos."

Montemorelos, she recalled. Yes. That was the name of the town near the Parrish rancho.

"What was her name?"

Delgado sat back, his eyes losing focus. "Her name… I can see her so clearly—small, with the most perfect heart-shaped face, the most glorious hair, black as a raven's wing, thick and smooth as satin…a waist a man could span with his hands…" He pantomimed what he was saying. "Her lips were like rosebuds. She was the only daughter of an Anglo rancher who had married a *méxicana* and settled there.... Her name began with a *P*, I think. Pabla? Pepita? No, that's not it. Pia? Pía means pious, and she was very devout, this girl, but I don't think that was it...." Something flashed in his eyes. "*Pilar!* That was it, Pilar. I don't remember her family name, though."

Thank you, Lord! "That doesn't matter," Tess said with a nonchalance she was far from feeling. "Tell me about her—about your romance."

Delgado's eyes were suddenly sharp again. "I'm not sure I should, Tess. I do, after all, want you to think fondly of Diego Delgado—*very* fondly, *querida.* And this tale does not reflect well on me. I had the excuse of being young, perhaps, but still...."

"You must think of me as your biographer right now, Diego," she reminded him. "Not as your...your friend."

"My very...good friend," he murmured thickly, slurring his words, reaching out to touch her hair. "What has this tale to do with the story of Diego Delgado, the greatest outlaw of all time? I think I should tell you of some of the great raids, the big prizes I have taken."

To come this close and then have him refuse to say more about Pilar? Tess fought a feeling of desperation, and knew she had to tread carefully. "Telling me about the women in your life reveals you as a full, well-rounded man, a man of feeling, with human failings," she said. "A man other men can sympathize with."

He sighed. "I suppose you're right. You are so wise, Tess Hennessy. Very well. I will tell you, but you must promise not to hate me, eh? I am not the same man as I was then."

Tess didn't believe for a moment he had changed. He merely desired her, and wanted her willing. She didn't

hate him, though. She hated what he did, and what he
had done, but hating him was a useless emotion and
one not becoming to a Christian.

"Go on."

"I first saw Pilar entering the church in Montemorelos just as I happened to pass by, and I was smitten with her beauty. I couldn't believe she was alone,
not with some relative or at least a duenna! I followed
her inside, but she went immediately into the confes-
sional, so I went back outside and waited for her. I cannot imagine what she was going to confess, for she was
the most innocent female I have ever known. Covet-
ing an extra sweet, perhaps? Anyway, when she came
out I introduced myself to her, and asked if I could escort her somewhere. I would have offered to buy her a
drink at the cantina, but this was not a thing a gently
bred girl like Pilar would have agreed to do, especially
not with a stranger, you understand?" He yawned. "I'm
sorry, I cannot imagine why I'm sleepy, after doing so
little today."

Perhaps from drinking so much tequila? Tess
thought.

Delgado took another deep draft from his glass before continuing. "She was shy, *so* shy. She blushed when
I first spoke to her, and said she could not, since we
had not been formally introduced. She said her duenna,
some elderly aunt, was ill, but it had been a full week
since Pilar had made her confession and she did not like
to miss it, so she had stolen out of the house to do so,
intending to go right back. I told her it was a matter of
honor to me that she was safe as she walked home, and
if she did not allow me to walk with her, I would be so
devastated that I would die of grief. At last she agreed."

Tess could not imagine any girl believing such fulsome flattery, even if she had enjoyed a very sheltered upbringing, but apparently it had been so.

"I was my most charming self," Delgado remembered. "It was obvious she did not know I was the outlaw who had been recruiting other young men to join me, so I soon had her laughing with me and chattering away as if we were old friends. Her *rancho* was perhaps a mile away, but the distance seemed like nothing.

"I meant to leave before anyone saw me," Delgado went on, steepling his fingers, "but I was so beguiled by her beautiful eyes—and she by my compliments and my funny stories—that we lingered under the arbor, talking. It was obvious to me that she had never flirted with a man before, and she was enjoying it immensely. I was just stealing a kiss when her father found us there."

"Oh, dear," Tess murmured. "Did he know who you were?"

Delgado chuckled ruefully. "I'm afraid he did. He was a big, strapping Anglo, and he snatched me up by my shirt and said if he ever saw me near his daughter again he would kill me. He threw me to the ground, and my cheek scraped against a stone. When I got to my feet I was bleeding. Pilar was very distressed and protested, but he ordered her into the house. She obeyed him, but not before I saw the sympathy in her eyes."

"So, how did you manage to see her again?"

Delgado grinned. "It wasn't easy. After that she was never alone. If she came to town that elderly aunt was always with her, or her gangly younger brother."

Sandoval.

"He was very vigilant, that brother. And he never came to the cantina, where I might have corrupted him with drink. But I was determined."

"What did you do?"

"I bribed an old man in town to write Pilar a love letter from me, and paid a child to deliver it to her secretly. I told her I would wait under the arbor that night, and if she did not come I would understand, but I said I had fallen in love with her. I told her I craved more of her kisses, more than I craved my next breath."

"How romantic," Tess said, injecting admiration into her voice. She could well imagine the appeal of his approach to an innocent like Pilar—the thrill of a secret rendezvous with a handsome stranger who had been hurt by her father because he'd dared to kiss her....

"She sent back a note saying she would be there, that she would kiss the wound on my cheek. It was exactly what I wanted to hear."

Delgado's face was changing now. Gone was the wistful romantic. As if he'd forgotten he was telling this story to Tess, his features became sly, cunning, predatory. "That night I lured her into my room at the cantina. I made her mine with promises that we would be married as soon as we were far enough away from Montemorelos. We made a plan to steal away at dawn, before she had been missed. I left word for my band of men to join us in that town. It was a risk, of course."

"That her father would find you?" Tess asked, fascinated in spite of her horror at the cold-blooded way Delgado spoke of ruining Pilar's innocence.

Delgado shrugged. "That, too, but the risk I meant was the risk that my men were not loyal enough to obey my order without my being there. We had not been together that long, of course. But they came, just as I had instructed them." He smiled triumphantly at the memory.

"And Pilar?" Tess reminded him.

"She was completely in love with me, and even with

her romantic idea of being an outlaw's wife—free as the wind, answering to no one but her loving husband."

He smothered a yawn again, and rubbed his eyes. Tess was tempted to apologize for keeping him from his bed.

"But her father never caught up with her? And you never married her?"

"No… We rode east for a while. We heard the Anglo was looking for us, so we headed west, north, south. We lived off the land. I had gathered all the men I needed, and eventually we stopped hearing of him chasing us."

Tess thought of Sandoval and Pilar's father, overcome with grief, never finding his daughter, and finally dying. Was *her* father grieving like that, too? The thought made her heart ache.

"By this time," Delgado continued, "naturally, Pilar had begun to suspect my promises were worth nothing. But it was not until we came to Monterrey, and she found me with another woman, that she realized that I was never going to marry her."

"What did she do?" Tess asked, keeping her voice level, nonjudgmental. As if she were asking about the weather, when the question meant everything.

Delgado rubbed his eyes, and it was a long time before he spoke. His speech was becoming quite slurred now. "She wept. But she did not rage at me, or demand I marry her or even apologize for my unfaithfulness. She had begun to look sad all the time, and she had lost weight because of the hard way we lived. She wanted only that I escort her to the local convent, where she said she would take the veil."

Tess felt a twinge of hope. If Pilar was in a convent, then she was safe. "So you left her at a convent?"

Delgado shook his head. "I was tired of her. I had

other things to do. I came to a brothel before I found a convent, so I left her there."

It was all Tess could do to control her reaction of shock and anger, to remain still in her chair and keep her voice calm.

"And you never saw her again? Never went back to see that she was all right?"

"No. I was a busy man. We had begun to raid across the river by this time, and I was caught up in the thrill of being the most feared outlaw in Texas." He smothered another yawn. "I'm sorry, I don't know what has gotten into me...." He closed his eyes.

"Perhaps we should continue our talk tomorrow," Tess said. She had gained the information she needed, but how could she tell Sandoval his sister was in a brothel? He would be so angry he'd want to kill Delgado on the spot!

She could not think of that now. What could explain his sudden drowsiness? Delgado drank every time liquor was available, but she'd never seen him overcome by it.

"No, please, Tess. Perhaps if we take a walk..." Delgado rose, wobbling to one side, but catching himself on the table.

Something wasn't right. "Really, it's getting late. We'll talk tomorrow."

"At least give me a good-night kiss." The word came out *kish*. Delgado lurched toward her, his arm outstretched to grab her, then fell forward, and lay prone on the stolen carpet.

Tess paused only long enough to hear him snore.

Chapter Twenty-One

Tess gave a start when she crossed the threshold into the night and a dark shape detached itself from the adobe wall.

"Did the tequila do its work?" Delores said, rising with some difficulty.

Tess automatically reached out a hand to help her, wondering what the old woman meant. "Um…yes, he must have drunk a lot of it before I came to show him the pictures. He…fell asleep, right on the floor…." She was sure she looked guilty to Delores, even in the shadowy light, even though she was mystified at the sudden nature of her deliverance.

Delores chuckled. "You think he is merely *borracho?* Oh, no, *señorita,* Delgado has been drinking tequila since he quit his mother's milk. The tequila he was drinking contained a sleeping potion I added. He will sleep like the dead until morning. That will help you make your escape, no?"

Tess's jaw dropped. She stared at the old woman's amused face, then darted quickly past her to check at both sides of the hut and in back of it to make sure no one lurked there, eavesdropping. She stared across the creek, where some of the others were still sitting by the campfire, or in some cases, already rolled up in their bedrolls.

"You *know*? You drugged him to help me escape?"

The old woman nodded, her lips curved and her eyes still dancing with delight.

"Of course. You cannot stay here much longer, *se-ñorita*. Delgado wants to make you his woman, and Lupe is out for your blood. You must get away from here."

"Yes…" How much did Delores know? Did she know Sandoval was part of the plan? Did she know he was a Texas Ranger whose ultimate goal was to capture Delgado?

"But why are you doing this?" Tess asked, hoping Delores's answer might indicate how much she knew.

"Because you are a good woman, and you do not want this—to be his *ama*, no? Lack of willingness would not matter to Delgado, but it matters to me. And I want to help you because you took such good care of my son."

Tess saw a figure cross from the corral and step onto the narrow bridge. She tensed, holding up a warning hand to Delores, but in a moment she saw that it was Sandoval.

"That is the man you love, yes?" Delores murmured as he approached, but it was more a statement than a question. "He is the right man for you."

Tess could only nod.

"Everything is ready. Is Delgado sleeping?" Sandoval asked both women. So Delores knew of Sandoval's part in the escape plan, at least.

"Sí," she said to Sandoval. "He will be no threat to you till morning. And my Esteban will do his best

to distract Lupe until the sleeping potion takes effect with her, too."

So Esteban was part of the conspiracy, also. Now they only had to sneak with two horses past several sleeping men.

Sandoval looked probingly at Tess. He had to know right away if she'd been successful, but he wouldn't ask the question in front of Delores. All of their survival might depend on Delores not knowing. The Delgados wouldn't hesitate to torture the old woman if they thought she knew anything.

Fortunately, Tess understood immediately and nodded with a tremulous smile.

She had discovered what had happened to Pilar, and she was alive! Tess knew where she was! Tears stung Sandoval's eyes. He fought the urge to let out a cry and resolutely blinked the tears away. There was no time for that now.

"Once I'm sure everyone's asleep, we'll leave," Sandoval told Tess. "Between now and then, bundle up your clothing in the saddlebag you'll find by your pallet."

Tess nodded her understanding.

"Esteban's much more recovered than he pretended to be, Tess," Sandoval went on. "He's worried that Ben will bray when he sees us leave and wake someone, so he's going to hold Ben's head while we're leading the horses out of the canyon. Then, when we're discovered gone, and everyone's haring off after us—in the direction they *think* we're going—Esteban's going to hitch Ben to your camera wagon and, with any luck, bring your precious camera and mule home by another route. He'll deliver the negatives of Delgado to your assistant, Francisco, who will take them to your godfather. That way they can be published much sooner than if we were bringing them, since we're going in a…a different direction," he said, after a glance at Delores. "He'll also assure your parents you are all right and coming home as soon as you can."

Tess clapped a hand to her mouth, clearly overcome with joy. "You've thought of everything, haven't you?" she cried. She hugged him fiercely for a moment, then turned to Delores, kissing the surprised woman on both cheeks. *"Gracias,"* she breathed, through her tears. "Tell your son I thank him, too…." Clearly too moved for words, Tess was silent for a moment. "Esteban is a good man. And I—I don't know why, but I love that old mule. And the camera…"

"De nada, señorita," Delores said, beaming. "I have wanted to get my son away from the life of a bandit for a while now, and he's finally seen the sense of an old mother's pleas. I am glad he can help you while helping himself."

"But what about you?" Tess asked, worry furrowing her brow. "I don't want Delgado taking his fury out on you when he realizes we've escaped."

The old woman chuckled. "I have a place to hide that that fox would never suspect. I'll wait there for my son to come for me when it is safe. Meanwhile, I'm going to drink some of the spiked tequila myself, so that when Delgado and Lupe wake to discover you two are gone, I'll be as hard to wake as they are now. Maybe they'll think you drugged me, yes? 'Ah, that red-headed *bruja,'* Delores said, mimicking Delgado's voice, "'We had no idea she was so devious!'" She laughed at her own joke. "Now, don't you two have things to discuss?" she said, making shooing motions toward Tess's hut.

"So he left Pilar at a *brothel* in Monterrey?" Sandoval repeated, when Tess had finished telling him what she had learned from Delgado. His stomach churned with nausea, his throat felt thick at the thought of his sister, broken and disillusioned, believing she had no alternative but that—a girl whose faith had always been important to her, who had never skipped her prayers. A girl who'd wanted to be a wife and mother, just like their mother. She'd asked to be taken to a convent, but he'd taken her to a brothel instead.

It was too bad he could only kill Delgado once, and that he couldn't do it right now, this minute, and with his bare hands.

Tess nodded, watching him with wide eyes, as if she feared he would explode. She reached out a hand and gingerly touched his shoulder. "*We'll find her, Sandoval.* We have only to ride to Monterrey and ask at every brothel until we find her. Is it far?"

"About fifty miles from here," Sandoval said. "Almost due east. Tess, I *looked* for her in *Monterrey*—it's the biggest city in Nuevo Léon," he protested. "I went to every *burdel.* I offered money as a reward. No one knew anything about her."

"Perhaps she hadn't come yet," Tess pointed out. "Delgado said she rode with him for a while before he left her there."

He winced inwardly, imagining his delicate, innocent sister living as he had been living, always in the saddle, roaming from place to place, eating poor provisions cooked over a fire or in shabby cantinas and, in her case, gradually losing hope in the man she'd been unwise enough to trust with her love. And then he had abandoned her to an unspeakable fate.

"Then, as long as we're lucky enough to evade Delgado, we should be able to find her…. What's wrong?" Tess asked.

How could he explain to an innocent girl like Tess what life must be like for Pilar in such a place? He could not imagine Pilar surviving it a week, let alone five years. He almost prayed that she was dead, that God had taken her to heaven to rescue her.

"What if she didn't stay there, in the brothel?" he asked, afraid to give voice to the full horror of his thoughts. "What if she was too full of despair after what had happened to her, and she couldn't bear the life of a—" He couldn't say the word. "What if she lost all hope, and became ill and died?'"

Tess pulled him into her arms. "What if she managed to find a way to escape such a place? You must hold on to hope, my love. I cannot believe God would allow us to find out where he left her," she said against his chest, while he allowed the tears he had held back to slide down his face, wetting her hair, "only to close the door in our faces, Sandoval. No, I believe we will find her in Monterrey. But we must have faith until we get there."

He pulled away only enough to look down at her, smiling through his tears. "You have enough faith for both of us, Tess. It's why I love you."

"I love you, too. She'll be there, Sandoval," she told him. "You'll see."

But there was more he had to know. "Tess, Delgado…he didn't hurt you…before he passed out, did he?" He already hated the man for what he'd done to Pilar, but if Delgado had even come close to molesting Tess also, it would be hard to leave camp without making the outlaw pay for hurting the woman he loved.

"No," she assured him quickly. "I saw in his eyes that he wanted to…" she said, flushing. "And I *was* afraid I'd have to fight my way out of there. But he passed out at just the right time. God bless Delores for her cleverness."

"Amen to that! Now, here's what we're going to do…"

"It's time," Sandoval said, waking Tess with a gentle touch.

Tess started awake, her gaze darting around the room before settling on him. "I can't believe I fell asleep," she murmured. "I felt tight as a fiddle string when you told me to lie down for a while." She sat up, stretching out her arms.

"It's good that you could get some rest," he said, watching fondly as Tess rubbed her eyes and smoothed back a few curling, errant strands that had escaped her braid. "We have a long way to go."

"I'm ready," she said, getting to her feet. "But how will we get past the guard at the mouth of the canyon?"

"The plan was for Esteban to go out and offer to share a bottle with Prieto to help him while away the lonely hours. The trick will be for Esteban to pretend to drink when the bottle is passed to him, without actually drinking, but in the dark that shouldn't be too hard to accomplish. We need him to be alert later to drive the wagon away while everyone is off chasing us. So if Prieto has imbibed enough, the only bandits we need to worry about are the ones sleeping out there. Are you ready?" he said, nodding toward the door.

"I think we should pray first," she told him.

"Yes. You go ahead," he said. How could he expect the Lord to listen to him when he'd doubted God cared ever since Pilar had disappeared? God would listen to Tess.

Tess surprised him by taking his hand before she bowed her head and closed her eyes. "Father, we come to

You believing that You can do anything, and that You'll give us safety as we leave the canyon tonight. Please stop the ears of the bandits as we walk past them. Make us invisible to their eyes. Prevent the horses from whinnying. And keep Delgado and Lupe and Prieto deeply asleep. Help us to find Pilar. Oh, yes, and give Esteban protection and success in bringing Ben and the camera home, and give Delores safety too as she escapes. For we ask it all in Jesus's name, amen."

"Amen," he said, adding his own silent prayer— *Lord, I don't know if You will do all this, but please, at least get Tess safely home. It's all my fault that she's here, so if anyone has to pay for my foolishness, it should only be me.*

Tess met his eyes after he raised his head. "Now we can go."

"Wake up! Wake up, you fool!" Lupe cried, kicking her brother again, viciously, in the ribs.

Diego Delgado slitted his eyes open and snapped out a hand, catching the offending foot. He jerked on it, succeeding in yanking Lupe off her feet to fall heavily on him.

She cursed at him and struck him with a fist.

"Quit that!" Delgado shouted, and shoved her off of him. "Why are you abusing me, Lupe? I was only sleeping—what have I done to you that you would treat your brother this way?"

"Let go of me, and wake up, you stupid oaf! While you've been sleeping, your little redhead has flown the coop, and Parrish with her. I *told* you he was not to be trusted, that half-breed. We have to go after them!"

Delgado roared, fully awake now. He sat up and,

grabbing Lupe, jerked her into a sitting position, too. "You say they're *gone?* Where? When?"

"I don't know," she muttered. "I just woke up myself—and I wasn't on my pallet in there," she said, jerking her head to indicate the curtained-off room that separated her sleeping area from her brother's.

"Where were you?"

"Lying in a bedroll by the campfire." At her brother's knowing snigger, she pounded the floor with her fist. "I can assure you, brother, I'd never sleep there! I don't even know how I got there."

"What do you mean?" Delgado said. He had risen to his feet and was already strapping on his gun belt.

Lupe looked confused. "The last thing I remember, I was sitting on the bank of the creek," she said, pointing toward the mouth of the canyon, "talking to Esteban and sharing a bottle with him—flirting, if you must know the truth. I remember getting very drowsy…and then the next thing I knew, the sun was shining in my eyes and Esteban and the rest of the men were all waking around me!"

Delgado rubbed his chin, a murderous certainty growing within him as he searched his memory of the night before. He remembered telling Tess about that girl from his past, while he drank. He remembered getting unusually drowsy, which didn't make sense. He'd always had a good head for tequila. And he'd never slept on the floor, not with his good bed—a prize he'd taken from a rancher near Brownsville—a few feet away.

"We were *drugged*," brother and sister said in unison.

"Where's Delores?" he said. "Tell her to make us something to break our fast. We ride within the hour."

"Good luck with that," Lupe snapped sourly. "I found

her asleep in the *gringa's* hut. I think she was given the same thing we were, because I pinched her till she woke, but she went right back to sleep."

"Then we'll ride without eating," he decided aloud. "We can catch up with them faster that way. They couldn't have gotten that far yet," he said, but it sounded like wishful thinking, even to him. "I'll kill that traitor when I see him!" he said, his hands tightening into fists. He'd trusted Sandoval like a brother, and made him his second-in-command because of his intelligence, even though he had only joined the banditos during the last year.

"Yes, I'll kill him," he snarled, "slowly and painfully. And I'll make Tess Hennessey wish she was dead."

Chapter Twenty-Two

"Thank you, Lord," Tess murmured, when the opening to the canyon lay in the distance behind them. So far, God had answered Tess's prayers. Despite the fact that one or two of the sleeping banditos had stirred in their slumber, none had awakened when first Tess had stolen past, then Sandoval had walked the two horses by their sleeping forms. Esteban had lain among them, presumably feigning sleep. They had seen no sign of Delgado or Lupe. Prieto had snored at his post, rifle propped against a boulder.

Dawn was breaking when they reached the little village of Santa Clara, not far from the border between the Mexican states of Tamaulipas and Nuevo Léon.

"It's not a big village, but we'll stop here, if we can find a place," Sandoval announced, peering at the dusty village from their vantage point on a little bluff. "Sleep awhile."

"I—I can ride farther if you want, after we water the horses," Tess assured him, thinking he was trying to spare her. The thought of stopping, when they were still so close to the canyon hideout they'd fled only hours ago, made her nervous.

His eyes swept back to her, caressing her with his approval. "I know you can, sweetheart, but even though I don't think they'll figure out we've gone this way, it's probably better that we travel by night and hole up during the day."

It was then that she saw the fatigue that shadowed his dark eyes. He'd been awake all night, while she'd had the benefit, at least, of a short nap.

"All right, whatever you think best," she acquiesced, "but where will we hide the horses?" The pinto gelding Sandoval rode was memorable for his flashy color, as Tess was for her red hair. But Tess could hide her hair under the broad-brimmed hat she wore.

Sandoval must have had the same thoughts, for he said, "You stay here. I don't want anyone to remember seeing you, or these horses."

Tess looked uneasily over her shoulder.

"No one's been following us," he said. "But take this." He handed her one of his two pistols. "If anyone threatens you, use it."

No one passed by Tess except a boy herding a dozen goats, who stared at her curiously but did not stop. Sandoval returned within minutes. Santa Clara boasted no inn, he'd discovered, and the rooms attached to the back of the cantina housed the owner and his family. But the priest at the small church, Father Aldama, had been able to direct him to a farmhouse on the edge of town where his sister, Josefina Padilla, a widow, lived.

She agreed to give them shelter for the day and hide their horses in her barn for the price of a few pesos— but not before she'd peered at them through her spectacles and interrogated them.

"Are you running from the law? I won't have outlaws under my roof," she informed him, leaning on her cane and staring up at Sandoval, who was a foot and a half taller than she.

Tess watched as Sandoval swept his hat off his head and gave the widow a smile that would have melted ice. "No, Señora Padilla, we're no lawbreakers. As a matter of fact, we're fleeing from outlaws. You have perhaps heard of Delgado and his band?"

"Diego Delgado? Bah!" The widow spat in the dust. "I would kill him myself if I got the chance. He lured my nephew into joining him, and Antonio—may God forgive him—was killed the very next time they raided across the border. That man and his cutthroats give Mexicans a bad reputation. What are your names?"

"It may be safer for you not to know, *señora.*"

The diminutive widow digested that fact for a moment. "What am I supposed to call you, Juan and Juana? I'm not afraid of that fool! Tell me your names."

Seeing she wouldn't take no for an answer, they did so.

"Are you two married?" she asked, directing her question at Tess.

Tess felt herself redden under the woman's scrutiny. "No, *señora.*" She chanced a glance at Sandoval, and the look in his dark eyes caused Tess's blush to flood all the way to her scalp.

The widow saw it. "I'll give you two rooms, then. I'll have you know I'll stand for no mischief under my roof."

"Yes, *señora,* we understand," Sandoval said meekly.

The old woman showed them to two rooms at opposite ends of a long back hall.

"I'll wake you when the sun goes down, and give you something to eat before you go on your way," she promised.

Tess had doubted she would sleep, but she did not

wake until the old widow came in bearing a basin of hot water, soap and a towel. She'd evidently done the same for Sandoval, and even unearthed her late husband's razor, for when Tess and Sandoval met at Josefina Padilla's table to enjoy a meal of spicy chicken stew, they both looked and felt a great deal better than when they had lain down.

After she had served them, Josefina sat down and ate with them—or rather, she took an occasional bite while they answered the numerous questions she peppered them with. They soon found themselves telling her their entire saga.

Josefina gasped at the perils they had endured and the danger they were still in, growled in outrage when she heard what Delgado had done to Sandoval's sister and shed tears when they explained why they were headed to Monterrey instead of Texas. But it was their growing love for each other that seemed most to capture her fancy. It was plain that the widow was a romantic at heart.

"So you love one another," she concluded after the meal, while they drank her delicious but strong coffee and munched on freshly baked, pastel-colored cookies. When they both nodded, she leaned forward, placing her hands on the table. "You will marry?"

Tess's gaze flew to Sandoval, and he met it steadily, asking a question with his eyes and receiving her answer, all without words. "Yes," he answered for both of them.

"When?" Josefina demanded, her birdlike eyes avid for his reply.

Sandoval looked at Tess. "I imagine that will be once we have safely reached Tess's home, *señora,* and I have asked her father for her hand, and a proper wedding can be planned. The kind of wedding she deserves, where she wears a beautiful dress like a queen as she places her hand in mine."

"Humph!" the widow said, crossing her arms over her chest. She looked vastly disappointed, almost disgusted.

They both looked at her, startled. It was the last thing they had expected her to say.

"Pardon me?" Tess said at last.

"You said you love one another. Yet you plan to travel alone together all the way to Monterrey, and with God's help, find Sandoval's sister, and return to Texas again, still unmarried. All so you, Tess, can have a proper, fairy-tale wedding. I can see that your motives are honorable, Sandoval, but this is not right."

Tess looked uneasily at Sandoval, and then back at Josefina.

"But we must find Pilar, if it's possible, before we can think of going home," Tess pointed out.

"Indeed you must," Josefina agreed. "But you are in love and you want to be married, and here you are in a place where my brother is the priest! He can marry you this very night. However much the Lord approves of your plan to find Pilar, you are not guaranteed tomorrow, you know. I have been a widow for ten years. My Tomás and I thought we had forever, but we did not," she said, wiping a tear from the corner of her eye with a lacy handkerchief from her apron pocket. "Do you really want to wait for some other day when you can wed at home, when you could be man and wife this very night?"

Sandoval cleared his throat. "Perhaps you would not mind if Tess and I stepped outside and discussed this alone for a few minutes?"

"Of course," Josefina said, gesturing toward the porch just beyond the back door.

Tess followed Sandoval outside on shaking legs. Was this really happening, or was she still lying in the back bedroom of the widow's house, dreaming? What would Sandoval say?

For a moment they just stood there in the gathering darkness, staring up at the stars, then through the window at the widow bustling to clear the table, then at each other.

"Sandoval, please don't let Señora Padilla pressure you into something you're not ready to do," Tess began. "I mean, we've hardly had a normal courtship…perhaps you'd prefer to wait until we're home, and can see each other in regular circumstances. Perhaps you wouldn't even like me then, let alone love me. I'm spoiled and selfish and I like to have my own way—"

To her astonishment, Sandoval threw back his head and laughed. "*You're* selfish? *You* like to have your own way? Tess, you're speaking to the man who had you *kidnapped* to achieve his goal to capture Delgado, who didn't concern himself about the danger it could put you in. And you fell in love with me anyway!" he said, taking her in his arms and gazing down at her.

"Yes, I did," she admitted, feeling she could never have enough of gazing into his dark eyes and seeing the love for her that radiated from them.

"I was wrong to have you taken as I did," Sandoval said, "but in one sense I'm not sorry at all, because now we're here together like this. I don't think you'd have ever given me the time of day back in Chapin, would you? You looked so suspiciously at me at your godfather's barbecue."

"You looked dangerous," she told him honestly. "And

mysterious. I was afraid of you, a little, but more afraid of the immediate attraction I felt. I was afraid of what it would cost me."

"Your independence, you mean? I know you have a goal, too."

"Yes..." she said, moved that he could so completely understand her and crystallize her thoughts so effortlessly. She'd never been so well understood before—not by her mother, who loved her but had no understanding of her dreams, not even by her father, who sympathized with her goals.

"Loving you means I want you to be yourself, Tess," Sandoval told her earnestly. "If you want to go to New York and be a photographer, we'll find a way to do that."

She couldn't believe her ears. "But what would *you* do? You're a Ranger. You live to enforce the law in Texas. That's who you are. I understand that."

Sandoval shrugged. "I reckon there's law to enforce in New York, or anywhere you are," he said.

She tried to imagine this tall, rangy man who'd been bred for the big sky over the warm Rio Grande Valley living with his view hemmed in by the tall buildings of a vast city, buffeted by the cold winds and snow blowing in a northern winter. "You'd be like a fish out of water," Tess said. "And so would I," she murmured in a whisper, and knew it was true. Photography would always be important to her, but Brady's studio in New York City no longer shone in her imagination like the promised land. The promised land was anywhere Sandoval Parrish was.

"I don't think I want to go to New York City anymore. Not to stay, at least. I'll probably never be a conventional wife like my mother, but I love you. And I want to be your wife this very night."

"You don't want to wait and be married in your church at home? In a beautiful dress? I'd wait for you, you know—it's not tonight or never. Don't little girls dream of such a wedding?"

"Little girls dream of the dark, handsome stranger," she said, reaching up to caress his raven-black hair and his angular cheeks, "who turns out to be their white knight."

Her mouth fell open as he knelt and took her hand. "A white knight always kneels to ask his lady's hand in marriage," he explained. "Tess Hennessy, will you do me the honor of marrying me tonight?"

Father Anthony Aldama was bemused at his sister's request, but nonetheless, obligingly dressed in his vestments and followed her back to her farmhouse, listening as they walked to her accounting of Tess and Sandoval's story.

"This is hardly a usual situation," he said, when he arrived. "But no matter. If you are Christians and you love each other, and you want to be married before journeying off to find your sister, Señor Parrish, I can only approve. Are you ready?" he asked, beckoning them forward.

"Wait, wait!" Josefina interposed herself between the couple and her brother, moving quickly for a woman using a cane. "I have just the thing for the bride…." She left the parlor, and returned in a few minutes carrying a lacy white mantilla that smelled of the lavender it had been packed away with. She draped it over Tess's head.

"I wore it to my wedding," she said, kissing Tess on each cheek. "You do not have a proper wedding dress, but at least you have a veil."

"Thank you," Tess said, embracing Josefina. She met

Sandoval's admiring gaze over the widow's back. His eyes told her she was as lovely as any bride ever born, the only woman he wanted.

"You are ready now?" Father Aldama said. "Dearly beloved…"

Afterward, when he had pronounced them man and wife, he said, "Will you stay here tonight, Señor and Señora Parrish? My sister can come back to my little house next to the church so you may have the privacy a newlywed couple needs."

Sandoval's heart gave a leap of joy as he saw Tess smiling at being addressed as his wife. "We appreciate the offer," he said, sensing Tess would not mind his decision, "but it's probably best if we go on tonight as planned. The less time we are here, the less danger for you both if Delgado figures out what direction we went." And there was something he liked about the idea of their wedding night taking place under all the stars in God's heaven.

"Delgado, humph!" piped up Josefina. "I'd like to see him try to bother me and my brother. I'd beat him with my cane!"

Tess and Sandoval knelt for the priest's blessing.

Chapter Twenty-Three

❧

They rode on until the middle of the night and finally sought refuge in a grove of venerable live oaks some distance off the road. After tethering the horses to a rope line stretched from the trunk of one tree to the other, Sandoval set to making a bed out of their combined bedrolls.

Tess deserved something better than this for her bridal bower, he thought. There was a glade in the middle of the ring of trees where the sun was able to reach, so the ground was grass-covered, but it would still be a hard bed. "I should have taken the priest and his sister up on their offer of the farmhouse," he murmured, watching as she approached the blanket and sat down on it. "Once we get back to Texas, Tess," he promised hoarsely, "you'll never have to sleep in the open again."

"Shh," she said, leaning back on her elbows and beckoning to him to join her. "Look, you can see the stars, and even the moon." He sat and peered through the space between the branches, admiring the celestial view with her. Then he turned to admire Tess, the way she looked by the light of the moon and the stars.

Thank You for this most marvelous gift, Lord, this

woman whom I do not deserve, whom You have given to me as my wife. And if I can believe that You gave me Tess, I should be able to believe You will also allow us to find Pilar.

"Sandoval…"

At first Tess did not know what had awakened her—the light of morning filtering through the leaves? The gentle breeze? Then she realized it was Sandoval, no longer lying supine and relaxed next to her, but standing tensely with his back to her, facing the direction of the road, one hand loosely holding the pistol he'd set next to him when they'd gone to sleep.

Tess shifted quickly from her back to her stomach and levered herself up on one elbow, peering at the space between the trees where a man sat on a bony brown horse, his eyes shifting from Sandoval to her and back. She was thankful that the cool night had impelled her to don her clothes again before sleeping. Underneath the blanket, she reached surreptitiously for the other pistol.

His broad, flat face and short, broad-shouldered stature revealed a heavily Indian heritage. Probably his ancestors had dwelled in Mexico long before the Spanish conquerors had come exploring. But his Spanish, when he spoke, was as pure as Sandoval's.

"*Señor, señora,* I apologize for disturbing you. I saw a flash of white as I walked past, and wondered if it was the lost goat I was looking for. But as I came closer, I realized it was a horse instead," he explained, smiling as he nodded over his shoulder at Sandoval's pinto. That he was lying, Tess knew by the battered old shotgun he held at the ready. She froze in place, knowing Sandoval needed no distractions right now.

Lord, help us!

"I mean you no harm," the man said, but he made no move to put away the shotgun. "That's a nice horse, that pinto."

"Yes, he is." Sandoval did not turn his head away from the man to look at his horse. "As it happens, I would be willing to trade him for yours."

The man blinked in surprise. "Why?"

"He doesn't get along with my wife's horse."

It was a patent falsehood, for the pinto gelding, who had raised his head alertly when the man started speaking, had returned to grazing with his head just inches from that of Tess's mare.

A grin spread across the man's broad, coppery features. "This is my lucky day," the man said. "You have a deal, *señor*." Darting glances full of avid curiosity at Tess, he dismounted, laid down his shotgun and offered Sandoval the reins of his nag.

Sandoval did not relax his vigilance, and kept the gun in his hand. "I'll keep my own saddle," he said.

Disappointment flashed across the man's face, then he shrugged as if to say, "you can't blame me for trying." He loosed the cinch on his own horse and pulled off the saddle; then, while Sandoval remained on guard, put his old saddle on the pinto.

"*Gracias.* It was a pleasure doing business with you, *señor*," he said, reining the horse out of the grove and back toward the road.

Tess waited until the fellow was out of sight to come out of her blanket. "There was no lost goat!" she cried, her voice indignant. "You shouldn't have had to trade your pinto for that sorry piece of horseflesh." Then she felt bad when she looked in the rawboned brown horse's steady, honest eyes.

Sandoval was philosophical. "You're right. I never gave him a name, but that pinto could really run. But the man went away feeling he'd gotten a prize, instead of staying and making trouble. I didn't like the way he kept looking at you."

"Neither did I," Tess admitted.

"I'd been thinking of trading the pinto for another horse somewhere along the way, anyway," Sandoval said. "His markings were too memorable. I still have money from my share of the booty. Now if Delgado comes asking about a man riding a black-and-white pinto, they won't tell him about seeing us."

"You can't get much less memorable than this horse," Tess said, but laughed as the nag nuzzled her hand.

"I can buy another horse at the next town or *rancho* we come across," Sandoval said. "We'll keep this old fellow for a packhorse."

Tess wondered what Delgado and his sister were doing now. Were they still searching furiously for them somewhere between the canyon hideout and her home in Chapin? Had Esteban, with her precious camera and mule, and above all the important negatives of Delgado, managed to evade the outlaw leader? Had Delores, his mother, escaped safely?

Five days later, after encountering no further trouble, they arrived in Monterrey, a city tucked at the foot of the Sierra Madres. The closest mountain was notched at the top like an uneven *M*.

"That's *Cerro de la Silla,* Saddle Hill," Sandoval announced from the back of the bay gelding he'd bought along the way. He peered out over the city and sighed. "There were a lot of brothels when I was here before.

But maybe we should check into lodging first, and find some food? It must be nearly noon."

"That sounds good." He was nervous, Tess realized, worried that they'd look at each bordello and still not find Pilar.

Near the main cathedral they found a decent inn that also provided stabling for their horses, and down the street, a humble restaurant that served excellent tamales. Then, refreshed, they began their search.

Sandoval had remembered that the seedy part of town, where most of the brothels were located, lay to the east of the grand plaza. It took them fifteen minutes to walk there, but once they had reached it, it seemed like another world to Tess.

The narrow, winding street was lined with cantinas and two-story buildings whose upper verandas jutted out over the street. On several of these, handfuls of women in gaudy-colored wraps lounged on couches and chairs, chattering with each other and calling out raucous greetings when they spotted Sandoval, despite Tess's presence at his side.

Sandoval stopped. "I'd better take you back to the inn," he said, glancing upward and then quickly back at her. "You shouldn't be here."

"I'm staying," Tess said, and essayed a grin. "You might need protection from *them*." And then she remembered that one of those women could possibly be Pilar, and sobered. *Please, Lord, guide us to the right place, and as soon as possible.*

They went into the first brothel, *Casa de Marías*. A frowsy older woman dozed in a threadbare armchair.

"Buenas tardes, señora," Sandoval said, then repeated himself more loudly until the woman blinked,

startled and nearly fell out of her chair. Bleary, beady black eyes focused on Sandoval with apparent difficulty.

"Good afternoon, sir," she said with a drowsy smile. When she spotted Tess at his side, though, her eyes narrowed and she crossed her arms over her chest. "I have enough girls. I don't need any more. You might ask Florita down the row, though—she keeps foreign women for her customers. Me, I think they're too much trouble."

"No, you don't understand," Sandoval said curtly. "This is my wife. We're looking for a woman named Pilar Parrish, or maybe Pilar Morelos."

The woman shrugged, clearly bored now that there wasn't any money to be made from Sandoval. "All my girls are named *María*. It's easier that way. I have María Angela, María Filipa, María Rosa…"

"No María Pilar?" asked Tess.

The woman shook her head, setting her jowls waggling. "She's not one of my girls. I don't know her."

"Thank you," Sandoval said, and they left.

It was the same story in the next five *burdeles*. No one knew of a woman named Pilar, or of any woman who might have been brought by Delgado five years ago, though some had heard of the outlaw.

Tess's heart was heavy as she saw Sandoval's shoulders sagging in disappointment as they left each establishment. There was only one more place to try.

At the seventh house, the elderly proprietress, who seemed afflicted with some kind of tremors, shook her head. "No, I don't have any girls named Pilar."

"Thank you, *señora*," Sandoval said, already turning to go.

"But wait, *señor*," she said. "She was brought by an outlaw, five years ago? I wasn't here then, you understand, but the woman who ran this place before me told me about all the girls, and that sounds like Magdalena."

Magdalena. Mary Magdalene had been a prostitute Jesus healed of evil spirits. Tess felt a spark of hope flicker in her heart.

Beside her, Sandoval had paled and gone still.

"C-can we see her?" Tess asked, because her husband seemed unable to speak.

The woman shook her head, the voluntary motion accentuated by her palsy. "She's not here."

Sandoval stifled a groan and Tess's heart sank. "She's not here anymore? Where did she go?"

The woman held up a hand. "I'm sorry, I meant she's not here right now. I sent her to the cantina to buy some more tequila for the customers. If I didn't send her out on errands occasionally, that one would never go outside. She's very quiet, doesn't mix much with the other girls. Keeps to herself. Some customers don't care, I suppose, but she's not a favorite. Ramón—he's the owner—he tells her always she needs to be more friendly."

Something in Sandoval's tight face must have warned the old woman, for she stopped. "Who is she to you, *señor?* Why are you looking for her?"

"If this Magdalena is really Pilar, she's my sister. And I'll be taking her out of here."

The old woman looked alarmed. "Oh, *señor,* Ramón would never allow that."

Sandoval's jaw set in a hard line. "I have money. I'll buy her freedom—"

He broke off as the door opened behind them, and a young woman entered, her arms laden with a boxful of a dozen or so bottles.

Tess stared at her, and beside her, Sandoval was

doing the same. It was hard to see her features, for she kept her head down, avoiding their gaze.

"Señor Alba says he'll put this on Ramón's bill, Joaquina, but Ramón needs to pay him soon. I'll just take them to the back."

Sandoval cleared his throat. *"Pilar? Pilar Parrish?"*

Chapter Twenty-Four

"*S-Sandoval?*" she queried, in a hoarse version of the voice Sandoval had thought he'd never hear again. "*Is it really you?*" She set down the case of bottles with a clatter of glass.

"Yes. *Yes!*" he cried, starting forward. His sudden movement seemed to alarm her, and she took a step back; then, as if realizing he told the truth, she took trembling steps forward, her arms outstretched, until they met midway.

He stood holding her, both of them shaking, while he smiled through his tears at Tess, who stood beaming at both of them.

At last he loosened his hold on her but, still touching her upper arms, smiled down at her tearstained face. She was still lovely, he thought, though older, and a world-weariness had settled in her eyes where shining joy with life had once lived.

"Why don't you come into the reception room?" Joaquina suggested from behind them, beckoning to a door that led off the entrance hall. "It's never busy at this time of day, and you will have some privacy to visit."

They followed her as she ushered them into a medium-size room where chairs were lined up against the walls. Here was where the women of this house greeted their customers in the evening, Sandoval realized with a pang as they pulled three chairs into a circle.

"I thought never to see you again in this life, brother," Pilar said shakily, as soon as they had sat down.

"Pilar…may I call you that? I will call you Magdalena if you prefer…"

Pilar shook her head. "You may call me whatever you like."

"Pilar, I have been searching for you ever since… since you were taken away. I had given up and begun to think you must be dead. I would not be here if Tess—" he beckoned for Tess to join them "—my wife, had not helped me discover where you were and insisted we come and find you."

Pilar shifted her gaze and, leaning forward, embraced Tess, kissing her cheek. "Thank you. It is so much more than I deserve. I am in your debt."

"You owe me nothing," Tess assured her. "We thank God He has led us to you."

"But what are you saying, 'much more than I deserve'?" Sandoval said, his voice impassioned. "None of what happened was your fault. I knew Delgado had taken advantage of your innocence and lured you from home."

"Before I say anything more, I must know where that monster is. We've heard of his doings, even in Monterrey. He…he did not come with you, did he? How did you find out where I was?" Her eyes darted to the door, as if she expected Delgado to materialize there.

"No, no, of course we wouldn't bring him with us," Sandoval said quickly. "Please don't worry. I'll never let him come near you again." He briefly summarized how they had come to be here.

Pilar listened, her eyes widening at some parts, her jaw dropping at others. "So you are a Ranger, but you have posed as an outlaw in an effort to bring him to justice? And you *kidnapped* Tess in an effort to achieve your goal, all because she can take photographs?" She shook her head disapprovingly, then turned to Tess. "And you not only *forgave* my brother for what he did, but *married him*? *Why*?" She blinked as if the story was almost beyond comprehension.

"I love your brother," Tess said simply. "However unconventional his methods are, I discovered he is the man the Lord planned for me to marry."

Pilar looked from Sandoval to Tess and back again, still shaking her head. "So, you, too, brother, have received more than you deserve."

Sandoval nodded.

"God gives all of us more than we deserve," Tess said.

"Pilar, we came to take you out of here," Sandoval said. "You don't have to stay here any longer."

Pilar stared back at him, her eyes bleak, and shook her head. "It is enough that I have seen you again, and know that you are happy. This is my life now, brother. There is nothing left for me out there," she added, nodding in the direction of the front door. "What would I do, where would I go, after what I've done? No, Sandoval, I will stay here."

"Pilar, what are you saying? You can't mean you like this life!" he cried, taking her hands in his. "You can go home—either to Montemorelos, which I will deed to you, or join us in Texas. Our mother will be overjoyed to see you. She has grieved for years, not knowing if you were dead or alive."

Pilar's eyes were huge in her still-beautiful face, and now they gleamed with tears, like rain on onyx. "*Madre?* She…she's still alive?"

Sandoval gave her hands a squeeze, sure that mentioning their mother would convince Pilar. "Yes! She lives on my ranch in Texas, but if you decide to go to Montemorelos, she might want to come back there. I am willing to share her, of course," he added with a laugh—a laugh that soon died when he saw Pilar's face subside into hopelessness again.

"You must not tell her you found me," she told him flatly. "It's better that she thinks I am dead than living in a brothel."

"But why? Are you blaming yourself for being here, where Delgado brought you? None of what happened was your fault. You were *innocent,* sister," he repeated.

Pilar shook her head, her eyes brimming with a sorrow too deep for words. "I was innocent when I first met him, yes. But then he seduced me with his blandishments and flattery, until I was willing to plot and scheme and lie to be with him. I thought he loved me because he said so, and I left with him because I was addicted to his kisses and caresses. I *gave myself to him,* Sandoval, knowing we had made no vows before God, because I couldn't bear to breathe without him. *I* did those things, brother. It was *my choice,* don't you see?" She struck her chest with a clenched fist. "And now I am here, where I deserve to be. My sin is too deep for me to go anywhere else. How could I go home to our village, where everyone knows what I've done? I would be shunned like a rabid dog!"

Sandoval knew she could be right about Montemorelos. People's memories were long, and they might treat Pilar like a pariah, as if she could contaminate them. "Come with us to Texas, then. You could start all over again."

"Pilar, no one's sin is too deep for forgiveness—" Tess began.

"Mine is!" Pilar cried, and with a shout of anguish, she jumped to her feet and ran from the room. A moment later, they heard the sound of feet running up the staircase.

Sandoval would have gone after her, but Tess stopped him. And then Joaquina entered the room.

"That is enough for now," the old woman said. "Your coming has been a major shock to Magdalena—or Pilar, as you call her. She will have much to think about. In addition, it's time for her to get ready for work tonight."

The idea of his sister conducting business as usual in this place filled him with horror. "But I don't want her doing that! I want to take her out of this place, with us."

The old woman was polite, but firm. "I'm sorry. You're welcome to come back tomorrow, if you wish. She has little to do then."

Tess spoke up. "*Señora,* may I speak to my husband for a moment?" She glanced meaningfully at the doorway, then back at the woman.

Joaquina looked from Tess's earnest eyes back to Sandoval's, while Sandoval fought the urge to run upstairs after his sister.

"*Seguramente, señora.* But please understand my position. Señor Ramón holds me responsible for what happens in this house. He would not like it if he believes you are upsetting one of his girls so that she cannot work, and might not allow you to come back."

Sandoval would have told the old woman just what

Ramón would have to accept, but for the tightening of Tess's hand about his arm.

Joaquina turned on her heel and left the room.

"Sandoval—"

"Tess, don't try to tell me that I must accept my sister staying here, doing…what these women do. I'll carry her out kicking and screaming, if I have to."

"Yes, you could do that," she said, "but, don't you see, you'd just have this Ramón and every other bordello owner coming after you, probably armed to the teeth? And Pilar isn't ready yet. She's convinced she deserves to be here. We will have to spend more time with her."

He stared at her, hardly able to tolerate what his wife was saying. "You're saying we must let her 'work' at night, while we come to visit during the day? I can't do that."

"I understand how you feel. You have money, you said. So what's to stop you from paying for her time? Come back tonight, and pay for the whole evening. We can take her for some dinner, if she's willing and they'll allow her to go, and then we can talk to her."

He stared at Tess, hardly daring to hope that would work. "Do you think the old woman would let me do that? After I told her I'm determined to take Pilar away from here?"

Tess shrugged. "You won't know until you try, will you? I think she has a kind heart, but she wants to keep her position safe—she probably has nowhere else to go, either. It wouldn't hurt to give her a little…shall we say, *incentive?*" She pantomimed rubbing a coin between her fingers.

Together, they went back to the entrance hall, where the old woman had resumed her seat on the sofa, where she was munching on a pastel cookie from a dish of them.

"Does Ramón allow his girls to be hired for the entire night, and leave the house?" he asked Joaquina.

"*Sí, señor.* It happens occasionally. But I warn you, the price is not cheap." She named a figure.

She had told the truth. The price was not cheap. But Sandoval's share of the money from riding with Delgado was the Mexican equivalent of some three hundred dollars.

"What time do the customers start coming?"

"We usually see no one until seven, *señor,* though we're open from noon till the wee hours."

"I would like to book Pilar's time for the entire evening then, starting at six o'clock." Sandoval said. "And here's a little something so you do not feel it necessary to tell Ramón I'm her brother." He dropped a handful of pesos into the woman's palm.

"Ramón will be very pleased," Joaquina said with a conspiratorial wink. "Magdalena—Pilar—is so shy and withdrawn she is always the last one chosen. And I am not going to tell Pilar who is coming for her."

Sandoval felt the pain of the woman's last sentence like a punch in the gut. "You think she might not be willing to go with me?"

Joaquina shrugged eloquently. "Who knows? She gave up hope long ago. I can't remember when she's left this place, except to go across to the cantina to buy bottles. It's as if she doesn't exist outside this place, as if she's hiding from the world. We will see you back at six."

It had been a long journey to Chapin, one fraught with peril. Esteban had traveled, always looking over his shoulder for pursuing outlaws, northward beside the Rio Grande. Once, Esteban had only avoided being seen by Delgado, Lupe, and his former compadres by hiding in a thicket of mesquite and cedar and holding the mule's nose as they swept past. He'd kept off the roads after that until he came to a ford that boasted a ferry so he could keep the contents of the wagon dry.

Now, after picking up Tess's assistant, Francisco, in the small town of Chapin, they'd arrived at the plantation home of Samuel Taylor. Esteban waited in the parlor, clutching the precious negatives wrapped in oilskin, while Francisco went with a maid to fetch the retired Ranger.

Samuel Taylor came into the room, his eyes narrowing at Esteban. "He speak English?" he asked Francisco.

"*Sí,* Señor Taylor, he talk it better than me," the youth told him eagerly. "He knows where Tess is!"

Taylor turned to Esteban. "That true?"

Esteban nodded warily.

"What's this yarn Francisco's telling me about you having a picture of Delgado that my godchild took? Where's Tess and that rascal Parrish?"

He listened while Esteban explained in his heavily accented, halting English; then, when Esteban had finished telling him how Parrish had sent him here to have the negatives developed and sent out while he went with Tess to find his missing sister, he sighed deeply.

"I don't know what Parrish was thinking not bringing that girl straight home to her mama and papa. They're worried sick, even though they've gotten a couple of messages sayin' she was all right. But if I know Tess, she probably talked him into letting her go along," he mused aloud. "Headstrong, that girl. In need of a firm hand."

"Señor Sandoval has that," Esteban assured him, daring to grin. "And he loves Señorita Tess."

Samuel Taylor looked at him sharply, as if he hadn't expected to be answered. "You don't say."

"Yes, I do. And she loves him!"

The older man blinked. "We'll just see about that. If he lets my godchild come to harm, there won't be enough of him to bury, I can promise you that. And don't bother to assure me of something you can't know," he warned Esteban. He shifted his stare to the package Esteban carried.

"Well, what are we waiting for? Francisco, can we go develop this negative and see if your amigo here really brought me a picture of Delgado?"

"Of course, *señor!*"

"Then run to the barn and tell my stable boy to saddle my horse. Lula Marie!" he bellowed. "I'm goin' into town."

Chapter Twenty-Five

Delgado's curses were bloodcurdling when they returned to the canyon after their fruitless pursuit and found no campfire burning, Esteban and Delores gone, and the photography wagon missing as well.

One of the bandits silently took Delgado's and Lupe's horses, avoiding their furious gazes, while the rest of them quietly unsaddled their mounts. No one wanted to give the outlaw leader cause to redirect his wrath to him.

"The pictures the *gringa* took are still there," Lupe assured him, after running inside her brother's adobe to check.

"Bah! As if that matters!" her brother snarled at her. "They've taken some of the negatives, if not all of them—of that, you may be sure. My face will soon be plastered all over the valley, and beyond. Maybe yours, too! But how could Esteban and Delores have gotten away with that heavy wagon so quickly? Delores is an old woman. We should have come across them."

"Perhaps they did not travel together," Lupe pointed out.

Delgado gazed at his sister, considering her words.

"You're probably right. But where—" He stared into the fire one of the men had hastily kindled, remembering the last conversation he'd had with Tess that evening before so mysteriously passing out.

"Monterrey," he said aloud. "Sandoval and Tess went to Monterrey. That's why we did not find them!"

"But why—"

Delgado told her about Pilar Morelos. "And that traitor Esteban, his shoulder miraculously healed, must have driven the wagon out of here and managed to avoid us. By now he's probably arrived somewhere in Texas where he can have the negatives developed. I will have to think of the most painful way possible for him to die when I catch up to him. But he will die no more painfully than Sandoval Parrish, that treacherous half-breed."

"I always told you you shouldn't have trusted him, brother. His heart is Anglo, after all."

"You seemed content enough to overlook that for a while, sister!" Delgado snapped.

"So, I was fooled," she retorted. "So were you, by that cursed redheaded *bruja.* You wanted to wed her, remember? Are you still enchanted with the thought of her lily-white face?"

He would have slapped Lupe then, but she danced out of reach, and her hand came up holding the dagger she always carried in her waistband. "Have a care, *hermano,* and remember that *I* am not the enemy. Sandoval Parrish and Tess Hennessy are the ones who've played you false. Save your fury for them. I will help you achieve your revenge, if you let me be the one to carve a design in that lovely face until it's not so lovely anymore. Then you can have her and do what you will."

Their shared laughter was chilling.

* * *

The Metropolitan Cathedral bells were just tolling four when Tess and Sandoval left the street of the brothels and cantinas. Realizing they had some time to kill before they could return for Pilar, they toured the cathedral, admiring its baroque loveliness, so different than any of the churches at home. Tess wished aloud that she had her camera, to attempt to capture its grandeur in a photograph—or at least with her sketchpad and pencils.

After that, they happened upon a goldsmith's shop and belatedly purchased a simple gold wedding ring for Tess.

"I'll buy you a better one someday," he told her, placing it on her finger.

But she shook her head, laying a finger on his lips. "I only want this one. I'll always remember Monterrey when I look at it."

Pilar was sitting alone in the reception room when Sandoval entered, and rose when she saw him.

"*Buenas noches,* sister. You look lovely."

And she did. He had worried what sort of clothing his sister would have available, but although her white silk blouse nestled low over her shoulders, she looked perfectly respectable.

"*Buenas noches,* Sandoval." She smiled crookedly. "Joaquina wouldn't tell me who was coming, but when she said he had paid for the entire evening in advance and was coming to take me out of here at such an early hour, I guessed it was you. I'm not usually in high demand, and no one ever offers to take me out. You always were persistent, brother. Where are we going?" she asked, as they walked into the entrance hallway.

Pilar stopped stock-still as Tess emerged from the

shadowy interior doorway. Tess had worried aloud that the owner of the establishment, Señor Ramón, would get suspicious if he saw a couple arriving for Pilar, but Sandoval had not been willing to let her wait on the street in such an area. God must have been watching over them, for Joaquina told them Ramón had not arrived yet.

"Good evening, Pilar," Tess said. "We wanted to take you out for dinner, so that you and your brother could get reacquainted and I could get to know you. Is that all right?"

Pilar looked like a wary wild mare that might bolt at any moment. Nevertheless, she shrugged her shoulders and said, "Sure. Why not?" But something in her guarded eyes warned Sandoval they would need to keep the conversation light, at least at first.

In one of the streets that led away from a plaza they found a restaurant that served excellent food at a reasonable price, and soon the three of them were laughing and talking like old friends. Pilar regaled Tess with a number of tales about Sandoval as a pesky younger brother full of mischief, and Sandoval responded in kind, telling Tess about how Pilar would achieve her revenge by making it seem that Sandoval had been the one who had stolen a hunk of freshly baked cake off the kitchen windowsill, or placed a toad in their old nursemaid's bed.

Sandoval felt full of joy as he and Pilar reminisced about old times at their home near Montemorelos. Then Pilar asked about their father.

"He is dead, sister," he said gently, reaching out to take hold of Pilar's hand, while Tess looked on in sympathy.

Tears ran down Pilar's cheeks. "I knew he must be when you did not mention him along with our mother."

"When?" Pilar asked.

"Almost five years ago." He did not say, Shortly after you left, he died of a broken heart. He saw that Pilar guessed as much, however.

They let her weep, but soon she was smiling through her tears to hear how their mother thrived on Sandoval's ranch, where she did the cooking.

"Ah, if only I could taste *Madre's pan dulce* again," Pilar said with a heavy sigh—then looked startled, as if she hadn't meant to say it aloud.

"Pilar, you *could*," Sandoval told her. "You could leave with us tomorrow. Just say the word."

Already, though, Pilar was sitting back in her chair, shaking her head. "No, I couldn't."

Sandoval leaned forward. "Why not?" he said earnestly, keeping his voice low so the other customers wouldn't hear them. "I have some money. I'll give whatever it takes for Ramón to let you go. And if he won't take money, I'll take you from him—at gunpoint, if necessary."

Now Pilar leaned forward, too, and whispered back. "Even if Ramón would allow me to go, I've told you, Sandoval—it's too late for me. I can't forget what I've become, or change it. Let's not discuss it any further."

Sandoval looked away, fighting the urge to argue with his sister, to somehow force her to see that he couldn't leave her where she was. He noticed that they were among the last customers remaining. The evening had flown, and he guessed the restaurant owner was ready to close his establishment. Sandoval paid their bill and they left.

"This has been wonderful, Sandoval, Tess," Pilar said, when they were once more out in the street. "I will remember it always. Thank you. But perhaps you should take me back now. You are newlyweds, after all." She laughed when Tess blushed in the lamplight.

"If we take you back now, you...will not have to..." Sandoval's voice trailed off.

"Work?" she said, her expression guarded once again. "No, you paid for the entire evening. Besides, Joaquina gave me the key to the side entrance. I can go up to my room without going through the entrance hall. Ramón won't even know when I return."

"May we...see you again tomorrow?" Tess asked.

"You will still be in Monterrey?" Pilar asked, looking surprised. "Sandoval, you ought to ride out to Saddle Mountain with Tess. I hear there's a lovely view of the city."

"I'd like to, but I'm worried that Delgado may have figured out where we've gone and be heading this way. I don't think he'd come into Monterrey looking for us—there are too many people around—but we'll have to be on our guard when we leave."

Mentioning the outlaw made Pilar's expression somber again. "Brother, you should leave at dawn—tonight, even. You shouldn't take a chance on him catching you. You have a wife to worry about now."

Sandoval's heart ached for her. "I'm not leaving without you, Pilar. Or at least until I convince you to leave the brothel and go somewhere else."

"Go where? Another brothel?" Pilar's laugh was harsh. "It's too late for me, Sandoval—I told you that. I can never forget what I am—what *he* made me."

"Pilar—"

"Sandoval, it's late," Tess said, interrupting him. "We're all tired. Let's agree to see Pilar again tomorrow—if you're willing, Pilar? We could come earlier in the day, and stroll through the plazas, perhaps have lunch somewhere?"

Sandoval saw that Tess was holding her breath, clearly fearing Pilar would refuse to see them anymore.

"I suppose," Pilar said at last with a shrug. "Anything is better than lolling around with those women, watching them trying different hair arrangements and listening to them chatter about the baubles their customers bring them."

Sandoval couldn't sleep that night, imagining how it would feel to leave Monterrey with Pilar remaining in a brothel, until at last his tossing reawakened Tess. Taking his hand, she insisted he share his worries with her.

"We must pray that Pilar becomes convinced that God loves her and will help her start anew," she said sleepily, after he had confessed his worries. "I think, now that Pilar sees that she has a choice, she is paralyzed at the thought of having to make a decision. She probably thinks it's possible that the new life could prove to be harder than the life she lives now. At least, where she is now no one expects too much of her."

"But, how?" he asked. "You heard her tonight, Tess. Her mind is set."

"God will give us the right words when we need them."

When they returned to the brothel at midmorning the next day, Joaquina informed them that Pilar was sick and unable to leave her bed. Tess's heart sank. She didn't believe that Pilar was ill—she was trying to avoid them, and so avoid making a decision.

Pilar had given the old woman a note to deliver to them, though, she said, handing Sandoval a folded piece of paper. The old woman's eyes were alight with curiosity. Tess suspected the woman was illiterate, or she would have read it already.

Sandoval unfolded it, looked at it, then handed it to Tess.

"Go home, brother," it read. "It has been wonderful to see you again and meet your lovely Tess, and I am happy for you. But you cannot change what happened to me. Go with God, and remember, tell our mother I am dead. Pilar."

Tess looked into Sandoval's sorrowful eyes, and knew they couldn't give up so easily.

"Tell her I want to see her—just me," Tess told Joaquina. "Tell her we won't go away until she agrees to speak at least with me."

Joaquina nodded, and five minutes later she was back, breathing a little hard from her exertion. "She will see you, *señora,* but only you. Her room is the third one on the right upstairs."

"Let me try, Sandoval," she said. "I'll try to convince her to see you."

Sandoval pulled her into his arms. *"Thank you,"* he breathed, against her ear. "I love you for trying."

"I have to go to the market, since Pilar won't leave her room," Joaquina told Sandoval, after they had watched Tess ascend the stairs. "You may wait in the reception room."

Sandoval nodded and watched the old woman leave. He tried to pray, but his prayers seemed to go no farther than the ceiling with its exposed beams.

Tess knocked, but received no answer. Checking to make sure she had counted the number of rooms from the stairs correctly, she knocked again, and at last tried the door. It was unlocked. *Help me, Lord.*

The room was lit only by an ill-smelling tallow candle

sitting in a bowl of melted wax. As Tess's eyes grew accustomed to the light, she saw a figure lying on her back in the bed, the dingy covers pulled up to her shoulders.

"I'm here, Pilar," Tess called out. "Thank you for agreeing to see me."

For a long moment, she wondered if Sandoval's sister was going to acknowledge her presence, but at last, slowly, Pilar turned on her side, gesturing for Tess to sit in the rickety chair beside the bed.

"Well, it didn't sound as if you'd take no for an answer." Pilar's eyes, so like her brother's in their color, shape and expressiveness, were shadowed with violet smudges. The lids were swollen and red-rimmed, as if she had spent much of her time weeping. A pallor underlay the olive tone of her skin.

"Is it true what you said yesterday, when you first came here?" Pilar asked.

Tess blinked. "Is...is *what* true?"

Pilar looked down at her hands and gave a short, humorless laugh. "I'm sorry. I've been wrestling with God for hours, knowing He can hear my thoughts, even if I do not speak aloud—I forget that other people cannot. I meant, is it true what you said, that no one's sin is too deep for forgiveness?" Her eyes, desperate to believe, searched Tess's, alert for any hint that Tess would try to placate her with an easy, comfortable lie.

Tess knew Pilar didn't want to be told yet again that the fault had been entirely Delgado's. However innocent a girl Pilar had been, she blamed herself for loving the outlaw, for putting her trust in him, for becoming a liar for the sake of his kisses and more.

Understanding that, Tess did not hesitate. "Yes, it's true. Completely and totally true. If God forgave the thief on the cross, who'd spent his life in crime, He will forgive you, Pilar, for whatever you have done. God loves you. He never stopped. You have but to ask for forgiveness, but He will not impose it on you by force. You must ask."

Pilar's face crumpled. "Is it so simple? There was a baby—Delgado's baby. They said he died because I had been living such a hard life, always on the run—but I know it was because of my sin."

Tess shook her head. "Oh, Pilar, I'm so sorry.... That baby is with God now. But all of us need forgiveness from God. He wants to come into our hearts and make us new."

Pilar was haggard in the flickering candlelight. "How is it I have spent five years here, when I could have just asked God for forgiveness?" And then her face crumpled and she was sobbing in Tess's arms, crying aloud for God's mercy, while Tess assured her it was there for her already.

She wept for an endless time, and Tess held her until the storm was past.

At last, Pilar raised her head. "It's *true!* I *am forgiven.* It feels so good!"

Tess hugged her. She didn't want to hurry Pilar when she had just come so far, but dare she ask if they could share the news with Sandoval?

Sandoval paced the reception room. Above him, he heard the women start to stir and chatter, and eventually, they began to stroll downstairs past the reception room on their way to the kitchen. A couple stared boldly at him as they passed, but he ignored them.

He wondered what was happening in Pilar's room above his head, but knowing he could do nothing but wait, he began to think of the state of his own soul. Had he been trying to earn the Lord's forgiveness for failing his sister by bringing about Delgado's capture? Had he ever just accepted that God loved him no matter what he'd done, and wanted to walk with him as Father and Friend, Sandoval's failings forgiven? He hadn't.

Tess had taken that step, he realized. Probably years ago, judging by the faith that seemed to infuse her every move.

It was past time that he did so, too. Alone in the reception room, he knelt and prayed. And he knew his prayer was heard. No matter what happened with Pilar, he was at peace.

Deep in thought, Sandoval started when a knock sounded at the door. Tess entered the room, followed by Pilar, who ran into his arms.

"I am forgiven, brother. The Lord has *forgiven* me! Your wife helped me see that all I had to do was ask to find my way to the Lord."

Sandoval smiled at Tess over his sister's head. "Yes, she has a way of doing that," he said. "I've experienced it, too." He knew Tess would understand that it had just happened while she was gone.

The smile Tess returned to him was radiant with joy.

"And there's more good news," Sandoval told the two women so dear to him. "While you were upstairs, Señor Ramón stopped by to see who has been calling on you for two days in a row, Pilar."

Pilar took an involuntary step backward, her face filled with dread, her body quivering in alarm. "What did he say? Am I...still allowed to see you?"

Sandoval put a hand out and touched her trembling shoulder. "Be easy, sister, I told you I had good news," he said. "You are free to leave this place. Today. Right now."

Chapter Twenty-Six

"Wh-what are you saying, brother? I cannot just leave with you. Señor Ramón would never allow it."

"Ah, but I did, Pilar," said a heavy-set, oily-faced man who came into the room at that moment. "Señor Parrish drives a hard bargain, but at last we came to terms. I finally decided that with the money he gave me for you, I can obtain another girl who is…shall we say… more suited to her duties? Farewell, Pilar, and good luck. Oh, and leave the dresses you were given for working."

Pilar only stared at him, as if she couldn't trust her ears, until he left the room.

"As if I would wear those things anywhere else!" she said with a laugh.

Joaquina came in then. "Oh, my dear, I just heard the news. I am happy for you, my dear," she added, embracing Pilar. "If you will wait a moment, I have a small *maleta* you can have to pack your things."

Later, as the three of them sat in a sunlit plaza opposite the cathedral eating a picnic lunch of tamales purchased from an open-air stand, Sandoval asked Pilar if she had any idea where they could buy a horse for her so she could come along with them. "Ramón thinks

I gave him my last *centavo* for you, and of course I was willing, but I managed to keep enough back for a mount for you, and another for me." They had already told her about being forced to trade Sandoval's pinto for the bony old horse.

"I... I hope you will understand," Pilar said carefully, looking from Sandoval to Tess and back again, "but I think I would like to stay in Monterrey for a while."

"What are you saying, Pilar? What would you do here?" Tess asked, her forehead furrowed in puzzlement.

"I... I think I will stay for a while with the sisters at the convent by the cathedral," Pilar said, watching thoughtfully as two brown-robed nuns walked by.

"Are you thinking of taking the veil?" Sandoval asked, trying to keep the apprehension from his voice. Had he regained his sister, only to lose her again behind the walls of a convent? Did she think this was the only place God had for her, because of her past?

Pilar faced him, her eyes thoughtful. "I don't know, brother. Perhaps. I... I just want to do some thinking, before I begin the next part of my life. Maybe I will visit Montemorelos, just to see it one more time. I'm not afraid of that now. And then if I do not stay with the sisters, I will find my way to you."

"But how will you come to us?" Tess asked. "We could leave some money with you—or send it to you, after we reach home."

"There is no need," Pilar said with a grin, and reached for the valise that held the few belongings she had taken away from the brothel. Opening it, she took out a gold pendant from which dangled a gold ring with a cabochon ruby as big as a pigeon's egg.

"I was given this by an old man who came to the

brothel several times. He was a lonely old widower, quite wealthy, and he really only wanted to talk, to enjoy some female company. He always asked for me. When he knew he was going to die soon, he gave this to me in thanks, and told me to keep it in case I ever needed it. I'm supposed to give Ramón all such presents, of course, but I kept this one well hidden. So you see, Sandoval and Tess, I am not totally without a source of money. I will sell it to pay for my traveling expenses, or if I decide to stay in the convent," she said, nodding toward the small building that nestled at the side of the huge cathedral, "it will be my dowry."

"Will you stay with us tonight, though?" Sandoval asked her. "We won't leave until the morning, so we could get you a room at the inn. I'm not ready to part with you yet."

"I would like that, brother, and Tess, my new sister."

It was morning, and the time had come for parting. They had to begin the dangerous journey back home. While a small boy held the reins of their horses—including a handsome bay gelding Sandoval had purchased yesterday afternoon—in front of the convent gate, Sandoval and Tess embraced Pilar.

"*Vaya con Dios,* Sandoval and Tess," she said, hugging each of them in turn. "May the good Lord guard you from all harm and richly bless you. I will pray for you," Pilar told them, a tear making its way down her cheek.

Tears welled in Tess's brilliant-blue eyes, too, Sandoval noted, and felt a thickness in his own throat. "We'll send word as soon as we reach safety," he promised, when he could speak.

"And we'll pray for you, too," Tess added, embracing her new sister. "I know you'll make the right decision, Pilar, whatever it is."

"With God's help," Pilar agreed.

"I wish there was some way to let the Rangers know when we're coming and where we'll cross, so they could be waiting to cover us," Sandoval mused aloud as they left the convent and headed for the road heading northeast out of the city. He'd decided it would be best not to try and cross the Rio Grande where it was closest to Chapin, thinking Delgado might well be expecting him to do that. Instead, he'd told her, they'd cross upriver at Roma.

Tess knew he was trying to distract himself from the pain of saying goodbye to Pilar, not knowing what his sister's ultimate decision would be.

"Yes, there's no way a letter could reach them ahead of us," she said.

And then they both saw it. They'd entered Monterrey from the east after fleeing the outlaw hideout, and they hadn't passed this way when they were sightseeing.

In a tone that indicated he couldn't believe his eyes, Sandoval translated aloud the Spanish sign over the door of the building—"Monterrey Telegraph Office. Tess, we can send a telegram home—it's perfect!"

"Patrick, I got a telegram. They're coming home!" Samuel Taylor said, brandishing the message he'd received just a half hour before. He was flanked by Esteban, whose grin was so broad it threatened to split his face.

"But why did they send it to you, not to us?"

"Because Parrish needs me to set up a Ranger reception committee. Go get your wife and I'll read the message to both of you—that'll explain it."

But summoning Amelia was unnecessary, for she'd heard Taylor's horse thunder up to the house and skid to a sliding stop at the front door. "What's that, Sam?" she demanded, flying down the stairs with a speed that belied her years. "You've heard from Tess? She's coming home? When? How?"

"This message is from her and her *husband,* Sandoval," He couldn't help but enjoy a little the way Amelia's eyes goggled and her jaw dropped open. "Yep, she and Parrish are *married.*"

"My little girl is *married?*" Patrick echoed. *"Tess?"*

"To *that man?*" Amelia cried. "The very one who had her kidnapped?"

"Now, Amelia, he's a good man, just like I told you both at the barbecue," Taylor said, conveniently forgetting the way he'd also growled at Esteban that Parrish would pay if any harm came to Tess. "Calm down. You wouldn't want her racketing about Mexico alone with him, without them bein' married, would you? And don't forget, thanks to Parrish, we have that scoundrel's ugly mug plastered all over southern Texas—and thanks, too, to Esteban, here, for bringing the negatives safely home," he said, clapping Esteban on the back. The Mexican beamed modestly.

"Yes, yes, are you going to read us the telegram, or just stand there blathering all day, man?" Patrick asked, making a grab for the telegram.

"Patience, Patrick, don't rip it," Samuel Taylor said, surrendering the paper to him. "You can read it same as I, I expect—if you don't suffer an apoplexy first."

"Married in Mexico, stop," Patrick read. "Coming home via Roma approx. three-four days, stop. Have

Ranger company meet us at ford, stop. Watch for Delgado, stop. Signed, Sandoval and Tess Parrish."

"That's *all?*" Amelia demanded. "That's all he wrote?"

"Telegrams aren't cheap, Amelia," Sam reminded her. "They charge by the word, so I imagine Sandoval couldn't afford t' be wordy. There'll be time enough to pry all the details outta your daughter the bride once she's home."

"Yes, and I'm going to give that Parrish a piece of my mind for denying my youngest child the wedding of her dreams, here in our very own church with Reverend Fothergill," Amelia threatened; then she froze. "Patrick! We've got to be there, at Roma. I have to pack."

"Now, Amelia, it'll be at least three or four days before they could possibly make it to Roma, maybe more. This here message was sent from Monterrey. You'd do a lot better t' stay here and plan a big party for when they do arrive."

Amelia brightened at the prospect. "It can be their wedding reception," she said. "No matter what kind of hole-in-the-corner wedding they had, my daughter will have a proper wedding reception."

"But where are you going, Sam?" he demanded, as Samuel Taylor took hold of his wide-brimmed hat again and turned to leave.

"To send a message to the closest Ranger company, and have 'em meet me at Roma," Sam said. "C'mon, Esteban—"

"I'll be coming with you," Patrick told him in a tone that brooked no argument, then added softly, so Amelia wouldn't hear, "I'm thinking you're expecting a battle there maybe, eh?"

"It's a possibility," Sam admitted.

"Then an extra rifle won't hurt. I don't care whose wife she is, Tess is my daughter."

"Come along, then."

He followed Taylor out of the house onto the porch, bellowing for Mateo to saddle his horse.

Patrick needn't have worried about Amelia overhearing, for his wife was already hollering for Rosa, the cook, to help her plan the food for the party.

Chapter Twenty-Seven

"It's only about twenty-five miles to the border now," Sandoval announced. They had left Nuevo Léon and entered Tamaulipas again.

It was encouraging news. Only about half a day's ride, and they would be in Texas once more. Then they would be almost home. Chapin lay some fifty miles east of Roma.

"We've been blessed so far," she said.

It was true. No one had treated them with suspicion. They were just a man and his wife, traveling on horseback.

"I'll be thankful when I can go outside without this rebozo to cover my hair," she said, pointing at it. "It doesn't keep the sun out of my eyes nearly as well as a hat."

It was the closest she'd come to a complaint. He knew she had to be feeling the tension as much as he was, knowing that these last few miles could be the most hazardous of their entire journey.

The head covering would only work from a distance, Sandoval knew. Up close anyone could see from the fiery-red curl that peeped out and the blueness of her eyes that she was a *gringa*. Just tonight, when they'd left the spare room behind the little cantina and claimed their horses, the *cantinero* had stared at Tess as if memorizing her features.

"An extra ten pesos to say you never saw her or me," he'd said to the man. It was a princely sum, but there was no guaranteeing that, after they'd ridden away, the man wouldn't turn around and inform anyone who wanted to know that a couple fitting their description had passed this way. Sandoval wouldn't rest easy until they were once again in Texas and he knew that Delgado had been captured or killed.

"I imagine Papa and Mama won't want us to leave Hennessy Hall for a few days, once we get across the river," Tess was saying. "They'll want to kill the fatted calf, as they say."

"If your father doesn't shoot me on sight."

"I'm sure they'll both come to love you in very short order," she insisted firmly. "How could they not?"

"Oh, let me count the reasons," he retorted. "You could start with the fact I had you kidnapped." And then, he thought, there's my mixed blood.

She gave him a look, and he realized how pessimistic he'd been sounding. "I'm sorry. I'm not normally such a gloomy fellow." *God is in control,* he reminded himself.

"I can't wait to meet your mother and see your ranch," Tess said, after a moment. He'd told her about his property north of Chapin, a sprawling thousand-acre place on which he ran cattle and goats. Sandoval hadn't spent much time there before, mostly leaving it in the hands of his old foreman while he spent his time rangering, but now it would be their home. He'd have to find a way to be there more than he had in the past, when he hadn't had a wife to come home to.

"The ranch house isn't much," he warned her. "But you can put your own touches in it."

"But your mother's been in charge inside," Tess said, a little uneasily. "She might not welcome another female in her kitchen, making changes."

Sandoval shook his head. "*Madre's* been saying for years that she wanted more time to relax, and that as soon as I brought home a wife, she wanted to spend her time playing with the grandchildren we would give her. So we'll have to make the place bigger."

"Sandoval!" She giggled, pretending to be scandalized.

Sandoval grinned back, unrepentant. He couldn't help wondering if she was already carrying his child—a son, to carry on his name, or a daughter, who'd look just like Tess.

"And there must be a guest room for Pilar when she comes to visit," she said. "Oh, Sandoval, I can't help hoping she doesn't remain in the convent."

"I'm happy as long as she's happy, whatever she chooses," he murmured. "Though I admit I feel the same way you do and don't want her to become a nun. Perhaps she'll decide she wants to stay in Montemorelos, after all. If so, I'll deed her the *rancho*…." He froze, listening. Had he heard hoofbeats?

"Then we can visit her there, too. I'd like to see where you grew—"

"Shh! I think I hear horses. Quick, off the road! Take cover behind that ruined house."

The three roofless walls of the adobe house would never have hidden them in daylight, due to a window in the middle wall. As it was, they had barely time enough to ride behind it, dismount and hold their horses' heads before half a dozen horsemen rounded the curve and trotted on past. It was too dark to see if it was Delgado and his men, but Sandoval was sure it must be. Who else would be abroad at midnight?

They waited an hour behind the house before going on at a cautious walk, straining to identify every night sound. There was no more chatter. Were Delgado and his henchmen waiting for them around the next bend in the road? Each time the road curved, Sandoval scouted ahead.

They encountered no one else.

The sun rose on their right, transforming the Rio Grande ahead of them into a shining silver ribbon. A tiny village, no more than a scattering of buildings, lay between them and the river. A grove of trees obscured the tiny town of Roma on the opposite bank, but he knew it was there.

He reined in and gestured for Tess to do the same. "I'm trying to decide whether we should make a run for it. What I wouldn't give for another hour of darkness," he said, staring ahead of him.

Tess's face was sober, her eyes wistful as she stared at Texas lying on the other side of the river. So close...

"Should we see if that village ahead has an inn, and wait till dark?" she asked.

He shook his head. "This close to the river, I'd be afraid Delgado's men would be searching every building. We don't know if someone might've seen us and reported to Delgado."

"Why don't we ride upriver a ways, or downriver?"

He considered the suggestion. "The river's a lot wider, and deeper, in both directions. That's why this is such a good place to ford."

He pulled the spyglass he'd taken from Delgado's loot and studied the opposite bank of the river, and this time he was rewarded with a gleam of sunlight reflecting on metal. He peered more closely.

"There are mounted men over there under the trees," he said.

"Oh, Sandoval, it must be the Rangers!"

"I can't be sure, from this distance. Stay here. I'm going to take the spyglass and creep over to that nest of reeds yonder to get a better look."

"Sandoval, what if Delgado's men are hiding in there?"

"If they were there, I think they'd have opened fire on us already."

He was back in just minutes, but it was obvious from Tess's worried face that it had seemed like an eternity to her. "It's Rangers, all right," he reported, allowing himself to smile. "And they're here in force—looks like an entire company. I didn't see any sign of Delgado. Ready to swim for it, Mrs. Parrish?"

She nodded, trust glowing in her eyes. "As soon as we pray." She reached for his hand.

"I hope this bay can swim as well as my pinto did," Sandoval said.

In spite of the prayer, fear still gripped Tess's insides like an icy fist. "First, kiss me, please, Sandoval," Tess said, and he did.

Would it be their last kiss?

"All right, here we go," Sandoval said, unholstering his pistol. In unison, they kneed their horses forward, leaving the road so as to skirt the little village on their left. There wasn't much to the place, so their course changed only slightly.

Tess feared each step their horses took toward the water could be their last. The blood thundered in her

head. She heard nothing but birdsong, the drone of
dragonflies and the occasional slap of water against
the riverbanks, but with each heartbeat she expected
the pounding of hoofbeats behind her and a volley of
gunfire.

Sandoval's bay led the way, proving he wasn't water-
shy. Her mare followed willingly enough, and soon the
horses' hooves left the bottom and they were swimming.

Wet to her waist, Tess let the mare have her head. She
clung to the sorrel's mane with one hand and the saddle
horn with the other. She could see and hear the group of
Rangers easily now. They stood beneath the trees, cheering them on, their lighter skin looking almost foreign
to her after she'd spent so much time in Mexico alongside men and women with skin several shades darker
than hers. Then she caught sight of her father, jumping
up and down, and Uncle Samuel, waving like a mad-
man with one hand, though he still held a carbine in the
other. And there was Esteban!

They were actually going to reach the opposite bank
without so much as a shot fired or a glimpse of the outlaws! Had Delgado given up? She saw Sandoval's bay
clamber ashore. Her mare's hooves hit bottom then and
a moment later the beast was walking out of the river,
water streaming off her flanks, shoulders and mane.

The Rangers surrounded them then, assisting her
to dismount her horse, and she was embraced by first
her father, then Uncle Samuel in turn. Through a haze
of joyful tears, she saw Sandoval being embraced and
clapped on the back and heard them all calling him a
hero.

"You made it! You're safe. Oh, thank God," her father was saying, tears flowing unashamedly down his
cheeks. "Ahem! I think it's time I met your husband?"

In spite of the noisy celebration, Sandoval heard him, and turned around now, offering his hand to Patrick Hennessy, who took it.

"Sir, I'm Sandoval Parrish, and I'm sorry for the worry I've caused you about Tess. And although it's too late for you to give permission, I hope you'll give us your blessing. I promise I'll love your daughter as long as I draw breath."

"Aye, worry me you did, and that's the truth. But you'll have a lifetime with Tess to make up for it, God willing," Patrick said. "Long life to you both, and a love that lasts for all of it and beyond. Welcome to the family, son."

Uncle Samuel was right behind him. "You couldn't have a better lady, Sandoval. And I should know—I've known this child since she was knee high to a prickly pear. I hoped you two would find a way to get together, though I had no idea it would go like this."

"Where's Mother?" Tess asked, fearing that her mother's blessing wouldn't be so easily given.

"Waiting at home for you, readying the guest cottage for you and your new husband. She's planning the biggest welcome-home and wedding reception Hidalgo County ever saw, for two days from now. Did you two sleep last night? Never mind, I can see you didn't," Patrick answered for her. "There's shadows under your eyes big as silver dollars. We'll be stopping in Roma, then, and let you catch up on your shut-eye. You'll need to change into dry clothes, anyway—which we brought, of course."

Out of the corner of her eyes, she saw Sandoval give him a grateful smile.

"No, really, I can go on. I'd rather get home sooner—" Tess began to protest, but her body betrayed her just then, a gray mist swimming in front of her eyes as fatigue swept over her in the wake of abating fear. It took half an hour and a mug of strong coffee before Tess could remount her horse.

"So no one's seen any trace of Delgado?" Sandoval asked, once they were all mounted and heading eastward, away from the river.

"Not since you sent Esteban with that picture, no," said Captain Skelly, riding beside him. "It's been posted in every spot in the road wide enough to be called a town. I've already sent a message to the governor asking for an official pardon for Esteban, by the way. Maybe Delgado's too scared to come into Texas, now that even a half-blind fella would recognize him."

"We figured Delgado might guess where y'all were plannin' t' cross, so we put together a little welcoming committee armed to the teeth for you two."

"We're just as glad you didn't need to use any of those guns, though," Sandoval said.

"Yes, I think I've heard enough gunfire to last me for a lifetime," Tess said. She glanced at Sandoval. His dark eyes remained troubled. Delgado had failed to strike during their journey or while they were crossing. She supposed it would take a while for both of them to fully realize they were safe, that they had won, for they had lived with danger for too long.

Chapter Twenty-Eight

"Now, *señores, señoras,* everyone hold still, and smile," called the voice behind the camera, underneath the heavy canvas flap.

Tess Hennessy Parrish found it easy to obey. Her husband stood beside her, tall and handsome, his arm about her waist. Her parents stood on either side of her, beaming, with her godparents and Sandoval's mother—whom Tess had liked immediately—flanking them. And it was Francisco, her assistant from the shop, with his head under the canvas flap on this hot August day, not herself. A bride had to be in the photograph, after all, not taking the pictures—even if the reception was several days after the actual wedding.

"Your older daughter's wedding dress is just beautiful on Tess," Lula Marie Taylor gushed. "As if it'd been sewn for her originally. It's a good thing your Flora's so good and quick with a needle, Amelia."

"Yes, she is, isn't she?" Amelia agreed, grinning. Her chest puffed up with pride. She was in her glory as the mother of the bride, a bride who was at last properly dressed, in Amelia's eyes, even if her complexion was an unladylike tan from her adventures in Mexico. Well, that could be amended, now that Tess was no longer racketing about with outlaws and taking their photographs. Amelia knew of a good lemon-based paste that Tess would have to apply diligently every morning and night to undo the sun's damage. It was bad enough that everyone in the Valley was gossiping about where Tess had been, but there were *freckles* dancing across her daughter's nose and cheeks.

"Your son sure is a good-lookin' fella," Lula Marie told Vittoria Parrish, who had just joined them. "So dashing, with that dark hair and those *eyes*. Why, the way he looks at Tess! And she's lookin' right back— your baby girl's in love, Amelia, and no wonder! If I was only thirty years younger and single…" she added, fanning herself.

"Remember your dignity, Lula Marie," Amelia said, although a part of her really did find herself weakening under the onslaught of her new son-in-law's considerable charm.

"What are all those tents for, beyond the back pasture yonder?" Lula Marie asked curiously, pointing.

Amelia pursed her lips. "Sandoval invited those Ranger friends, the ones who waited at the river for them in case there was trouble, to camp there for a few days."

"So they could attend the reception? That's nice, Amelia, but where are they? I don't see any unfamiliar gents at the party…." She shaded her eyes as she looked over the guests on the lawn and under the veranda.

Amelia shrugged. "I suppose they're staying in their camp out there," she said, nodding toward the back pasture. "And, yes, they're still keeping watch for Delgado. As if that outlaw would *dare* to bother us now that the picture Tess took of him is hanging everywhere! But Sandoval's convinced that Delgado won't give up and stay on his side of the river, so in the meantime those boys are eating us out of house and home," she groused.

"I'll have Sam send over a side of beef or two and a couple of smoked hams," Lula Marie promised. Then her eyes went back to Tess, standing in the shade of the veranda with Sandoval and her father. "I bet they'll have beautiful babies," she burbled, her attention easily diverted at the romantic sight.

"I've had refreshments taken out to the men, son," Tess heard her papa tell Sandoval.

"Thank you, Mr. Hennessy."

"That's Papa to you," Patrick insisted. "Or Patrick, if you'd rather. We're family, remember?"

"Papa, then," Sandoval agreed. "Thank you. I know the men appreciate it."

"I just wish they'd come and join the party," Patrick Hennessy said, half turning to gaze over his shoulder at their tents, just visible beyond the back field. "They could bring their firearms with them, if they felt the need."

"You know Mother'd have a conniption if they did that, Papa," Tess reminded him gently, "dressed as roughly as they are. It wouldn't matter to me, though."

"We'll take them slices of cake, too, once you two slice it. Isn't it about time for that, daughter?"

"I suppose so, Papa. Francisco!" she called, spotting her assistant chatting with Flora, their hands gesticulating. "Ready to take another picture?"

"*Sí*, Tess—that is, Señora Parrish," Francisco said with a grin, after giving the maid one last wink. He moved the camera in front of the veranda where the bride and groom would be cutting the cake.

Her father went to the side door on the veranda and called for Rosa to bring out her four-tiered masterpiece.

Tess and Sandoval took their places behind the table in front of the cake. Tess felt Sandoval's warm, big hand atop hers as she sank the flowerand ribbon-trimmed knife deep into the edge of the cake, and they both looked up into the camera lens. She faintly heard a soft, long whirring as the shutter opened, then closed.

And over that, in the distance, the thudding of distant hooves—coming closer.

"Riders comin' up the lane!" cried a voice from above them.

"It's Delgado! Everyone take cover!" shouted another voice.

Simultaneously, amid the roar of gunfire and the screams of running women, Sandoval dropped the cake knife and shoved Tess toward the side door. "Get inside, Tess!"

For a moment she froze, her horrified eyes taking in the sight of Delgado galloping up the lane at the head of his men, shooting as he came. Out of the corner of her eye, she saw Sandoval retrieving a rifle he'd apparently hidden in the eaves of the veranda roof, shouldering it in one swift blur, and firing back.

She spotted Lupe riding at Delgado's side, looking evil and grim as a Fury. She recognized an individual face or two of the bandits—Garza, maybe, and Mendoza—but most of them were just a blur as they galloped toward the house.

"Tess, *Madre,* go!" Sandoval shouted at her again. Other women, shrieking, some carrying children, others helping older women—one of them Sandoval's mother—were running past them toward the side and front doors.

A bullet hit the punch bowl next to them, sending scarlet liquid and crystal shards flying.

Above her, deafening gunfire erupted from every window and, above that, from the roof. The Rangers hadn't remained at their tents in the back field, she realized in that instant. After the guests had begun arriving and she and her family had gone out on the lawn to greet them, they had entered the house from the back at Sandoval's direction, stationing themselves in the bedrooms and waiting for the trouble Sandoval had been so sure was coming.

He'd been right.

A bullet whistled past her, just above her head.

She moved to obey Sandoval and flee inside. Then she saw her mother go down on the lawn in a flurry of rose-colored skirts.

"Mama!" All thoughts of taking cover, of safety, fled from her brain. Where was her father? Where was Uncle Sam? Lula Marie? She jumped from the veranda, heedless of her veil as it caught on a branch of crepe myrtle in the flower bed and was pulled off. Someone running past knocked over her precious camera, and this, too, had no meaning for her as she ran toward the fallen figure.

Out of the corner of her eye, she saw her father dive behind a table that had held people's used plates, pushing it down, china, silverware and all, to take cover. His back was to his wife, so he had not seen her fall, and he was firing a pistol Tess had not known he was carrying. Uncle Sam was also shooting from underneath a guest's carriage.

It was up to her to rescue her mother. *God, please protect me!*

Bullets whizzed above her, to the side of her. All Tess could see was her mother, struggling to rise. She couldn't see any blood....

"My ankle...fell..." her mother grunted as Tess reached her side. Then, as she struggled to get an arm under her mother and help her to her feet, her mother began screaming and gesturing with flailing arms.

"*Tess!* Run! Get away!"

A horseman was bearing down on them, his grinning face and the ebony blackness of his horse like creatures from a nightmare. *Delgado!*

He'd holstered his pistols and held no reins, riding with his knees like a marauding Comanche. In one swift, graceful motion, he leaned over, arms extended to pull her off her feet and into the saddle.

Time stopped. She couldn't hear the bloodcurdling cry of one of the bandits as he was shot off his horse and fell, dead before he touched the ground, or the panicked whinny of a horse grazed by a bullet, or the splintering of glass as windows and abandoned punch glasses were hit. All she could do was wait, knowing that if she fled, Delgado would ride her mother down, wishing she had some weapon other than her fists. Sandoval probably couldn't fire without the risk of hitting her.

And then Delgado was wrenching her off her feet, heedless of her twisting struggles to free herself as the horse turned in a wide circle, away from the house and the gunfire.

"*Let me go!*"

He laughed, the sound demonic next to her ear. "Not a chance, *gringa!*"

The cake knife! She suddenly realized she had been

unconsciously clutching it as she had run. She still held it, wide-bladed, long and frosting-smeared.

She stabbed at him, hoping she could at least make him drop her and that it wouldn't hurt too much when she landed. But the knife was meant for cake cutting only, and wasn't sharp edged, and she was too close to him to do much damage anyway. Her stabs landed harmlessly against his leather chaps and the saddle. He grabbed at the knife. In a moment he would yank it out of her grasp and drop it—*Lord, help me!*

She stabbed again, frantically, and this time she managed to evade his grabbing hand and hit the galloping stallion in his shoulder.

The stallion reared, screaming in outrage. Delgado, caught unaware, let go of her. Stunned, the wind knocked out of her, Tess could only watch, helpless, as Delgado was forced to leave her in the grass and fight to keep his seat on the plunging beast.

Then a roar split the air, then another, and Tess saw Delgado slump, boneless as a rag doll. In the split second before he fell off the horse a few yards from her, she saw twin crimson holes flooding the front of his leather vest.

She closed her eyes and struggled to bring air back into her lungs before a blackness overwhelmed her.

Chapter Twenty-Nine

"Shh, he's dead, Tess," Sandoval was saying, before she even realized she was sobbing, or that her husband had reached her side. He held her against his chest. "He can't ever hurt you again."

Still dazed, she opened her eyes, and saw that someone was covering the body with a tablecloth, but not before she caught a glimpse of white frosting incongruously smeared on the legs of Delgado's trousers. There was no sign of the black stallion he'd ridden, or of Lupe.

"The others?" she tried to look around Sandoval's side, but he held her too tightly.

"Gone, the ones who weren't killed. Lupe was among the ones who fled. The other Rangers have gone after them, though of course the bandits had a long start on them."

"Mama?"

"She's all right, thanks to you—though I aged about a hundred years, sweetheart, seeing you running out there to her—"

"I had to help her…."

"I know," he said, kissing the top of her head. "I

think she's all right. Your father carried her into the house with your godfather's help."

"Was anyone else hurt?"

"Not as far as I know. Let me get you to the house, Tess, and we'll make sure."

Tess felt him lifting her up into his arms, and began to protest, "Sandoval, I can walk—"

He ignored her, and she was glad, for even the motion of him shifting her weight against him set her head spinning. She let her head fall against his chest as he strode over the lawn.

The door was opened as he reached it. Everyone flocked to them, exclaiming over Tess as Sandoval lowered her gently onto a brocade-upholstered couch. She saw her mother first, sitting next to the couch with her foot propped up on an ottoman and wrapped in a wet towel. Her father stood next to her, happy tears standing in his eyes at the sight of Tess. And there was Sandoval's mother, crying tears of joy and murmuring "Thanks be to God" over and over again in Spanish as she hugged her son.

"Oh, Tess, thank God you're safe!" cried her mother. "Are you hurt? When I saw that monster snatch you up I swooned. My dear girl, if my clumsiness had caused you to be kidnapped again—"

"I'm fine, Mama," Tess assured her quickly. She saw her godfather sitting with Lula Marie nearby, his arm bandaged. "Uncle Samuel?"

"One of them banditos winged me, but I'll mend, I reckon. Esteban here shot him, and although the fella was still on his horse when they galloped down the lane, he thinks he was hit worse than me. And it seems I was the only one of us hit, so we can thank God for that. I figure they came for only one purpose—you."

Tess gulped, knowing it was true. She stared at Esteban, trying to imagine how hard it must have been for the Mexican to shoot at men he had once called compadres. "Thank you, Esteban."

He smiled steadily back at her. "I have chosen a new path, Señora Tess. I don't want to be an outlaw anymore."

"I'm glad."

"He says he'd like to work on my ranch," Sandoval told her. "As I told you, my foreman's getting old, so I reckon Esteban could work into the job. And when Delores arrives, she can help you in the kitchen."

"I am going to go look for her tomorrow," Esteban said. "She has a sister in Reynosa. She told me that she would wait there for me."

"But the other banditos—Lupe—" Tess began, alarmed that Delgado's sister might seek vengeance against the old woman.

"We never told any of them that my mother's sister lives there. I think my mother knew she might have to get away from Delgado someday. The other men… I think if they are not caught by the Rangers before they reach the border, most of them will stop raiding and go back to their villages. I hope so, anyway," he concluded with a sigh.

The friends and neighbors who had been guests at the party came forward now, expressing their relief that she was all right, and taking their leave. Doc Evans, who was already there as a guest at the reception, took Uncle Samuel into another room to tend his wound. He was followed by Lula Marie. Before long, only Tess, Sandoval and her parents remained in the room.

Amelia cleared her throat. "I have something to say to you, Sandoval Parrish."

On the couch, Tess tensed. By this time, Sandoval was sitting on a chair by the couch. She placed a hand on her husband's wrist, ready to spring to his defense. Now that the danger was over and the guests were gone, was her mother about to blame Sandoval for what had happened?

"Now, Amelia," began her father, apparently worried about the same thing.

Her mother held up a hand. "I need to say this. Sandoval Parrish, when I first saw you, and heard what they said about you, I thought you were up to no good. And if I'd had a gun, after Tess went missing and we found that note in her room, I might've used it on you."

Beside her, Sandoval said, "I understand, Mrs. Hennessy. I can't say I'd blame you. It was wrong of me to use your daughter to try to capture Delgado—"

Her mother held up a hand again, forestalling him. "Yes, it was. But she seems to have survived it all right, thanks to you. My Tess is an adventurous girl—I'm not sure *where* she gets that from, but there it is."

Beside his wife, Patrick grinned.

"I don't think she would have ever been content to just marry some planter's son around here and settle down to raise babies and give teas and help the Ladies Aid Society. She's always been different, my Tess." She smiled at Tess then, and it was a proud smile. "I want to thank you for bringing her safely home."

Sandoval rose to his feet. "Mrs. Hennessy, I—"

"That's *Mama* to you, Sandoval Parrish, or Mother Hennessy, if you must be formal. Welcome to the family. I know you're the only man the Lord could find who could keep up with my Tess."

Sandoval smiled at Tess, then went to Amelia, kneeling so they could embrace without her getting up on her sprained ankle.

"But what about this plan of yours to go to New York City and work with Brady, Tess?" her mother asked, after Sandoval had returned to the couch. The question surprised Tess yet again, especially the lack of disapproval in her mother's tone.

"Oh, I wouldn't mind going up to see his studio someday," Tess said, after gazing into Sandoval's eyes. "But now that doesn't seem so important. I'm a wife now, you know—and if the Lord blesses us with babies…" Her voice trailed off and color flooded her face. "In any case, I'm afraid the camera may have sustained some damage," Tess said, remembering how it had been knocked over in the midst of the attack. "I'm not sure it'll work anymore."

"Excuse me…" said a voice hesitantly from the door. It was Francisco. As Tess watched, he turned and began pulling something into the room—her camera.

There was a scrape on the side of the box, and a small rent at the lower edge of the heavy canvas flap in the back.

Tess braced herself, unable to hope for one more bit of good news. "Francisco, is it…?" She could not bring herself to say the word *broken*.

He held up a finger. "One moment, please." He walked out of the parlor again and when he returned, he was carrying a photograph that was apparently still wet. He held it out. It was a photograph of Ben, her mule, grazing out in the pasture.

"I took this a few minutes ago, Tess, just to test it. Your camera, she still works."

A month later, Tess and Sandoval found themselves walking into the office of the governor at the state capitol building in Austin.

"Thank you so much for coming," Governor Oran Roberts, a solemn, gray-haired and gray-bearded, long-faced man said, welcoming them into his office.

"It's an honor, sir," Sandoval said, speaking for both of them.

"I'm the one who is honored by your presence," Roberts insisted. "And on behalf of the entire state of Texas, I'm pleased to present you with these medals, with the thanks of the grateful citizens of this fine state." He pinned on each of them a bronze, five-pointed star of Texas dangling from a horizontal bronze bar by means of two slender bronze chains. "Thanks to you, the depredations committed by Diego Delgado and his band have ceased, and reports of raids by other marauding bands from south of the border have been nearly nonexistent."

Tess experienced a moment of sadness as she thought of Diego Delgado, a man whose vainglorious pride had brought about his destruction. He could have done so much more with his life. He could have served as an example for his avaricious, cruel sister. But now he was dead.

They'd never caught Lupe Delgado, or any of the other bandits who had lived to flee Hennessy Hall the day of the attack, but reports out of Mexico had it that she had married Andrés Cordoba, the wealthy *ranchero*. Perhaps Lupe would learn from her narrow escape and turn her life around—or at least make only this one last man wish he'd never met her. Tess resolved to pray for her, and for all the men who had been part of Delgado's band.

"I was merely doing my job as a Ranger, sir," Sandoval told governor. "It's my wife, Tess, who went above and beyond anything she might have been expected to do as a private-citizen photographer who happened to be of the fairer sex." He smiled down at Tess, who returned his smile, her heart glowing with pride and love for the man next to her.

Roberts's eyes twinkled underneath bushy brows. "I'm told there is much more to the story, that you actually had her kidnapped?"

Once again they found themselves telling their remarkable story.

"I've seen some of your photographs, Mrs. Parrish. A contingent of Rangers went down to the Delgado's canyon hideout—with permission from the Mexican government, I might add—and brought out the pictures Delgado had left behind there. You have a remarkable talent, ma'am."

"Thank you, sir."

"Are you planning to write a book? This yarn you've told me would make a great dime novel, complete with your drawings."

Tess smiled. "Maybe someday…" She doubted it, though.

"Might I commission you to take my photograph sometime, ma'am?"

Tess blinked in surprise. "I… I'm afraid I didn't bring my camera with me to Austin, sir." She imagined traveling all the way to Austin in the wagon and was glad she hadn't known Governor Roberts would make this request. "But we'd be honored if you'd like to visit our ranch down in the Rio Grande Valley. I could take your picture then."

"Perhaps I'll do that, Mrs. Parrish, and thank you. Mr. Parrish, do you plan to continue your career as a Ranger?"

Sandoval smiled regretfully. "I'm afraid I've ten-dered my resignation, sir. I was honored to serve that way for many years, but rangering is a job that can take a man away from his home for months on end. It's not a job for a man who's newly married. But I've told my captain that I'm willing to help out if Texas needs me."

"I understand," the governor said. "Congratulations on your marriage. And once again, thank you for your service to the state of Texas."

Epilogue

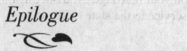

October—the Rio Grande Valley north of Chapin

Tess watched from under the shelter of the grapevine-twined lattice over the patio as Sandoval helped first his mother and then Pilar up into the carriage Esteban was driving. She was amused to see Esteban turn around and dart a look at Pilar, a look that Sandoval's sister returned with a flirtatious smile.

Pilar had arrived last week from Monterrey, joyous and confident, completely unlike the regretful, shy girl they had encountered in the bordello. Her time of contemplation had done her a world of good. She now knew that God loved her, and had always loved her, and she was ready to live the rest of her life in search of His will for her.

Pilar had decided to live with their mother, at least for the time being, and so Sandoval had started building an addition on the ranch house. They were going into town now to buy furniture and fabric for curtains for the new rooms.

As the carriage started down the road, Sandoval strode back to the house and sat down, smiling appreciatively as Tess handed him a glass of freshly made lemonade. For a moment both of them just savored the breeze that fluttered the tendrils of red hair over Tess's forehead. Now that the cooler days of autumn had replaced the steamy humidity of a Valley summer midday, they often sat out here, enjoying the view that spread before them— grazing horses and cattle, cotton fields and sturdy barns against the backdrop of thick tropical foliage.

"If I'm not mistaken, I think our Esteban is sweet on my sister," Sandoval said, gazing after the carriage disappearing down the road.

"And she on him," Tess responded. "You don't mind, do you?"

"Not a bit. Esteban's a good man, steady and dependable," Sandoval said, smiling lovingly at his wife.

"It's fun watching them fall in love, isn't it?" she said.

He nodded. "Our life is just about perfect, isn't it?"

It was time, Tess decided. She had waited until she could tell him alone. "It's about to get more perfect," she murmured.

"What? How?" he asked, puzzled; then, as she continued to smile, he blinked. "Tess…do you mean…are you—are we—"

"Going to have a baby? Yes. I've thought so for a week or two, but I wanted to tell just you first."

"When?"

"I think he—or she—will come in mid-May, if I'm figuring right." The baby had been conceived while they were still in Mexico, she figured, on the run, but it would be born amid peace and safety.

Sandoval pulled Tess into his embrace and kissed her. "I don't know why God gave me such gifts—I mean *you,* my darling Tess, and our coming child— but I thank Him every day."

* * * * *

Florida author **Louise M. Gouge** writes historical fiction for Harlequin's Love Inspired Historical line. She received the prestigious Inspirational Readers' Choice Award in 2005 and placed in 2011 and 2015; she also placed in the Laurel Wreath contest in 2012. When she isn't writing, she and her husband, David, enjoy visiting historical sites and museums. Please visit her website at blog.louisemgouge.com.

Visit the Author Profile page
at Harlequin.com for more titles.

LOVE THINE ENEMY

Louise M. Gouge

Behold, thou desirest truth in the inward parts:
and in the hidden part thou shalt make me
to know wisdom.
—*Psalms* 51:6

To Kristy Dykes (1951–2008), a godly, gifted author who encouraged me to write about Florida, her home state and mine. Kristy was a beautiful Christian lady, a light in my life and in the lives of countless others. She is greatly missed by all who knew her.

Also, to my husband, David, who accompanied me on my research trips and found some excellent tidbits for this book. Thank you, my darling.

Chapter One

St. Johns Settlement, East Florida Colony
May 1775

Through the window of her father's store, Rachel watched the Englishmen ride their handsome steeds up the sandy street of St. Johns Settlement. Their well-cut coats and haughty bearing—as if they owned the world—made their identities unmistakable.

"Make them pass by, Lord," she whispered, "for surely I'll not be able to speak a Christian word to them if they come in here." She glanced over her shoulder at Papa to see if he had heard her, but he was focusing his attention on a newly opened crate of goods.

Rachel turned back to the window. To her dismay, the two young men dismounted right in front of the store. One snapped his fingers at a small black boy and motioned for him to care for the horses.

Her dismay turned to anger. How did they know the boy could take time to do the task? Did they care that the child might be beaten by his owner if he lingered in town?

"What draws yer scrutiny, daughter?" Papa approached to look out the window. "Aha. Just as I hoped. From the cut of his clothes, that's Mr. Moberly, no mistake. Make haste, child. Go behind the counter and set out those fine tins of snuff and the brass buckles. Oh, and the wig powder and whalebone combs. Mayhap these gentlemen have wives who long for such luxuries here in the wilderness."

The delight in his voice brought back Rachel's dismay, even as she hurried to obey. Until six months ago, Papa had been a man of great dignity, a respected whaler who commanded his own ship. Why should he make obeisance to these wretches? These popinjays?

When the two men entered, the jangling bells on the front door grated against her nerves, inciting anger once more. But for Papa's sake, she would attempt to control it.

"What did I tell you, Oliver? Isn't this superb?" The taller of the two men glanced about the room. "Look at all these wares."

Rachel noticed the slight lift of his eyebrows when he saw her, but he turned his attention to Papa.

"Mr. Folger, I presume?"

"Aye, milord, I am he. How may I serve ye, sir?"

The young man chuckled. "First of all, I am not 'milord.'"

"Not yet." His companion held his nose high, as if something smelled bad. "But soon."

The taller man shrugged. "Perhaps when the plantation proves as successful as Lord Egmount's." He reached out to Papa. "I'm Frederick Moberly, sir, His Majesty's magistrate for St. Johns Settlement and manager of Bennington Plantation. This is my friend and business associate, Oliver Corwin."

For the briefest moment, Papa seemed uncertain, but

then he gripped the gentleman's hand and shook it with enthusiasm. "How do ye, my good sirs? I'm pleased to meet ye both."

"And I'm pleased to see your fine store ready for business." Moberly surveyed the shelves and counters. And again his glance stopped at Rachel.

Papa cleared his throat. "My daughter, Miss Folger."

Moberly swept off his brimmed hat and bent forward in a courtly bow, revealing black hair pulled back in a long queue. "How do you do, Miss Folger?"

She forced herself to curtsy but did not speak. The very idea, a gentleman giving a shopkeeper's daughter such honors. No doubt the man was a flatterer. The one named Corwin made no such gesture, but his intense stare brought heat to her face. Rachel could not decide which man would require her to be more vigilant.

Moberly's gaze lingered on her for another instant before he turned back to Papa. "Your store and the village's other new ones are what I've been hoping for. If St. Johns Settlement is to succeed as a colonial outpost, we must have every convenience to offer our settlers. Tell me, Folger, do you have any concerns about your shipments? With all that nonsense going on in the northern colonies, do you expect any delay in delivery of your goods?"

"Well, sir, I had no difficulty sailing down here from Boston. I expect all those troubles to be behind us soon. The rebels simply haven't the resources. I'll wager wiser heads will prevail. I'm from Nantucket, ye see, and we're loyal to the Crown."

Corwin snorted, and Moberly glanced his way with a frown.

"Ah, yes, Nantucket." The magistrate appeared interested. "From whence whalers set out to harvest the world's finest lamp oil. Will you be receiving goods from there?"

"Perhaps some, sir. My own ship will sail to and from London until things are settled."

"Good, good." Moberly nodded. "And are you a Quaker, as I've heard most Nantucketers are?"

"I was reared in the Society of Friends," Papa said. "But I don't mind wearing a brass button or a buckle."

"We don't need any dissenters here." Corwin's eyes narrowed.

"Now, Oliver, the man said he wasn't a zealot." Moberly gave Papa a genial look. "Moderation in all things, would you not agree?"

"Precisely my sentiments, sir."

Rachel inhaled deeply. She must not display her feelings. This was not Nantucket, where women spoke their minds. Nor was it Boston, where patriots—both men and women—clamored for separation from England. Until she got the lay of the land here in East Florida Colony, she must not risk harming Papa's enterprise.

"Miss Folger." Moberly approached the wide oak counter which she stood behind. "What do you think of our little settlement?"

She caught a glimpse of Papa's warning look and stifled a curt reply. "I am certain it is everything King George could wish for." She ventured a direct look and discovered his eyes to be dark gray. His tanned, clean-shaven cheeks had a youthful yet strong contour. Young, handsome, self-assured. Like the English officers who ordered the shooting of the patriots at Lexington and Concord just over a month ago.

Her reply seemed to please him, for his eyes twinkled, and Rachel's traitorous pulse beat faster. *Belay that, foolish heart. These are not your kind.*

"Indeed, I do hope His Majesty approves of my work here." A winsome expression crossed his face. "As you may know, in England, younger sons must earn their fortunes. But if we are clever and the Fates favor us, we too can gain society's interest and perhaps even its approval."

Rachel returned a tight smile. "In America, *every* man has the opportunity to earn his fortune and his place in society." With the help of God, not fate.

He grinned. "Then I've come to the right place, have I not?"

The man had not comprehended her insult in the least. How she longed to tell him exactly what she thought of his King George and all greedy Englishmen.

Papa emitted a nervous cough. "Indeed ye have, my good sir. And so have we." Again, his frown scolded her. "Now, sir, is there anything in particular we can help ye with?"

"Hmm." The magistrate effected a thoughtful pose, with arms crossed and a finger resting on his chin. "My Mrs. Winthrop requested tea, if you have some." He tapped his temple. "And something else. Oliver, can you recall the other items she mentioned?"

"Flour and coffee." Corwin's languid tone revealed boredom, perhaps even annoyance. "She wanted a list of his spices, and of course she'll want to know about those fabrics." He waved toward the crates Papa had opened.

At Papa's instruction, Rachel wrote down the items they had imported from Boston, things an English housekeeper might want. She snipped small samples of the linen, muslin and other fabrics, and wrapped them in brown paper. All the while, she felt the stares of the two men. Despite the summer heat, a shiver ran down her back while a blush warmed her cheeks.

None too soon, they made their purchases and left, but not before Mr. Moberly once again bowed to her. Why did he engage in such courtesy? Neither in England nor in Boston would he thus have honored her, nor even have acknowledged her existence.

"Well, daughter, what think ye?" Papa held up the gold guineas they had given him. "His lordship didn't even ask for credit."

"Papa, will you listen to yourself?" Rachel leaned her elbows on the counter and rested her chin on her fists. "You were raised a Quaker, yet hear how you go on about 'milord' and 'his lordship.'"

Papa harrumphed. "I suppose ye'll be after me to take up my 'thees' and 'thous' again. Ye, who abandoned the Friends yerself, going off to that other church with yer sister and her husband." He lumbered on his wounded leg toward the back room. "I should never have sent ye to Boston to live with Susanna."

He disappeared behind the burlap curtain, and soon Rachel heard crates being shoved roughly across the hard tabby floor. Sorrow cut into her. Had he not been injured on his last whaling voyage, Papa could still captain his own ship, and she would still be in Boston helping the patriots' noble cause. Instead, here she was in East Florida helping him.

He must feel as cross as she did about their differences of opinion, both about the revolution and the Englishmen. But she had not chosen to flee Massachusetts Colony to avoid the war against the Crown. How could he expect her to treat the English oppressors with civility?

"Pleasant fellow, that Folger." Frederick flipped a farthing to the Negro boy who held their horses. "Good job, lad. If you get into trouble, tell your master Mr. Moberly required your services."

"Pleasant fellow, indeed." Oliver grasped his horse's reins and swung into the saddle. "'Tis the little chit you found pleasant."

"And you did not?" Frederick mounted Essex and reined the stallion toward the plantation road. "I saw you watching her as if she were a plump partridge and you a starving man."

Oliver drew up beside him. "Of course I was watching her. Your father sent me along to this forsaken place to make sure no provincial lass sets her cap for you. And if she does, I'm to nip the budding romance."

Frederick swallowed the bitter retort. Oliver's reminder ruined the agreeable feeling that had settled in his chest the moment he set eyes on the fair-haired maiden. Here he was at twenty-three, and the old earl still treated him as if he were a boy sitting in an Eton classroom. As for the girl, she was no chit, but fully a woman, possessing a diminutive but elegant figure. Spirited, too, from the liveliness he had noticed in her fine dark eyes. But he would not say so, for Oliver would only misunderstand his generous opinion of her.

"Have no care on that account. I've no plans to pursue American women." He glanced at the rolling landscape with its sandy soil and countless varieties of vegetation. While the weather could inflict heat, lightning and hurricanes upon inhabitants, he found East Florida a pleasant paradise, as satisfying as any place for building his future.

"You cannot fool me," Oliver said. "Need I remind you that if you fail here, Lord Bennington will ship you off to His Majesty's Royal Navy? You'll end up wearing the indigo instead of growing it."

Frederick glared at him. "Fail? My father sent me to rescue the plantation from Bartleby's mismanagement, and that's exactly what I have accomplished. He will not be quick to snatch me home."

"You know as well as I it's moral failure he's concerned about."

Frederick gritted his teeth. How long would he have to pay for the sins of his older brothers? "Rest easy on that account. I'll not risk my business association with Mr. Folger by dallying with his daughter. However, if you will recall, we're supposed to be building a settlement here. Before we can bring English ladies to this wilderness, we must provide necessary services. This man Folger may have friends up north who want no part in the rebellion. We must court him, if you will, to lure other worthies to East Florida Colony, even if it means socializing with the merchant class."

Oliver regarded him with a skeptical frown. "Just be certain you don't socialize with the little Nantucket wench while you await those English ladies."

"Enough of this." Frederick slapped his riding crop against Essex's flanks and urged him into a gallop.

The steed easily outdistanced Oliver's mare, and Frederick arrived home far ahead of his companion. At the front porch, he jumped down and tossed the reins to the waiting groom.

"Give him a cooldown and brushing, Ben. He's had a good run in this heat."

"Yessuh, Mister Moberly." The slender black man led the stallion away.

Three black-and-white spaniels bounded around the corner of the house to greet Frederick. He ruffled their necks and patted their heads. "Down, boy. Down, girls. I'm on a mission."

He took the four front steps two at a time and crossed the wide porch with long strides. The door opened, and the little Negro girl who tended it curtsied.

"Welcome home, Mr. Frederick."

"Thank you, Caddy." He pulled a confection from his coat pocket, handed it to her and patted her scarf-covered head.

Inside, he strode across the entry toward the front staircase. "Cousin Lydie, I'm home." He listened for his cousin's response. Soon the soft rush of feet sounded above him.

"Dear me." Cousin Lydie hastened downstairs, shadowed by Betty, the housemaid. "I expected you to be in the village much longer. Dinner is not yet prepared."

"Don't fret. I only announced my homecoming because I have this for you." He pulled the fabric samples from his pocket and handed them to her. "Oliver has the other items, but I wanted to give you these myself. Be quick to order the dress lengths you desire, or the vicar's wife will beat you to it." He winked at her.

"Why, sir." Cousin Lydie's gray eyes exuded gratitude as she spoke. "You're too kind."

Frederick noticed the longing in Betty's expression. The once cheerful maid had become a sad little shadow after an alligator caught her skirt and almost dragged her into the river. If Oliver hadn't shot the beast, Frederick would have had a bitter letter to write home to Father's groom to report the loss of his daughter.

"And be certain to choose something for Betty, too. Something to mark her status in the house." He felt tempted to pat the girl on the head as he had the child at the front door, but thought better of it. Such innocent contact with serving girls had been the beginning of troubles for his older brothers.

"Thank you, sir." Betty curtsied, and her pale face brightened.

"Think nothing of it."

"Mr. Moberly." Cousin Lydie insisted on addressing him formally in front of the servants. "A flatboat arrived bringing mail. Summerlin put several letters on your desk."

"Ah, very good." Frederick proceeded down the hallway to his study and sat at his large oak desk. Trepidation filled him as he lifted the top letter and broke Father's red wax seal.

As expected, he could almost hear Father's ponderous voice in the missive. The earl always seemed to find something wrong in Frederick's correspondence and scolded him about nonexistent offenses. Yet the abundant shipments of produce and the financial reports sent by Corwin confirmed everything Frederick claimed about the plantation's success.

Through the tall, open window beside him, he stared out on the distant indigo field where slaves bent over tender young plants. Last year's crop had been modestly successful, and this year should produce an abundance, perhaps even rivaling the success of Lord Egmount's nearby plantation. Why did Father doubt the veracity of Frederick's reports?

He blew out a deep sigh. Pleasing his father had always proven impossible, so he cheered himself with Mother's letter. She chatted about a party she had given in London and said how much she missed him. As always, she thanked him for giving her widowed cousin a home where she could feel useful. Frederick would make certain he responded that Cousin Lydia Winthrop did more for him than he did for her, managing the household with skill.

Marianne's letter brought him laughter. His younger sister had rebuffed yet another foolish suitor who, despite an august title and ample wealth, possessed no wit or sense of adventure. "I shall remain forever a spinster," she wrote. Frederick pictured her dramatic pose, delicate white hand to her pretty forehead in artificial pathos. How he treasured the memories of their carefree childhood days.

The letters had done their job. Father's dire warnings had been mitigated by Mother's and Marianne's gentler words. Frederick rested his head against the back of his large mahogany chair and gazed out the window again.

In his most amiable dreams, he considered that his success in East Florida might move His Majesty to knight him, as Oliver had said. Then, in due time, he could complete the picture by returning to England to choose a woman to be his wife from one of the families who once had shunned him. But how could he win the king's favor when his own father gave only disapproval?

He recalled the words of the pretty young miss he had met two short hours ago. In America, every man had the opportunity to earn his place in society. Not be born to it, as his eldest brother had been, but to earn his fortune by his own honest sweat. More and more, that peculiar idea appealed to him, for he found great satisfaction in his work. And the sort of woman Frederick required for a wife must be willing to leave her cushioned life to establish a new home, just as Miss Folger had done for her father.

Frederick would do well to foster a friendship with the merchant and his daughter to discover what kind of woman would make the perfect wife to bring to this savage land. Perhaps inviting the two to some sort of social gathering would be beneficial. A party such as

Mother had given in London, where no expense was spared to please her guests.

Eager to enlist Cousin Lydie's help in the project, he rose from his chair, but noticed another letter bearing Father's seal lying facedown on the desk. Two reprimands? What had the old earl forgotten to scold him for?

Frederick snapped the wax and unfolded the vellum sheet, not caring if he tore it. The salutation made him blink twice.

My dear Oliver—

Frederick turned the missive over. Oliver's name was clearly written in Father's hand across the outside. A coil of dread tightened in Frederick's stomach. Father had never addressed *him* as "My dear Frederick."

He should not read this letter. Summerlin had left it here by mistake. Yet Frederick could not resist.

Received your letter of December 20. You have my gratitude for your faithful reporting of the matters we discussed. I shall make my decision accordingly. Please continue your endeavors to keep my son from further overspending. As to the chit from Oswald's plantation, do all in your power to keep them apart.

Gratefully, Bennington

Frederick slumped back into his chair. What matters? What overspending? What *chit?* Frederick had visited the manager of Oswald's plantation last year, but met no young woman.

And Oliver knew it. Oliver, the illegitimate son of a well-born lady, who had depended on Father's generosity since childhood. Oliver, Frederick's lifelong friend.

His hands curled into fists, crushing the heavy paper into a ball. He thrust it into the fireplace, then snatched a piece of char cloth from the box on the narrow mantelpiece. But before he could strike flint against steel to light it, other thoughts stayed his hand.

Working to subdue his anger, he pressed the page out on his desk, refolded it and then consigned it to the hidden compartment beneath his desktop. He must not let Oliver know that he had discovered his treachery.

Frederick paced back and forth across the room. All his hard work might come to nothing because Father believed Oliver's lies. He reread the earl's letter. At least Father had not called him home at once. But he must discover a way to prove himself.

The party. That was it. He would throw a grand affair and earn the friendship of the newly arrived residents of St. Johns Settlement. If they required help, he would give it. In his judgments as magistrate, he would continue to be firm but fair. He would solicit a letter of praise from his plantation physician, Dr. Wellsey, regarding the health and productivity of the slaves. He would foster friendships with the leading citizens of the growing settlement and petition for recommendations, as well.

And he would watch Oliver as a falcon watches its prey.

Chapter Two

"Captain James Templeton. How impressive your new title sounds." Rachel sat across the table from her cousin in the parlor of the Wild Boar Inn. "Papa could have chosen no better man to succeed him as captain of the *Fair Winds*."

"Thank you, Rachel." Jamie grinned. "Of course, I've learned my trade from the best. When Uncle Lamech chose me as his cabin boy those fifteen years ago, he may have wondered how this orphaned boy would turn out."

"We will miss you, but I shall pray for a good voyage." Rachel took a sip of tea from her pewter cup. "But why must you go to London? Are there no other ports to supply Papa's store?"

"In these turbulent times, English settlers might not favor French products. And after all, London has the best merchandise." His brown eyes shone with brotherly affection. "I do wish you'd charge me with some special purchase to bring you."

"You know what I want. News of the revolution." She exhaled a sigh of annoyance. "I cannot even discuss it with Papa, for he will not listen to my opinions. With you gone, I will need to find another friend in whom I can confide…and complain to." She glanced beyond him at the British soldiers in red uniforms seated across the entry hall in the taproom.

He followed her glance, then turned back with a frown. "Don't get yourself in trouble. These soldiers are here for your good. They'll protect you and your father and every other British subject in East Florida."

"I am *not* a British subject." She leaned toward him and whispered. "When will you join us, Jamie? When will you accept that we *will* be free from British rule… or die trying?"

Now he stared into her eyes with an almost scolding look. "My dear little rebel, why do you think your father brought you so far away from the troubles? Why, you'd have been fighting alongside the militia at Concord or Lexington if you'd had your way."

She straightened as high as her short stature permitted. "When I sought to become a servant in General Gage's home, I planned to gather information to help the patriot cause."

He sat back, shaking his head. "Humph. Your feelings are always written across your face, and you never fail to speak your mind. You'd fail as a spy. You'd be discovered and hanged, but not before they wrested the name of your every accomplice from you."

She clenched her jaw and stared down at her teacup. He was wrong. She could have learned how to withhold the truth, perhaps even to lie, as Rahab in the Bible had done to save the Hebrew spies. Sometimes the desperation to do her part in the revolution ate at her soul. At other times, she felt nothing but despair that Papa had made her participation impossible.

"Dear cousin." Jamie reached over to nudge her chin.

"What shall I do with you? After watching you grow into a beautiful woman, I see you slip back into the childish imp who bedeviled the crew in '68."

Rachel granted him the change of topic without protest. "Wasn't that a grand voyage?" She smiled at the memory of dressing as a cabin boy and climbing riggings to watch for whales. Then she sobered. "But for Mama's death, Papa never would have taken me."

"Your father's never ceased his grieving." He patted her hand as if she were a child. "Please, Rachel, do not grieve him further. Forget the revolution." A frown flickered across his youthful but weathered face. "Rebellion, I should say."

She pulled back her hand. "'Rebellion' makes it sound as if the patriots are naughty children instead of sound-minded adults who have suffered enough of King George's injustices."

"Whatever you call it, just stay out of trouble."

"What trouble could I find here in this remote wilderness?"

He gave her a playful wink. "Who knows? Maybe one of these handsomely uniformed soldiers will catch your eye and you'll be married before I return."

"You may wager all the *Fair Winds*'s profits that no Englishman will ever win my hand." Again she cast a cross glance at the soldiers across the hall, who now harried Sadie, the innkeeper's daughter, demanding rum despite the early hour.

Jamie shoved away his teacup. "It'd be a winning wager, no mistake. Now, may I escort you to the store? The captain will keelhaul me if I make you late."

"He'd do no such thing to his nephew and new partner." She scooted her wooden chair backward across the plank floor. "Wait while I fetch my bonnet."

He sent her a playful smirk. "By all means, protect your face. The English value a fair complexion."

She wrinkled her nose and laughed, but not too loudly for fear of drawing the soldiers' attentions. In spite of Jamie's assurances of their protection, she had no doubt that, given the chance, they would harass her as much as they did the innkeeper's women.

As she hastened up the rickety steps to the inn's second floor, she sent up a silent prayer of thanks that soon she and Papa would move into their own more stable home above their store. Under the supervision of Mr. Patch, the carpenter from Papa's ship, the crew had labored for weeks to raise the roof and build the apartment. It was almost completed.

From her room at the end of the inn's second-story corridor, she snatched her straw bonnet from a peg on the wall. Passing the room next to hers, she heard a soft whimper through the slightly open door. She glanced toward the stairway, then peered into the room.

There, in a rough-hewn pen no more than three foot by four, sat the innkeeper's grandson, his dark, soulful eyes staring up with sudden hope when he spied her. Flies buzzed about the two-year-old's face and crawled over a dry crust of bread beside him.

"Up. Up." His winsome, tearful expression nearly undid her.

"Dear little Robby." Unable to resist his entreaty, she lifted him. "My, my, you need a change. And look at all these mosquito bites." She felt a twinge of anger that the innkeeper had not provided his grandson with mosquito netting, but perhaps he could not afford it.

Several clean diapers hung on a rope line near the window. Rachel started to call the baby's mother, but compassion filled her. No doubt Sadie was kept busy serving those awful soldiers and could not care for her child as she ought to. Laying the child on the bed, Rachel quickly changed him, cooing to him all the while.

"There, little one. I've not forgot how to do this. Gracious knows I changed my nieces and nephew often enough these past few years." And the three of them healthily plump, while this wee tyke's ribs were all too visible.

The baby whimpered as she set him back down in the pen, a splintery structure made from an old shipping crate and far different from the sanded, polished beds her sister's children slept in. And nothing more than an old tin cup, empty at that, for a toy.

"I must go, sweet boy." Rachel thought her heart would break. "I'm certain Mama will come feed you soon."

Only by force of will could she hasten down the stairs to join Jamie in the entry hall.

"What is it, Rachel?" With a frown, he stared into her eyes. "You look distraught."

"Sadie's little one." She bent her head toward the staircase. "He spends his days alone in her room while she must fend off those dreadful soldiers."

Jamie's face softened. "You have a kind heart, cousin. Hmm, didn't Sadie say her husband is a soldier, too?"

"Aye, but that doesn't seem to protect her." She lowered her voice. "And I've learned he's serving under General Gage. Perhaps he even fought against our men at Concord."

"Rachel—"

"Yes, yes, I know." She moved past him out the inn's front door.

The East Florida heat blazed down on their covered heads as they walked the sandy road toward the sturdy wooden structure Papa had purchased for his mercantile. But Rachel could be concerned with only one matter—a poor, hungry little baby left alone in a room all day.

"I've changed my mind," she said as they reached the store. "There is something I want you to bring me when you return."

He swept off his broad-brimmed hat and gave her an exaggerated bow. "Name it, milady, and I'll sail the seven seas to obtain it."

She dipped a playful curtsy. "Why, thank you, kind sir. But there's no need for that. Just bring a toy for little Robby." She sobered. "Do you mind?"

"Anything for you, milady." He caught her hand and placed a noisy kiss on it.

"Ah, such gallantry." Caring not a whit what onlookers might think, Rachel reached up and kissed his cheek.

After a week of planning with Mrs. Winthrop, Frederick rode into town to invite more guests to his party. His first visit had been to Major Brigham, the garrison's new commander, who along with his stylish bride had responded eagerly to his invitation. Several others also promised to attend. With a similar response from the merchants, the party would be complete.

Frederick rode past the inn and saw the innkeeper's wife and daughter hanging laundry on a line. Mrs. Winthrop had been aghast when he had suggested inviting them, and now her wisdom was confirmed as he observed their unkempt appearance and heard their uncouth language.

A half mile from the inn, he spied Miss Folger with a brawny fellow who was bent over her hand like an adoring swain. The young lady then reached up to kiss the man's cheek, and an odd pang coursed through Frederick's chest. Did she dole out kisses to every man, or was this one a particular friend? He shook his head. Why should it matter to him?

The fellow straightened and offered his arm, and the two entered Folger's Mercantile. Frederick tethered his horse to a post under a nearby oak tree and followed them inside.

The door had no sooner shut behind him than the three inside turned to him in surprise. Was that a glare emanating from the young lady's face, or were her eyes merely adjusting to the inside light, as were his?

"Good morning, sir." Mr. Folger limped forward to welcome him. "How can I help ye?"

"Good morning, my good man. Miss Folger." Frederick removed his hat, nodded to the father and daughter, and cast an inquisitive glance toward the big man behind Folger.

"Ah, ye've not met my partner." Folger urged the man forward. "Mr. Moberly, this is my nephew, Captain Templeton, who now commands my old ship."

The younger captain's steady gaze was a clear and bold appraisal of Frederick.

In an instant, the air seemed sparked with invisible lightning. Instinctively, Frederick took on the unassuming pose he had perfected as the youngest of four sons to keep from being whipped into his proper place. Hating himself for it, he nonetheless feigned amiability and reached out to shake the other man's hand rather than meet his challenge and put him in *his* place. Who was this man that he would boldly stare at a superior?

"Captain Templeton," Frederick said.

"Moberly." Templeton's guarded frown softened as they shook hands. "You've done a right fine job in building St. Johns Settlement. Perhaps we can do business in the future."

"Indeed?" Frederick glanced at Folger.

"Aye." The older man's broad smile suggested his eagerness to foster a friendship among the three of them. "A wise man's always on the lookout for good business associates."

"Well said." Frederick wondered if he had been mistaken about the younger captain's earlier demeanor.

The conversation turned to weather, the war up north, anticipated shipping problems, the feasibility of planting more citrus groves and prices of goods. All possible storms were dispelled as the three men enthusiastically expressed their concerns and opinions as if they had been in trade together for years. The amity in the air felt good after Oliver's betrayal.

He noticed Miss Folger had busied herself with the bolts of lace and ribbons behind the counter. With her back to him, he could see the delicate lines of her ivory neck, with a few blond curls escaping from her mobcap to trail over the white collar of her brown dress.

Templeton must have caught the direction of his gaze, for he cleared his throat. "Did you wish to speak with my cousin?" His tone sounded like the growl of a protective bear.

Irritation swept through Frederick, but again, he was all amiability. "Indeed, I did."

She turned around, puzzlement lifting her eyebrows into a charming arch. "To me?"

Frederick hesitated. "Perhaps I should say to you

and your father." He nodded to Templeton. "And now to you, as well."

Folger appeared more than a little pleased. "Say on, sir."

"I am planning a dinner party for those whom I consider the leading citizens of this community and surrounding areas. I should like to invite you and Miss Folger—" He included Templeton with a quick glance. "All three of you to join us one week from Saturday at my plantation."

Their stunned expressions nearly sent Frederick into a schoolboy's guffaw. Did these people know nothing of parties? Had they never received such an invitation?

"Why, that's quite an honor, sir." Folger straightened as if he had been knighted by the king himself. "Of course I accept."

"And you, Miss Folger? Will you attend with your father?"

Her wide-eyed gaze darted from him to her father to Templeton and back to him again. "Why, I—I haven't anything to wear to such a grand occasion."

"Why, Rachel, what a thing to say in front of these gentlemen." The color deepened in Folger's ruddy cheeks. "As if yer papa couldn't provide a proper gown for ye."

The young lady's corresponding blush bespoke her modesty, a pleasing sight.

Frederick looked at Templeton. "And you, captain?"

Templeton shook his head. "I thank you, sir, but I'm afraid I'll be on my way to London by then. I'm setting sail from Mayport in a few days."

"Ah, I'm sorry to hear it." Frederick found himself meaning those words. After those first sparks had been extinguished, the fellow had inspired a certain confidence.

As for doing business with him, Frederick had much to consider. After Oliver's betrayal, how could he ever trust another man? Especially an American.

Chapter Three

"Can ye beat that?" Papa stared after Mr. Moberly as he rode away. "Inviting us to a dinner party. Calling us 'leading citizens.'"

Jamie raised one eyebrow and traded a glance with Papa. "A good opportunity."

"What do you mean?" Rachel looked from one to the other. Was this another of those secrets they kept from her, things they called "men's matters"?

"Why, business, daughter." Papa took up his shipping log and quill and made notes. "'Tis a great honor for Mr. Moberly to stamp his approval on us. It'll bring more customers."

"Indeed it shall." Jamie leaned back against the counter and crossed his arms. "Now what do you suppose I could bring from London to further foster his good opinion?"

Papa tapped his quill against his chin. "Hmm. He hires ships to deliver the plantation's products to England and bring back what's needed here." He stared out of the window for a moment. "I've got the notion they'd like to increase the population with decent folk, more tradesmen and such, not the low-life camp followers that plague the regiment, nor the Spanish who stayed on after England seized these lands."

"Humph," Rachel said. "Please do not tell me you want Jamie to import more Englishmen, tradesmen or no. It is beyond enough that English sympathizers from the Carolinas are arriving here every week."

"And welcome to them." Papa bent toward her in his paternal fashion. "The more that come from South Carolina and Georgia, the better it will be for everyone, for they'll understand the land more than an Englishman. And consider this. King George gave the good citizens of New England plenty of opportunities to populate both East and West Florida. Ye can see how few have accepted his invitation."

"And, if not American colonials," Jamie said, "why not more English?" He sent Rachel a brotherly smile. "The ordinary Englishman's no threat to your patriot cause, especially way down here in East Florida. They're like Uncle Lamech here, people who want a chance to build a life in a new place."

"Yes, so you both have said. Never mind that they will all be willing to join a militia in support of the Crown." Rachel would not add that she had never wanted a life in a new place. Papa had announced she would accompany him to East Florida, and that was that. With a sigh, she ambled across the room toward the material display and ran a finger over a bolt of fabric. "Papa, will you let me take a length of this mosquito netting to protect Sadie's baby? He's a mass of bites this morning, poor boy."

"And how's Sadie to pay for it, might I ask?" Papa had returned to his accounting and now peered at her over his reading spectacles, eyes narrowed.

Rachel lifted her chin and stared back, mirroring

his look. She had backed down in the discussion about the English, but she would not back down in this matter. For countless seconds, she faced his "captain" glare that had always made his whalers tremble.

Jamie coughed and hummed a flat tune, then drummed his fingers on the counter. The hammers of the men working on the living quarters echoed above them. A bird of some sort sent out a plaintive cry in the marshes behind the store.

Papa did not flinch, nor did Rachel.

"If you do it for the least of these—" she began.

Papa slammed his logbook shut. "What shall I do with ye, my girl? Given yer head, ye'd give away the entire store."

Pulling the bolt from the display, Rachel hurried to his side and placed a kiss on his gray-stubbled cheek. "Perhaps Mr. Moberly will make more purchases with his gold guineas. That should balance everything out."

She glanced at Jamie, whose face had reddened in an obvious attempt to stifle his amusement. She never would have put up such a fight in front of any other of Papa's crew. Measuring out an appropriate length of the sheer material, she cut, folded and wrapped it. "May I take it over right away?"

"There's a limit to my surrender, daughter. Look." Scowling, he pointed out the window. "Customers are headed this way. Ye can take it when ye go for yer noon meal." His expression softened. "Have ye noticed the mosquitoes come out in the evening? The tyke will be fine until then."

"Thank you, Papa."

Jamie left, and customers entered to shop. Several soldiers came to purchase tobacco, and one bought a new pipe. An Indian family, speaking in their Timucuan language, studied the various wares and selected a large cast-iron pot. The tanner's wife bought a box of tea. One of the slatterns who followed the soldiers eyed the finer fabrics with a longing eye. Repulsed by her sweaty smell but also filled with pity, Rachel watched the woman move lazily among the displays. Papa greeted one and all as if they were old friends, even taking time to learn a few native words from the Indians.

The morning passed quickly, and soon Papa gave Rachel a nod. She placed her bonnet over her mobcap, fetched the wrapped mosquito netting, and then hastened out the door.

The sun stood at its zenith like an angry potentate pouring fiery wrath upon all who dared to venture beneath him. Perspiration slid down Rachel's face and body, stinging her eyes and dampening everything she wore. Perhaps she should ask Jamie to bring her a new parasol from London, for her old one was bent and tattered.

As she passed the large yard beside the inn, she heard a commotion—Sadie's shrill voice screeched for help above the chaotic squawking of chickens and geese. Rachel hurried around the corner of the clapboard building, where she saw the young woman tussling with a soldier amidst the innkeeper's fowls, a plump goose the object of their struggle.

"Let 'er go, ya blunderhead." Sadie tried to kick the red-uniformed man, without success. "Ya've no right to take 'er."

The man cursed and continued to grasp the goose's neck. "Gi' way, girl. I've a right as the king's soldier to take what I need."

"Ya've got yer own provisions in the regiment," cried Sadie.

Her sob cut into Rachel's heart, stirring memories of the time a brutish soldier invaded her sister's house and took food from the children's plates. Then he had threatened Rachel and Susanna with something far worse. Enraged by the recollection, she dashed toward the altercation.

"Brazen wench, let go." The soldier cuffed Sadie on the face, but though she cried out, she held on to the goose.

"Stop it, you horrid monster." Rachel dropped her package and, with hardly a thought of what she was doing, grabbed a length of wood from the nearby woodpile and slammed it into the man's ear. Her hands stung from the blow, and she dropped the weapon as his tall, black leather cap flew to the ground.

"Ow!" He grabbed his ear and released the now-dead beast. Turning to Rachel, he glared at her with blazing eyes and took a menacing step toward her.

Lord, what have I done? Terror gripped her, and she searched for an escape.

But he glanced beyond her and stopped.

"What's all this?" A familiar English voice resounded with authority behind her.

Rachel turned to see Mr. Moberly astride his horse, staring down his aristocratic nose at the scene. His gray eyes flashed like a shining rapier in the shadow of his broad-brimmed hat. Despite the day's heat, a strange shiver swept through her body.

"Good thing ya come along, gov'ner." The soldier tugged at a lock of his hair in an obeisant gesture. "This wench refuses me a soldier's right to provision, and this 'un…" He waved at Rachel. "She done assaulted a king's soldier, is what she done." He stepped toward her as if about to return the blow. "'Tis a hangin' offense."

"Take another step—" Moberly bent forward and pointed his riding crop at the soldier "—and you'll be the one to hang."

The man stopped, his eyes wide. Rachel could see his fear in his slack-jaw expression. Did Moberly really have that kind of power?

"Chiveys, gov'ner," Sadie cried, "he just killed one o' Ma's brood geese."

"I've a right to take provision as needed." The soldier retrieved his tall cap and shook off the sand clinging to it. He winced as he placed it above his bloody ear.

"I shall speak to Major Brigham about the matter." Moberly dismounted. "I shall also see he requires you to repay the innkeeper for the loss of his goose."

"Repay—?"

"Are you contradicting me?" Moberly's stately posture forestalled any appeal.

"No, sir, yer lordship." The man stood straight and lifted his hand into a salute.

"What is your name, private?"

"Buckner, sir."

"Well, now, Buckner, get back to your duty." Moberly pointed the riding crop toward the street.

"Yes, sir." The soldier hastened around the corner of the inn and disappeared from sight.

Moberly stepped near Sadie, and his stern expression softened. "Hurry to pluck and dress it, girl, so it won't be a complete loss."

Her face still flushed, Sadie cast a confused look at Rachel and then at Moberly. "Aye, sir. I'll do that." She curtsied to each of them. "Thank you, miss." And away she dashed.

Moberly now gave Rachel a gentle smile, and she thought the heat might flatten her on the spot. Gratitude for his rescue warred within her heart against her scorn for all things English.

"I must say, Miss Folger, I have never seen a lady quite so, um, bold in defense of a less fortunate soul." His gray eyes twinkled. "But I must also say I quite admire you for it."

"Indeed? I did no more nor less than the citizens of Lexington and Concord this past month when your British soldiers attacked them." Rachel could not believe her own words. The man had just saved her from assault.

Puzzlement swept across his face, as if he had no idea of the matter. "I beg your pardon?" Then his eyebrows raised in clear comprehension. "Ah. I see. May I surmise you favor the cause of the thirteen dissenting colonies?" His thoughtful expression held no condemnation or disdain.

Before she could respond, the injury to her left hand began to sting, and she looked down to see several splinters embedded in her bloody palm.

"Why, Miss Folger, you've been wounded in battle." He stepped forward and seized her hand to inspect it. A frown creased his forehead. "I shall send my personal physician immediately to make certain no infection sets in. If left untended, this sort of wound can become quite serious, especially here in the tropics." He drew a white silk handkerchief from his waistcoat and wrapped it around the injury. "This should protect it until he arrives."

Shame dug into her. Had she misjudged this man? She pulled her hand away.

"Thank you, sir, but please don't trouble yourself." She tried to brush past him, but his large horse stood in the way. Confusion filled her. She spied the forgotten package of material.

Anticipating her direction, he hastened to retrieve it and held it out.

"Yours?"

"Yes." She took it in her uninjured hand. "Thank you."

"May I escort you to your destination?"

Rachel's pulse raced. A hundred arguments warred within her, yet she felt a strange, strong impulse to accept. Was this nudging from the Lord? "Yes. Thank you. To the inn."

He offered his arm, and she set her bandaged hand on it, wincing slightly at the pain.

"You must accept my apology for that soldier's conduct." Mr. Moberly's tone rang sincere, reinforced by his troubled frown. "I shall speak to his commander. You may trust me when I promise we shall have no conflict between citizenry and soldiers here in St. Johns Settlement."

Once again, the day's heat almost proved her undoing. *Lord, I've judged this man without knowing anything about him. That's nothing less than a sin. Please forgive me.*

They walked to the front of the inn, and Mr. Moberly tethered his horse to a post. "Are you always this quiet?" His tone betrayed amusement.

She again took his offered arm. "Papa would say I am all too loquacious."

"Ah, I see. Then I shall have to spend more time in your company to ascertain who the true Miss Folger is."

As they passed through the open door, his posture transformed from relaxed to imperious. He surveyed the taproom, where a half-dozen soldiers sat drinking. Then, in a voice raised so they could hear, he said, "Miss Folger, you and your father may count me as your friend. If you need anything at all, send one of these fellows to my plantation." He waved his riding crop toward the soldiers. "And you shall have it posthaste." He took her injured hand and placed a gentlemanly kiss on it. "Good day, dear lady."

Filled with wonder, Rachel watched him depart. A good Englishman. An aristocrat who treated her with dignity. Who, through one simple sentence or two, had made clear to these brigands that she and Papa must be respected. Surely the word would pass through the entire regiment, and her fears of mistreatment could be set aside.

"Chiveys, Miss Folger, what do you think o' that?" Sadie stood at her elbow. "The gov'ner's a right decent fellow, ain't 'e?"

Rachel shook off her stupor. "Why, yes, Sadie. I do believe you are right."

Frederick barely noticed the landscape as he rode slowly back to his plantation. How could one brief encounter with a dark-eyed beauty answer all his questions about the sort of woman he must marry?

He had caught a glimpse of the brawl behind the inn, not realizing who was involved, and had ridden around the building in time to see Miss Folger strike the soldier. In that instant, he knew two things. First, her courage could not be matched in any titled young lady he had known in his life. Second, his position as magistrate demanded that he protect this young woman from the irate soldier. Because of the troubles up north, Major Brigham might be offended by Frederick's actions, but he would stand by them.

And then there was a third thing he knew…and felt as deeply as any truth he had ever encountered. He did not need to ask Miss Folger for advice on the type of young lady to marry, for she herself embodied everything he could ever desire: beauty, spirit, wit, pluck and more. The list seemed endless.

Was he mad? Possibly. Impetuous? No doubt. Yet, at this moment, Frederick's heart felt so light, he longed to turn Essex back to the settlement, where he might spend more time in Miss Folger's delightful company.

But that whimsical impulse was cut short by the specter of Oliver and his lies to Father. He had invented an imaginary female at the Oswald Plantation. Well, now Frederick's attention had been captured by a real, living young lady, and he must do all within his power to keep Oliver from destroying his chances with her... and from telling Father about her.

Chapter Four

"Oh, Señorita Rachel, this lace, it is very beautiful." Inez carefully stitched the delicate white trim to the neckline of the blue gauze gown. "Your papa, he is generous to make such expense for you." Her dark eyes shone with appreciation for the fabric. "He wants you to look nice for the party, *si?*"

Rachel sat beside her newly hired servant in the corner of the store and hemmed the gown's striped panniers. Inez had already moved into the kitchen house behind the store and awaited the day when Rachel and Papa would take up residence in their apartment over the store. When he announced he had hired someone to cook and launder for them, Rachel had been delighted and more than a little surprised at his willingness to bear such an expense.

Now Papa had once again set aside his frugal ways for the party and insisted she use an expensive fabric. Rachel didn't know what to make of his interest in her clothing. Perhaps her claim to have no appropriate gown for the party wounded his pride, especially spoken in front of Mr. Moberly.

"So you think *el patrón's* fiza…" Inez wrinkled her forehead, then shrugged. "Fiza-something."

"His physician?" Rachel asked.

"*Si,* the fiz-iz-cion." Inez laughed, and the age lines around her eyes deepened. "The one who fix your hand. He will be at the party, no? This one, he is not married, is nice to look at, is not so old for—" She gave Rachel a sly look. "Hmm. Maybe Inez say too much?"

"Not at all. You may speak freely when you and I are alone." Rachel studied her stitches to make certain they gathered the delicate fabric without puckering it. "But perhaps you don't understand the English. Dr. Wellsey is a member of the gentry and no doubt regards himself as being above a shopkeeper's daughter. For my part, I would not consider receiving the attentions of an Englishman."

"No?" Inez stared at her. "You do not like the English?" She busied herself with the lace again, muttering to herself in Spanish.

"What is it, Inez?"

"Have we not agreed, señorita, *Dios* has love for every man? *Jesu Christo,* He die for every man?"

"Yes, of course."

"Then if we do not like the English, is the love of *Dios* in us?" Maternal warmth glowed in Inez's eyes. "Does He not say to love others as He love us?"

Rachel concentrated on her work without answering. Inez had not abused her freedom to speak her thoughts, and her words conveyed great wisdom.

In truth, Rachel had hated the English for as long as she could remember. They stole from the colonists, both in taxes and in seizing men and property for their own use. Yet she had not considered that God might love them, as He did every soul. Her Quaker mother would be disappointed in her, for she had taught Rachel the Bible verse Inez quoted.

The jangle of the bell over the front door startled her from her thoughts.

"Hello, is anyone here?" Mr. Moberly stood inside the door, hat in hand, blinking his eyes as everyone did to adjust to the dimmer store light after being out in the sun.

"Yes, sir." Rachel set aside her sewing and hurried to greet him. "How may I help you?"

"Miss Folger." His smile seemed almost boyish. "Good afternoon."

"Yes, sir. How may I help you?" *You just asked him that.* She gazed up into his dark gray eyes, transfixed by the intense look he returned. At the memory of his rescuing her from the soldier, she felt her cheeks grow warm. Now, as then, she thought perhaps some Englishmen might not be purely evil. His black hair was swept back in a queue, but one stray lock curled over his forehead like an unruly, and utterly charming, black sheep.

"I, well, um," he said, "I wondered how your father's business is faring. I have been telling everyone they should patronize your store. Even written the news of your establishment to other plantations along the St. Johns River. Settlers have done without many necessities and nearly all luxuries here in the wilderness and waited a long while for a proper mercantile close by…" He pursed his lips. "Now who's being too loquacious?"

Rachel laughed. Her face grew hotter. To think he had recalled her silly comment. "Papa will be pleased to hear that you are, um, pleased."

"Yes." He glanced around the store and then back at her. "Ah, I should have asked straightaway. How is your hand?" His right hand moved toward her slightly, then retracted, as if he would take her injured one but thought better of it. "Did Dr. Wellsey serve you...well?" He grinned.

"Oh, indeed, he did." Forbidding herself to laugh again, Rachel flexed her fingers to show the hand was on its way to complete recovery. "Although I must say he seemed to regard my little injury as a scientific experiment." The pleasant young doctor had never once looked at her face and seemed disappointed at the ease with which the splinters came out. "But, gracious, the smell of that salve." She waved her hand beneath her nose at the memory.

"Dreadful stuff, I agree." Mr. Moberly gave her a comical frown. "Yes, the good doctor is a serious scientist. But a competent physician must be, do you not think?"

"Why, I've never considered—"

"What's this?" Papa's voice boomed from behind Rachel as he entered from the back room. "Ah, Mr. Moberly. What can I do for ye today?"

Jamie followed close behind Papa and raised an eyebrow to question Rachel. She shrugged one shoulder and hoped Mr. Moberly did not see their silent communication. For some strange reason, she felt an urge to remind the Englishman that Jamie was her cousin, not a suitor. But why should he care about such things?

"Good afternoon, Mr. Folger." Mr. Moberly extended his hand. "Mrs. Winthrop has sent me for thread and, oh, several other items. I can't recall them all." He pulled a crumpled paper from his pocket and handed it to Rachel. "Do say you have everything she wrote down, Miss Folger, so I may continue to recommend this establishment for its many and varied wares."

"Yes, sir." Rachel walked to the counter and pressed the paper flat with her hand so she could read it. Mr. Moberly reminded her of a little boy who had not yet learned to be entirely neat, but she found it charming. Darning needles, twenty ells each of red and blue bunting, cinnamon, black pepper, several shades of thread, plus other needs. She gathered the items on the front counter but kept her ears open to the men's lively conversation.

"I did not know if I would see you again, Captain Templeton." Mr. Moberly's tone was jovial, as if chatting with an old friend. "Were you not to sail to England this week?"

"I'll sail day after tomorrow, weather permitting." Jamie's expression brightened to match Mr. Moberly's. "But since you've been here for some time, I hoped to ask your advice about the merchandise I should bring from London."

"Of course." Mr. Moberly clapped Jamie on the shoulder. "This is truly fortuitous. We have had many newcomers whose needs we failed to anticipate. I shall make a list for you."

"Very good." Jamie grinned. "List as you will, and I'll obtain it. And if you give me a letter of introduction, I shall be pleased to call upon any of your associates for you."

"I shall prepare that letter this very day. Do you have time to ride to my plantation this afternoon?"

"Sir, that is most agreeable." The last reservation fled from Jamie's expression, replaced by a broad smile.

"Excellent." Mr. Moberly perused several items on display: knives, flintlock pistols, a barrel of cast-iron nails. "While I am here, I should like to enlist your assistance."

Rachel's ears tingled, and she leaned closer to the men.

"Ask as ye will, sir," Papa said.

"A dissident agitator has entered our settlement and tried to stir up sympathy for the rebellion in Massachusetts and the other colonies." Mr. Moberly toyed with a length of rope coiled for sale. "The chap slips into the Wild Boar Inn or Brown's Tavern and makes a few remarks while men are in their cups, then slips away before anyone can apprehend him."

Rachel's heart raced. Another patriot, right here in St. Johns! She must learn his identity and try to contact him.

"Of course, no man here is of that mind." Mr. Moberly settled a placid smile on Papa and Jamie.

"Not that I've discerned," Papa said.

"Certainly not." Jamie sent Rachel a wárning scowl. She wrinkled her nose in return.

"In any event, a reward awaits the man who can supply any information leading to his apprehension."

The men continued their business discussion, and by the time Rachel had assembled and packaged all of Mr. Moberly's purchases, they seemed to be lifelong friends. The gentleman paid Papa, bowed to her and afterward left the store.

"Don't that beat all?" Papa crossed his arms and watched Mr. Moberly leave. "Looks like the path is smooth before us."

"To be sure." Jamie sent a glance Rachel's way. "With Moberly's letters, we'll have access to the best products London can offer."

"Indeed we will." Papa moved behind the counter and pulled out a logbook. "Now let's take a look at those figures."

The two men hovered over the book and continued their discussion of Jamie's imminent voyage. To Rachel's annoyance, they never once mentioned the dissident agitator.

She wished they would include her in their consultations, but most often, they shooed her away. Her heart torn between wanting Mr. Moberly to come back and longing to go find the patriot right away, she returned to her corner. Inez was stitching the last inches of lace to the gown's neckline, and Rachel resumed her own work. With their shoulders almost touching, Rachel felt Inez shake and looked over to see the older woman working to hide her mirth.

"Shh. What is it?" Rachel glanced toward Papa. As kindhearted as he was, he had no patience with chatty or giggling servants.

Inez leaned toward her and whispered, "Señorita, I think we both make mistake."

"Oh?"

"*Sí*. My mistake is thinking the physician is for you. No, no. It is *el patrón* who admires my mistress, and more than a little."

"What nonsense. Mr. Moberly is an English aristocrat. He would never consider...*admiring* me." Rachel sniffed at the thought of it. "Furthermore, as I said before, I would never receive the attentions of an Englishman."

"Mmm—mmm." Inez hummed softly. "From the happiness I see in your eyes, mistress, you have receive them whether you wish it or not."

Rachel forced herself to frown. "What nonsense."

But if the notion were truly nonsense, why had her face felt hot the entire time the gentleman spoke to her? Why had she felt keen disappointment when Papa and Jamie entered the store? And why did her heart now pound as if trying to leap from her chest?

Nonsense. Utter nonsense.

* * *

While Mrs. Winthrop prepared a list of household needs, Frederick carefully penned the letter to Father recommending Captain James Templeton as a worthy business associate. While he had nothing to lose after Father's last correspondence, he did not wish to further anger him. Despite a bit of rusticity, Templeton had an air about him that Father should admire, as one might esteem a capable horse handler or even a household steward. The captain possessed clear eyes that seemed to hold no hidden motives, unlike Oliver, who had always been a bit sly.

How ironic that Frederick had never noticed Oliver's wiliness. Yet since he had read Father's revealing letter, Frederick began to recall many instances where his innocent antics had brought unwarranted censure. But only when Oliver was involved.

Perhaps he was mad to entrust to Templeton the rebuilding of his own reputation with Father. But at this point, the captain's good reference was all he had.

Templeton arrived midafternoon. Frederick met him in the drawing room and welcomed him like a brother.

"You've a fine house, sir." The captain surveyed the room with interest, but no envy clouded his tone or expression. "I've often thought to build a house, but the sea's been my home since boyhood. I don't know if I could abide solid ground beneath me for too long."

"You may have the sea, sir. I gladly welcomed the feel of that solid ground after my stormy voyage across the Atlantic to East Florida."

They both chuckled, but before Templeton could offer a rejoinder, Oliver sauntered into the room. Frederick reluctantly made introductions.

"Well, captain," Oliver said, "what brings you to our humble home?"

Templeton's eyes narrowed for an instant, but he seemed to purposefully brighten his expression. "Just a bit of private business with Mr. Moberly."

Frederick withheld a laugh. His new friend was no fool. How quickly he had seen through Oliver's facade.

"Then let us adjourn to my study." Frederick enjoyed the dark look on Oliver's face. "You will excuse us, Oliver."

"Of course." Oliver's terse tone came through clenched teeth.

Once in the study with the door closed, Templeton stared at Frederick, an earnest look in his eyes. "Moberly, you don't know me well, but let me advise you not to trust Corwin." He gave his head a quick shake. "Something about him—"

"Yes, I agree." To think this man had seen it in less than five minutes. Perhaps as first mate to Captain Folger and now a captain himself, he had honed his skills in human understanding, whereas Frederick had taken a place of leadership only a few short years ago. He still had much to learn.

He sat at his desk, retrieved his letters and lists, and checked them once more to be sure all was in order before applying his seal. "Thank you for taking these to my family. I hope the introduction will serve us both well."

"I'm honored that you trust me." Seated opposite him, Templeton took them in hand, all the while appearing to search for words. "I sense you are a trustworthy man, too, Moberly, and therefore I must address a subject of some concern."

Frederick swallowed hard. He wanted to be open

with this man, but he was so used to posing to achieve advantage that he hardly knew how to be genuine. Perhaps in that manner he had been playing the same game as Oliver. But at least he had never betrayed anyone.

"Say on, friend." He felt as if he had just unlocked his soul.

Templeton's brown eyes bored into his. "My cousin Rachel, Miss Folger, is like a sister to me. Captain Folger raised us together, and I couldn't love a sister by birth any more than I love her." He studied the letters in his hand, yet seemed not to see them. Again, he stared at Frederick. "If harm of any sort should come to her, whether to her person or to her heart, I'd have to require it of the man responsible for her grief."

Frederick's lower jaw fell slack, and he closed it as casually as possible while overcoming his shock. "I find Miss Folger to be a remarkable young lady, one whom I admire far too much to grieve in any way." He offered a half smile. "You may count on me in your absence to require it of anyone who might think to harm her."

Templeton's gaze softened. "I believe you."

An unfamiliar sense of comradeship filled Frederick's chest. Before he could speak his gratitude, Templeton added, "I hope Lord Bennington knows what an extraordinary job you've done in developing St. Johns Settlement. If he doesn't know it now, he will after I've finished talking with him."

Again warmth filled Frederick almost to bursting. "I am grateful, captain, more than you can know."

They stood, shook hands, and then proceeded to the front of the house. After another handshake, Templeton set his hand on Frederick's shoulder.

"Please know that the Almighty will be receiving my frequent petitions on your behalf."

Frederick coughed away the emotion that threatened to overwhelm him. "And I shall pray for you, as well." An onlooker might think them lifelong friends. "God speed you on your way."

He stood on the porch and watched Templeton ride away on a lop-eared mule. The chap did not ride any better than Frederick kept his footing on a ship. But their new friendship soothed away some of the ache left by Oliver's betrayal.

As if conjured by his thoughts, Oliver appeared beside him on the porch.

"Hmm. I wonder if his departure will put a stop to the seditious gossip in the taverns."

Frederick would have struck him if the suggestion had not sent a sting of suspicion through his chest.

Chapter Five

"Papa, the heel of my shoe has loosened." Rachel would not mention that she had helped it to that condition. "May I go to the cobbler?"

Seated behind the store counter, he took off his spectacles and peered over his logbook. "Aye, 'tis best not to delay such repairs, else it'll cost more. We've no customers, so hurry along." He glanced down the length of her skirt, which covered her shoes, and wrinkled his forehead.

For a moment, Rachel thought he might have comprehended her ruse. She shifted from one hidden foot to the other and gave him a bright smile. "Thank you. I shall return as quickly as possible." She turned to go before he could change his mind.

"Avast." He stood and crossed his arms.

"Yes, sir?" Her pulse quickened.

"Whilst ye're there, see if the cobbler can make ye some slippers to match yer new gown." From his tone, he could have been ordering her to swab the deck. He sat down, put on his spectacles and studied the logbook again.

Yet his words brought a blush of confusion and shame to Rachel's cheeks. "Slippers?"

"Aye." He did not look up. "I'll not have ye tramp through a fancy plantation house in yer old shoes."

Surprised again by his generosity, she nonetheless hurried from the store and up the street, glancing at the various structures as she passed. While much needed to be done to transform the settlement into a true town, the streets had been laid out and cleared, and tabby foundations now supported numerous wooden buildings in various stages of completion.

In the distance, Rachel noticed a group of people loitering in the village's common. One tall figure in a wide-brimmed hat stood above the crowd. Mr. Moberly! Her feet—and her heart—tried to carry her toward the gathering, but she forced herself to turn aside at the cobbler's building two blocks from Papa's store.

As she stepped inside, the heavy smell of oiled leather almost pushed her back into the street. She inhaled shallow breaths and glanced around the small front room, where lasts, buckles, buttons, needles and countless other shoemaking supplies covered three tables.

The middle-aged cobbler looked up from his work and acknowledged her with a nod. "Miss Folger, what can we do for you today?" He rose to greet her.

"Good morning, Mr. Shoemaker. Would you be so kind as to fix my heel?" She slipped it off and held it out.

He turned it in his hands. "Tsk. Looks like someone tried to pry the heel off with a nail." Carrying it back to his workbench, he began his repairs.

Rachel moved across the bench from him. "Is Mrs. Shoemaker well?"

"Yes, thank you. She and the children are working in the kitchen house. Shall I call her?"

"No. No doubt she is too busy to chat." Rachel glanced around and saw no fabric for slippers, but another matter held priority. "Tell me, sir, what prompted your removal from Savannah to this wilderness? Surely the city had sufficient work for a cobbler."

"Humph. Let those rebels look to their own feet." He hammered her shoe with considerable force. "After they tarred and feathered Judge Morgan for speaking against their wicked rebellion, any sensible man would take his family elsewhere." He held up the repaired shoe and rubbed it with an oil-stained cloth. "Just let those rebels dare come to East Florida. We're raising a militia here, and there'll be no mercy for any who rise up against the Crown."

Rachel gulped back a tart reply. Clearly this man was not the unknown patriot seeking to stir up sympathy for the cause. She would have taken her shoe and left, but Papa would only send her back. Ordering the slippers helped her collect her emotions. Mr. Shoemaker agreed to send his oldest daughter to Papa's store for the needed fabric, and the two men would negotiate the payments.

Glad to leave the stuffy shop, she breathed in the warm, fresh breeze drifting down the street. To her right, loud voices drew her attention to the common. She glanced at Papa's store and back toward the crowd. Once again her feet seemed determined to carry her there. This time she did not deny the impulse.

To her relief, several women from the settlement and nearby plantations stood among the men on the newly planted grass poking through the dark, sandy soil. She stayed at the edge of the crowd, surprised to see Mr. Moberly seated at a rough table beneath a spreading oak tree. He was writing in a leather-bound ledger. So this was how he dispensed his duties as magistrate.

Rachel's feet once again seemed to move of their own will, drawing her closer to him.

In front of Mr. Moberly's table stood a barefoot young man in rags with his hands tied behind his back and fear in his eyes. Nearby stood a man whom Rachel recognized as the owner of a small plantation close to the village. He held in his arms a plump pink piglet that wiggled and squealed until he covered it with a burlap bag.

Laughter and rude comments from the crowd nearly sent Rachel on her way, but she could not bring herself to leave. Surely the Lord had directed her steps to this place so she might learn more about Mr. Moberly through his judgments.

She noticed two red-coated soldiers beside a hangman's noose that dangled from a branch of the vast tree, and an icy shiver ran through her from head to toe. Several yards away, out in the sun, newly made wooden stocks suggested a less severe sentence. But in this East Florida heat, who could endure even that?

A storm of emotions swirled through Rachel. The young man must have stolen the piglet. Such a crime must not go unpunished. Praying for justice and mercy, she found herself barely able to breathe.

Frederick felt the urge to squirm like the hapless young man who stood bound and trembling before him. He hated holding court, hated making judgments, hated having the eyes of everyone in the settlement look to him for wisdom. Why Father had arranged for him to be the magistrate, he could not guess. And with Oliver leaning against the trunk of the oak tree, arms crossed and chin lifted, Frederick felt certain whatever he did would be reported to the earl…and would be wrong.

Heretofore, the disputes had been easy to solve: uncertain boundary lines, drunken brawling, that sort of nonsense. But the theft of a pig must be dealt with severely. In England this thief most likely would be hanged. Surely in this remote part of East Florida, where men sometimes were forced to do desperate things in order to survive, English law need not be enforced to its fullest extent. And after reading of former Governor Grant's harsh decision in a similar case where he sentenced the hapless servant to death by hanging, Frederick shrank from inflicting such an unforgiving sentence. Should a Christian not offer mercy and redemption to the miscreant?

Frederick surveyed the crowd, glad that the broad brim of his hat shielded his eyes from their view. He kept his mouth in a grim line and assumed a stiff, formal posture. In the corner of his eye, he saw Miss Folger approach, and his heart sank. He must not look at her, must not care what she thought of his coming decision. He must forget her, forget Father, forget Oliver, forget everything but the men in conflict before him.

Lord, grant me wisdom as You have promised in the Holy Scriptures.

"Mr. Baker, come forward." Frederick beckoned the pig's owner.

Shifting the sack holding the pig, the man snatched off his hat and then stepped up to the table beside the accused. "Yes, sir."

"This is your indentured servant, John Gilbert? And that is your pig?" Frederick pointed to the sack.

"Yes, sir."

Frederick noticed that Baker's expression held more worry than anger. Interesting. Did he hope for leniency or vengeance?

"Now, John, you have been accused of stealing this pig. Did you do it?"

Misery clouded the lad's blue eyes. "Aye, sir. 'Twas not just fer meself. Mr. Baker don't feed us aught but gruel. A man's gotta have meat now and then or he can't work the land."

Frederick saw color rush to Baker's cheeks. He did not deny the charge.

Lord, grant me the wisdom of Solomon. Frederick recalled that Governor Grant had required one man under judgment to hang his more blameworthy friends.

"Well, Mr. Baker, this man belongs to you to do with as you will. If you want him hanged, you will do it yourself." Frederick pointed his quill pen toward the noose hanging from the oak tree.

A great gasp and much murmuring rose from the crowd, some approving, some grumbling. Frederick would not permit himself to look at Miss Folger to see what her reaction might be.

"Now, Mr. Moberly, sir," Mr. Baker said, "if I hang him, I'm out a servant to work my land. I paid his fare to these shores, and he owes me six more years."

Frederick shrugged. "Then what do you consider a just punishment?"

Baker scratched his head. He glanced toward the stocks. "Forty lashes and a week in the stocks should teach 'im a lesson."

And kill him in the process. Frederick set down his quill and crossed his arms over his chest. "Three days in the stocks and ten lashes afterward. And you will scourge him yourself."

Baker's posture slumped, and he hung his head. After several moments, he gave John Gilbert a sidelong glance, then raised his eyes to Frederick. "That'll do justice. Thank you, sir."

The crowd burst into cheers and applause. John Gilbert slumped to the ground on his knees. "God bless ya, Mr. Moberly, sir. God bless ya."

Emotion flooded Frederick's chest, but he managed a gruff dismissal. "Are there other quarrels?"

With none coming forward, Frederick made notes in his ledger, blotted the ink, and closed the book. As the crowd dispersed, he cast a hasty glance at Miss Folger and barely contained a smile. Her head was tilted prettily, and a look of wonder filled her lovely face. Once again he swallowed a rush of emotion. Whether or not his judgment had been correct, her obvious approval was all he required.

Rachel knew she must turn and walk away like the others, but her feet refused to move. To her relief, Mr. Moberly approached her. She struggled to think of a Scripture verse to relate to him in praise of his decision. But she could think only of some words from Shakespeare that nonetheless imparted an eternal truth: *The quality of mercy is not strained. It droppeth as the gentle rain from heaven upon the place beneath. It is twice blest: It blesseth him that gives and him that takes.*

"Miss Folger." Mr. Moberly gave her that boyish smile of his that belied his august position. "What brings you to the common on this lovely day?"

Unable to meet his gaze, she stared down at his well-polished black boots, now covered with sand. "Just a trip to the cobbler."

"Ah. And did Mr. Shoemaker serve you well?"

She looked up to see a twinkle in his gray eyes. "Indeed he did." At least with her shoe.

"Very good." He nodded his approval. "If I am not being too bold, may I escort you to your father's mercantile?"

Happiness swept through her. On the way, she could recite her Shakespeare to compliment his judgment. "That would be—"

"Moberly." Mr. Corwin approached them with a determined stride. He barely glanced at Rachel. "The tavern keeper had a visit from that rabble-rouser last evening. He can give us a description."

Mr. Moberly drew in his lips and shot a cross look at his friend. "I am certain he can wait for an hour."

Rachel's heart thumped wildly. The patriot was still at work.

"No, he cannot wait." Mr. Corwin's frown matched Mr. Moberly's. "He must meet his suppliers on the coast before nightfall."

Mr. Moberly blew out a cross sigh. "Miss Folger, will you forgive me?"

"Of course." A riot of confusion filled her mind. How could she long to become better acquainted with this gentleman when he represented everything she opposed?

For the briefest moment, she thought to delay him so he would miss learning more about the patriot. Or she could follow him and try to discern the man's identity herself. But both actions would be shocking improprieties. She would wait until next Saturday's party at Mr. Moberly's plantation. Surely there she would learn something useful to the revolution.

Chapter Six

"Are you certain I should wear this one?" Frederick studied his reflection in the bedroom mirror while his manservant fussed with the turned back tails of the gray linen coat. "Why not the red brocade?"

"Sir, if you will permit me, the red most assuredly is your finest coat." Summerlin brushed lint from the gray garment's padded shoulders. "However, I despair that you would waste it on these rustics." His lip curled. "Should you not save it for the day when you are called once again to the capital of this wilderness?"

Frederick shot him a disapproving glance in the mirror, but Summerlin had shifted his attention to the lace at Frederick's cuffs. Never mind. He hated to scold the old fellow, who had been ordered by Frederick's father to leave the comforts of London and come to East Florida, a crushing change for a man in his fifties. Perhaps he was another spy like Oliver, sent to make certain Frederick brought no scandal upon the family, as his brothers had. But, white hair and stooped shoulders notwithstanding, Summerlin's talents as a valet could not be matched.

"Very well. I shall accept your choice of attire but

not your attitude toward my guests." Frederick kept his tone soft. "Some of these 'rustics' can be quite charming, not to mention intelligent and clever at business."

Summerlin straightened in his odd way and stared at Frederick. "Charming, sir? Oh, dear. Has some young lady caught my master's eye?" The clarity in his pale blue eyes and the half smile at the corner of his thin lips removed any doubts about where his loyalty lay. "Well, then, perhaps the red—"

"No, this will do." Frederick breathed in the orange and bergamot cologne Summerlin had concocted for him. "Now that I think of it, if I were to dress as for an audience with the governor, my clothing might intimidate my guests. Since my purpose is to ensure their loyalty to the Crown and foster a feeling of community, I should avoid strutting before them like a peacock."

"Ah, well said, young sir." Approval emanated from Summerlin's eyes such as Frederick had longed for in vain from his father. "Lady Bennington would be proud."

Summerlin's words further encouraged him. Indeed, Mother would understand his choice of clothes, despite her own exquisite wardrobe, for she always sought to make even the lowliest of her guests comfortable.

"Forgive me, sir, for disparaging your new friends." Summerlin glanced over his shoulder toward the closed bedroom door and bent toward Frederick with a confidential air. "I am your servant in all things."

Frederick mirrored his move. "Thank you. But there will be no trysts. The young lady will be courted properly." He caught Summerlin's gaze. "Only time will tell, of course, but I believe Miss Folger is all I could wish for in a wife."

Serene comprehension washed over Summerlin's

face, softening his pale wrinkles. "As I said, sir, I am your servant in all things."

A sharp rap sounded on the door. "Moberly, your guests are arriving." Oliver's tone sounded almost jovial.

Summerlin's expression flickered with distaste for the briefest instant before giving way to his customary formal air. In that half second, Frederick knew without doubt that his devoted servant had purposely left Oliver's letter on his desk, and warmth filled his chest, as it had over Templeton's friendship.

Father would sneer at his idea of calling these lower-class men "friends," but Frederick could consider them nothing less. And how relieved he had been to discover that Templeton was not the agitator, as Corwin had suggested.

"Coming, Corwin." Frederick strode toward the door.

Summerlin hobbled close behind, brushing lint from Frederick's coat all the way. "Have a good evening, sir."

Visions of the lovely Miss Folger danced before Frederick's eyes as he grasped the door latch. "That I shall, my good man. That I shall."

The wagon rattled along the well-packed sand and seashell road beneath a canopy of oak, pine and cypress trees. Seated beside Papa on the driver's bench, Rachel held her poorly mended parasol overhead while the late afternoon sun blasted its heat through the tree branches. Perspiration had begun to wilt her freshly pressed gown, and her curls threatened to unwind. Nevertheless, excitement filled her as she anticipated the party. She would try to discover if the patriot was among the guests. And she hoped to find the opportunity to tell Mr. Moberly how much she admired his wisdom in the case of the stolen pig.

Savoring the fragrances of the tropical forests, she studied the undergrowth for evidence of panthers, bears or poisonous snakes. Papa had assured her that this road lay too far from water for them to chance upon an alligator, yet she watched for them, as well. Several times she thought to have seen one of those fearsome dragons only to realize the object was a fallen tree.

As they rounded a stand of palm trees and a large white building came into view, Papa pointed with his wagon whip and whistled. "Thar she blows. Now that's a house, if ever I saw one."

Rachel laughed at his understatement even as her own feelings swelled. The two-storied mansion sat elevated several feet off the ground on a coquina foundation. A broad wooden porch extended across the wide front, and four white Doric columns supported the porch roof. Eight tall front windows, four on each floor, suggested airy rooms inside.

The blue and red bunting Mr. Moberly had purchased from the store now hung around the columns in a festive display. Their crisscross pattern against the white background vaguely suggested the British flag, a nettling reminder to Rachel of who ruled this land. With some effort, she dismissed the unpleasant thought. Even if their host had deliberately hung them that way, he was after all an Englishman who no doubt loved his homeland.

On the left side of the main house, smoke curled from the kitchen house's chimney, and a warm breeze carried the aroma of roasting pork.

"That'll set a man's mouth to watering." Papa steered his two mules into the semicircular drive before the

front entrance, where several liveried black grooms
awaited.

As Papa pulled the reins, one groom grasped the
harness, and another stood ready to take control of the
equipage. Rachel saw Mr. Moberly hastening from the
house, followed by a slave carrying a small white box-
step. At the sight of him, finely dressed but by no means
haughty, her heart missed a beat.

Papa jumped to the ground and hobbled to her side
of the wagon. But Mr. Moberly reached her first.

"Good evening. Welcome." Mr. Moberly shook Papa's hand. "Will you permit me to assist your daughter,
Mr. Folger?"

"As ye will." Papa bowed.

"Put it here." Mr. Moberly motioned to the slave and
indicated a spot on the ground. "Miss Folger, may I?"
He held out both white-gloved hands.

"Yes, thank you." She grasped them with pleasure,
and her face warmed as she climbed from the wagon.
Never in her life had she received such attention.

"Welcome to Bennington Plantation." Mr. Moberly
offered Rachel his arm. "Won't you please come inside?"

The entrance to the house was a welcoming red door
with an oval etched-glass window. Inside they were introduced to Mr. Moberly's cousin, a tall, older woman.

"Do come in. We're pleased to have you." Mrs. Winthrop wore a black linen gown, and her hair was pinned
back in a roll. A kind look lit her finely lined face, and
her voice resonated with sincerity.

Dr. Wellsey greeted the newcomers, and even Mr.
Corwin spoke pleasantly to them. They met a Reverend
Johnson and his wife, and the minister invited them to
his church services. To Rachel's surprise and delight,

Papa accepted. Mrs. Johnson, however, showed no interest in further conversation.

Several other couples were in attendance, and Rachel studied each face upon introduction trying to discern if any of them might be the patriot. Although everyone seemed friendly, not one person lifted an eyebrow upon meeting the Folgers from Boston. Had they not heard of the British invasion and the battles of Lexington and Concord?

While servants passed trays of hors d'oeuvres and cups of citrus punch, the men stood in a group and chatted about crops and weather. Rachel passed by as one man mentioned the "agitator" who frequented the taverns, and she glanced about the group to see if anyone appeared nervous. Not one expression informed her.

"The problem is," Mr. Moberly said, "his description does not match anyone we know along the St. Johns River or in the settlement. So, if you see a stout fellow with a long red beard, do mention it to the nearest soldier."

While the other men accepted the charge without much concern, Rachel felt a tremor of delight. Now she had one description, but perhaps there were other patriots.

She joined the other ladies, who stood on the opposite side of the drawing room making polite conversation about the challenges of living in the wilderness. The youngest woman in the group, Rachel listened more than she spoke, as propriety demanded. But she prayed for an opportunity to mention the matter close to her heart. In Boston, all the talk had been of the revolution. Here, none of the women seemed aware that their counterparts up north were sewing uniforms for their soldier husbands and weeping for those who had died for freedom's sake a short two months ago.

"Miss Folger," Mrs. Winthrop said, "I understand

your father's store has many wares we are generally deprived of here in East Florida."

"Yes, ma'am." An unexpected wave of pleasure swept through Rachel at being addressed so particularly by this kind, elegant lady. "We have been fortunate to import many useful items for sale, and my cousin will bring more from London."

The other women cooed their approval.

"Then I must come and see for myself," Mrs. Winthrop said, "for I am certain Mr. Moberly has not told me everything that would be of interest to ladies." A proper hostess, Mrs. Winthrop now turned her attention to another guest. Yet her comments put an approving stamp on both Rachel and Papa's business *and* their presence at this party.

Rachel cast a casual glance across the room and found Mr. Moberly staring at her. Her breath caught, and she hastily turned away. Her glance had also taken in the pleasant look Mr. Corwin sent her. Heat filled her cheeks. Why would these high-born gentlemen thus regard her? She recalled her mother's cautions regarding men.

Outside the drawing room, a large commotion captured everyone's attention. Servants hurried past the doorway, and soon the stout black butler entered to announce "Lady Augusta and Major Brigham."

"Moberly." Lady Augusta marched into the room with both hands extended toward him. "How good of you to invite us."

While the vicar's wife, Mrs. Johnson, released a sigh suggesting envy, Rachel almost gasped at the newcomer's appearance. Perhaps ten years older than Rachel, Lady Augusta wore a tall, white-powdered wig and a green silk gown with broad panniers and a low-cut bodice. Her face, which seemed well-formed, bore a mask-like covering of white. A single black dot, clearly not a blemish, had been placed to the right of her rouged lips, perhaps to suggest a dimple.

Rachel had seen a few ladies wear such a facade in Boston, but surely here in East Florida, the heat would melt that mask off of her face—if indeed the substance melted—before they sat down to dinner. And there stood her husband, dressed in his full regimental uniform, a glaring red banner of British pride emphasized by the haughty lift of his equine nose. Rachel shook away her distaste. She must do nothing to damage Papa's favor among these people.

Mr. Moberly did all the proper honors to welcome the two latecomers. Their rank demanded that other guests be presented to the couple, so the company filed past them. Major Brigham languidly studied every person up and down through his quizzing glass, as though trying to decide if each were some sort of miscreant. Not one guest elicited a smile or even a polite nod from the officer or his wife.

Instead, Lady Augusta looped an arm around Mr. Moberly's. "Dear Moberly," she simpered, "you must show me your house. How clever of you to bring a bit of English country charm to this horrid jungle."

"Of course, my lady. Come along. All of us shall go." Mr. Moberly waved his free hand to take in the whole room.

Lady Augusta's arrogant expression soured into a frown. Rachel could not help but wonder whether the woman had wanted to be alone with Mr. Moberly.

He guided his guests through the house's ten rooms, each of which inspired Rachel's admiration. While elegant in all appointments, the rooms were not ostentatious or gaudy. She particularly liked the library and would have been happy to spend the rest of the evening perusing the many books there. Lingering by the gentleman's desk, she thought she spied a familiar pamphlet partially covered by a book. She longed to know what Mr. Moberly had been reading, but the party moved on, and propriety required her to follow them into the hallway.

"Shall we see the grounds?" Mr. Moberly addressed Lady Augusta, for everyone understood her approval alone would permit the expedition.

"Of course. I should not wish to miss anything."

Mr. Moberly offered his arm to Lady Augusta, and Rachel noticed with surprise that Papa also offered his arm to Mrs. Winthrop.

The party moved outside, where a cool breeze from the east gave some relief as they walked along the narrow pathways among the plantation's many trees. Mr. Moberly gave commentary as he showed them the sugar mill, the fields of sugar cane, cotton and indigo, and the fragrant, flourishing orange grove. He took them to the springhouse, a covered coquina cistern that caught water flowing from the earth's depths, where a house servant dipped in a pitcher and filled goblets for the guests. From there, they moved to Bennington Creek, across which lay vast rice paddies.

As the party wended its way back to the house, Rachel noticed countless slaves, both men and women, at work in the fields, and her heart sank. How she despised slavery, an evil that had been abolished in Nantucket in 1773. Did Mr. Moberly approve of it or merely tolerate it by necessity?

Ahead Mr. Moberly was assisting Lady Augusta up the front steps. How courteously he behaved toward her, and even toward Rachel and his other guests of lower rank. But how did he treat his slaves? The men and women in the fields did not wear chains, but iron bands on some slaves' ankles suggested they were chained at night. On the other hand, the black servants in the house seemed truly devoted to Mr. Moberly. In particular, Rachel had noticed the little slave girl who sat in the corner of the drawing room to wave the palm fans. The child had gazed at Mr. Moberly with clear adoration.

But despite Mr. Moberly's frequent friendly glances in Rachel's direction during the tour of his plantation, she came to know one thing. As proven by the ease with which he socialized with Lady Augusta, any kind attentions he gave Rachel were merely the actions of a gentleman displaying good manners. If she received them with any sort of expectation, she was nothing short of a fool.

In the dining room, they sat down to supper at a long, damask-covered oak table laden with exquisite bone china, delicate etched crystal and heavy silverware with an ornate floral pattern. A vast array of delicacies graced the board.

Rachel found herself seated between Señor Garcia and Reverend Johnson, neither of whom she could imagine to be the patriot. The Spaniard seemed to prefer eating to conversation, but the vicar made pleasant conversation.

"What do you think of the alligator, Miss Folger?"

"I find it surprisingly tasty, especially seasoned with these exotic herbs. And I should far rather eat alligator than for one to eat me. As we came by skiff from the coast, a large one bumped our vessel so hard I thought we would be swamped and devoured." The memory made her shudder.

"How dreadful. Thank the Lord you were spared."

Major Brigham and Lady Augusta, on either side of Mr. Moberly, spoke to no one but their host, although the officer seemed to take an inordinate number of opportunities to peruse the company through his quizzing glass. From his perpetual frown, Rachel guessed the haughty man might be having difficulty controlling his temper, but she heard and saw nothing to suggest why. When his stare fell on her, she stared back, and his frown deepened. But what did she care about the opinions of a rude British officer and his equally rude wife?

At the end of the meal, Mr. Moberly directed his guests to the drawing room, where rows of chairs faced the magnificent pianoforte in the corner. "Mrs. Winthrop, will you entertain us with your delightful playing?"

"Now, Mr. Moberly." The lady shook her head. "Surely someone else can play better than I." She gazed around the room. "Mrs. Johnson? Señora Garcia?"

All the ladies declined, denying any musical skill.

Standing beside Rachel, Papa looked down at her with a clear question in his eyes, but she warned him off with a frown. As much as she longed to play the beautiful instrument, she refused to put herself forward in this company, where Lady Augusta might ridicule her and who knew what Major Brigham might say.

"Very well, then." Mrs. Winthrop sat down to play, and the other guests took their places.

Rachel chose an armless brocade chair in the back row where her panniers would not poof out in front. When Mr. Moberly took the chair next to her, her pulse quickened. This was the first personal attention he had given her since helping her down from the wagon. Foolish hope assaulted her, and she had no weapon with which to defend herself.

"I do hope you're enjoying yourself, Miss Folger." His eyes beamed with kind intensity. "Did you find the meal satisfactory?"

Against her best efforts, Rachel's cheeks warmed. "Oh, yes, it was—"

"Moberly." Lady Augusta appeared beside him. "I must speak with you, and I fear the noise of your aunt's playing will drown me out. May we find a quiet corner?" She waved her silk fan languidly, and her eyes sent an invitation Rachel could not discern.

"Of course, my lady." Mr. Moberly glanced at Rachel and offered an apologetic smile. "Forgive me, Miss Folger. I shall return in a moment."

"Of course." Rachel echoed his words, working hard to keep the sarcasm from her tone.

Once again, certainty shouted within her. She was nothing more than a trifle in Mr. Moberly's eyes. He would always defer to those considered well-born. Why had she ever permitted herself to think otherwise?

But just as Papa claimed the empty seat beside her, another thought quickly replaced her disappointment. She stood and moved past him, determined to discover Mr. Moberly's true character. When Papa raised his bushy eyebrows to question her, she whispered "the necessary." Instead of searching for that room, she tiptoed down the hallway just as Mr. Moberly disappeared into his study. Rachel stopped outside the door, still ajar, leaned against the wall and, heart pounding, prayed no servant would discover her eavesdropping.

Chapter Seven

"Dear Moberly, I congratulate you on a delightful supper." Lady Augusta gazed into Frederick's eyes with a doelike expression, her own dark orbs encircled by dreadful black lines and her face covered with white lead ceruse. A despicable fashion, if ever he saw one, especially when the lady seemed not to have suffered the ravages of smallpox that required such a covering.

He shifted from one foot to the other and glanced beyond her toward the open door. Brigham could come down the hallway, see them poised close to one another, and misunderstand. Worse still, Miss Folger might do the same. Where was his watchdog Corwin when he needed him? Frederick stepped back from Lady Augusta to sit on the edge of his desk, glad to distance himself from her heavy rose perfume.

"Thank you, my lady." He crossed his arms. "I hope you did not find the wild boar too gamy."

"Not at all, silly boy." She tapped his arm with her closed fan and gave him a coquettish smile. "It was delicious."

"Excellent." He tugged at his cravat. "Well, then,

was there something in particular you wished to say…
to ask…to offer complaint about?" He grinned.

The brightness in Lady Augusta's eyes dimmed, and
the coquette vanished. "I want…no, I *require* a favor
from you." Her voice wavered, and she swayed lightly.

"My lady, you have but to name it." He uncrossed
his arms, ready to catch her if she fainted.

She clutched her fan. "You must know my husband
is the bravest man in His Majesty's service, so you must
not think ill of him or tell him of my request."

Frederick leaned against the desk. "Madam, you may
depend on me."

"Thank you." She exhaled a soft sob. "Will you write
to Lord Bennington on my behalf? Ask your father
to use his influence with His Majesty to keep Major
Brigham in East Florida, say that you cannot do without him, that only he can manage the Indians, that—"

"Shh." Frederick lifted a finger to his lips. "My lady,
your voice grows louder. Surely you do not wish Major
Brigham to hear this unusual request." Nor did Frederick wish to hear it.

She sent a furtive glance toward the open door. "No,
no. He must not know." She pulled a lace handkerchief
from her sleeve and dabbed the corners of her eyes,
smudging the black kohl. "I would never ask such a
thing except for the rebellion in Boston. I cannot bear
it if Brigham is sent there to fight."

Even as understanding welled up in Frederick's chest,
another thought intruded. His brother Thomas, who
served in His Majesty's navy, would be deeply shamed
before the admiralty if his wife were to beg this favor.

"Oh, Moberly." She lifted her hands in supplication.
"Say you will write the letter." She straightened, seem-
ing to gain a measure of self-control. "In turn, I will

write a letter to *my* father asking him to look with favor upon you."

"Me? I did not know Lord Chittenden knew of my existence, much less that I am out of favor with him."

"Oh, he doesn't, and you aren't. But I have four sisters, each of whom has her own small inheritance." Her voice lilted slightly. "I know how difficult it is for a younger son to find a bride among his peers."

"I, uh, that is—"

"With your successes here in East Florida, surely His Majesty will soon bestow a knighthood upon you. And, if I ask Father, he will receive you, and you may choose among my sisters for your wife." She opened her fan, once again the coquette. "They are beauties, one and all."

"My lady, I am honored, but—" A month ago, this proposal might have filled him with hope. Now he had a sudden urge to seek out Miss Folger and spend a pleasant hour in her company to clear his memory of this conversation.

"Please." Transparent honesty now emanated from Lady Augusta's eyes.

Frederick sighed his surrender. "You must permit me to write what I deem best."

"God bless you, Moberly. I shall never forget this." Her tears washed the ghastly black substance down the mask on her cheeks. Dabbing with her handkerchief, she seemed unaware of the mess she had made of herself.

"My lady, there is a looking glass in the necessary room."

She gave him a sheepish smile. "Yes, of course. Thank you." She walked toward the door, then turned back. "I believe Eleanor would suit you well. She is sweet-tempered and—"

"Please do not trouble yourself, Lady Augusta." If memory served, Lady Eleanor was one of the young ladies who had refused to speak to him at Lord Abingdon's party some four years ago.

"Or perhaps Margaret, the youngest." Her voice trailed off as she left the room.

Frederick leaned back on the desk and exhaled his relief. Hearing Cousin Lydie's music, he forced himself to recover, for he must return to the drawing room. Her arthritis might flare up if he left her playing the pianoforte for their guests too long.

As he stood, one hand brushed over an unfamiliar paper stuck halfway under a book. Lifting the pamphlet, he read its title, *A Declaration of Rights and Grievances.* A copy of the disgruntled colonists' complaints against King George! Frederick's heart leapt into his throat. Where had this come from? Who had placed it on his desk? He rubbed his forehead. This could bring him serious trouble if Brigham saw it when they toured the room. Perhaps that accounted for the man's ill humor during supper. Frederick started to tear it up and throw the pieces into the unlit hearth, but mad curiosity stayed his hand. He thrust it behind the books on one of his shelves and hurried to the drawing room.

While the other guests sat listening to Cousin Lydie's lovely music, Brigham and Corwin stood across the room in intense conversation. The officer gave Frederick a dark glare, and Frederick's pulse quickened. His father's influence with the king might not be sufficient to save him if he could not convince the major he knew nothing about the pamphlet.

He sensed Lady Augusta's presence beside him and gave her a quick glance—a mistake, for she gazed at him over her fan flirtatiously. Now Major Brigham's glare grew even darker. Did he suspect them of a tryst?

Seated again with Papa near the doorway, Rachel had difficulty not laughing. Lady Augusta's furtive rendezvous was the furthest thing from an assignation, and poor Mr. Moberly's discomfort had been apparent in his conciliatory tone of voice. He truly was an honorable gentleman.

Rachel turned her attention to Mrs. Winthrop, even as her own fingers itched to play the fine mahogany pianoforte. The lady's playing was adequate but uninspired, and she often hit a wrong key. But propriety forced everyone to sit with rapt admiration.

Guilt nudged at Rachel for such ungenerous thoughts. Throughout the evening, Mrs. Winthrop had shown her nothing but the kindest of attentions, and the dear lady exhibited modest awareness of her shortcomings at the instrument.

Footsteps behind them drew Rachel's attention to the doorway, where she saw Mr. Moberly enter the room. Against her will, she glanced behind him to see if Lady Augusta had followed. When the lady entered a moment later and gave Mr. Moberly an intimate look over her fan, Rachel again wanted to laugh. But Mr. Moberly wore a troubled frown as he looked toward the lady's husband.

The moment Lady Augusta sat down, her husband and Mr. Corwin crossed the room to Mr. Moberly, and the men stepped out into the hallway. With a casual air, Rachel leaned back to hear their conversation. Perhaps these men would say something useful to the revolution. She glanced at Papa, but his gaze was focused on

Mrs. Winthrop, who now played a rousing tune at full volume.

"Now, see here, Moberly." Major Brigham's words came out in a low growl. "I'll not see my wife involved in a scandal."

Rachel smothered a gasp and forced herself to remain seated. But if necessary, she would tell that odious major that his wife was the one at fault.

"I will not have Lady Augusta disgraced in this manner." His voice low and menacing, Major Brigham placed one hand on the hilt of his ceremonial sword and waved the other fist at Frederick.

Frederick felt certain his heart had stopped. "But, my lord, I assure you—" He glanced toward the lady in question, who now sat listening to Cousin Lydie's concert, oblivious to his dilemma.

Brigham marched toward the front door and back again. Frederick sent a questioning grimace toward Corwin, who shrugged and shook his head.

"How dare you entice my wife off in some corner for who knows what?" Brigham's cheeks flamed, and his blue eyes sent out an icy glare. "I demand to know what you did."

Frederick swallowed hard, praying for the right answer. He forced himself to assume a relaxed pose. "She will be disappointed in my telling you, but since you insist…"

Lord, give me an answer, please.

"Well?" Brigham took a step closer, his hand still on his sword.

"Ah, very well, then." Frederick studied his fingernails and brushed them against his jacket shoulder. "She asked me to help her arrange a, um, surprise for you."

"What? A surprise, you say?" Brigham drew back, and his eyes widened. After several moments, his raging scowl melted into a slow smile. "I see. Well, then, I'll ask no more questions." He gazed at his wife tenderly, then frowned again. "But there is another matter which I will not so lightly dispense with."

Frederick had difficulty maintaining his composure. Was this a parlor game this couple played? "And whatever might that be?"

"The very idea," said Brigham in terse, quiet tones, "that you invited the daughter of an earl into company consisting of nothing more than shopkeepers, sailors and Spaniards, to sit at table with her as if they were her equals, why, it's preposterous. An affront not to be borne."

Frederick struggled to keep the sarcasm from his tone. "I beg your indulgence, sir. I thought it was clear when I invited you and Lady Augusta that you'd have no peer here. No one holds a rank equal to yours outside of St. Augustine, a bit far to go for a simple supper." He pasted on a smile that had often won over his older brothers in times of conflict.

Corwin coughed away a laugh.

Brigham glared at Frederick, and he blustered out a few huffing breaths, as though he was trying to maintain the intensity of his anger. "Humph. A poor excuse for forcing us to mingle with this rabble. Do you have any idea of the scandal it would bring upon my wife if anyone in her London circles found out about this? Why, she would be humiliated, pitied behind her back." As he looked in her direction, his threatening stance relaxed, and his dark frown softened into an expression of unmitigated affection.

Frederick also relaxed. After all, the man was merely a gallant knight defending his lady.

"If I may say so, sir, Lady Augusta appears to be enjoying herself." Frederick wished he could say the same for Miss Folger. Her posture stiffened noticeably during Brigham's tirade. He and Brigham spoke softly, but no doubt she heard every cruel word. Would that he could shield her as Brigham now attempted to shield his wife from perceived injury to her reputation.

"Perhaps she is. Yes, you may be right. The dear, brave girl has put up with much since I dragged her away from her friends and brought her to this beastly wilderness."

"And who would tell those friends about this evening's innocent gathering?" Frederick could see the man relenting. "Not I. Not Corwin here. Not Mrs. Winthrop."

Brigham turned a stern face to Corwin. "I suppose not. But—" He stood squarely in front of Frederick and studied him up and down through his quizzing glass, as if inspecting one of his insubordinate dragoons. "There is yet another matter that cannot be easily explained away."

"Indeed?" Frederick crossed his arms and tilted his head to feign interest. But in truth, this man was beginning to irritate him. Frederick was His Majesty's magistrate and, peerage notwithstanding, possessed more authority than Brigham in this part of East Florida.

"Indeed." Brigham's eyes took on a steely glint. "Corwin here tells me you have permitted an Indian village to remain in the southeast corner of your plantation. Is that right?" Again, his anger was too excessive for the matter at hand.

"Yes, of course. The Timucuan people know the land

as no Englishman possibly could. They're peaceful, and fostering their friendship benefits all of us."

"I want them out." An order, not a request.

Frederick studied the major while countless responses warred within him. He saw Miss Folger watching over her shoulder, her face solemn. Suddenly he felt like a spineless toady.

"Major Brigham, I will be responsible for the people living within my domain." A strange thrill shot down his spine. "All of them."

Brigham lifted his chin and sneered. "Do you refuse my orders?"

How many times in his life had Frederick disarmed such animosity with a joke, a smile, a feigned surrender? But this man would not tell him what to do on his father's land. This time he would not give way, must not give way. Not in front of Miss Folger.

"Sir." He kept his voice low. "You do not have the authority to give me orders. If you have a grievance or question about the manner in which I manage my father's plantation or St. Johns Settlement, we can take the matter before Governor Tonyn in St. Augustine."

Brigham stared hard at him for several moments. "Very well, then. I shall inform His Excellency of your refusal to send those savages to Cuba, where the rest of their kind went when we took possession of these lands." He snorted. "If I did not know better, I would think you were one of those traitors, like the fools up north who are demanding *independence*." The last syllable sizzled with his distaste.

"Haven't we Englishmen always been fond of our independence?" Frederick relished the unfamiliar courage surging through him. "You know, the *Magna Carta,* and so forth?" A renegade grin forced its way to his lips.

Brigham's eyes narrowed. "Be careful, Moberly. Lord Bennington may have His Majesty's ear, but I have my own resources, including my esteemed father-in-law."

Frederick offered a genial shrug. "We should not be enemies, my lord. We have too much to gain through friendship."

Brigham drew himself up into a stern military stance, as if to forestall any attempt at alliance. "You will excuse Lady Augusta and me. I must take her away from this rabble and convey her safely home before complete darkness."

Frederick bowed slightly. "Of course."

Courtesy required him to see the couple to their carriage, where mounted, torch-bearing soldiers waited to guard their passage up the darkened road. Facing away from her husband, Lady Augusta gave Frederick a conspiratorial wink that made him shudder. He must keep his promise to her and plead for Brigham's continued posting in East Florida when his preference would be to see the man sent straightaway to the very location she feared.

As he walked back into the house, disappointment crowded out the pleasure he had felt over standing up to Major Brigham. He had planned this party to get better acquainted with the lovely Miss Folger but hadn't had but two separate moments to speak with her. Hardly the way to impress or interest her. But now he inhaled a deep, refreshing breath. He still had time to redeem the evening. He would seek out Miss Folger straightaway.

Chapter Eight

While the other guests adjourned to the terrace for dessert, Rachel lingered behind at the pianoforte. She brushed her fingers over the surface of the keys, not making a sound but longing to bring forth music.

"Aha." Mr. Moberly appeared and pulled up a chair to sit close beside her. "You play, Miss Folger." His masculine citrus scent, perhaps his shaving balm, sent a wave of agreeable dizziness through her head.

"You have discovered me, sir." Her pulse quickening, Rachel rested her hands in her lap. "I am guilty."

He tilted his head. "Why did you not confess earlier? I'll warrant Cousin Lydie would have gladly surrendered the instrument to you."

She studied his well-formed face, and her pulse hammered in her ears. "Everyone enjoyed her playing."

"She does play well."

The soft light in his eyes proclaimed his affection for his cousin, a sentiment that clearly kept him from seeing her musical shortcomings. But then, Rachel thought it might be pleasant to be the object of Mr. Moberly's generous opinions.

As before, she forced herself to dismiss such foolish

thoughts. This gentleman treated everyone with kindness. She must protect her heart or risk the devastation of her soul. Still, her esteem for him grew due to his proper behavior with Lady Augusta and his courage in the face of the woman's terrible husband. What might it cost Mr. Moberly if Brigham became a true adversary?

"Well." He put on a severe expression. "I suppose I should pronounce sentence on you for failing to confess that you play."

Heat rushed to her face. "I am at your mercy, sir."

His unnerving smile reached all the way to his eyes, and she could not look away. The smile faded, and he seemed to move closer, focusing on her lips. Would he kiss her? Right here and now? She tingled in anticipation, even as she struggled against such impropriety. Yet she could not break free from his invisible hold on her.

"Rachel." Papa's distant voice broke through the fog in her mind.

Mr. Moberly inhaled sharply and moved back from her. "Forgive me, Miss Folger," he murmured. "That was most unseemly."

Rachel jumped up, knocking over the pianoforte stool.

"There ye are." Papa halted at the double doorway across the room. A quizzical look crossed his face, and he looked from Rachel to Mr. Moberly, who was righting the piano stool. He stared again at Rachel. "I wondered what become o' ye."

Rachel edged past her host. "At the piano, of course." Her voice wavered. "You told me I should offer to play, and now I'm sorry I didn't."

Mr. Moberly stayed her with a light touch on her hand. "Please say you'll forgive me," he whispered, his dark gray eyes exuding regret. "Although my actions were unforgivable."

"I am not without fault, sir." She kept her voice low. "But it will not happen again." She moved beyond Mr. Moberly and joined Papa. "Shall we go to the terrace? I need some of that coffee Mrs. Winthrop offered. I do hope it's strong."

They proceeded to the wide tabby terrace, where a refreshment table awaited. A servant handed her a delicate china cup, and she took a sip. "Mmm. Excellent coffee, Mr. Moberly. Don't you think so, Papa?" She could hear the strain in her voice. "Are you ready to go home?"

Papa turned to their host. "Ye'll excuse us, won't ye, sir? I've promised Reverend Johnson we'll attend services tomorrow, and Rachel'll need her rest."

"Of course." Mr. Moberly looked the picture of misery, with his forehead wrinkled in sorrow and his posture slouched. He crossed the terrace and reached out to Papa. "Mr. Folger, it has been my pleasure."

"And mine, sir." Papa pumped his hand with his usual enthusiasm.

While Papa drove back to town, once again with the musket across his lap, Rachel held a lantern and kept watch for predators. This time as she stared out into the darkness, she wrestled with thoughts very different from her earlier happy anticipations. Not only had she not found the patriot, but Mr. Moberly had behaved most disrespectfully toward her.

Did he think she was a strumpet to be kissed when they barely knew each other? Mother had warned her about certain types of men, wealthy ones in particular, who regarded less affluent girls as nothing more than casual entertainment.

Rachel had hoped for, yes, even longed for Mr. Moberly's attentions. But certainly not in the manner he had delivered them. All the way home, she chided herself for expecting more and for almost permitting the kiss. As the dimly lit inn came into sight, she resolved never to permit her heart to betray good sense, no matter what emotions Mr. Moberly might stir there.

What's more, her duty here in East Florida was not to seek a romance but to help Papa with his mercantile. And of course, to discover ways to help the revolution.

Frederick lounged across a settee in the darkened drawing room, staring at the ceiling and rubbing his forehead. What a muddle he'd made of this evening. Why had he even arranged the event? He'd antagonized Brigham, made a foolish promise to the man's wife and came far too close to kissing the young lady for whom he'd planned everything. After all his mistakes, he'd not even managed to have a true conversation with Miss Folger. Instead of being drawn by her thick blond curls, delicate lavender scent and those full pink lips, he should have sought to know her mind, her heart, her soul.

"Freddy?"

He glanced over the settee back and saw a dark form in the doorway.

"Come in, Cousin Lydie." Reassurance swept through him. Throughout his life, quiet, intimate moments with his older cousin had often soothed Frederick's worst anxieties. He sat up to make room for her.

Already in her dressing gown, with her hair bound in a long braid, Cousin Lydie settled beside him. "Could you not sleep?"

"No."

"Have you made your rounds?"

"Corwin offered to do it."

She hummed her approval. "Very good. You deserve a rest after your hosting duties."

"Thank you for playing tonight." He reached over to pat her dear, wrinkled hands, which often had chastened and more often calmed him in his boyhood. "I hope it did not cause you pain."

"Not excessively." She gently squeezed his fingers. "Mr. Folger says his daughter also plays, but modesty keeps her from asserting herself. I thought that was charming."

Frederick's pulse quickened. "You found her charming?"

"Why, yes, of course. Her modest dress and proper deportment are entirely pleasing. And one finds it more than a little surprising to see such refined table manners in a merchant's daughter living here in the wilderness." Cousin Lydie gasped softly. "Freddy, have you formed an attachment with the young lady?"

"No." He emitted an ironic laugh. His own foolishness had spoiled that effort. Yet he longed for an ally in his endeavors. Perhaps Cousin Lydie would help him. If not, at least she would never betray him to Corwin. "But I would like to."

"Oh, dear."

With his cousin's face shadowed, Frederick could only imagine her arched eyebrows and pinched-together lips.

But she grasped his hand. "Dear boy, have you counted the cost of such a decision?" Distress filled her voice. "Do you know how my entire life has been affected by one such choice I made at nineteen?"

Guilt shot through him. He'd never inquired about

Cousin Lydie's life, even though she knew every detail of his. "You must tell me about it."

"Simply put, I fell in love with a man of no prospects, then compounded the offense by marrying him against my father's wishes."

Frederick's mind reeled. His cousin's loving heart had led to her impoverishment. "What happened to Mr. Winthrop?"

"A fever took him less than a year after our marriage."

Frederick would not ask her why she never remarried, for her tone conveyed sorrow even after these many years. How she must have loved him. Such constant love would be a treasure.

"But…" Her brightened tone, tinged with humor, startled him. "The wealthy man my father wanted me to marry was a dreadful beast who turned out to be dishonest. Father was most pleased not to be connected to him. Of course, he never confessed that to me."

He felt her lean against the settee back.

Soon she continued. "If given the opportunity, I would do exactly as I did, however short-lived my happiness."

For a moment, the meaning of her words lingered above him. When at last they flowed into his mind, he nearly sprang to his feet.

"Cousin Lydie, do you hear what you are saying? What you are suggesting? Do you know what that means to me?"

She sighed. "I fear I do. That is why I hesitated to tell you. But things will go well for you, dear boy."

"Only if you help me."

"I?" Her maternal laughter grew more musical. "Oh, what fun we shall have. Now, tell me what to do. Shall

I write to Lady Bennington and ask her to influence your father?"

"There will be a time for that, but it's a bit too soon." Guilt once again gripped him. "I must tell you all that happened this evening." He related his encounters with Major Brigham and Lady Augusta. After a pause to gather his courage, he confessed to almost kissing Miss Folger.

"I cannot imagine what I was thinking," he said. "No, I wasn't thinking. That was the problem. After I'd suffered Major Brigham and Lady Augusta's nonsense, Miss Folger's presence was entirely refreshing, and thus I almost surrendered to unseemly emotions. I would say I could not help myself, but I should have. Were a man to treat my sister thus, I should have called him out."

"Oh, my, I can see we have some repair work to do. I have already promised the young lady I will visit her father's shop."

His enthusiasm renewed, Frederick gently squeezed her hand. "Thank you, dear cousin. I shall arrange for Ben to drive you into the village on Monday."

"But I heard Mr. Folger say they would be at church tomorrow." Her tone turned conspiratorial. "That is not too soon to begin our strategy. Here is what I advise..."

"Think of it, Papa. Only one more breakfast in this place." Rachel glanced toward the tearoom door to be certain Sadie was not nearby. "On Tuesday, we will awaken in our own home to Inez's fine food." She took a bite of the greasy ham on her plate only because she needed sustenance.

"And good riddance, if ye ask me." Papa devoured a large slice of fresh-baked bread dripping with honey.

"I'd sooner try to sleep through a storm at sea than in this rickety pile of wood with no decent foundation."

Rachel glanced at the broad boards beneath their feet and wondered why the innkeeper had not built on tabby or coquina. Perhaps he had been in a hurry to build it and begin his competition with the settlement's other tavern.

"If not for my promise to the reverend," Papa said, "we could move the last of the furniture in today." He puffed out an impatient sigh. "Church. Why did I ever agree to go?"

"We should have attended when we first arrived last month." Rachel tried to keep a rebuke from her tone. "Reverend Johnson seems to be a godly man. And perhaps his wife will demonstrate more courtesy in church than she did last evening."

"Ah, well." Papa dug into his porridge. "That was a motley gaggle of geese in Moberly's barnyard. More than one had no idea of how to comport himself."

Heat filled her face as she pushed her overcooked eggs around the plate. If Papa learned what happened with Mr. Moberly, she could not guess what he might do. "But, Papa, I noticed you had no trouble engaging the attention of Mrs. Winthrop."

Lifting his coffee cup, Papa washed down his last bite and seemed to focus on some distant point. "Aye, she's a true lady. All manners and all sincerity. The genuine article."

Rachel stared at him, her eyes wide with surprise.

"Why, captain, have ye formed an attachment with the lady?" She imitated Papa's inflections.

Papa shot her a guilty glance. "O'course not." He blustered and mumbled under his breath. "Can't a man compliment a lady without being accused of impropriety?"

"But it wouldn't be improper, Papa." Rachel had long hoped he would find a suitable companion. "You're both widowed. And if you're both agreeable to it, why not keep company?"

Papa set one elbow on the table and scratched his fresh-shaven chin. "Hmm. Well, now. I don't know. Perhaps 'twas mere courtesy that urged her to take my arm when I offered it. I'd not have ye ashamed of me for being an old fool."

"I'd never be ashamed of you." Rachel patted his hand. "You have my permission to call on Mrs. Winthrop." The instant she spoke, she wondered whether the genteel lady would consider herself above Papa. *Lord, please do not let me advise Papa amiss. Let my heart break, but not his—again.*

"Well, now, let's not be hasty." He fussed with his cup. "I s'pose I could see if Mrs. Winthrop treats us with the same courtesy today." He repositioned his napkin in his lap. "Well, now, if I go calling on her, ye must come with me. If I've misunderstood, she'll be none the wiser, for she'll think ye initiated the call and I'm only along to protect ye as ye travel."

"Oh." Rachel could not think of going back to the plantation, especially unannounced.

"What is it, girl?" Papa eyed her. "You disapprove? Say it right out."

"Nothing, Papa. Nothing at all."

"Well, then." Papa tossed his napkin on the table. "Let's be off." He stood and moved toward the hall. "Come along, now. We don't want to be late."

Delighted with his change of attitude about attending services, Rachel nonetheless followed him slowly.

At the prospect of seeing Mr. Moberly again within the hour, she found her heart misbehaving once more, and she had no idea how to control it.

Walking beside Papa, she breathed in the fresh pine and sweet magnolia fragrances of the warm, rain-washed June morning. They skirted a few puddles spotting the road, but most of the previous night's showers had disappeared into the sandy soil or run down into the many creeks flowing through the hilly landscape.

The small rough-wood church had been built on a sturdy base of coquina, the same foundation supporting Mr. Moberly's plantation house. The granite quarries of Massachusetts offered no better foundation stone than this.

Rachel recalled the verses in Matthew that spoke of a wise man building his house upon a rock, and she sent up a silent prayer that Papa would begin to build his life on Jesus Christ this very morning. Old Reverend Johnson might have an unfriendly wife, but he seemed to possess a true concern for souls. Rachel had been pleased to see Papa talk so easily with him. If the vicar expounded a clear revelation of Christ's love and sacrifice, how could Papa resist?

At the church door, her heart began to race as she followed Papa inside. The half-filled sanctuary held an assortment of people. Soldiers and indentured servants sat behind the free white tradesmen, and black slaves stood in the galleries above. Instead of boxed family pews like those in Boston churches, the room was furnished with benches that held perhaps a hundred souls, far fewer than Rachel's home church. Yet the familiar peace she had always experienced when she entered a house of worship now filled her chest. Strangely, the peace intensified when she spied Mr. Moberly seated near the front with Mrs. Winthrop and Mr. Corwin.

Perhaps he sensed her gaze, for he turned, and a soft smile graced his lips. Now Rachel almost stopped breathing, and she turned her eyes toward the cross above the altar. She would not permit this man's presence to intrude upon her time of worship. But as she moved into the row behind Mr. Moberly and his companions, she feared that, instead of worshipping, her pious soul would spend the next two hours at war with her disobedient heart.

Soon Reverend Johnson entered, accompanied by other church leaders to assist him. Dressed in pale brown cotton cassocks with little ornamentation, the four men moved through the holy rites with the ease of those used to serving together.

Rachel followed the liturgy in her prayer book, holding it for Papa to read along. Yet her gaze kept straying toward Mr. Moberly, who never cast a second glance in her direction.

As Rachel had hoped, the vicar gave a brief but wisdom-filled homily concerning the simple path to salvation, summing up his discourse by reciting John 3:16. While he spoke, Rachel prayed Papa would comprehend the love of God. She could not bear to think of his perishing for want of faith, and promised the Lord she would endeavor to do everything to win his soul to Christ, though Papa rarely listened to her opinions.

When the last prayer had been spoken and Reverend Johnson had pronounced the benediction, her thoughts flew to the awkward situation sure to erupt when she and Mr. Moberly stepped out into the heat of the East Florida sun.

Chapter Nine

"A fine message, Reverend Johnson." Frederick shook hands with the vicar while watching to see if he could reach Miss Folger and her father before they walked too far away. Running after her would be most unseemly for the settlement's magistrate, yet Frederick's legs ached to do just that. He forced himself to maintain propriety and bowed to the vicar's wife. "Mrs. Johnson, you look lovely, as always."

She beamed at him. "Thank you, Mr. Moberly. And thank you again for a delightful party last evening. Lady Augusta was the very picture of charm and elegance, and I was so delighted to be introduced to her. You simply must have another party because—"

"Mrs. Johnson, what a pretty bonnet." Cousin Lydie stepped to Frederick's side. "Do tell me the name of your London milliner. I shall ask Mr. Moberly to order something for me."

The younger woman blushed and fell into conversation with Cousin Lydie, apparently forgetting the wonders of Lady Augusta.

Frederick moved away, wishing he could kiss his dear cousin. Their talk last night had resulted in a plan to rectify his misdeed, but Mrs. Johnson almost ruined it.

To his relief, the Folgers had not wandered far from the church. They stood talking with the innkeeper and his family in the shade of an oak tree. Squinting in the morning sun, Frederick approached the group and waited for their conversation to conclude.

"'Tis the Lord's truth, miss." The innkeeper tipped his hat to Rachel. "Having you and the captain stayin' at me inn has been a blessin'." He bent his head toward Papa.

"Thank ye, sir," Papa said.

"Thank you, Mr. Crump." Rachel searched for some compliment to return. "Mrs. Crump, we are so grateful for the clean sheets every other week. That is a special kindness to your guests. You and Sadie have enough work."

The heavy, red-faced woman beamed. "'Twas a special kindness fer you, miss. Don't do that for ever'one."

"You have my gratitude." Rachel felt a sting of remorse for her heartless thoughts about this hardworking couple. In truth, they were the salt of the earth, the same sort that comprised the militia back home. She regarded the stout, red-haired innkeeper, but his clean-shaven face precluded his being the red-bearded patriot. Or perhaps not. Perhaps a disguise?

"Mr. Crump, I am curious." Rachel glanced at Papa but proceeded anyway. "Have you had any visits from that patriot, uh, the agitator who has been spreading news of the revolution taking place up north?"

"Rachel." Beside her, Papa exhaled a lengthy sigh.

"No, miss," Mr. Crump said. "He'd find no welcome

at the Wild Boar, and no doubt he knows it." His cross frown and grumbling tone underlined his words.

Mrs. Crump put a plump hand on her hip. "He'd better keep his ideas to hisself, or I'll set on 'im with my rolling pin."

Mr. Crump looked beyond Rachel and jerked to attention. "Well, Mrs. Crump, 'tis time to quit gabblin'. We've a meal to serve the boarders." He tipped his hat. "Cap'n Folger, good day t'ya. Miss Folger, you can be sure we'll miss yer kind face onc't ya've moved."

"Thank you, sir." Rachel gave a little wave of her hand while a familiar ache of disappointment filled her. She lifted a prayer that she could soon find just one person, any person, who agreed with her sentiments regarding the revolution.

She turned to find Mr. Moberly standing not two yards away, a frown on his handsome face. A strange shiver swept down her spine. Had he heard her question the Crumps?

"Good morning, Mr. Folger, Miss Folger." Mr. Moberly swept off his broad-brimmed hat and bowed, but still no smile touched his lips.

"Good morning, sir," Mr. Folger said in a hearty tone.

Miss Folger's curtsy looked unsteady, and she quickly stared down at her prayer book rather than meet his gaze. He wished he could address her in particular, wished he could give her a reassuring smile, but that would spoil the plan.

"Miss Folger." Cousin Lydie appeared beside Frederick. "How charming you look. I'm pleased to see you this morning. Did you enjoy the service?"

"Yes, indeed." Miss Folger bestowed a pretty smile on Cousin Lydie.

Frederick yearned to be the recipient of such radiance. He hoped his attempt to kiss her had not destroyed forever the chance that she might smile at him again.

"Mr. Folger," Cousin Lydie said, "may I borrow your daughter for a moment?"

"Aye, madam." His eyes wide, Mr. Folger nodded. "Of course."

She looped her arm in Miss Folger's. "My dear, you must see the garden behind the vicarage."

As the two ladies walked away, Frederick noticed Mr. Folger's gaze followed Cousin Lydie. Curious.

"Well, sir," Frederick said, "I suppose you miss Captain Templeton."

Mr. Folger seemed reluctant to turn his attention away from the ladies. "Aye, my nephew's more like a son to me." He now focused on Frederick. "And we thank ye for sendin' along the oranges and lemons with him. Scurvy can be a blight on any voyage, but we'll not worry about that striking the crew due to yer generosity."

Relief swept through Frederick. The young lady's father seemed unaware of his misstep the previous evening. "And I am grateful to the captain for taking letters to my family. They do not hear from me often enough to suit them, so they will be pleasantly surprised. So you see, we have done each other a favor." Especially if Templeton kept his promise to tell Father of Frederick's successes.

"As befits a budding partnership, do ye not think?"

"Yes, I agree. In these wilds, and troubled times, one can never have too many friends."

"True, true." Mr. Folger stared off toward the path

the ladies had taken. "I think I'd like to see that garden. Do ye think the ladies'd mind me comin' alongside?"

"Surely not." Frederick shook his head. "In fact, I'll go with you." All according to plan.

Rachel reminded herself that Mr. Moberly had smiled at her in church, but just now he barely addressed her. Without doubt, he heard her speaking to the Crumps and caught her use of the word *patriot*. Surely that would bring to an end any interest he might have in her. She tried not to care. After all, he was an Englishman in authority. Hardly the right man to attract her interest. And yet...

She yielded to Mrs. Winthrop's gentle guidance as they walked to the backyard of the vicarage. Mrs. Johnson's lush fenced garden bloomed with an abundance of vegetables and flowers.

"Reaping two garden harvests a year will always seem odd to me," Mrs. Winthrop said. "In most parts of England, we complete our single harvest by mid-October."

"Boston is much the same." Seeing the corn and squash, Rachel felt a pang of hunger. But dinner could wait. Mrs. Winthrop's interest in her filled an empty spot food could never satisfy. Beyond her own concerns, she thought of Papa and prayed he and the lady might establish a friendship. With Papa's lack of interest in the revolution, he would have no conflict of beliefs with an English lady.

They wandered arm in arm around the garden's border, peering over the fence to see tiny melons with withered blossoms still attached, string beans ready to harvest, and thumb-sized green tomatoes clinging to their vines.

"Ah, there ye are, ladies." Papa limped toward them across the grass, Mr. Moberly following a few steps behind. "We thought we'd like to take in the garden with ye."

Mr. Moberly's expression remained sober, and he bent over the squash plants with apparent interest. Rachel decided she must act as if nothing were amiss.

"Papa, we must have a garden like this behind the store."

"Indeed, daughter, many things bloom well here." Papa gazed not at the garden but at Mrs. Winthrop. He cleared his throat. "Mrs. Winthrop, will ye join us for a repast at the inn?"

Rachel winced, knowing what the effort cost him. She prayed he would not be rebuffed.

But like a flower blossoming in the rain, Mrs. Winthrop's whole face broke into a wide smile, and a delicate blush touched her ivory cheeks. "How kind of you to ask, sir. But I fear my duties at home demand my attention straightaway. Perhaps another time?"

Disappointment flickered briefly in his eyes. "Ye have but to name the day and time."

Now Rachel's spirits lifted. She glanced at Mr. Moberly to see his response. Although he continued to study the garden, she could see his smile in profile, and contentment filled her.

Soon he turned to face them. "Cousin Lydie, are you ready to go home?"

"Yes, dear." She did not remove her gaze from Papa.

"Then we must take our leave." Mr. Moberly bowed to Rachel. "Miss Folger. Mr. Folger." Mrs. Winthrop stepped over and squeezed Rachel's hand. "I shall see you soon."

Wondering at her remark, Rachel took Papa's arm

and watched the two depart. Perhaps she had been wrong about Mr. Moberly hearing her remarks to Mr. Crump.

As she and Papa began their trek across the lawn, a long black snake slithered through the grass and almost ran over her shoe. She jumped back with a gasp. "Oh, my."

Papa gripped her hand. "Stand still till it's gone, daughter."

"Harmless, I assure you." Mr. Corwin walked around the corner of the vicarage, swinging a fine ebony cane. "They keep the garden free of rats and other pests. But they certainly can surprise a person."

Rachel willed away a shudder. "And of course, one must make certain they're not poisonous."

"Indeed." Mr. Corwin swished the grass with his cane. "I say, Mr. Folger, may I speak with your lovely daughter for a moment?"

Papa stared at Rachel, his eyes twinkling. "Well, daughter?"

Her face burning almost as much as her curiosity, she nodded. Papa limped away toward the road.

"Yes, Mr. Corwin?" The overhead sun burned through her bonnet, making Rachel dizzy, and she hoped this would not take long.

He lifted an eyebrow, and a wily expression crossed his handsome face. "I'd like to discuss Moberly's intentions toward you."

Chapter Ten

Rachel stood aside as stocky Mr. Patch carried her trunk up the stairs, his shoulders bent to the task. The sweat pouring from him pushed her back, but her heart warmed toward this former member of Papa's whaling crew, who now helped with the store.

"Please put it in my room." She motioned toward the door.

"Aye, miss." He placed the heavy trunk on the floor with care. "That's the last of it."

After he left, she surveyed the boxes piled throughout the four rooms, and sadness filled her. Once she unpacked, once she set Mother's vase on the mantel and her porcelain tableware in the china cabinet, this would be home, whether she liked it or not. She had no energy to start the task. Life would soon become very dull, Mr. Corwin's daft remark notwithstanding. If Mr. Moberly were smitten with her, why had he barely spoken to her after church?

"Rachel, come quick, daughter." Papa's voice boomed up the stairs. "Ye're needed down here." The joviality in his tone eased her sadness.

"Coming, Papa." She glanced in the tiny mirror over

her bureau, brushed back a few stray hairs, and hurried downstairs. "Yes, sir?" She stopped short. "Mrs. Winthrop."

The lady stood across the counter from Papa, but no wares had been laid out. Instead, she held a bouquet of fragrant white flowers.

"How nice to see you again so soon, ma'am." Rachel's face warmed.

"And it is a pleasure to see you, as well, Miss Folger. I hope you do not mind my calling at this early hour, but one does best to travel before the day's worst heat." She handed the flowers to Rachel. "From my garden."

"How lovely. Thank you." Rachel breathed in the large blossoms' sweet smell as she glanced at the empty counter again. This truly was a social call. "I am so pleased to see you." A nervous twinge tickled her insides. Did Mr. Moberly know his cousin had come here? She smelled the flowers again. "What pretty, sweet-scented flowers. What are they?"

"Gardenias. The bushes were recently imported from China. Isn't the fragrance lovely?" Mrs. Winthrop leaned close to Rachel. "Miss Folger, if I am not being too forward, I thought I might help you arrange your apartment."

Rachel could barely withhold a gasp. She could not think it proper for such an elegant lady to engage in such work. Yet turning her down would be an insult. "How kind, ma'am. I do not know how to thank you." She glanced at Papa, whose face radiated his delight. Rachel wondered how long they had chatted before he called her downstairs.

"No thanks are necessary, my dear. I would imagine the task will take some time, perhaps all day. Shall we get started?" Mrs. Winthrop laughed, a pleasing sound. "Forgive me. I do not intend to manage things, merely to help you."

"I am very grateful," Rachel said. "And I will appreciate every suggestion. Shall we go?" She turned toward the burlap-covered door to the back room, aware of the store's humble look compared to Mr. Moberly's grand house. A sudden longing filled her. How pleasant it would be to have a proper front door where she could greet her guests.

Mrs. Winthrop followed her up the rough wooden staircase and looked about the apartment with an appraising eye. "What excellent accommodations and what spacious rooms." Her maternal kindness radiated from her gray eyes. "Nothing invigorates me more than a scheme of this nature."

Her own energies renewed, Rachel found Mother's cut-glass vase for the gardenias and set them on the maple dining table. Their scent filled the room with a fragrance as sweet and welcome as Mrs. Winthrop's offered friendship. Perhaps this new home would be happier than expected.

They spent the morning unpacking china and other small items. After a quick midday meal, they proceeded to the trunk in Rachel's room. In it, Mrs. Winthrop found a small framed drawing of Rachel's mother. "She was quite lovely."

Rachel gazed at the picture. "Yes, ma'am. But she did scold my sister for sketching her likeness, for she considered it a vanity." A soft chuckle escaped her.

"Ah, yes. But then, perhaps the Quakers are correct in their humility. There is far too much vanity and self-ishness in this world."

"I agree. That is why your kind help means so much." Rachel bent over her trunk, and musty but pleasant ocean smells met her senses, stirring memories of her carefree childhood on Nantucket's windswept shores.

Mrs. Winthrop reached across to pat Rachel's hand. "It is my privilege."

The gentle expression in her gray eyes brought a lump to Rachel's throat. Were the lady not Mr. Moberly's kinswoman, Rachel would confide in her regarding him.

"What have we here?" Mrs. Winthrop unwrapped a carved whalebone fan and spread it open to reveal intricate lacelike filigree. "What delicate workmanship."

"Isn't it exquisite? Papa carved it for Mother on one of his whaling voyages."

Mrs. Winthrop tilted her head. "Indeed? Your father is a gifted artist." Her cheeks grew pink, and she waved the fan in front of her face. "How useful here in the tropics."

Rachel wanted to laugh. Instead of thinking about her own hopeless romantic interests, she should foster the romance right in front of her. "Papa has many talents."

"And a prodigious wit, as well."

"I'm pleased you think so." Rachel was smitten with playfulness. "A man who has been long at sea can forget his manners. But I have noticed that in your presence, he remembers them very well."

"Oh, my. Well, a true gentleman does not require much reminding." Mrs. Winthrop waved the fan with vigor. "Do you mind if I use this?" She glanced at her wrist. "Oh, I have my own." She set down the borrowed one and used her own. "My, this East Florida heat."

Rachel ignored the lady's chagrin. "Indeed, it can be quite oppressive."

Mrs. Winthrop lifted a drawing of Papa from the

trunk. "It must be difficult for a man to lose his wife and be left with two young daughters, especially when his work takes him to sea." She held Mother's portrait side by side with Papa's. "Perhaps just as difficult as being left with three unruly sons but having to spend all of one's time in the king's service instead of seeing to their behavior."

A little twinge struck Rachel's heart. "Of whom do you speak, madam?" Mr. Moberly had mentioned being a younger son. Had he grown up without a mother's care?

"Lord Bennington, the proprietor of this settlement."

"Mr. Moberly's father?" Rachel risked another question. "What did Lord Bennington do about his sons?"

Mrs. Winthrop's eyebrows arched. "Why, he remarried, of course, as soon as he could do so within propriety." She set the pictures on Rachel's desk. "To my cousin Maria, who presented him with two more children, young Frederick and his sister, Lady Marianne." She heaved a great sigh. "Alas, dear Maria could do nothing with those three older boys, rapscallions all. They grew up entirely untamed."

Rachel's mind spun with more questions. Mr. Moberly had a sister, a *titled* sister. Why did he not have a title?

"May I ask…" Mrs. Winthrop set a pewter vase on the desk. "How did your father see to your care?"

Rachel hesitated. Would Mrs. Winthrop think it scandalous? "He took me on his next whaling voyage."

Her eyebrows arched again. She appeared not quite shocked, but perhaps amazed and even a little amused. "Gracious, young lady! What an adventure you had. No wonder you are doing well here in East Florida. You are a hardy soul."

Relief filled Rachel's heart. "Thank you. I was eleven when Mother died, and Papa had difficulty deciding what to do with me. After the voyage, I went to live with my married sister in Boston." Curiosity prompted another question. "Did Mr. Moberly take after his older brothers?"

"Mercy, no. He and Lady Marianne have brought nothing but joy to their mother. Lady Bennington is a woman of great faith, and she personally saw to their catechisms." Seated beside the trunk once more, Mrs. Winthrop folded her hands in her lap. "She is also the soul of generosity. My Mr. Winthrop died not long before her marriage, and my sweet cousin insisted I come to live under Lord Bennington's protection." Tears glistened in her eyes. "She would have nothing else for her wedding gift from him."

Rachel struggled to stop her own sudden tears. "A true Christian."

"Yes." Mrs. Winthrop bowed her head. "My, I did not intend to speak of such things." A frown crossed her brow, but it softened. "What I did intend to say was this. Mr. Moberly is a kindhearted soul like his mother. A true gentleman. And he is so utterly mortified by his behavior on Saturday evening that he has enlisted my assistance in ascertaining whether he has lost all hope in regard to…becoming your friend."

At first, the words seemed so implausible Rachel could not grasp them. Her throat constricted, preventing any response other than a tiny, silly squeak. To think he had confessed his misdeed to his kinswoman.

Mrs. Winthrop's eyes twinkled. "Miss Folger, your face is a study. May I assume you are amenable to friendship with Mr. Moberly?"

Rachel thought her head might explode. Friendship? He desired friendship with her? His coolness and strange responses had not been a snub or suspicion but, rather, continued mortification over his actions. She recalled Mr. Corwin's claim that Mr. Moberly was smitten with her, but she had not believed him. Nor had she accepted Mr. Corwin's offer to advise her as to how she might "snare" Mr. Moberly. Instead, she had politely thanked him, then walked away before he could further insult her. Now this kind lady had made a milder, yet just as startling claim. But could she, *should* she accept such a connection with him, knowing where it might lead? Knowing where it must not lead?

"Oh, dear lady." She stood and paced across the room. "How shall I respond?" Returning to kneel in front of Mrs. Winthrop, she grasped the lady's hands, breathing in the delicate gardenia fragrance clinging to her. "In your eyes, I see no deception, only goodness and truth. You must answer me truly. How can Mr. Moberly, an earl's son, seek a pure and proper friendship with a shopkeeper's daughter?" Until this moment, the attraction she felt for him had seemed a foolish fancy. Yet even if he felt an equal attraction to her, were they not mad to think a romance could follow? Every force of man and nature seemed against it.

Sadness flickered over Mrs. Winthrop's face. "I cannot promise you an easy path, my dear. But having loved deeply and without regret myself, I would not deny it to anyone else."

Rachel stared up into her kind gray eyes. "Then we each must count the cost before taking even the first step down that path."

Mrs. Winthrop caressed Rachel's cheek with her soft, smooth fingers. "You are wise for one so young."

Rachel shook her head. "Only time will reveal whether that is true or not."

"Then you will receive him?"

A giddy laugh bubbled up from within her.

"Yes, I will receive him."

Frederick paced the inn's taproom, his boot heels thumping noisily against the wooden floors. He ignored the nervous glances and murmuring of the off-duty soldiers lolling about the nearby tables. These men steered a wide berth around their magistrate and showed almost reverential respect when they did encounter him. Frederick supposed it worked to his advantage, for people had treated his father with a similar cautious respect, but even after more than two years, he had yet to become accustomed to it.

Would that Oliver held the same respect for him. Just this morning Frederick had discovered another betrayal. Clear discrepancies had appeared among Oliver's financial reports to Father, the books he kept for the plantation and the funds in Frederick's safe. Did Oliver think he would not be found out? Now Frederick must confront him, a task he dreaded almost as much as receiving another letter of censure from Father.

At every thought of Father, Frederick prayed that Captain Templeton would find favor with the old earl. Surely the man would make a good impression on Father, proving to him that Frederick possessed good judgment and an astute business sense. And Mr. Folger had made it clear he welcomed Frederick's patronage and partnership. Now if only he could receive the same welcome from Miss Folger, he would be more than satisfied.

The hot breeze blowing through the windows carried the smell of pigs and other barnyard creatures and made normal breathing a chore. The proprietor really should keep his animals farther from the inn. Frederick would speak to him in that regard.

What on earth was keeping Mrs. Winthrop? Surely it could not take long to unpack a few trinkets and trifles, have a bit of conversation—about him, of course—and have done with it.

Frederick sat down at a rough-hewn table. How foolish and selfish of him to think Cousin Lydie would be content with a pretense of helping Miss Folger. The old dear would have her elbows deep into the packing barrels. She might not want to leave until the entire project had been completed. Frederick would not have her any other way.

"Mr. Moberly, sir?" The innkeeper approached him. "Yer man Ben's out back. He asked me to tell ya the lady's ready to leave. Will ya have a drink afore you go, sir?"

"No." His pulse racing, Frederick dug a coin from his waistcoat and handed it to the man. "But I thank you for the message, my good man."

He hurried out the front door to meet Ben.

"Missus Winthrop's called for the rig, sir. I'll fetch it from the livery barn."

"Very good, Ben. I'll ride down and meet her."

His horse Essex quickly covered the half mile from the inn to the mercantile, where Frederick peered in the window and observed Mrs. Winthrop perusing the shop's wares with Miss Folger. At the doorbell's jingle, the ladies turned to greet him. Mrs. Winthrop gave him a triumphant smile. Miss Folger blushed.

His pulse hammering, Frederick swept off his hat

and bowed. "Good afternoon, ladies. I hope the day has been productive."

"Prodigiously so." Mrs. Winthrop donned her straw bonnet. "Shall I assume Ben is awaiting me outside?"

"Indeed he is." Frederick hoped his grin did not appear foolish. "May I take you to your chariot, my lady?"

"No, no." She gave her head a little shake. "You need not bother. Ben can assist me. I am certain you have other business to attend to."

"Ah, very good."

"Good day, Miss Folger." Mrs. Winthrop passed by Frederick with a swish of her skirts and a hint of gardenia.

Frederick gazed at Miss Folger, and she returned the same.

"This is madness, you know." Her sober expression belied the lilt in her voice. "You are mad, and so am I."

He chuckled, a strained and foolish sound in his own ears. "But it is a merry madness, do you not agree?"

She looked down, as if trying to hide the smile spread across her lovely face. A blond curl fell over her cheek, a mere wisp, delicate like her.

He longed to brush it back, to lift her chin, to reclaim her gaze. But he dared not risk another temptation to kiss her. So he cleared his throat and glanced about the room, trying to discover some safe topic of conversation. He settled at last upon a bolt of blue gauze.

"Miss Folger, I admired your exquisite gown the other evening." Perhaps not the best beginning, for he would not wish her to recall his blunder. "Most ladies would hide the bolt—" he pointed to it "—so no other lady could purchase the same material."

She glanced at the fabric, and the pensiveness in her eyes gave him pause. Had he spoken amiss? The air here in the shop, with its strange mix of cinnamon, lavender and new leather, was decidedly more pleasant than in the inn, but he still found it difficult to breathe.

"I must admit I was tempted to hide it." She gave a charming little shrug. "But gauze is hard to come by, and Papa will make a tidy sum on the remainder. I could not deny him that." Her melodious voice shook slightly.

"Ah. The dutiful daughter. I understand."

Her face took on a beguiling radiance. "I believe you do. And that brings up a matter that deeply concerns me. I would not have you disappoint your parents."

Frederick felt as if he had been struck in the chest. She had uncovered the core of his dilemma, for he did not yet know if he could surrender all his former dreams for the sake of marrying her. Could she help him reason it out? "But may a man not decide his own destiny? Must he always seek his parents' approval?"

Voices sounded on the street. Frederick hoped desperately the speakers would not enter the store. He felt tempted to lock the door, but that would reek of impropriety.

Her lips formed a pretty little bow, and her brow wrinkled, as if she were considering his question. "You must count the cost, Mr. Moberly. You have more to lose than I. No doubt your father will disown you or, at the very least, devise some form of discipline for you."

"Perhaps so. Perhaps not. But what of you? I would not have you suffer on my account."

"I risk only my heart, as women have done since time began."

He turned his hat in his hands. "If your heart suffered, I would grieve being the cause of it." A memory surfaced. "Someone once told me that in America every man has the opportunity to earn his fortune and his place in society. As a younger son, I will inherit no part of my father's fortune, for it is entailed by law to my eldest brother. Perhaps it is time for me to earn my own."

If a man could snap his fingers and bring forth light, it might resemble the brilliance in Miss Folger's eyes, in her entire beautiful face.

"Why, then, sir, I believe our friendship might prosper, after all."

Chapter Eleven

Rachel continued to study Mr. Moberly's handsome face, which reflected her own happiness.

"Shall I call for tea?" Her decision made to receive him, she relaxed at last. Until this moment, she had felt as if her feet were rooted into the floor, and all her senses seemed suspended. Now the fragrance of lavender wafted about her, and the day's heat felt like a cozy caress. "We can sit over there." She pointed toward the table and chairs in the corner.

"Alas, I must see to matters at home." A wry grimace claimed his handsome features. "Duty is a cruel master to tear me away just now, but unfortunately I must obey."

"Of course." Her mind churned with dozens of questions, for she longed to learn more about him without delay. "I understand."

"I fear that same duty will keep me at the plantation throughout the week. But perhaps on Sunday you and Mr. Folger will come for dinner?" His hopeful, eager expression soothed her disappointment.

"I shall ask Papa. He loves fine cooking, so I do not imagine he'll say no."

Mr. Moberly chuckled. "I do not exclude myself when I say that describes most men."

"Indeed? Then I shall return the invitation. Will you dine with us the following Sunday?" Rachel decided to offer a modest boast. "I would be pleased to discover if you like my mutton stew, a specialty my mother taught me to make when I was a child."

He stared at her for a moment, his mouth open slightly. "You cook?"

"Why, of course I cook." She laughed but quickly sobered, for earnest concern emanated from his eyes.

For the longest moment, they merely looked at each other. Rachel could think of nothing to say, and she could see from his slackened jaw that he was struggling to grasp her revelation. Her own memories added to her turmoil, for she recalled that the wealthy ladies in Boston disdained such common chores. Rachel would not ask if Lady Bennington or Lady Marianne prepared the family meals. For as surely as cooking had been a part of her training for womanhood, it just as surely would have been consigned to servants in the home in which Mr. Moberly had been reared. By confessing her skill, she no doubt reminded him of the stark differences between their classes.

This attempt at friendship was a mistake. Never mind that everyone required food to survive or that people of wealth demanded meals tasting nothing short of splendid. Ladies of his social rank simply did not cook.

"I say, Miss Folger." His face brightened. "No wonder your good father depends upon you. Is there anything you cannot do?"

Rachel turned away to hide a grin, while her sinking heart returned to its proper moorings.

"Did I speak amiss?" He touched her shoulder.

Startled, she spun around. He was so close she could smell his shaving balm, a heady bergamot scent.

He pulled back his hand as if burned. "Ah, forgive me."

"No, no, I am not offended." Not at all. In fact, his touch had bestowed further reassurance on her. "I thought perhaps you were…that you thought—"

"I would never think anything but the best of you, Miss Folger." He seized her hand. "I can only hope to be worthy of the same consideration in return." He bent forward and held her fingers to his lips for a half second beyond propriety. When he straightened, his gaze sent a wave of joy through her.

He released her hand and put on his hat. "I must go now." His voice was husky, but also a bit playful. Then he turned and strode toward the door, stopping there to glance over his shoulder. "Until Sunday, Miss Folger." Then he was gone.

"Until Sunday," she whispered. But her heart shouted with happiness.

A wild whoop burst from Frederick, unbidden and unbridled. He kicked his heels against Essex's sides and bent forward in the saddle as the stallion leaped into a gallop. People on the street—workmen, soldiers, servants on errands—gawked, but he shook off concern. Let them think their magistrate was mad, for he was. Mad with love.

Love? Was he ready to call this wild exhilaration *love*? Inner voices advised caution, the caution that had always saved his neck and kept him from getting into scrapes like his older brothers. But happiness clamored for preeminence, for mastery. And for once in his life, he would rip caution from his soul and cast it to the wind, as the roadway sand was dug out and tossed aside by Essex's hooves.

Another impulse seized him. He would find some rare gift to present to Miss Folger, something to delight her. But where could he find such a gift? Mrs. Winthrop would have to help him find something appropriate. Perhaps Captain Templeton would bring such a gift in his London cargo.

Laughter seized him. What an adventure this would be, this courtship. He'd seen merriment in the young lady's eyes and knew she was a cheerful soul. They would laugh together. Real laughter such as he had never known, except when he and Marianne had played about the manor house as children.

Dear Marianne. She would love Rachel. Perhaps he should write his sister and beg her support in this matter. Marianne was a romantic soul and determined to marry for love. Perhaps she would understand his plight and sway Father, who always gave her whatever she asked for.

Father. The thought of him sobered Frederick, and he tugged on Essex's reins. As the stallion slowed his pace, Frederick's pulse slowed, as well. For a brief half hour, if that long, he had managed to forget his father. Where he had savored the refreshing fragrance of magnolia blossoms, he now smelled his own sweat and that of his hard-run horse, pleasantness supplanted by reality. But he would not draw back. Some force perhaps even stronger than the fear of Father had gripped him, and he would not lightly dismiss it.

Yesterday during church, as the congregants repeated the general confession, Frederick had asked God's forgiveness for almost kissing Miss Folger. The assurance that filled him gave him confidence to ask the Lord's favor in pursuing the young lady. Today's events could be nothing less than proof of God's approval of that pursuit.

If only he did not have to confront Oliver this evening, he could have stayed for tea with Miss Folger. He had many questions to ask her. Did she like to read? If so, what sort of books? What did she think of the turmoil in the northern colonies? Would she be interested in traveling to Europe? He could imagine a wedding trip to his maternal grandfather's villa in Tuscany. Could see her dipping her toes into the Mediterranean Sea. Could hear her melodious voice squeal with delight over every new adventure. Would that these fantasies might be fulfilled.

But first he must contend with the reality of Oliver's betrayals.

Consumed with that objective, he could barely keep his peace during supper. He did not mind addressing the subject of the mismanagement of the books in front of Dr. Wellsey. In fact, he might need the good physician for support. But Cousin Lydie should not be subjected to such a conversation, especially if things turned out badly. Fortified by prayer, he plunged ahead with the distasteful task.

"Oliver." He used a sober tone. "I should like to see you in my study after supper."

A sneer curled Oliver's upper lip. "You sound like your father. Have I been a bad boy?"

Cousin Lydie gasped softly.

Dr. Wellsey gaped. "Now, really, Corwin."

Frederick sent the doctor a look, and tilted his head in the direction of the hallway, hoping the usually preoccupied man would understand. He was rewarded with a narrowing of the doctor's eyes and a slight nod.

Few words were spoken for the rest of the meal, and in short time, the men had gathered in Frederick's study. He sat behind his desk and indicated two chairs for the others.

"Oliver, I won't waste your time or mine. We have been friends since boyhood. My father thought well enough of you to send you to Florida as my companion." At Oliver's continued sneer, Frederick emitted an ironic laugh. "In truth, Lord Bennington felt that I needed your assistance in managing the plantation finances."

A flicker of some sort crossed Oliver's face. Apprehension? Guilt? But he sat back, arms crossed. "What of it? You've always been a spendthrift. Someone has to tighten the purse strings."

"Tighten them, perhaps. Not dip into that purse and help yourself." Without proof of theft, Frederick could only imply wrongdoing to see Oliver's reaction.

Eyes wide and mouth hanging open, Oliver appeared to be rendered mute. Yet the darting of his eyes told Frederick that the other man's mind was working. "Are you calling me a thief?"

Frederick shrugged. "If you are blameless, you won't mind my examining the discrepancies in my bookkeeping and yours." He casually repositioned his ink bottle and quill. "Further, we should discuss a certain letter to you from Lord Bennington that accidentally found its way to my desk. Oh, and I shall need to have your keys until this matter is fully examined."

Shaking with rage, Oliver stood and leaned over the desk. "My, my, aren't we getting bold. Little Freddy takes charge of the plantation."

Long accustomed to deflecting his brothers' taunts, Frederick nonetheless barely managed to keep his hands relaxed. He ached to stand and smash his fist into Oliver's scorn-filled face. Instead, he leaned forward with his forearms resting on the desk and stared up at his lifelong friend. "Yes, in fact, I am taking charge. Will you take these matters to heart? Or shall I simply send you home straightaway with a letter of dismissal?"

With a distasteful curse, Oliver retrieved his set of household keys from his jacket and slammed them down on the desk. "You will not take this position away from me. I will appeal to Lord Bennington, and then we shall see who prevails, especially when I tell him of your dalliance with a certain shopkeeper's daughter." He spun around and strode from the room. In a moment, the back door banged shut, jarring the paintings on the walls.

Dr. Wellsey stood and stared at Frederick. "I thought for a moment I might have to step into the middle of a fight." He released an unsteady breath. "Thank the Lord for your cool head."

Frederick shook his not-so-cool head. "I don't know what's become of him. Perhaps he has always been this way but managed to hide it." He waved Dr. Wellsey back to his chair. "Can you think of any reason for his changes?"

Seated again, the physician pulled his lips into a thin line and gazed toward the night-darkened window. "Of course you know he suspects Lord Bennington of being his father."

Nausea leaped into Frederick's throat, and he rested his forehead on his hands. In all their years together, how had he failed to comprehend the source of Oliver's torment? Such a vile, wicked lie. Wasn't it? Mad doubts stretched across his mind, followed apace by the urgent need to defend Father's honor. "Preposterous. And I am certain we will have no difficulty proving it."

"Even if it were true, what has he to gain by discrediting you? Our English law prevents his inheriting anything."

"True." Frederick drummed his fingers on the desk. "But, should I be removed from my positions here, he could convince Father that he is the perfect replacement for me."

The back door slammed again, and soon Oliver raced into the room. "Fire! Fire in the settlement."

Chapter Twelve

"Rachel!" Papa dashed up the stairs with energy that belied his age. "The inn's going up in a blaze."

Her heart racing, Rachel set aside her mending and sprung up from the settee.

Papa paused to gasp a few hurried breaths. "Shut the windows. The wind might shift our way, and the smoke'll ruin everything it touches."

"Yes, Papa." Rachel hastened to the front windows, catching the scent of smoke as she shoved the lower panes into place.

"I'm going now," he called from the top of the stairs.

"I'll come, too." Rachel started toward her room to change into an old dress.

"No. Stay here."

"But perhaps I can help."

"There'll be nothing for women to do." He spoke in his sharp captain's voice. "You'll get in the way." He ran down the steps, losing for a moment his limping gait.

Rachel clamped her lips together to keep from answering crossly. Of course she could help—somehow. After she closed the windows upstairs and down, she locked the shop door and hastened out into the night.

After a quick glance into the empty kitchen house, she guessed Inez had already gone to help.

Her pulse pounding, she lifted her skirts and ran toward the inn. Even from a hundred yards away, she could see the bright orange glow that lit every front window and the tongues of fire that reached out from under the eaves to lick the shingled roof. Without doubt, the inn would soon be burned to the ground.

Rachel permitted herself a moment of relief that she and Papa had removed all their belongings. But poor Mr. Crump and his family would no doubt lose everything.

A throng of settlers—both men and women—hastened toward the conflagration. Most watched in horror, but Rachel saw a few brave men cautiously venture near enough to retrieve items of value: an oxen yoke, a harness, a wooden tray, a pewter pitcher. Screams and cries rose up in discord against the roaring crackle of the flames. Terrified animals shrieked as men released them from the livestock pens and herded them away.

Soldiers had cast off their red coats and formed a bucket line from the creek to the building. Papa joined them and, with powerful arms that had harpooned many a whale, flung the contents of the pails to quench the raging blaze.

Her own arms aching to help, Rachel searched for a useful task. The acrid smoke filled her lungs, and she moved upwind to the back of the building. There, she looked up in horror to see Sadie standing immobile inside an open window holding her baby.

"Sadie," Rachel cried, "come down. Oh, do come down." But even as she screamed out the words, she knew it would be impossible, for the stairs were surely on fire. "Jump, Sadie, jump!" Her heart twisted as she saw the flames behind the mother and infant.

"Sadie, girl!" A soldier appeared beside Rachel. "You've got to jump. Come on, now, be a brave lass. We're here to catch you."

"She's scared to move," another soldier said.

"Sadie, Sadie," the first man shouted. "Toss me the boy. Don't let him burn."

"She can't even hear you," the other soldier said.

"Bring a wagon, Henry," shouted the first soldier. "Bring something. I've gotta climb up."

"It can't be done, Bertie," Henry said. "There's no time. The whole place'll soon collapse."

With a dark scowl, Bertie grabbed his friend's shirt. "Will you look Rob in the eye and say you didn't try to save his wife and son?"

"All right, then. I'll get something." He dashed away.

"Sadie!" Rachel screamed out her name again. "Drop Robby down to us. Please, Sadie." A sob caught in her throat. *Dear God, please make her hear us.* She found a rock and threw it as hard as she could, but it fell far short of the window.

"Yes, that's the idea." Bertie also grabbed a rock and flung it, striking a glass pane with a loud whack.

Sadie jerked, then glanced back at the flames and screamed. "Mercy. Dear God, have mercy." She knelt by the open window's lower half. "Miss Folger, my baby!"

"Let him go, Sadie," Bertie called. "I'll catch him. I swear I will."

Weeping hysterically, Sadie pushed the terrified child out the window. He clawed for her as she held him at arm's length. With an agonizing cry, she shoved him away from the building but clutched at the air an instant after he left her fingers. "Robby!"

The screaming infant landed in Bertie's able arms. The soldier handed him to Rachel, then gripped her shoulders. "Take the boy to safety." He gave her a little shove toward the road.

"Yes, of course." With one last look at Sadie, one more prayer for her to be saved, too, Rachel clutched the wailing child and retreated from the roaring fire. Her heart screamed at the unfolding horror, but she forced herself to coo reassurances to Robby.

As she rounded the building, five soldiers bustled past, rolling a large shipping barrel, with Major Brigham in their wake. As they passed her, Rachel turned back to watch.

"Put the barrel against the wall," Brigham ordered in terse tones. "Banks, Carter, Smith, steady it." He stared up at Sadie, who now lay draped halfway out of the window. "Sims, Martin, climb up and bring her down." His stern expression bore not a hint of his former arrogance.

Henry and Bertie climbed on the barrel and braced their feet against their comrades' shoulders, forming a pyramid. Stretching their bodies upward beyond natural reach, they none too gently pulled Sadie through the window. As they lowered her to the ground, smoke billowed from her skirt and petticoats, and her leather shoes and long auburn hair smoldered.

Major Brigham pulled off his jacket and smothered the flames in her skirts, while another soldier found a bucket of water to douse her hair. The soldier named Bertie pulled off her ruined shoes and cast them aside.

"Move her away from the building." Brigham pointed toward the road.

The entire troop ran thirty yards to a place of relative safety, with Sadie bobbing limply in the arms of two soldiers.

Rachel followed and watched, praying all the while.

With a whimpering babe in her arms, she could do no more. Unconscious, Sadie moaned and cried out.

A thunderous roar sounded behind them, followed by a blast of heat. A hundred terrified cries filled the air. Rachel fell to her knees, managing not to drop Robby, then turned back to see the crowds running from the collapsed building. Fed by splintered wood, the fire once again roared out its fury. All the people moved a safe distance away. There they inspected themselves and their neighbors for injury. Cries of pain pierced the night.

Blackened and breathing heavily, Papa stood among the other helpers watching the disaster play itself out. Inez emerged from the throng and hastened to Rachel and helped her up.

"Señorita Folger! Are you well?"

Rachel nodded. "Yes, but Sadie isn't." She glanced toward the girl. "We must take care of her, Inez."

"*Sí*. God would have us do this." Inez moved to where Bertie, Henry and Brigham still knelt beside Sadie. "Señors, you have done your job." Her grandmotherly tone held a hint of authority. "Now you take this *pobre madrecita,* the poor little mother, to my kitchen house where I can care for her."

"Indeed?" Brigham glared at Inez. He glanced at Rachel, and his sneer relaxed. "Miss Folger?"

"Yes, of course. We'll take responsibility for her." She glanced over her shoulder.

The bucket line reformed and made progress in dousing the outer edges of the blaze. Three soldiers who had helped with Sadie hurried to join them.

"Major Brigham." Rachel's eyes stung with tears and soot, and her lungs felt as if they might burst. "Do you know…where the Crumps are?"

A sad, almost kindly expression filled his eyes, and he shook his head.

Comprehending his meaning, Rachel groaned. But she shuddered away her feelings. Robby had fallen asleep in her arms, and she would not waken him by weeping for the deaths of his grandparents.

"Mr. Sims, Mr. Martin," she said to the soldiers. "You saved Sadie's and Robby's lives. You were very brave."

Bertie Martin shook his head. "No, miss, 'twas yourself. If we hadn't heard you cryin' out, we'd've never known she was still in there. We never saw her in the window when we checked around back."

"Well done, men," Major Brigham said. "Well done, Miss Folger. I shall write of your courageous actions in my reports to the magistrate and the governor." He started back to the fire. "You men carry the girl to Miss Folger's store and make haste to return."

The soldiers lifted Sadie and followed Rachel and Inez home. The smoke set all of them to coughing. But the wind had not shifted, and the small party soon moved beyond the worst of the choking air.

"Señorita Folger, will you let me carry the child?" Inez's slumped posture revealed her exhaustion.

"No, Inez, I can manage." In truth, Rachel could not bear to surrender her precious burden, though he seemed to grow heavier with each step she took.

"Ah!" Inez cried out, her eyes round and white in her soot-covered face. "Another fire."

"Miss Folger," one soldier shouted, "it's your store."

Frederick's stomach knotted as he rode hard toward the settlement, with Corwin and Dr. Wellsey close behind him. During the three-mile journey, he mentally checked off the list of orders he had given at the outset of Corwin's alarm. Mrs. Winthrop was to wake Cook and have her prepare food for those who would fight the fire. His overseer would assemble the male slaves least likely to run away to come help in the settlement. Frederick ordered Dr. Wellsey to bring his bag and tend the injured. But amidst it all, he had only one prayer: *Dear God, please don't let it be the Folgers' mercantile.*

Nearing town, Frederick saw flames above the distant trees and gauged that the fire was far beyond the store. Relief swept through him. But the blaze rose so high that, even though the wind blew at his back, he smelled the stench of burning wood. He slowed his mount to a brisk trot as he tried to locate the tragedy somewhere beyond the trees. His companions followed suit.

"Oliver, check the church and vicarage." He pointed his riding crop toward a side street. "If all is well, come into town."

Without answering, Corwin rode away.

As they came around a giant oak tree, Dr. Wellsey reined his horse alongside Frederick. "The only buildings large enough to kindle such a fire are the store, the church and the inn."

"True." Frederick stared toward the darkened settlement, which seemed lit from behind by an eerie red glow. Muted shouts and cries met his ears. "You'll have many patients this night, doctor."

"Not what I would wish for, sir."

"There. Look."

A little more than a half mile away, red and orange flames blazed over the inn, and people darted about in a frenzy to save it. A great sudden roar filled the air as the building collapsed, sending people running in all directions. Their cries of fear rose in a crescendo above the bedlam. The flames diminished briefly. But fueled by the broken wood, they soon roared upward into the sky.

His eyes on the conflagration, Frederick cast a glance at the store as they rode by. A movement caught his attention, a dark form and a flicker of fire in the shrubbery next to the building. Fear for Miss Folger shot through him, and he pulled back on Essex's reins.

"Wait," he called to the doctor. "Here." He nudged Essex nearer just as a large bush burst into flames. The horse reared up and shrieked. Frederick nearly lost his seating. "Whoa, boy." He pulled to the side and jumped from the saddle, letting the reins fall free. "You there," he called to the fleeing man. "Stop."

The man ran into the forest behind the store, and Frederick charged after him.

"Sir," cried Wellsey. "It's starting to burn the building."

Frederick stopped short and spun about, racing back to the fire. He pulled off his coat and beat at the flames, but the linen fabric snagged on a branch and caught fire. He yanked it free and threw it in the sand where it could do no harm, then cast about for something to stop the blaze. A memory of something he had seen earlier in the day shot through his mind.

"Burlap. In the back room." Thankful the door was not locked, he dashed inside and grabbed several burlap bags. "Mr. Folger. Miss Folger," he called up the back stairs. When no one responded, he ran up the staircase to find an empty apartment, then hurried down the stairs and out the door. "The stream. Over there." Twenty feet from the store, a lazy spring ambled from beneath a limestone outcropping and wended its way toward the creek.

He and Wellsey plunged the bags into the water and ran to slap the drenched material against the burning wall. The battle raged for countless minutes. The flames seemed to die, but another spark ignited, and the dry bushes farther down the wall lit up the night.

Frederick and Wellsey alternated in their trips to the stream to rewet the burlap. Soon Frederick's arms and lungs ached. Wellsey seemed not to fare much better as he frequently stopped to gasp for breath. Just when Frederick thought he might fall to the ground in exhaustion, two men appeared beside him.

"Here, sir." A soldier grasped the damp bag and tugged it from Frederick's hands. "Let me take that."

His companion relieved Wellsey.

Frederick bent over, hands on his knees, and gulped in smoke-streaked air. After a violent bout of coughing, he rejoined the two new men.

Oliver appeared on the scene and set to work beside them. "The vicarage is unharmed. The vicar and his wife are safe at home."

Still struggling to breathe, Frederick shook his head. "Go back. I saw someone starting this fire, and I've no doubt they set the one at the inn. Watch over the Johnsons."

"Yes, sir." Oliver left without another word. No complaint about his assignment. No disputing Frederick's authority. Perhaps that was one fire quenched.

With the soldiers' help, they beat back the flames. One man found a hoe and chopped away all the vegetation near the building, removing it to the sandy area where Frederick lately had tossed his burned coat.

"Mr. Moberly."

A soft, shaky voice came from behind him. Frederick turned to see Miss Folger silhouetted against the glow of the still blazing inn. He hurried to her, longing to pull her into his arms, but stopped short at the sight of a sooty, ragged moppet in her arms.

"Are you well, dear lady?" He gently turned her to the light and found his reward: her fair face was blackened but unburned.

"I am well, sir." Her glistening tears caught the fire's red reflection and washed down her cheeks in black rivulets. "But poor Sadie is badly burned." She glanced beyond him. "You have saved our home." Sniffing, she wobbled where she stood but did not appear faint. "We shall be forever grateful." She gave her head a little shake. "We must see to Sadie. She's beside the road." She tilted her head. "Back there. Inez went for Papa."

He held her shoulders, then cupped her chin with one hand. "Carry the boy to the kitchen house. I'll bring Sadie." At her nod, he added, "Don't go into the store until I've made certain no live embers remain."

Again she nodded, but her eyes did not seem to focus.

"Wellsey, come see to Miss Folger."

As the good doctor led her away, Frederick sent up a prayer that she had not breathed in enough smoke to make her ill. At the thought of such a possibility, a nettling pain lodged in his chest. He must not lose her. *Must not.*

The urgency of his emotions startled him. His regard for her had deepened far beyond all previous contemplations, and he could do nothing to guarantee she would recover.

Chapter Thirteen

After assuring Dr. Wellsey that she had suffered no injury, Rachel requested that he assist Frederick in bringing Sadie to the kitchen house. There, at the doctor's direction, Rachel and Inez inspected beneath Sadie's skirts and found blisters on her feet, ankles and lower legs. He gave Rachel a small tin of salve, the same vile-smelling medicine he had put on her injured hand, and instructed her to apply it liberally to the wounds.

"We can treat the external injuries," he said, "but I fear she inhaled a great amount of smoke. Only time will tell whether she will recover." He closed his bag and walked toward the door. "I'll come back once I've seen what's needed at the inn."

After he left, Inez sniffed the salve and wrinkled her nose. "Why ruin aloe with bear grease?" She snorted as she began to spread the medicine on Sadie's wounds. "The aloe works good alone. Many people in the islands use it since my *antepasados,* ancestors, bring it there."

While Inez administered the healing balm, Rachel leaned over and wiped Sadie's face with a damp cloth.

Sadie moaned, and her eyelids fluttered. "Robby. Save my Robby."

"Shh. Don't fret, Sadie." Rachel blinked back tears. "Robby is safe." She glanced across the kitchen house. Inez had made the baby a bed in an old crate, and there he slept soundly. Rachel released a weary, broken sigh.

Inez eyed her. "Señorita, you must rest. Go to your new house and sleep there. I will see to the señora and *su niño.*"

"No, I should stay here. You're exhausted, too." Rachel slumped on a wooden bench. "Besides, Mr. Moberly wants to check the store to be certain the fire won't begin again." Fear gnawed at her. Why would someone want to burn down the inn and Papa's store?

"Miss Folger." Mr. Moberly stood in the doorway. "May I come in?"

"Please do." At the sight of his soot-covered hair and face and his singed shirt, a flurry of anguish and appreciation gripped her. He had risked his life to save the store.

"Oh, how will I, *we*, ever thank you?" The tears that had threatened for the past two hours now seized control. Choking sobs burst forth, and she covered her face in her hands.

His strong arms pulled her up into a comforting embrace. "Shh, there now. Everyone is safe." His gentle voice strummed a soothing chord in her soul, but she wept harder, gulping in air between sobs. After several moments, he gripped her upper arms and moved back a half step to look into her eyes. "Your father has returned from the fire."

She gasped. "Is he all right?"

"Believe me, Miss Folger, he is well." Mr. Moberly's even gaze conveyed the truth of his words. "He will come here after inspecting the store." He settled her back on the bench and sat beside her, draping an arm around her shoulders. "And you? Are you recovering?"

"Yes I believe so." Her words seemed to ease the tension in his face.

She leaned into his broad chest, discounting the impropriety and relishing the reassurance of his embrace.

"My overseer has brought workers from the plantation. They will sort through the debris at the inn and carry it away after the fire has been completely extinguished."

She nodded, but a nettling displeasure stung her conscience. When he said "workers," of course he meant slaves.

A cooling wind gusted in through the doorway, bringing a sprinkle of moisture.

Mr. Moberly bent down to capture Rachel's gaze. "Listen. Can you hear the rain? Would that it had come four hours ago."

His comment brought fresh tears to her eyes. "Yes. It might have saved Sadie's parents, if not the inn, too."

"Rachel. There ye are, my girl." Papa entered the kitchen house brushing raindrops from his filthy shirtsleeves.

"Papa." She stood and hurried to him. "Are you hurt? Burned? I saw your courage." She leaned into him, hoping for a hug. "You'll forgive me for disobeying, won't you? I had to help."

"I'm unharmed." Papa embraced her briefly, placing a quick kiss on her forehead. "And I do forgive ye. Mr. Moberly here told us how ye saved the girl and her babe. That's Nantucket courage, no mistake." The tenderness in his eyes belied his casual tone.

"Inez and I will take care of them." Rachel glanced at her servant, who nodded her agreement. "I knew you would wish it."

"Aye." Papa's scratchy voice revealed the fire's effects.

"I'd be ashamed if ye didn't take on the task." He looked at Mr. Moberly. "I've checked all over the house and store. A few boards are needed to replace the scorched ones, but we're in no danger. Ye saved my property, and I thank ye for it."

"If you need lumber," Mr. Moberly said, "I can provide it from my sawmill."

Papa appeared flustered. "Indeed. That's more than generous. Thank ye, sir."

Rachel noticed the heightened color in Mr. Moberly's soot-streaked face, and her heart delighted to see such feeling in a man of his position.

"I must go now." Mr. Moberly brushed a hand through his hair, sending soot cascading down his shirt-sleeves. "Major Brigham will want details about the man who started the fire. He's ordered the entire garrison to patrol the settlement until the man is caught." He took Rachel's hand and kissed it with more feeling than a mere courtesy. "Good night, Miss Folger, Mr. Folger."

He walked out into the growing rainstorm, and Rachel followed, stopping at the doorway to watch him mount his horse. As he rode out of sight, she ached to ride away with him, far away from the disaster.

Stinging rain pelted Frederick's head and back, but he ignored the discomfort, for the events of this night had secured more than one matter in his life. That Miss Folger's fondness and respect for him were growing, he felt more than hopeful. That he could manage Corwin and his dishonesty, he felt likewise sanguine. But the fire had tested him to a greater degree than any previous event in his life, and he had emerged triumphant. At the outset, he had known what to order, what to do. By God's mercy, he had seen the fire at the store and sent the culprit running. And never once had he surrendered to his fear.

How he longed to report the whole of it to Father, like a child seeking praise for well-formed letters or clever computations—anything to discredit Oliver's evil reports. But Father would dismiss it all if Frederick boasted. Best to make an objective list of events, leaving out his concerns for Miss Folger, of course, and point Father to the community's collective efforts. Perhaps Brigham would lend a note of praise, and Frederick would dispatch the same in return. He had yet to ascertain how to win the fellow over. Perhaps this event would seal that matter, as well.

When he reached the garrison, the guards recognized him and gave him entrance. One man led his horse away for grooming and oats. At the commander's house, a servant greeted him and offered a change of clothes.

"No, thank you, my good man. I won't be here long, and it's not cold."

The man brought towels to sop up moisture from his dripping shirt. Some of the soot had washed off in the rain, so he would not do too much damage to the commander's house.

"Mr. Moberly." Lady Augusta joined him in the small, elegant drawing room. She wore a modest dressing gown. And without her dreadful makeup, she seemed younger, prettier and decidedly more pleasant.

"Forgive me, madam, for my frightful appearance. Major Brigham asked me to come, but I shan't stay for long." He offered a lighthearted chuckle. "I promise I shall not sit down."

Her soft laughter sounded free of intrigue. "Thank you, sir, for then I should be required to have my chair recovered at your expense."

"As tired as I am, I should sit and pay the consequences. This night has brought its challenges."

At her second laugh, he relaxed further, but the memory of their last private meeting still cautioned him.

"You must know, madam, that your husband performed brilliantly tonight. In the thick of the fire, he executed his duty with unflinching courage." Frederick had not seen Brigham's performance, but others had praised the officer's valor.

A blush touched her cheeks. "Yes, I am certain of it." She glanced at the closed door behind her, then turned back to him with pleading eyes. "Will you temper your praise when you report the incident? Please?"

Frederick drew in a breath. "No, madam. That I cannot do."

"But our bargain—"

He glanced at Major Brigham's portrait above the fireplace. Dressed in uniform, he appeared the perfect British officer. "A fine picture. Gainsborough, if I'm not mistaken."

"Mr. Moberly."

He turned back and stared hard at her. "Madam." He leaned toward her and spoke softly lest Brigham enter the room and hear him. "Are you unaware that a man like your husband would rather die than face dishonor?"

Tears sprang to her eyes, and her jaw jutted forward. "Yes," she hissed. "And if forced to make such a choice, I would rather he be dishonored than die."

"Surely you do not mean that."

Her defiant expression answered him.

"Moberly." Brigham entered with a hand extended, but his stern look shot back and forth between Frederick and Lady Augusta.

"Brigham." Frederick shook his hand heartily, determined to ignore the suspicious stare. "What are your plans? I should like to accompany you as you pursue the culprit."

Brigham shook his head. "A man would be mad to order troops out in this weather. You've experienced an East Florida hurricane. This storm shows every sign of becoming one. If it diminishes tomorrow, we can decide about pursuit then."

"By then all tracks will have washed away, as they no doubt already have." Frederick grunted. "But you're right, of course."

"Will you have some tea, Mr. Moberly?" Lady Augusta asked.

He shook his head. "Thank you, madam, but no. I should like to be at home before the storm worsens."

Essex met the challenge of carrying Frederick through the blinding rain on the road back to the plantation. Along the way, Frederick bent into the headwind, wishing for his hat, which had blown off on the ride into town.

Just as the rain battered his head, Lady Augusta's request beat against his conscience. He had written the requested letter and came close to sending it with the latest mail delivery going to Father, but something had held him back. The letter sat in his desk, and now he would destroy it. Brigham was a brave man, the kind of soldier needed to help quash the rebellion up north. He would be shamed to know of his wife's machinations, seemingly on his account. And he would blame Frederick for his part in it.

What did a woman know of men's matters? Of a man's need to succeed in the world? Clearly, Frederick would have to choose between keeping his promise to Lady Augusta and honoring her courageous husband.

Chapter Fourteen

After a two-day storm, Frederick surveyed the damage to the plantation and gave orders for cleanup and repairs. Although the storm had prevented travel and all but the most necessary outdoor work, it was nothing like the previous year's hurricane. This time the overflowing creeks did not reach severe flood levels and had already receded to their natural banks. Branches littered the ground, but no trees had been blown down. And the slave quarters had escaped serious loss due to Frederick's recent orders to reinforce the structures to make them as sturdy as his other outbuildings.

Frederick had more reasons to be encouraged. During the fire, Oliver had obeyed orders without complaint. He had also displayed exceptional valor in rescuing plantation animals in the storm. Perhaps his letters to Father had been written out of frustration over his future. While Frederick faced the challenges of a younger son, Oliver's illegitimacy presented a far more formidable barrier to advancement. No doubt he had been tortured all his life by not knowing his paternity, and Father's generosity must have seemed like the actions of a guilt-ridden parent. Oliver's courage called for extending another chance to work out their conflicts.

The air smelled fresh and clean, and the fragrance of pine wafted on the breeze. But the sun returned from its two-day absence eager to make up for lost time. It beat down smartly on Frederick's back as he rode toward town along the leaf-strewn road. Yet he would endure a fiery furnace to reach the mercantile and discover whether the Folgers had suffered any loss from the hurricane. With Mr. Folger there, Frederick had some assurance that the man who started the fires could not cause any further mischief. But until he saw Miss Folger himself, he would feel no peace.

At the edge of town, he encountered Major Brigham on horseback overseeing the removal of a fallen oak tree lying across the road. The officer hailed him.

"Moberly, how fares your plantation?" His military demeanor bore not a hint of his former arrogance.

"Very well, sir. A few repairs are needed, but nothing to complain of. And the garrison?"

"Likewise." Brigham reined his horse closer. "You will want to know we have a suspect in the matter of the fires."

"Indeed?" Frederick felt an odd mix of disappointment and satisfaction. He would gladly have caught the man himself and seen to his punishment. "Did you apprehend him?"

"No." Brigham shook his head. "As we surmised, he fled into the wilderness. But we are confident of his identity. You recall of course the innkeeper's dead goose."

"Buckner." Frederick spat out the name and felt a mad desire to hunt the man down forthwith.

"He is the only man unaccounted for in the regiment,

and we assume he's deserted." Brigham snorted. "Sims reported that Buckner carried a great deal of resentment after the goose incident. He vowed to make everyone pay dearly for his demotion. Vile coward."

"And a murderer."

"Too bad the man cannot be hanged twice."

"Beggin' yer pardon, sir." A soldier carrying an ax approached Brigham.

"Yes, sergeant."

"We're goin' ta need a winch to haul this tree off the road, sir." The man brushed sweat from his face. "It's too big to chop apart so we can clear the road in a timely way."

"Very well. See to it." Brigham turned back to Frederick. "If you're in agreement, I'll write letters to the commanders of other garrisons around East Florida to watch for Buckner."

Surprised, Frederick took a moment to consider the proposal and the manner in which it was delivered. Brigham had changed much in a short time.

"Yes, of course. Your signature will carry as much weight as mine in this matter." Frederick saluted Brigham with his riding crop. "If you need a winch, send someone to the plantation, and Corwin will make mine available."

"Thank you, sir." Brigham nodded his appreciation. "I'll do that."

Frederick took his leave, anxious to tell Miss Folger about Buckner. If the man dared to return to the settlement, she would need protection.

He left Essex in the shade of an oak tree and walked through a maze of puddles to the store, giving the building a cursory inspection before he stepped up on the narrow wooden porch. Inside, he found the object of his concern and immediately cast aside all worries. Serenity floated on the air with the scent of lavender.

As lovely as ever, Miss Folger stood behind the counter measuring a length of linen for the customer who stood on the other side. Frederick recognized the woman as a servant indentured to an upriver planter.

Miss Folger glanced up, and her face brightened. "Good morning, Mr. Moberly. I shall be with you in a moment."

The slender servant gasped. "Oh, no, miss. You must help the magistrate. I can wait."

"Not at all," Frederick said. "I'm in no hurry. Complete your transaction."

"Thank you, sir." Miss Folger turned back to the customer.

The other woman bent near her and muttered something in urgent tones.

Miss Folger shook her head. "Be at ease, Esther. Unlike other British aristocrats, Mr. Moberly does not insist that the waters should part before him."

The woman cocked her head and then glanced at Frederick. "If you're sure, miss."

Miss Folger folded and wrapped the linen. "There. Two dress lengths of brown, one dress length of white and thread to match. Will there be anything else for Mrs. Allen?"

"No, miss." The woman gathered her mistress's purchases and hurried out, but not before casting a nervous glance Frederick's way.

Struggling not to laugh, he sauntered to the counter. "So you do not find me an ogre—like most aristocrats?"

"I've not yet made up my mind." Miss Folger returned a box of snuff to the display case. "It is difficult to change an opinion one has held for a lifetime."

He leaned his arms on a small cask on the counter and tilted his head. "And such a terribly long lifetime, too." Emotion flooded him such as he had never felt for any young lady, but what to name it, he did not know. Surely his face must proclaim his feelings for her, for she blushed and her hands shook as she rewrapped the bolt of linen. He gently gripped them, enjoying the silken feel of her skin. "It is good to see you well and unharmed by the storm."

She pulled one hand loose and placed it on top of his. "And you, as well, dear friend." Her soft rush of words revealed feeling that seemed to match the depth of his own.

The jingle of the doorbells shattered the sweet moment. Miss Folger quickly freed her hands, but Frederick leaned against the counter and crossed his arms in a tranquil pose. He would not be ashamed of their friendship, even if Father himself should walk through the door.

Still, he did not wish for anyone to misunderstand his lingering presence. He straightened and sauntered toward the gun display to peruse the small selection. But his gaze frequently turned toward Miss Folger.

"Good morning, John," she said to her customer, the settlement's new wheelwright. "May I help you?"

Like the woman before him, the young man glanced at Frederick and asked whether he should not be served first.

"The magistrate is still considering his purchases." Miss Folger gave the man a reassuring smile. "John, am I correct in assuming congratulations are in order?"

"Yes, miss." John grinned broadly. "'Tis our first, a fine, healthy boy."

"Do you have a name for him?" Her lovely dark eyes

exuded genuine kindness, a rare quality that Frederick found endearing.

"'Twill be William, if I have my way," John said. "George, if she has hers."

Miss Folger's merry laugh echoed in Frederick's heart. "Knowing Mary, I think you will be calling him George."

John's laugh held somewhat less mirth. "'Tis true, miss. But I love 'er all the same, and I'd like to buy her some small gift. Can you suggest anything?"

"Indeed, I can." She pulled a tray from beneath the counter. "We have several whalebone items carved by our Mr. Patch. Thimbles, combs, a candlestick and the like."

While John hunched over the tray and consulted with Miss Folger, Frederick found himself captured by the scene. This lovely young lady had a grace about her that entirely enchanted him. Like Mother, she did not hold herself above the common man, but treated the wheel-wright with the same courtesy she had shown the more prominent guests at Frederick's party. No arrogance, no hauteur, nothing artificial. Except for his own sister, he had never known a young lady with such a generous demeanor—and good humor, as well.

While John argued for the practicality of a thimble, Miss Folger insisted his wife deserved nothing less than a pretty comb. In the end, Miss Folger won, but John seemed as pleased as she when he left the store with his purchase.

Frederick set his elbows on a tall display, rested his chin on his fists and gazed across the room at her. He re-called the tender emotion that had filled him as this de-lightful creature leaned into his embrace after the fire, thus revealing her trust in him. Now, deep sentiments for her stirred within him, feelings so strong he wondered if he could speak to her again without declaring his love. But no, he must wait. Must not play her false. Must examine his emotions to be certain of their depth and nature…and ensure that they would last forever.

Rachel's hands shook as she arranged the whalebone carvings in their tray. In the corner of her eye, she saw Mr. Moberly staring at her with twinkling eyes and a half smile, his admiration clear. With her own emotions in such a muddle, she feared even to speak to him again.

While waiting on John, she had wanted to ask the wheelwright's opinion of the revolution, but Mr. Moberly's presence prevented that. Yet she did not want the gentleman to leave. Indeed, recalling how much she had enjoyed his comforting embrace after the fire, she would not have him leave at all. Ever.

But with all their differences, could they ever truly be friends…or more? *Lord, let me not mistake Your leading in this.*

She sent a tentative glance in his direction. "Did you find something of interest, Mr. Moberly?"

"Indeed, I have found something of interest, Miss Folger. But the price is very dear—far beyond that of rubies."

Rachel could think of no response, for doubtless he would indeed pay dearly if they proceeded. Yet neither of them seemed to possess the power to stop. As he approached, she saw the ruddy color in his face was heightened, as hers must be.

He set one hand on the tray of wares, preventing her from moving it below the counter. "May I look at these? Ah, what fine craftsmanship. You must commend your Mr. Patch for me."

"I shall do that." Inhaling a deep breath, Rachel forced her racing pulse to slow. "Perhaps you would like to purchase something for dear Mrs. Winthrop."

He raised his eyebrows. "What an excellent idea. What do you suggest?"

"This candlestick is quite exquisite, do you not think?" Holding up the round article with a two-masted ship carved on its side, Rachel risked a glance into his dark gray eyes. Her pulse raced again.

"Perfect." He took it in hand, brushing her fingers with his, and a pleasant shiver shot up her arm and tickled her neck. "I will take it."

While Rachel wrapped the gift, Mr. Moberly stared at her again, while a teasing grin played across his lips.

She tried to tie twine around the package, but it slipped. "If you expect me to accomplish this, you must stop staring at me."

"Never." He stuck his finger against the string while she completed the task.

"Thank you." Rachel continued to stare at the package and prayed for some objective matter to discuss. A memory sparked in her mind, and her prayer became thanks. "For some time, I have wanted to tell you how much I admired your decision about the indentured man who stole the pig."

He straightened, and a frown swept over his fine features. "Truly? I still wonder about it."

Rachel's heart reached out to him. He seemed so young to hold the fate of hapless souls in his hands. "You must set your mind at ease. You displayed the wisdom of Solomon, and shame forced the owner to relinquish his demands for punishment, since he could not bear to administer it himself. You were guided by mercy, as our heavenly Father is merciful."

His countenance lightened, and he breathed out a long sigh. "Miss Folger, your words have dispelled my anguish. I am grateful."

Now she could gaze at him without shyness. In fact, she felt infused with courage. "'Tis nearly noon. Will you join us for our midday meal?"

"I should like to very much, but duty calls. I must ensure that the rest of the settlement has survived the storm." He claimed his hat from a nearby display. "And I must examine the ruins of the inn."

"Yes, of course." At the memory of the tragedy, Rachel's heart hitched. "Dr. Wellsey came to see Sadie early this morning. He suggests that she is not yet well enough to be told of her parents' deaths."

"I am grieved for her." He glanced away with a grimace. "After our pleasant chat, I despair of telling you this, but I must. Major Brigham has informed me that the culprit is none other than Private Buckner, who sought to steal the Crumps' goose."

"Oh, my." Rachel shuddered at the memory of the brutal soldier.

"He fled into the wilderness, and with the weather improved, the entire garrison will search for him. You may rest assured that he will be apprehended. But we all must keep watch for him and prevent him from doing more harm." Mr. Moberly touched her hand. "I do not think you need to fear."

"I promise to be vigilant."

But as he walked out the door, Rachel sorted through another muddle of emotions, as her delightful memories of Mr. Moberly's visit vied with her fear of the murderer who had yet to be apprehended.

Chapter Fifteen

"Reverend Johnson's homily certainly suited our town's recent trials," Mrs. Winthrop said. "Do you not agree, Mr. Folger?" Seated across from Rachel and Papa in Mr. Moberly's fine carriage, the lady appeared the picture of serenity.

"Aye, madam." Papa's voice rang with enthusiasm. "The vicar's passage from the Book of James expresses the thinking that's guided my life for fifty-two years."

Rachel glanced sideways at him, working to keep shock from her expression. In vain she had tried these many years to extract a claim to faith from Papa. Yet Mrs. Winthrop had drawn out his deepest thoughts with a simple question.

"How so, sir?" Mrs. Winthrop's lined face seemed smoother as she gazed at him.

Papa scratched his chin, which lately he had kept clean-shaven, no doubt on Mrs. Winthrop's account. "As we saw last week and, I'm sure ye'd agree, ofttimes in our years on this earth, our lives truly are vapors that appear for a short time and then vanish away. A man'd be a fool to presume his own plan to buy and sell and get gain was equal to divine will."

While he and Mrs. Winthrop turned their conversation from the sermon to other matters, Rachel eased back into her seat and looked ahead, where Mr. Moberly and Mr. Corwin rode horseback side by side, leading the way to the plantation. Papa's response had not been what she had hoped for, but it did reveal something new. At least he believed God existed. She offered up a silent prayer that Mrs. Winthrop would draw him closer to the Almighty.

Traces of delightful aromas—baked chicken and peach pie—met them as they came around the familiar stand of palm trees, and Rachel's stomach rumbled softly. Smoke from the kitchen house sent a gauzy curtain over their view, but a breeze from the east soon unveiled the elegant white mansion. Today, the front columns wore no festive bunting, and no slaves worked the distant fields. Rachel did, however, see uniformed black servants out front awaiting the arrival of their master and his party.

Did Mr. Moberly provide church services for those who worked his fields and cooked his meals? Did he grant them at least part of each Sunday as a Sabbath rest, according to Scripture as Papa did for Inez? Now her heart rumbled in rhythm with her stomach, and her mind churned with more questions, especially regarding overseers and chains. If Mr. Moberly could not answer them to her satisfaction, she must find a way to silence forever the siren call of...*friendship* that sang both night and day in her heart.

Oh, why was she using that word? What she felt for dear Mr. Moberly was far more than friendship. It was nothing less than the painful pangs of love.

Yet as she stepped from the carriage, climbed the front steps, and walked through the mansion's red front door on Mr. Moberly's arm, she felt as if she were coming home—a bewildering sensation.

Inside, familiar servants stood ready to attend to every need of their master's guests. The same sweet little slave girl sat in the dining room corner waving a large palm branch to direct the indifferent breeze drifting in through two tall windows.

Seated with the others at the dining room table, Rachel surrendered to her appetite and enjoyed the many courses the servants set before her. She noticed with interest that no trace of fear or unhappiness could be found on any of their faces, a credit to their master. Did they yearn for freedom beneath their placid smiles? Uncovering their true opinions would be difficult.

After many light pleasantries, Papa eyed Mr. Moberly. "Tell me, sir, have ye discovered the identity of the man who's trying to stir up trouble in the tavern?"

Rachel choked on her rice. Should Papa discover the patriot, surely he would not betray the man, despite his indifference to the cause.

"Unfortunately, no." Mr. Moberly buttered a piece of bread. "But we continue to get reports of his appearances at the oddest times and places."

"Well," Papa said, "I've been keeping an eye out for him amongst my customers, but no stout, red-bearded man's come in the store."

"We are grateful for your vigilance," Mr. Moberly said. "But in truth, I do not believe he has found any sympathizers for the rebels' cause."

"True, true." Papa savored a bite of chicken. "We shouldn't have to contend with the likes of him when we've got renegade soldiers starting fires."

"Mr. Folger," Mrs. Winthrop said, "you and your daughter have been so kind to take in Sadie and her son." Her eyes soft with sympathy, she turned to Rachel. "Who is caring for them today?"

"Our servant, Inez." Rachel served herself a second helping of greens from the bowl held by a liveried slave. "She's very good with both mother and child and willingly gave up her Sunday morning off to attend to their needs."

"What a comfort." Mrs. Winthrop looked at Mr. Moberly. "What is to be done with the little boy if Sadie does not recover?"

"Can you not guess, madam?" Papa set down his food-laden fork. "Rachel and I will care for the lad."

Mrs. Winthrop's face seemed to glow with beatific beauty. "Why, sir, that is more than generous."

"Indeed, it is." Mr. Moberly gave Rachel a merry grin. "He's an active little scamp. Do you not tire of chasing him?" His well-formed lips gave way to a teasing grin.

"You may be surprised to learn that Papa keeps little Robby out of mischief more than I do and enjoys every minute of it."

"'Tis no more tiring than gamboling with my eldest daughter's little ones." Papa grinned broadly, then sobered. "Too many years was I out to sea chasing whales while my daughters grew up without me. Should need arise, I'll be a father to the boy and rear him, as I did Captain Templeton." Papa's eyes shone with feeling, and Rachel knew he missed Jamie. But she acknowledged sweet surprise at hearing of his regrets over missing much of her childhood.

"Then the boy will be well reared, sir." Mr. Moberly gave Papa an approving nod. "I must tell you, however, I asked Major Brigham to send word to Sadie's husband about the tragedy. With the insurrection in the northern colonies, it may be some time before he replies to advise us about any relatives in England. Until then, we must pray God's mercy for this family, that they might not suffer another loss."

"Amen," Papa said.

Rachel pursed her lips and concentrated on eating the aromatic, spicy greens on her plate. Perhaps her prayers had been answered. Perhaps the fire had changed Papa's thoughts about trusting the Lord. As for Mr. Moberly's encouragement to pray, how could it mean anything other than that he was a Christian who sought to do God's will?

After dinner, the party stepped outside for an afternoon stroll. Papa and Mrs. Winthrop lagged behind while Rachel took Mr. Moberly's offered arm with gratitude, for many roots and rocks covered the unfamiliar ground.

The East Florida skies were filled with wispy, meandering clouds and not a hint of rain. The scent of oranges filled the air, and the oyster-shell pathways crunched beneath their feet. Beside the unpainted shacks in the slave quarters, men, women and children tended private gardens or hung laundry they had washed in the stream. Around many of the humble homes, youthful slaves swept the sandy brown earth into tidy patterns with pine bows. Here and there, pansies and marigolds flourished in broken crockery or little wooden boxes.

As Rachel and Mr. Moberly walked past the humble homes, the slaves stopped their work to offer a respectful greeting. To each one, Mr. Moberly responded kindly and by name, the latter of which Rachel regarded as a remarkable accomplishment. She clasped his arm more firmly, a gesture that must have pleased him, for he set his hand over hers as they continued their walk.

"Shall we visit the springhouse?" He pointed toward a pathway meandering through the pine forest. Overhead, tree branches met to shield them from the harsh summer heat.

"Yes. I would like that." Rachel glanced behind to see Papa and Mrs. Winthrop walking arm in arm, their heads tilted toward one another as if they were old friends.

"They will follow." Mr. Moberly squeezed her hand. "Mrs. Winthrop is exacting in matters of propriety. She'll not permit us to go unchaperoned." He glanced behind them. "And I'm sure your father is of the same mind."

Rachel nodded her agreement. Papa had come close to calling Charles out—with a harpoon, no less—when he began courting her sister Susanna. But he had never mentioned Mr. Moberly's attention toward her. Surely after today, Papa would perceive the depth of their mutual interest.

When they reached the springhouse, Mr. Moberly led Rachel to a little arbor woven of tender oak branches. She sat on a cushioned cast-iron bench while he fetched cups of water. After the first tasty sip, she inhaled a deep breath, knowing she could no longer put off the inevitable conversation. She considered several ways to begin but found none satisfactory.

"Is it all right?" Mr. Moberly lifted his own cup. "Seems good. The servants are instructed to keep leaves and other debris from the cistern."

Rachel's heart leapt. A perfect opening. "Why, yes, it's every bit as delicious as before. But forgive me, sir. Do you not mean 'slaves' instead of 'servants'?"

Seated beside her, he blinked in the most charming

way, and she could not help but notice how his black eyelashes enhanced the appeal of his dark gray eyes.

"What an interesting question." He placed one finger against his chin in a thoughtful pose.

The pleasant fragrance of his shaving balm threatened to undo her senses. She detected the scent of bergamot and perhaps a bit of petitgrain. "Had you never considered it?" she managed to ask.

"Cannot say I ever have. But that is not to say I should not." He sat back against the arbor wall, extended his legs and crossed his arms. With a winsome grin, he added, "I shall consider anything you wish, dear lady."

Heat rushed to her face, as much from annoyance as from the pleasantness of his being close to her.

"Thank you. For I have many questions to ask you."

"Many?" His eyebrows arched. "Then let us begin."

She bit her lip to keep from smiling. "I am in earnest, Mr. Moberly."

Amusement disappeared from his face. "Forgive me. Please proceed."

She gazed beyond the bower opening to see Papa and Mrs. Winthrop seated on the cistern's wide coquina wall. From his broad gestures, she could tell Papa was relating one of his whaling adventures. The two of them spoke together easily. Perhaps that came with age, for they certainly had not known one another long enough for familiarity to have engendered such harmony. Or perhaps it was because neither of them demonstrated a passion as strong as Rachel's for matters that ate at her soul.

With a quick breath, she stared up at Mr. Moberly, noting against her will how his softened expression enhanced his handsome features. "Sir, I despise slavery of any sort. When my Quaker ancestors settled on Nantucket Island, they vowed before God that they would never enslave a person of any race or gender or age. While some of us have left the Society of Friends, we have not lost our hatred of slavery."

"Ah." He uncrossed his arms and placed his hands on his knees, while understanding filled his eyes. "I see. And so, of course, you are concerned about the slaves who work my plantation."

"Yes." Her answer came out in a breathless rush.

He seemed not to notice but, rather, studied the ground at his feet as if thinking over her words. "It may surprise you to know my mother shares your sentiments." He looked away and broke off a green twig from the arbor's latticed wall. "Father, of course, remains detached from all his New World enterprises so long as they are prosperous."

Hope surged through Rachel. "But how do you regard the matter?"

"I am my father's agent, Miss Folger. I must do his will just as my servants...*slaves* must do mine. That is, if we are to make this plantation a success." His firm tone conveyed no displeasure, only that to him his statements were simple facts.

Rachel's pulse pounded. Could he hear it? "Success means much to you, then?"

He sat up, and his eyes widened. "Why, of course. What man worth his daily bread does not seek to succeed?" His lips twitched with merriment, and her pulse increased. "Perhaps you are aware that in England younger sons do not inherit any portion of entailed estates, as my father's is. Therefore, we must make our own way in the world."

"Yes, you mentioned something to that effect the day we met."

"I am honored you recall my words."

Rachel gave him a sly look. "'Twas merely good business. You were a new customer and an important one. I took care to remember." Someday she would confess she had disliked him that day simply for being English.

"Ah." He chuckled. "A commendable habit if one wishes to—dare I say it?—*succeed*."

"Humph." She could not quite pucker away her smile. "I was merely tending to my father's interests."

"Of course," he murmured. "That is something I fully understand."

Somehow she must turn the conversation back to the slaves. But before she could begin, he inhaled as if about to speak, and so she waited.

"Lately, I have felt an even stronger desire than before to prove myself." He seized another twig and twirled it between his thumb and forefinger. "May I tell you why?"

"Certainly. I shall keep your secret."

"Can you not guess, Miss Folger? If I continue to do well for my father, he can have fewer objections to our…oh, bother, I'm weary of calling this a 'friendship' when to me it is nothing short of a courtship." He sat back as if disconcerted, and his face was flushed, as if he were embarrassed. "There." He tossed the twig to the ground. "I've laid my heart bare before you. Do with it as you will."

Compassion filled her, along with the desire to reveal her own heart. But caution swept unbidden into her mind. "Sir, I shall always regard your heart as worthy of the tenderest care."

He stared at the ground and frowned, his disappointment evident. "I have spoken too hastily. Forgive me."

"Not at all." Rachel set her hand on his forearm. "I would but remind you there are differences in our opinions on certain essential matters. Such disparities do not make tranquil marriages. Did we not agree to discuss these things?"

His brow furrowed. "Yes, we did. Again, forgive me." He ran his hand through his hair, loosening several black strands from his queue. He brushed them back behind his ear. The ever-present stray curl graced his noble brow and enhanced his charm. "Tell me what concerns you. The slavery issue, of course. What else?"

"The revolution."

"The—? Ah, yes. The revolution." He stared out of the arbor with a dark frown. But he sent her a playful glance. "Now, really, Miss Folger. Do not tell me you are the red-bearded agitator trying to incite rebellion in our midst."

She smirked. "If only I could be." She dismissed her levity. "We...that is, the thirteen northern colonies mean to have their independence from England." She swallowed. "And had I not been forced to come here with Papa, I would be in Boston doing everything in my power to help their grand cause."

Dismay filled his eyes for a moment, and he gave her a sad smile. "I would expect nothing less from you, brave lady that you are. And so we have much to consider, do we not?"

Rachel bent her head in agreement, but a knot filled her chest at the thought of losing his regard because of their differences. Would it truly come to that?

Chapter Sixteen

He had not meant to declare himself to her. What had incited him to such an extreme? Her eyes, of course. Those dark questioning eyes that made him turn to soft butter inside. Those inviting lips, which had tempted him nearly to distraction as he sat close to her in the arbor. That pert little nose, which wiggled in the most charming way when she spoke with passion about her interests. The scent of her lavender perfume, the modest cut of her gown that nonetheless enhanced her feminine form.

Frederick exhaled a happy sigh at the memory of her seated later at the pianoforte, enchanting the entire household with her exquisite playing. Despite months away from an instrument, she had quickly regained her skills. What an accomplished young lady.

He sat in his library with both feet propped on the desk, a pose that had earned him more than one scolding from Father. But somehow the earl's specter seemed less ominous than before. Now Miss Folger's image pervaded his every thought, his every feeling. His desire for her approval had begun to weigh more heavily upon him. While not quite supplanting Father, she had nearly attained preeminence. But pleasing her might turn out to be every whit as difficult.

Managing the plantation without slaves was a preposterous notion, of course, but somehow he must convince her of his kindly intentions toward his workers. Perhaps he could convince her of the good she herself could do for the slaves as the plantation's mistress, much like Mother's ministrations to the villagers near Bennington Manor.

As for the foolish rebellion up north, he had no doubt that would soon be quashed. A farmers' militia had no chance against trained British forces, and the colonists had no navy to fight His Majesty's unparalleled fleet. Frederick had not meant to deceive Miss Folger in regard to his opinions about the conflict, merely to diffuse her concerns about his feelings. Of course, he could never say so, but soon enough their differences would be settled by the course of history. He only hoped her friends up north wouldn't suffer for their participation in that rebellious cause.

With her departure, he felt the ache of missing her presence mingled with hope that they could soon resolve everything. If only he could comprehend her thinking and satisfy her concerns.

"Ah! Of course," he exclaimed.

Frederick rose from his desk and strode to the bookshelf. From behind John Milton's *Paradise Lost,* he retrieved *A Declaration of Rights and Grievances.* His fingers touched the pamphlet, and he had to force himself back to the desk rather than to the fireplace to burn the seditious paper. He read it over in a few minutes and wondered about its implications.

Everyone had known for some time of the difficulties in the dissenting colonies. Father would rant about it from time to time, especially after a session of Parliament. Undoubtedly, the earl had been one of those who had voted in favor of the choking restrictions placed on Massachusetts Bay. But now that Frederick had settled in the New World, he found the punishments leveled against the colonists to be harsh in the extreme, despite their throwing a shipload of tea into the Boston Harbor in '73. Many times he himself had longed to lodge a protest against the taxes on the plantation's produce, but Father would permit no complaints against His Majesty.

"Interesting reading?" Oliver appeared in the doorway, and his gaze shot to the pamphlet. He sauntered across the eight feet from door to desk as Frederick struggled to fold it with nonchalance.

"Merely passing the time." Frederick opened the desk drawer, put the document inside and then casually closed the drawer. Later he would place it where Oliver would never find it.

Oliver sat down and lounged in a wingback chair in front of the desk. He leveled a smug look at Frederick. "So you've fallen for the little Nantucket wench."

Rage shot through Frederick. Leaning forward, he clenched his fists on the desk and glared at Oliver. "If you use that word to describe her again, I shall call you out."

Oliver blinked and frowned. "Now, now, Freddy, no need for anger. I'll call her whatever you wish." He studied his fingernails, then stared at the ceiling. "Except Mrs. Moberly."

Frederick sat back, grasping for the appearance of calm while his emotions stormed within. "Suit yourself. There will be no need for any form of addressing her when you've returned to London." The quaver in his voice betrayed him.

Oliver's face flamed red clear up to his ears. "When my letter reaches Lord Bennington, *you* will be the one who returns to London."

Frederick went cold for the briefest moment. But the warmth returning to his chest was not anger, rather, an odd reassurance. So Oliver had indeed written the letter, and Father would soon know about Miss Folger. So be it. Let the dice fall as they would. He had not yet crossed the Rubicon, but the bridge was in sight.

"Why did you come in here, Ollie?" Frederick used the name he had called this former friend in childhood. Alas, when had they ceased to be friends?

Oliver smirked. "I thought you should know that I have written to Lord Bennington about your *courtship*." Sarcasm laced his tone.

Frederick drummed his fingers on the desk. "Oh, my friend, what makes you think I have not sent a letter to Father, as well? Did you think I would let him continue to regard me as a wastrel when in truth I have discovered proof of your dipping into plantation funds?" Despising the tremor of anger in his voice, he focused on his quill pen and raised his gaze only when he could speak in a tranquil tone. "My father is no fool. He will quickly discern your purpose in accusing me of impropriety."

"Do you think he will believe you, since you have showed such poor judgment in regard to other matters?" With a snort, Oliver stood and walked to the window, from whence he sent a sneering grin over his shoulder. "Besides, it is not as if I have absconded with the money. I have merely held it in trust for you against the day when you overspend and have need of it."

"Ha!" The tension in Frederick's chest burst free. "If

that is true, then return it to me with a full accounting of your expenditures."

Oliver stared out the window. "And if I do not?"

Once again, Frederick drummed his fingers on the desk. "I do not wish to discredit you to my father. However, you have already betrayed me, and I think it only fair—"

"I have not 'betrayed' you…yet."

"But your letter?" Hope sprang up once more.

"Awaiting the next shipment to Lord Bennington." Oliver coughed out a mirthless laugh. "Surely you don't think I would be fool enough to entrust it to just any merchant vessel, do you?"

"Ah. I see. So no harm has truly been done." Frederick permitted a wave of jubilation to flow through him. "Oliver, let us put aside all this foolish rancor between us. There is no reason we cannot help each other achieve our desired goals." He offered him a genial grin. "Give me the money and the letter, and I shall help you devise a satisfactory future for yourself."

Oliver crossed his arms and clenched his teeth. "I suppose you mean away from St. Johns Settlement."

"Do you not agree that would be best?"

Oliver puffed out a mild snort. "I shall give it some thought." But as he left the room, the sly narrowing of his eyes did nothing to reassure Frederick.

Rachel stood inside the kitchen house door. "How is Sadie?"

"Shh. We must speak softly." Inez tilted her head toward the cot where Robby lay asleep. "She slept well through the night. I think the lemonade made this possible."

"I'm glad. Mr. Moberly sent a generous portion, for

Dr. Wellsey is convinced that lemon can heal fever."
Rachel lifted Sadie's sheet to inspect her injuries, but
shuddered at the blackened, peeling skin visible at the
edges of the fresh bandages.

"Ah. Mr. Moberly." Inez gave Rachel a sidelong look.
"A very kind man, *si?*"

"Yes." Rachel covered Sadie's feet. "And I know you
want to hear all about my conversation with him yesterday."

"*Sí.*" Inez leaned close. "You must tell me everything."

Rachel glanced out the door. "I have to help Papa in
the store soon, but I can tell you this. I lay awake long
into the night considering what we discussed." She motioned for Inez to sit with her on the raised edge of the
brick hearth, where a cast-iron pot hung above the embers keeping warm the cinnamon-flavored oat porridge.
The room had a cozy atmosphere, with garlic, onions
and dried peppers hanging from the low rafters, and
the fragrance of other spices blending into an aromatic
stew for the senses.

"Mr. Moberly says he can no longer refer to us as
mere friends." Rachel enjoyed the grin creasing Inez's
angular face. "Instead, he insists we are courting."

Inez's whole body shook as she clearly tried to contain her mirth. "Did I not tell you?"

Rachel struggled to mute her own laughter, but truth
soon seized her. Soberly, she gave Inez the details of
the previous day. "How can I receive his courtship until
we resolve our differences over slavery and the revolution?" Her heart aching, she studied the maternal concern in Inez's expression.

"Mistress, this thing I have heard of *el patrón*. He is
a kind master." She held her hands in a prayerful pose,

and her eyes moistened. "If a man must live in *la esclavitud*, enslavement, then he must pray to belong to such a one as Mr. Moberly."

The intensity of her words brought tears to Rachel's eyes. "But why must anyone, man or woman, be enslaved?"

Inez took Rachel's hands in her soft grasp. "This I do not know. It is *simplemente* the way of this world." Her brow furrowed. "Mistress, I know how this matter troubles you, but I cannot advise you. Only *Dios* can."

As they rose from the hearth, Rachel embraced Inez. "I know. But you can pray for me."

"*Sí*, señorita, that I always do."

Rachel left the kitchen house and hurried across the patchy grass yard to the store's back door. She wished for more time with Inez, for no one else could be trusted to keep her deepest secrets. Inez possessed a true servant's heart, such as the apostles exhorted Christians to have. Rachel could not imagine her friend ever rebelling against her servanthood. Nor, for that matter, could Rachel picture her encouraging the revolution. Although the Spanish woman had seen much injustice in her long life, she accepted it with grace that could come only from God. Yet surely there was a time when one should and must stand up against the forces of evil domination, whether by a slave master or a wicked king.

Once inside the back room, she heard Papa's cheerful banter, and curiosity propelled her through the burlap curtain and into the shop. At the sight of Major Brigham, she almost withdrew. Before she could retreat, both Papa and the officer turned and saw her.

"Here she is." Papa beckoned to her. "Come, daughter. Hear the good major's news."

Her face burning, Rachel forced a curtsy. "Good

morning, sir." Her feet seemed reluctant to obey as she forced herself across the floor. True, just one week ago, she and this man had helped to save Sadie and Robby. But though Major Brigham and Lady Augusta had attended services yesterday, they had left the church immediately afterward, speaking to no one. If Lady Augusta had pointed her aristocratic nose any higher, she would have fallen over backward wearing that ridiculous wig and enormous bonnet.

"Miss Folger." Major Brigham nodded briefly, but he also smiled. Rachel was not the fainting sort, else she might have required smelling salts at receiving such courtesy from the man. "I bring you and your father good tidings from Governor Tonyn."

"The governor?" Rachel grasped for an air of nonchalance, but her squeaking voice no doubt gave her away.

If the officer noticed, he gave no sign of it. "Indeed. You are both invited to the capital for the governor's ball." He seemed proud of himself for bestowing such news.

Her jaw slack, Rachel looked at her father, whose chest was puffed out as though he had harpooned a particularly large whale.

"Say something, child." Papa's tone chided her. "Do ye not wish to know what brings us such honor?"

Rachel's belly clenched. Her proud father, once one of Nantucket's most respected whaling captains, now in obeisance to this officer in that despicable King George's army.

"Forgive me, Papa. I fear I am stunned into silence."

"Of course." Major Brigham smirked. "It is stunning news, after all. But as His Majesty's representative, the governor endeavors to do everything to make our colonists happy in this vast wilderness."

Rachel nearly bit her tongue to keep from adding *and no doubt to avoid the troubles King George has caused with the northern colonists.* "But why invite us?"

"Ah, well." Major Brigham fingered a nearby bolt of lace and inspected it through his quizzing glass. "I sent word of the fire to His Eminence immediately after the storm. My messenger returned last evening with the news that the governor insists upon rewarding the community's efforts to extinguish the fire before it destroyed the entire settlement."

"The storm would have put it out even if we had not lifted a hand."

"Rachel." Papa glared at her, fury riding on his brow.

Major Brigham turned his quizzing glass toward Rachel and looked at her up and down. "Perhaps so. Perhaps not. But on the battlefield, the soldier who acquits himself with courage receives his reward, no matter how the battle is won."

"Well said, sir." Papa's stormy frown forbade Rachel to deny it.

"In any event, the governor asked me to choose appropriate representatives, for we cannot have the entire populace sail down to St. Augustine, now can we?" He inspected his glass, blew on it and then brushed it against his red coat. "I could think of no better choice than you and your courageous father. And of course, Mr. Moberly, if he can get away."

A pleasant shiver swept through Rachel. This changed everything. "Pray tell, sir, exactly when is the ball to take place? For I must have a new gown." She sent Papa a sweet smile and batted her eyelashes.

Major Brigham snickered at Papa. "The ladies always require a new gown, do they not?"

Papa grimaced, but if he truly resisted the expenditure, Rachel would remind him that Lady Augusta had already seen her blue gown.

"July eighth, two weeks from this Saturday, Miss Folger. You should have plenty of time to prepare."

As the major left, several customers entered in his wake, casting cautious, curious glances at the officer as they bustled into the store. Taking care of the newcomers' needs, Rachel and Papa had no chance to talk until Mr. Patch came in to tend the store while they ate their noon meal upstairs. When they sat at the table, she waited in vain for him to address the subject, for he seemed lost in thought as he ate.

"Papa, how can you sit there and devour your dinner when you know I am anxious to hear all Major Brigham said before I entered the shop."

He looked at her with surprise. "Are ye, then? 'Twasn't much. Same as he said to ye." He shoved a spoonful of bean soup into his mouth.

Rachel tapped her foot under the table. There was more, she felt sure of it.

"Come to think…" Papa took a large chunk of bread and dipped it in his broth. "The major also mentioned that some loyalists from South Carolina will no doubt be there. With all the rumpus going on up north, they're feeling a mite fretful about the dangers to wives and children." He shrugged. "Not unlike me bringin' ye down here afore ye got yerself in trouble with those addlepated plans to spy on General Gage."

She stared down at her plate, her appetite gone. This old argument never solved anything.

"Seems to me," he said, "ye'd do yerself some good

by makin' friends with some of these English. Where d'ye think yer people came from? England, that's where."

Rachel sent a sly look in his direction. "Do you not think your friendship with Mrs. Winthrop is enough fraternizing with the enemy for both of us?"

"Well, now, if ye recall, ye gave yer approval—" A glint lit his dark brown eyes, and a smug smile formed on his lips. "And I s'pose ye think I've not noticed yer moon eyes over Mr. Moberly, nor his lovesick stares in yer direction."

Heat filled Rachel's face that had nothing to do with the day's warmth. "Well. Good. I am glad you noticed. At last."

To her shock, Papa's expression sobered and he narrowed his eyes. "Aye. I've noticed from the first day he walked into the store that he was smitten with ye. And why wouldn't he be?" He frowned. "And ye, girl, *ye* be the one fraternizing with the *enemy*." He stood and tossed his napkin to the table. "Finish yer meal. I'll be downstairs."

She couldn't read his expression as he left the room, and her heart ached with confusion. Did he approve or disapprove of Mr. Moberly?

But another thought interrupted her musings. If she did become friends with the English in St. Augustine, perhaps she could learn something of value for the patriot cause. Surely all the ladies would not be snobbish like Lady Augusta, at least not the ones from South Carolina, whose ancestors had settled there long after the Folgers had made Nantucket their home. But, if those ladies had taken on airs, Rachel would simply have to resort to eavesdropping. For was that not the quintessence of spying?

Chapter Seventeen

"An excellent plan, sir." Frederick leaned against the indigo vat and dabbed sweat from his forehead with a linen handkerchief. "A trip to St. Augustine will be exhilarating."

Brigham also used his handkerchief, heavy with perfume, but he held it in front of his nose, no doubt to deflect the indigo's stench. "Of course you understand this will be more than a ball to please the ladies."

Frederick gave him a slight nod. "Understood." A weight sat heavy on his chest. Governor Tonyn would be ascertaining the loyalty of East Florida settlers, something that would not have bothered him before he met Miss Folger. Or before he read that vexing pamphlet.

"With John Stuart in the capital, we can expect a full appraisal of his talks with the Choctaw." Brigham wore a sober expression. "The Indians trust him, and Governor Tonyn will want to spread that influence to all the settlements."

"Does this mean they're concerned the Indians will cause trouble here?" Frederick would not inquire whether Brigham had changed his views on the Timucua, who still dwelled in the southeast corner of

Bennington Plantation, lest the officer repeat his order for them to leave.

"I suppose His Excellency simply wishes to ensure their loyalty. With traitorous militias active in Georgia and South Carolina, we could use a buffer if they turn their sights southward."

Frederick grunted his agreement.

At the approach of several slaves leading a horse-drawn wagon filled with linen bags for drying the indigo, he stepped away from the vat. "May I offer you some refreshment?" He waved his hand toward the path to the house.

"Certainly." As they walked, Brigham continued to fan his handkerchief in front of his nose. "How do you bear it? I would rather smell a stable in need of cleaning than indigo being processed."

"Ah, well, the king's navy must have its blue." Frederick inhaled a hint of magnolia on the fresh easterly breeze and blew out the bad smell from his lungs. Long ago he had resigned himself to the unpleasant elements of managing the plantation.

"Well said, sir." Brigham eyed him. "In the future, I shall endeavor to more fully appreciate those of you who must do such distasteful work for king and country." His light tone and easy candor seemed sincere and quite different from his previous arrogance.

Encouraged by his friendliness, Frederick ventured a request. "Milord, I would be remiss if I did not request an invitation to the governor's ball for my cousin. That is, if you do not consider me out of order."

"Not at all. I had intended to include Mrs. Winthrop in my invitation. I know Lady Augusta will appreciate her company. My gallant little wife has endured much.

She will be put out in the extreme when she learns the shopkeeper and his daughter will be along."

"Indeed?" Frederick coughed to hide his excitement. "Why would they be invited?"

"Ostensibly to honor them for their courage during the fire. But of course, Tonyn will be interested in learning of their loyalties. His letter conveyed his desire to meet strong leaders in the community, men like Folger with experience in leadership, the type who might foment rebellion such as happened in Boston." His eyes gleamed with sudden feeling. "Boston. Now that's the place to be. What I wouldn't give to be on the front lines instead of in this remote wilderness. In fact, before I even arrived here, I requested a transfer to Massachusetts. And I have every intention of asking the governor to use his influence to make that happen." He shrugged. "Of course, Lady Augusta will be disappointed."

As they passed the slave quarters, relief settled into Frederick over his decision not to keep his promise to the lady. If Brigham was determined to serve where the action occurred, so be it. Frederick would support his choice.

"In fact," Brigham said, "I think it best to send her back to London. She will be happier there. I cannot tell her until I receive my orders, of course." He tilted his head and lowered an eyebrow, inviting confidentiality.

"Of course. I'll not mention it to anyone."

They reached the house, and when Caddy pulled open the front door, Frederick followed his guest inside and called for refreshment.

Brigham's relaxed posture revealed that he felt comfortable here, but in his eyes Frederick read the longing for a future in another place. Pity. Now that the man had become more sociable, he might have proven to be a good friend. As for Lady Augusta, no doubt she would be glad to leave this wilderness, even though it would mean separating from her husband. And, in time she would be grateful for her husband's anticipated elevation. Then she could sail through the finest London drawing rooms with her head held high, deferring to no one and never having to socialize with those whom she considered rustics.

For his part, Frederick regarded their marriage as a good one, worthy of emulation, despite the couple's differences. Perhaps on the excursion to St. Augustine, he could observe how Brigham planned to sway his wife to his views, for that might prove useful in Frederick's own marriage some day. A marriage that might come about later rather than sooner if he and Miss Folger found their opinions too conflicting.

But then, Mother and Father often held different opinions, and their deep affection for one another was obvious to any who would see it. Yes, that was it. Couples must expect to have differences. It was the duty of the man to set the course for the marriage and the duty of the wife to follow him. As long as their love was constant, Frederick need not be troubled by Miss Folger's disagreements with him regarding the futile rebellion or the necessity of slaveholding. Nor need he feel forced to reveal all to her. As he'd seen with Major Brigham and Lady Augusta, there were some things women could not comprehend and therefore did not need to know.

"Señorita Rachel." Inez's voice held a note of humor. "If you do not stop lifting the lid, the lamb will never cook."

"Yes, I know." Rachel replaced the lid, then removed her apron and hung it on a wall peg. "You know when to add the vegetables." She counted tasks on her fingers. "The pies and bread are baked, the butter fresh-churned, the tea and lemonade are—"

"Please, señorita." Inez took her arm and gently tugged her toward the door. "I have cooked much food in my life, and no one complains about its taste." She tucked a loose strand of hair into Rachel's coiffure. "See, you are going to ruin my hard work."

Rachel squeezed Inez's hand. "Thank you for giving up another Sunday morning."

Inez's eyes shone. "It is my gift to *Dios*. Now, go to church. Pray for us. And we will pray for your nice dinner for *el patrón*."

With a laugh, Rachel hurried across the yard just as Papa emerged from the back door.

"Papa, you look quite handsome. Mrs. Winthrop will be impressed." Mischief got the better of her. "That is, if you mind your manners and do not slurp your stew."

"Is that how you show respect, girl?" With his chin lifted and his broad-brimmed felt hat cocked at a rakish angle, he put his fists at his waist as a breeze caught his coat and blew it wide like a cape.

Rachel's breath caught. How truly handsome he looked—as grand as when he had stood on the quarterdeck of his ship shouting orders to his whaling crew above the roar of ocean waves. How she longed to throw her arms around him and kiss his fresh-shaven cheek. But he would only tell her to belay such foolishness.

"Is this better?" She gave him an exaggerated curtsy.

"My lady, may I be so bold?" He offered his arm, and the glint in his eyes revealed his merry disposition.

"Yes, good sir, you may." She set her hand on his arm, feeling the strength that had propelled countless thousands of harpoons. "Papa, I am pleased you and

Mrs. Winthrop have formed a friendship. Today Mr. Moberly and I will be discussing our friendship further." She dared not say *courtship*. "Will you give your approval?"

"Ye know yer mind, Rachel. I'll not deny ye yer happiness, even as I never denied Susanna hers."

"But the other day, you seemed concerned about it. You said I was making friends with the enemy. You, who care nothing for the revolution."

She felt him stiffen for the briefest moment.

"I would not have yer heart be broken, child." His tone was soothing but sad. "Do not give it away too freely. But when ye do, give it entirely."

Happy tears stung her eyes. That sounded very near a blessing to her.

As the church came into sight and parishioners gathered from around the settlement, two thoughts struck her. First, Papa, always so straightforward before, had not answered her question about making friends with the enemy. And second, with no time to question him, she must set aside her concerns and prepare her heart for worship.

Visiting this humble church for the third Sunday in a row, Rachel felt at home. She nodded or spoke soft greetings to other parishioners as she and Papa found their pew. Even though the pews were not bought or assigned, everyone seemed to sit in the same place they had before, like well-mannered children taking their seats around a large family dinner table. The Father's table.

Seated beside Papa, Rachel offered up her customary prayer that he would understand the message of salvation. Soon peace swept into her soul, but she could not be certain whether it was an assurance from the Lord or because Mr. Moberly and his party moved into the pew in front of her.

Reaching his accustomed spot, Mr. Moberly turned. "Good morning, Miss Folger, Mr. Folger." His dark gray eyes communicated good humor, and his soft voice rumbled in a rich baritone against Reverend Johnson's opening intonations.

Although she managed to return his smile and nod to Mrs. Winthrop, Rachel's knees went weak. *Lord, forgive me. This is our time to worship You.* But once again, for the next two hours, she required much self-control to remember Whom this service was about.

Chapter Eighteen

"I ate entirely too much of your excellent stew, Miss Folger." Mr. Moberly patted his stomach.

"Indeed," said Mrs. Winthrop. "I do not imagine anything we will be served in St. Augustine could be any finer. The taste of your tender lamb took me back to Warwickshire."

"Thank you." Rachel's cheeks warmed. "But I would guess Governor Tonyn will serve the best of everything to his guests." She still could not grasp that she and Papa would have such a grand adventure with Mr. Moberly and Mrs. Winthrop.

"Ye've got yer mother's touch, daughter." Papa beamed. "Now, about that pie."

"Yes, of course." Rachel started to ring for Inez.

"Ah, dessert." Mr. Moberly's voice sounded reserved. "Where to put it? Perhaps we should take a stroll before our pie. I've not been in town for over a week, and I would like to see if the workmen have satisfactorily cleared away the ruins of the inn." He turned to Papa. "That is, with your permission, sir."

Papa nodded. "A brisk walk is good for the health, I always say. Mrs. Winthrop, will you join us?"

From the opposite end of the table, Rachel glared at him, willing him to understand that she and Mr. Moberly would not need a chaperone, in fact, must not have one if they were to freely discuss important matters.

"Why, yes, I should like a stroll." Mrs. Winthrop regarded Papa. "However, I wonder if you and I might walk back toward the church. Mrs. Johnson has promised to give me some of her daffodil bulbs, and I would like to collect them. We did not have time after the service."

"Ah, a fine idea." Papa's jovial tone soothed Rachel's concerns.

Out in the blazing, late-June heat, as Papa and Mrs. Winthrop walked in the opposite direction, Rachel cast an envious glance toward the lady's parasol, plain and black though it was. She could not think of bringing out her old patched one and hoped she would not suffer too much for her pride. Instead, she pulled her wide straw hat low and prayed the East Florida sun would not reflect off the white sand-and-seashell road to redden her face. At least her white gloves would protect her hands from burning.

"Is everything well with you, Miss Folger?" Walking beside her, Mr. Moberly wore a round, broad-brimmed brown hat to top off his skirted brown linen coat and blue breeches. With his tanned complexion, he bore the look of a handsome country gentleman.

"Everything is very well, sir." Rachel's pulse quickened. Here they were at last, and all she could do was fret about the sun. "Well, there is one small matter of complaint."

"Ah, that will not do. Tell me what it is, and I shall do all within my power to amend it."

A dog cart driven by a young slave boy rattled past, stirring up sand and dust. Mr. Moberly took Rachel's arm and moved her away from the onslaught. At his touch, she felt a pleasant shiver run up her arm.

"Will you call me Rachel?" Her heart pounding at her audacity, she tilted her head and glanced at him from beneath her hat brim.

His charming smile dispelled her anxiety. "Only if you will call me Frederick."

"Agreed."

A few people wandered about town, some strolling and others going about necessary business such as tending animals, as befitted the Sabbath day. In the shallow inlet, great white cranes poked their long golden beaks into the water and pulled out frogs, insects or small fish, then lifted their heads to swallow. On the other side, gauzy Spanish moss hung on the nearby oak trees, swaying in the summer breeze like the gray hair of an old crone. The last magnolia blossoms spread over their giant leaves as if loath to end their season.

"Rachel." Mr. Moberly swung his riding crop at a fly. "What a lovely, biblical name."

"Yes. On Nantucket Island, most children received scriptural names."

"Ah. What a strong testimony to their faith."

"Truly, it is a fine heritage to have." Rachel felt her heart flood with joy. Their conversation was proceeding naturally. Surely that signified good things to come.

The tanner shouted his greeting from his front door, and Frederick responded with a majestic nod. Several mounted soldiers gave friendly, informal salutes as they rode past, and indentured servants stopped to bow or curtsy to Frederick. Rachel felt a measure of modest pride and pleasure for being seen in his company.

They reached the scene of the tragedy and found only a large charred patch to mark the ground where the two-story building had stood. Despite the rains that had washed over the site, the stench of the tragic fire remained. Some distance beyond, the stable had survived, as had the various animals Mr. Crump had kept for feeding his guests. The creatures now resided at Bennington Plantation.

"You were kind to purchase Sadie's livestock," Rachel said as they walked toward the stable. "The money will be more than enough to meet her needs."

Frederick shrugged. "No other course would have been acceptable." He studied the stable. "Do you mind if I look inside?"

"Not at all." Rachel stood by the empty stockyard. "I shall wait here."

His quizzical look was charming. "Would you not like some relief from the sun?"

"Indeed I would." She located a nearby giant oak across the road. "And that fine tree will provide it."

He grimaced and shook his head. "Forgive me. I wasn't thinking. I need not inspect this place. I shall send Oliver tomorrow."

Rachel sent up a silent prayer of thanks that Frederick understood why they must remain in plain sight of the townspeople enjoying this Sunday afternoon.

They found a seat on one of the ancient tree's arching branches that lay across the ground, extending some thirty feet perpendicular to the main trunk.

Toying with a tender stem beside her, Rachel decided not to waste time, for Papa had granted them only one hour. "Have you considered the matters we discussed last Sunday?"

Frederick did not meet her gaze, and a frown replaced his smile. "Yes."

Fear crept into her mind. "And?"

He reached over to take her gloved hand. "Dear Rachel, what can I say? How can I argue against your concerns? For they come from a pure Christian heart."

Her hand felt so right in his. So safe. So protected. His eyes exuded nothing but kindness and concern. And, perhaps, even love.

"Then you agree with me?" Surprised to feel the sting of tears, Rachel blinked and sent them splashing down her cheeks.

His gaze seemed almost paternal. "Dear one, many of these matters are beyond our human comprehension."

Pain stabbed into her deepest sensibilities. "No, they are not beyond our comprehension. If men are evil and do evil, it is easy to comprehend that they must be stopped." She pulled her hand away and immediately felt adrift.

He released a long sigh, and she turned to study his face. How she ached to reach out and touch his cheek, to reclaim those strong hands. But to do so would be a betrayal of her most cherished beliefs.

"Frederick..." How she loved the feel of his name on her tongue, in spite of their differences. "This is the essence of who I am. If you cannot accept the things I hold dearest to my heart, then you cannot love me."

His gaze grew intense, burning into her. "Do not tell me I cannot love you, Rachel." His voice resounded with feeling. "I have loved you almost from the moment I met you. And it has cost me...*will* cost me everything, yet I count it nothing for the love I have for you." He grasped both of her hands this time. "Do you understand? I love you."

She could not breathe. Could not think. Could only feel. "And I love you."

Frederick gazed into her eyes, barely able to breathe. She loved him in return! With all his being, he longed to kiss her. Longed to rush back to the church to marry her this day. After much inner struggle, he settled for brushing his hand across her tear-stained cheek and giving her what he hoped was a reassuring smile.

"Are you well, Rachel?"

The smile she returned was radiant. "I am well, Frederick."

As if in silent agreement, they released each other's hands, a concurrence that could only portend future harmony between them.

"Will you free your slaves and pay wages to those who want to stay and work for you?" The innocence in Rachel's eyes and the tenderness in her tone stirred his soul.

"Would that I could. But they are not my property. They belong to my father. To set them free would be nothing less than thievery." Even as he said the words, they sounded hollow.

"I see." Rachel waved at a little brown boy walking past on the road. "You must know that I will never own a slave."

Frederick gazed off beyond the stable and across the marshy inlet where a myriad of birds, great and small, foraged for sustenance. "I would not ask it of you. But will you grant me what I must do for my father?" He grunted, considering the question's irony. "That is, for as long as he permits me to continue as his agent."

Rachel's eyes widened, and she stood and walked several feet from the tree. Hoping she did not intend to leave him, Frederick stood, ready to pursue her. But she turned back, and her lips were drawn in a decisive line.

"Perhaps the Lord will provide you with another occupation, one that does not require slaves."

Frederick stared at the ground and nudged an old seashell with the toe of his riding boot. Just when he felt he had succeeded beyond Father's expectations—with God's blessing—she wanted him to leave the work he loved. Again, his soul wrenched over this absurdity. Must he lose one dream to gain another?

But a sudden insight took him by surprise. He had not the slightest doubt Father would disown him for choosing to love and marry Rachel. He would be forced to find another occupation. That being true, he could seek one for which slave labor was not required.

He looked up to see Rachel staring at him, doubt and hope at war in her expression. He walked to her and reclaimed her hand. To his relief, she did not pull away.

"We must depend upon the Lord to show us what He would have us do."

Her little gasp of delight sent a strange mix of optimism and trepidation down his spine.

"Oh, Frederick, God will bless you for this. And should your earthly father reject you, your heavenly Father will take you up in His arms."

Nothing could have encouraged him more. She believed in him, and that was enough.

Glancing up at the sun's position, Frederick felt certain an hour had passed since they had left the store. "I must take you home. If I am to remain in your father's good graces, I must keep my word to him."

"Yes." She looped her arm in his as they once again

took to the road. "But you know there is another matter we must discuss."

"Ah, yes. The rebellion." Frederick hardly had to
concern himself with it. Like the certainty of Father's
disowning him, he had no doubt the uprising would fail.

"Revolution."

"Very well. Revolution." What difference did a word
make? The color of the sky seemed richer, deeper to
him today, as if a vat of indigo had splashed across the
fields where woolly cloud sheep frolicked. Below, pine
trees waved their good wishes to any who walked by.

"Well?" There was a slight tug on his arm.

Frederick glanced down into the dark brown eyes of
an Inquisitor. But he could not be cross with her. "I recently read an interesting pamphlet called *A Declaration
of Rights and Grievances*." He enjoyed her wide-eyed
shock. "I am convinced that the cause of the thirteen
rebelling colonies is not without merit."

"Truly?"

"Truly. But you must give me more time to consider
it."

"Oh, I shall. But we should discuss it, too."

"Certainly." Frederick sent up a prayer that all conflict would be over before he was forced to tell her of
his sworn loyalty to the king, a pledge he felt no urg-
ing to abandon.

For the present, her contentment revealed itself in her
light steps beside him. He felt a little like a playful colt
himself. Yet they managed to keep a respectable pace
as they strolled along the sandy road. The townspeople
now greeted them with open stares and knowing winks,
as if privy to a delightful secret. Let them look, then.
Let them talk. For he had crossed the Rubicon, and he
would not go back.

Chapter Nineteen

Early Friday morning, Rachel and Papa made their way to the plantation. At Bennington Creek, twenty-foot flatboats waited in boat slips to carry them on the first leg of their journey. The boats' red and yellow canvas awnings flapped in the soft breeze like birds taking flight, reflecting Rachel's soaring excitement.

Already awaiting the company's departure, Lady Augusta whispered to her husband in urgent tones. Major Brigham shook his head and assisted his wife across the wooden planks into the boat. Lady Augusta sent an angry glare toward Rachel before plopping into her seat and staring off into the distance.

Rachel's merry mood plummeted. But what had she expected from the pompous aristocrat? At least Lady Augusta had the good sense not to wear her hideous wig and makeup for this outing. In the dim morning light, she appeared at least ten years younger, and her dark brown hair framed a truly pretty face, marred only by her arrogant scowl.

In contrast, Frederick shook Papa's hand as if greeting an old friend, then placed a kiss on Rachel's fingers as the pleasant scent of bergamot wafted into her sphere. She must ask him about that enchanting fragrance one day.

"Let me assist you, Miss Folger." Frederick's formal address bespoke their agreement to keep their declarations of love a secret, but his gentlemanly manners restored her bruised feelings. "I ordered these cushions for comfort and the awning for shade."

"How lovely. Thank you." Rachel took his arm and stepped into the boat. With the boatman's help, she settled into a down-filled canvas cushion at the opposite end from Major Brigham and Lady Augusta. Soon Papa and Mrs. Winthrop joined them.

"A lovely day for an excursion, my lady," Mrs. Winthrop said to Lady Augusta. "Do you not think so?"

Chin lifted, Lady Augusta snapped her head toward her. As her gaze settled on the older woman, she offered a slight smile, one that enhanced her natural beauty. "Yes. Quite." Again she peered out across the marsh.

In short time, the boatmen shoved the flatboat from the slip and steered it northward into shallow Bennington Creek, rowing toward the St. Johns River. A second boat conveyed the servants and baggage, with a small squad of soldiers divided between the two vessels. Each red-coated soldier clutched a loaded musket. Rachel felt a mixture of relief for their protection from present dangers and distaste for the offenses of their fellow soldiers up north.

She saw that Lady Augusta had brought two trunks, her lady's maid and a slave girl. Mrs. Winthrop had packed a small trunk and also brought her housemaid. Rachel had one valise, which held her new pink gauze gown, her blue dress, a dressing gown and a night rail. She was used to dressing herself, but her hair was another matter. Inez had given careful instructions on how to create a stylish coiffure, but Rachel had little practice doing it.

The sun rose higher, and the ladies lifted their parasols for additional shade. Even though Rachel feared her old black one would embarrass Frederick, she'd decided she must use it. Last Sunday's walk had reddened her face, and she could not bear to further spoil her complexion.

Lady Augusta took one brief look at the tattered apparatus and rolled her eyes, even emitted a ladylike "humph" before lifting her own delicate lace parasol. Rachel cast a quick glance at Frederick, but he had engaged Papa in a discussion about fishing. Mrs. Winthrop reached over to squeeze Rachel's hand. With that bit of reassurance, Rachel reclined against the cushions to enjoy the passing scenery. She would not let the haughty aristocrat ruin this rare expedition for her.

She had forgotten the beauties of the river—the many varieties of trees, bright red and purple flowers she couldn't name, and myriads of birds calling to their own kind in a cacophonous symphony. Peeking over the boat's side, she could see fish large and small—bass with their gaping mouths, sword-nosed gar, giant spiny sturgeon. Occasionally one would leap into the air to devour an unfortunate insect before splashing back into the water. It seemed to her that a thousand streams fed the vast, shallow waterway, and numerous islands divided it along the way. How easy it would be to get lost without experienced boatmen navigating their course.

Yet always in the back of Rachel's mind was the memory of the alligator nearly as long as this boat that had noiselessly approached through the tall river grasses and slammed into their vessel upon their arrival those long weeks ago. Even now groups of the great hideous dragons sunned themselves on the river banks or slithered into the water in their ominous way.

She noticed Lady Augusta's hand draped over the boat's side and trailing in the water, and thought to offer a warning. Her husband doubtless saw the danger, too, for he spoke to her, and she snatched back the endangered appendage. Rachel shuddered.

"Are you well, Miss Folger?" Frederick leaned toward her, gentle concern in his eyes.

"I am well, Mr. Moberly." Warmth that had nothing to do with the sweltering heat rushed to her face. She would never tire of his loving gazes.

When the sun reached its meridian, Mrs. Winthrop ordered a basket brought forth, from which she dispensed bread and cheese to the hungry travelers. Lemonade, made from springwater and kept cool in an earthen crock, slaked everyone's thirst.

Shortly after their meal, the party reached Mayport, where the two-masted sailing ship *Mingo* lay anchored and crewmen bustled about, ready to welcome them aboard.

There the travelers joined an Amelia Island plantation owner, Mr. Avery Middlebrook, along with his wife and two daughters, and an agent of Dr. Fothergill of London, Mr. Bertram, a naturalist who was writing a book about the flora and fauna of both East and West Florida.

Once aboard the brigantine, the Middlebrook women flocked to Lady Augusta like clucking hens, and she basked in their adoration, deigning to speak a generous word to each. Then, as the time drew near for departure, the ladies sought shelter from the sun in the stateroom. When their conversation offered no useful information, Rachel grew restless and joined the gentlemen on the foredeck.

Hiding under her parasol, Rachel stood between Papa and Frederick, eager to experience the delight of wind and salt spray on her face once again. The brigantine soon dropped its mooring lines, hoisted sails and then charged across the pounding waves into the Atlantic Ocean.

"See now," Papa said, "how strange this St. Johns River is. Not only does the water run north, but see how its lethargic outflow is nearly overpowered by the ocean's waves. What should carry us out to sea with ease puts up no fight against the breakers."

"Ah, yes." Frederick wore an amused expression. "But that lethargy works to our advantage on the return trip. If the tides are right, the boatman will have little trouble rowing us back home."

"Ha. I'll grant ye that, sir," Papa said. "I've heard tell sharks and other sea life can be found inland far beyond the cow ford."

"'Tis a wonder of nature, one must agree." Rachel copied his Nantucket dialect as she stood on tiptoe and peeked over the rail. From the safety of the merchant ship, she could regard the creatures below without trepidation.

"Do you like to sail, Miss Folger?" Mr. Bertram brushed gray hairs from his sweat-covered forehead.

"Indeed I do, sir." In fact, she had found her footing as well as Papa, while the other men clutched the rail. The smell of wood and tar and the slapping of lines against the mast reminded her of pleasant days aboard Papa's whaler.

"Remarkable young lady." Looking a little green, Mr. Bertram pulled a folded piece of paper and a pen-

cil from his coat pocket and made notes. "Remarkable."
He hurried away, but whether from seasickness or inspiration, Rachel could not tell.

Once beyond the reef, the vessel caught the wind
in its sails and headed southward. While Frederick,
Mr. Middlebrook and Papa discussed the weather and
fishing, Rachel strolled about the deck. Seeing Captain
Newman at the wheel, she climbed to the quarterdeck.

"A fine day for sailing, sir."

Coming closer, she noticed that the whiskered, fair-
haired officer was younger than her first estimation. Of
medium height and well formed, he had a handsome,
ready smile.

"Yes, miss." He tipped his tricorn hat and gave her a
little bow. "The current is mild. Would you like to take
the helm?" Still gripping the wheel, he stepped aside
and beckoned with his free hand.

"Oh, yes." Rachel tucked her parasol into the lines,
then took hold of the wheel with one hand and a spoke
with the other. How good it felt to direct the vessel,
even if only to keep it on course with the captain's help.
Waves surged beneath them, rolling the ship from side
to side as it moved through the water parallel to land.

"Steady as she goes." He reached around her and
gripped the wheel with both hands, pressing close to
her back. "You're doing well."

A blend of sweat, wool and sea salt met her nostrils,
and breathing became difficult, and she could feel the
captain's hot breath on her neck. Maybe this wasn't a
good idea, after all.

"There you are, Miss Folger." Frederick bounded up
the steps to the quarterdeck, albeit a little unsteadily,
and a glower rode on his brow. "I hoped we might take
a turn around the deck."

"Why, of course, Mr. Moberly. Captain, will you excuse me?" Cheeks aflame, Rachel ducked under his arm, almost ripping her bonnet off. "Thank you for letting me steer."

"Of course." He gave her a crooked grin. "You may take the wheel again at your pleasure."

Tugging her bonnet back into place, Rachel whipped around and quickly descended to the main deck. What must Frederick think of her? How could she explain? She heard his booted steps behind her and hurried to a deserted place at the rail. She must confess her foolishness and ask his forgiveness.

"I saw the whole thing." Frederick stood beside her, staring out to sea, his arm grazing hers. "What a blackguard."

"What? But I—"

Frederick faced her now and grasped the rail as the ship dipped into an unexpected trough, sending a light, foamy spray across them. "Rachel, you did nothing wrong. One of your most admirable traits is your adventurous spirit. Of course you would like to steer a ship when the captain invites you." He gave her a gentle smile. "I wish I could have a portrait of your expression as you held the wheel. I have no greater wish than to secure such happiness for you." His frown returned, and he reached out to complete the job of straightening her bonnet, brushing her face in the process with a featherlike touch. "Captain Newman, however, stared at you as if he might devour you on the spot."

Rachel gasped. "Oh, my." Had she known, she would have slapped the man.

Now the salt spray had begun to sting, and she swiped a hand across one damp cheek.

"There, now, don't cry." Frederick pulled her hand up and gave it a lingering kiss. "I'll watch over you."

"But, I—"

"And to ensure that nothing of this sort happens again, I will make it clear to everyone that you and I are courting. That is, with your permission."

His bright eyes and tender smile dissolved her protest, and she nodded. One day, when they had been married many years, she would explain she had not been weeping at all. For now, she would bask in Frederick's adoring gaze and forget the ungentlemanly captain and the unfriendly ladies below.

The fragrance of Rachel's hair wafted up to enchant Frederick at the same moment he decided to call the captain out, thus thwarting that plan. What was the matter with the man? Could he not see her innocence? She even tried to take responsibility for the man's evil intent. That very moment, Frederick knew he could no longer act as if she were merely an acquaintance, a denizen of his father's settlement. He must let everyone from pompous Lady Augusta to scoundrels like Newman know that Rachel Folger, merchant's daughter, formerly of Boston and Nantucket, was his own true love, the woman he would marry and love for the rest of his life.

He glanced beyond her to see Mr. Folger eyeing them, a frown shadowing his leathery face. In another time, Frederick might have wilted under such a glare. But Rachel's sweet and trusting gaze emboldened him.

"I must speak to your father."

She peeked over her shoulder. "Now?"

"Yes, now." Frederick shot a quick look at the ship's captain. Another crew member stood by, perhaps to take the helm, leaving him free to approach Rachel while Frederick was engaged elsewhere. "I want you to join the other ladies below. This might take some time."

Rachel's eyes twinkled. "I have no doubt it will. Do not let him intimidate you."

"No, of course not. Your father and I are friends." Frederick swallowed hard and sent up a quick prayer that they would still be friends at their conversation's end.

After escorting Rachel to the safety of the ladies' stateroom, he returned to the foredeck, where Mr. Folger stood at the rail, an inscrutable expression on his age-lined face.

Frederick's knees felt as if they might buckle, much like the times when he had been called before his father for a lecture. Until just minutes ago, he had not considered that Mr. Folger might deny his request for Rachel's hand. How foolish, how arrogant to presuppose his superior rank would guarantee this man's acceptance. That assumption disappeared when he caught something in the old gentleman's glare that cast doubt on his success, a truly humbling thought. In London, Frederick never had to consider how to approach anyone's father, for the young ladies had been thoroughly schooled in rejecting younger sons all on their own. But then, none of them ever found their way into his heart, as Rachel had, and he could not think of losing her. Thus, he must face Mr. Folger whether the man planned to accept or reject him.

In their previous conversations, Folger had demonstrated a refreshing affability, a temperament Frederick himself always strove to project. For him, it was often a matter of survival, but this former whaling captain feared no one. Nor did he seek to strike fear into any-

one else, at least never in Frederick's presence. Until
now. Until he looked at Frederick with an expression
that reflected Frederick's own anger at Newman for his
improper behavior toward Rachel. But surely after all
this time, Mr. Folger believed in Frederick's integrity.

Heart pounding, Frederick turned to face him.

"Captain Folger, it will come as no surprise to you
to hear that I am devoted to Rachel. I have come to ask
your permission to propose marriage to her."

There. The words were out. But the inner trembling
did not cease. *Lord, what a coward I am, using his former title to gain approval.*

Mr. Folger's jaw muscles worked, and he breathed
like an angry bull. Still staring out to sea, he gripped
the rail until his knuckles turned white beneath a per-
manent tan.

Above them, seagulls called to one another. A pel-
ican swept down to scoop up its dinner. The canvas
sails captured the wind with a majestic *whoomp*. The
ship's bow cut through the waves, and salt-scented foam
dampened everything on deck, including his hopes.

Frederick tried to shake off bitter childhood memories and his drowning sense of inadequacy. Why did
Mr. Folger not answer? Why should he not answer, if
for nothing more than courtesy's sake? Frederick had
done nothing to offend him, had done all to advance
his business in both St. Johns Settlement and London.

As for Father, Frederick longed to face him this day
and show him how the failing plantation had been rescued by his efforts. How his kind treatment of the slaves
encouraged energetic productivity. How the crops flourished so prodigiously that his indigo shipments would
soon rival those of Lord Egmount. With bold determination, he had succeeded despite his father's doubts,

despite his brothers' taunts, despite Oliver's lies, even beyond his mother's generous expectations. For Rachel, he would take that same determination into his marriage. For himself, he would never again wilt under the fear of every threat, real or imagined.

I will care for Rachel as if my life depended upon it. Her happiness is my only purpose for living.

"Aye. I can see that." Mr. Folger cast a sidelong glance his way. "No need to shout it."

"Ah." A little breathless, Frederick could not believe he had spoken aloud his heartfelt declaration. But it sounded good in his ears, felt good on his tongue. Felt good clear down to the depths of his soul. And yet—

"You are not pleased, sir. I entreat you to tell me why."

Mr. Folger turned halfway and stared hard into Frederick's eyes. "I'll grant ye love her, lad. Ye wear it all over yer face. But do ye *know* her? Do ye know what stirs her soul? Do ye care about those matters?"

Frederick started to assure him that he did know of her concerns over the useless skirmishes up north *and* for the slaves. But somehow the words would not come forth, for he knew nothing of Folger's thoughts on either subject and thus could plot no strategy to avoid potential conflict. *Coward.* Again his conscience accused him. He would not so quickly fall back into his old ways.

"We have discussed our deepest interests, sir, and have resolved our differences." Not quite true. "I should say, we have found ways to compromise."

"Hmm." Mr. Folger's stare softened. "I've no doubt ye'll be the one who finds ways to compromise. For a while. Until the wedding's rosy bloom is off yer cheeks."

Frederick laughed, and the weight in his chest lightened. Those words sounded like approval.

"Well, then, take her to wife." Mr. Folger's shoulders slumped, as if in surrender. "And may the Almighty bless ye both."

"Thank you, sir." Relief flooded Frederick's chest.

Contrarily, sorrow and surrender—neither of which Frederick could comprehend—emanated from Mr. Folger's eyes. He set a callused hand on Frederick's shoulder and gave him a little shake. He chuckled, but no smile lit his eyes. "No reason it should not go well for ye, as it did for my wife and me."

"Thank you, sir," Frederick repeated. Although Mr. Folger clearly felt some reservations, kindness filled his voice, another sign that he had granted his blessing to the union. To honor that, Frederick vowed he would stay by Rachel's side and love her, no matter what forces sought to divide them. As attested to by both her parents and his own, a happy marriage was the greatest success, the greatest happiness of all.

Seated on a stool beside Mrs. Winthrop's cot, Rachel fanned the sleeping woman and brushed damp strands of gray hair from her face. This morning, the poor dear had confided to Rachel her aversion to sea travel, but with her cheery disposition, she made no complaints, not even about the smells of mold and putrid bilge water filling this cabin. Rachel hoped she would remain asleep for the rest of the voyage and be revived by the time they reached St. Augustine.

The Middlebrook women sat or reclined nearby as Lady Augusta held court, expounding on what had been fashionable in London when she left six months ago. Earlier, when Rachel entered the stuffy stateroom, no one acknowledged her. But she refused to be wounded.

Poor Frederick. Rachel prayed he would be able to

face Papa without too much apprehension. She recalled how Papa had struck fear into Charles when he courted her sister Susanna. Perhaps every father felt the need to frighten his daughter's suitors. No doubt it served some purpose, though she could not imagine what that might be. At the completion of the dreaded discussion, Papa would grant his permission and then Frederick would be free to propose marriage. At the thought of it, Rachel's heart nearly sprang from her chest.

As for these silly women, she would simply ignore them as they ignored her. Frederick's love was all she required for happiness.

"*Rachel.*"

Lady Augusta's sharp tone shattered her thoughts, and Rachel jumped.

"What?" She would not call this woman "my lady."

The Middlebrooks seemed to gasp in one collective breath, and their eyes widened until they resembled three owls preparing to descend on a mouse. Lady Augusta arched her eyebrows and glared down her nose at Rachel.

"Do come fan me, Rachel. I'll wager Mrs. Winthrop has no notion of your ministrations."

Rachel noticed the elegant lace fan at Lady Augusta's wrist. She saw in the corner of her eye the gaping stares of the servants seated along the bulkhead. Comprehension filled her. This woman meant to cast her as a servant, a lower being, rather than someone whom the governor had invited to his ball on equal footing with his other guests, including aristocrats. Indignation filled Rachel. Or was it something else?

Lord, help me. Must I bow to her? Is this Your way of subduing my pride?

Warm certainty swept through her. Like the patriots of Boston, she must not submit to English oppression.

"Well, what are you waiting for?" Lady Augusta's voice cut through the tension-thick air like a newly sharpened razor.

Rachel stood and walked toward the hatch. "If you are overly warm, perhaps you should join me on the deck. The sea breeze is delightfully stimulating."

More gasps and much murmuring trailed behind her as she climbed the narrow steps and emerged into the fresh air. Try though she might, she could not dismiss the sick feeling in her stomach. No doubt Lady Augusta would seek reprisal for such defiance. Once the woman learned of her engagement to Frederick, she might seek to harm him, too. But just as the northern colonists had cried "Enough!" regarding British rule, she would never bow to such despotism. Like the brave patriots at Lexington and Concord, she had fired her cannon in self-defense and would not back down, no matter what revenge that woman devised.

"Rachel." Frederick hurried forward with his hand extended. "Come, my dear. We're sailing into St. Augustine. Let us go forward and watch."

The love in his eyes and excitement in his voice told her everything she needed to know. Frederick loved her. Papa had said yes. Why should she bother with any other matter?

As they stood at the bow watching the pilot boat tow the *Mingo* safely past the barrier islands and into Matanzas Bay, Frederick placed one hand at her waist, almost but not quite embracing her, as propriety demanded. She rested against him and let his lean strength soothe her soul. Soon the other guests joined them, exclaiming over the beauties of the century-old Spanish fort guarding the harbor.

Major Brigham and Lady Augusta stood several yards away. The officer bent to speak in his wife's ear, and she swung her gaze toward Rachel and Frederick. Major Brigham nodded to them, approval evident in his good-natured expression. Lady Augusta blanched, and her mouth gaped for an instant before a red rage marred her pretty countenance.

Rachel glanced up at Frederick, whose attention was focused on the fort. Clearly, he had no idea of Lady Augusta's outrage. Feeling slightly wicked, Rachel gave the woman a sidelong look and the sweetest smile she could muster. An uncontrollable giggle erupted from deep within her. This ball promised to be more enjoyable than anything she'd ever experienced.

Chapter Twenty

Lulled by the comfort of the goose-down mattress, Rachel tried not to awaken, tried to continue the sweet dreams of her beloved Frederick. But the early morning breeze blew in through the open windows and brushed over her like a feather, inviting her to rise. The cool air carried the fragrance of some sweet flower she could not identify, along with the aroma of baking bread. On the guest room bed beside her, Mrs. Winthrop's soft, even breathing indicated she had rested well and recovered from yesterday's short voyage.

Rachel stretched out her limbs ready to greet the new day, but murmuring came from across the room. She lay still and strained to listen to the Middlebrook women.

"And Mr. Middlebrook said our contact wants all the information we can gather without risking exposure." Mrs. Middlebrook's alto whisper carried across the large chamber. "Fort Ticonderoga was a smashing success, and even after the defeat at Breed's Hill, our militia is more determined than ever. We must discover how much support they may count on in East Florida."

A shiver of astonishment ran through Rachel. These ladies supported the patriots' cause? She never would have guessed it. The two locations Mrs. Middlebrook mentioned must have been the battle sites. Oh, how Rachel longed to learn what was happening in her old home city. Why, Breed's Hill was right across the Charles River from Boston, visible from the upper floor of her brother-in-law's mercantile shop. Had the militia suffered great losses?

"Did you learn anything from Lady Augusta?" That was the unmistakable nasal voice of Ida Baldwin. That meant their hostess was also a sympathizer.

"Humph." Mrs. Middlebrook spoke again. "She cares for nothing but fashion and position." A pause. "We must play our parts well. We don't yet know whom to trust, nor do we know who our contact is. Take care. Trust no one."

As they continued to talk in low tones, Rachel felt a small measure of shame for thinking so little of them. But after their fawning over Lady Augusta, she could not be faulted for assuming they were loyal to King George. Should she tell them of her own sympathies for the revolution? A sense of caution filled her. None of these people knew her. Even at their introduction, no one had mentioned she came from Boston. Best to keep her own counsel. Why, they did not even know the name of their contact.

Yet if Rachel could discover who that person was, perhaps she could let him know she too was a patriot. Perhaps he would give her an assignment, as he had these ladies. She would befriend them, at least as much as they would permit her, and try to learn all she could.

She inhaled a noisy yawn and rolled over to stretch. The women abruptly stopped speaking and stared at her as if she were an intruder.

"Good morning." Sleep filled her voice, and she rubbed her eyes.

They murmured their greetings in return.

"I'll send the servants with hot water." Mrs. Baldwin left the room.

"Oh, Mother," Elsie Middlebrook simpered. "Do you think that handsome Mr. Moberly will ask me to dance at the ball?"

"If he asks either of us to dance, I should be the one," Leta said. "After all, I'm the oldest."

Rachel buried her face in the pillow to hide her mirth. They had resumed their roles as silly girls, and she would do nothing to interrupt their performance. As for Frederick, she would make certain he had no opportunity to ask either of them to dance, for she planned to fully occupy his time during the ball.

After morning ablutions and dressing, the ladies gathered in the breakfast room. Mrs. Baldwin announced that the men had eaten earlier and had then gone hunting. Rachel missed Frederick, even though she had not expected to see him here. As befitted their stations, he and the Brighams had spent the night at the governor's mansion. And although Mrs. Winthrop treated Rachel with kindness, the others still seemed uncertain how to place her in their social hierarchy. She could stave off loneliness only by thinking ahead to when she would see Frederick.

With all the exuberance of a woman who loved her city, Mrs. Baldwin gave the ladies a tour of St. Augustine, especially King George Street's many shops. Rachel's interest was piqued at the two rival mercantile stores. She would be certain to inform Papa about their displays of fabric, sewing supplies, spices and other wares. Like their own store, one mercantile bore the fragrance of lavender, while the other did not. She surmised that the scent must encourage customers to linger and perhaps make more purchases. The millinery shop also attracted her attention with its many broad-brimmed hat styles, for the fiery sun blasted down upon the women of St. Johns Settlement, as it did upon their counterparts in East Florida's capital.

As the ladies emerged from the milliner's, the Middlebrook daughters stared off across the sandy stretch of ground toward the fort.

"Mrs. Baldwin," said Leta Middlebrook, "may we not visit Fort St. Marks? I should love to see all the renovations and the grand new cannons."

"Renovations? Cannons?" Her sister Elsie giggled. "It's the soldiers you want to see."

Leta put on a pout. "And I suppose you don't wish to see a certain handsome lieutenant posted there."

While Mrs. Baldwin assured them that a tour of the regimental headquarters had been arranged for later in the day, Rachel studied the two sisters with interest. Beneath their bickering lay an affection she had never known with Susanna, whose nine year seniority had made her more mother than sister, especially after their mother died. But these two had another bond to incite Rachel's envy. United in the colonists' cause, they no doubt wanted to tour the fort to garner information for their father's patriot contact. Rachel would try to do that, too.

After a midday meal of bread, cheese and fruit, the ladies retired to the guest room. Rachel pretended to sleep, hoping the Middlebrooks would once again talk of spying. But they all lay quiet. Soon hazy, happy dreams of Frederick fogged her mind, and in no time she felt herself being shaken.

"Wake up, my dear." Mrs. Winthrop gently shook her. "Mr. Moberly has come calling."

With a gasp of delight, Rachel jumped out of bed. "He's here? Oh, my!" While hurrying to freshen up and put on her blue dress, she cast a nervous glance toward the other beds, but the Middlebrook ladies were no longer there. "How do I look?"

"Hmm." Mrs. Winthrop studied her up and down, then led her to the dressing table. "Let me see what I can do to help." She brushed Rachel's long, thick hair into a smooth roll at her neck and used a tortoiseshell comb to keep it in place. "And now the hat." She secured Rachel's straw bonnet with a long hatpin. "Lovely. Now go and enjoy your tour. And take this." She held out her own parasol.

Rachel's face warmed. "Thank you. But won't you be going on the tour?"

Mrs. Winthrop's eyes twinkled. "Why, yes." From her small trunk, she removed a wide-brimmed hat that sported silk flowers and a large fluffy feather, which she gently shook back into its natural shape. "Mr. Folger is escorting me."

Rachel grasped Mrs. Winthrop's hands. "I am well pleased, madam. Very well pleased." She placed a quick kiss on the lady's cheek. "Enjoy your afternoon."

She descended the marble stairway and found Frederick alone in the large airy drawing room, staring up at a painting of King George III above the mantel. Her pulse raced. How handsome Frederick looked in his brown waistcoat and fawn breeches. With difficulty, she suppressed the desire to hasten across the tile floor and embrace him.

"Good afternoon, Mr. Moberly."

He turned, his eyes aglow with affection. "Rachel."

With long, quick strides he reached her and enfolded her in his arms.

She rested against him and let every concern flow away like water after a rain.

After a few sweet moments, he moved back. "Come sit with me." He waved one hand toward the carved mahogany settee in front of the hearth.

"Are we not going to the fort?" Her words rushed out on a quivering breath. "I mean, if you wish to talk instead, I've no objections, but—"

"Yes, I do want to take you there. But first we must settle a matter." Frederick sounded a bit breathless, too.

"Oh." Every nerve seemed to dance within her. "Very well. What is it?"

"Would you not like to sit?" A mixture of happiness and confusion skipped across his brow. He took her hand and tugged her to the settee.

Working hard not to laugh with excitement, Rachel surrendered to his lead. He sat beside her and folded both of her hands in his.

"Rachel, I—" He blinked. "No, that will not do." Still grasping her hands, he slid down on one knee before her and cleared his throat. "Rachel, we have not known each other long, but, that is…"

Bursting with happiness, her heart nevertheless ached for his discomfort. "Yes, I will."

Again he blinked. "You will?"

"Must I say it again? Yes, I will."

A sheepish grin crept across his whole face. "I feel foolish." He moved to sit beside her. "Thank you for making it easy for me."

Rachel reached up and stroked the dark midday stubble on his unlined cheek. "Please set your mind at ease, dear Frederick. I would not have you feel foolish with me."

His expression relaxed into sublimity. "Nor would I have you anything but happy, my dear."

They gazed at each other in silence for some time, enjoying the moment. But soon, Rachel felt a twinge of impatience.

"You may kiss me now."

To her surprise, Frederick frowned. In fact, he stood and walked to the hearth. "I don't know, Rachel. I promised Captain Templeton I would never do anything improper regarding you."

"Jamie? What does he have to do with us?" She jumped up and strode to his side, gripping his arm to turn him around. Another grin played at one corner of his lips, and mischief beamed from his eyes. Rachel laughed. "Oh, I will scold him thoroughly when he returns. As for you, Mr. Moberly, I am certain it's perfectly proper to seal an engagement with a kiss, and it is nothing short of nonsense to wait any longer."

Just as she stood on tiptoes and tilted her head to kiss him, he bent down, and their lips met with a painful bump.

"Ouch." She touched her burning lips and wondered if her front teeth had been knocked loose.

"Unh." He touched his lips and wiggled his jaw. "Well, I must say that was not what I was expecting." Clearly trying to recover, he began to chortle. "Our first kiss, and I make a muddle of it."

Rachel joined him in laughing. "I did my part to spoil it, too." She turned towards the door. "Shall we go to the fort now?"

He caught her and spun her back, pulling her into his arms. "Do you not want to try that kiss again?"

Her breath caught at his gentle assertiveness. "Perhaps one not so painful."

"Very well, then. Hold still." His gray eyes twinkled.

She tilted her face upward and closed her eyes. At the gentle touch of his soft lips on hers, a rush of joy and certainty filled her heart. She loved him. He loved her. Whatever the coming days brought their way, they could work out their differences and face the future together.

Chapter Twenty-One

As Frederick escorted Rachel to the fort, he thought he might burst with happiness. Tonight at the ball, he would ask Governor Tonyn to announce their betrothal. And if Rachel agreed, they would marry as soon as they returned to St. Johns Settlement. Although Frederick would like to marry her this very day, Reverend Johnson would appreciate the honor of performing the ceremony. And of course, Mrs. Winthrop would insist that they post the banns.

Rachel placed a dainty hand on Frederick's arm, and he covered it with his. She glanced up from time to time, giving him smiles he felt from his chest to his toes. The sparkle in her dark brown eyes revealed that her joy equaled his.

Now and forever, he would do everything in his power to ensure she remained happy, as Father had always endeavored to please Mother. Only now had he begun to appreciate Father's better side. No matter how much Lord Bennington disapproved of his youngest son, he had always been a tender, generous husband, an example Frederick aspired to follow with all diligence. With sweet Rachel as his bride, he would find the task easy.

Rachel seemed particularly interested in exploring the fort, and Frederick would use his influence to see her every wish was granted. His dear little dissenter might feel some sympathy for the northern rebellion, but nothing in St. Augustine should stir her concern. This morning during their hunt, the governor informed the men that the situation was firmly in hand. Despite the presence of a few dissidents in the colony, no strong rebel leaders had arisen to bring the mounting conflict this far south. Loyalist militias had formed in many areas. And with the able help of Mr. Stuart, the Choctaw Indians had been persuaded to help guard the border between East Florida and Georgia. That should settle the matter.

"Look, Frederick." Rachel nodded toward the couple some fifteen yards ahead. "Do you not think it dear that Papa and Mrs. Winthrop have become friends?"

"I do." Frederick watched his elegant kinswoman, graceful even as she walked along the rough, sandy path on Mr. Folger's arm. "I wish them to be as happy as we are."

Rachel repositioned her hand, looping her arm through his. "Surely no one could be happier."

"Surely not." He forced his gaze away from her tempting lips. Of course he would not demonstrate his affection for her in full sight of others. But more than the heat of the day brought warmth surging up to his face. Both their first disastrous kiss and the sweet one that followed had only increased his love for her. They must marry soon. Until then, he would direct his thoughts toward learning more of her interests.

At the fort's wooden drawbridge, guards stood at attention with their muskets shouldered, while the corporal in charge saluted and waved them beneath the raised iron gate. Beside him, Rachel shuddered. "Are you well?" Frederick asked.

Her pretty little nose wrinkled as if she smelled something foul. "Yes, thank you."

She sent him a quick smile that did nothing to reassure him. But as they walked through the shadowed passageway leading to the fort's open courtyard, Frederick took in the odor of the unwashed soldiers who stood on either side. Their crimson uniforms might have the look of courage, but surely something lighter than wool would be more appropriate for this tropical climate. He would make inquiries in his next letter home. For now, he would try to shield Rachel from the stench that seemed to displease her.

Many other guests had already assembled in the courtyard and divided into smaller groups. A slender young officer approached Frederick and Rachel and bowed.

"Mr. Moberly, I am Lieutenant Cobb, sir. I'll be your guide." He pointed toward a wide stone staircase. "Shall we begin with the upper gun deck?"

They ascended the steps and emerged onto the wide bastion where a row of cannons jutted toward the sea through the battlement openings. Guard towers stood sentinel at each arrow-shaped corner of the fort. Above them, the red, white and blue Union Jack snapped proudly in the breeze, lifting Frederick's soul with love of country and king and life itself.

He noticed that Rachel's gaze swept over the impressive guns and nearby powder kegs as if she were counting them.

"Tell me, lieutenant," she said, "if a ship fires a cannon from the harbor, can it blow a hole in this wall?"

The officer chuckled. "No, miss. You've no need to fear. There's not a cannon made that can break through it. Even if a vessel sailed close enough without our navy blasting her out of the water, the cannonballs would bounce off the coquina and barely make a dent. The Spanish were right smart to use the natural stone to build this fort." He pointed across Matanzas Bay to a sandy promontory that guarded the inlet. "They quarried it from that island."

"Ah, I see." She brushed her gloved hand across the low wall. "Then how did the British, I mean, how did we gain control of it? Was there a battle?"

Frederick noticed her word change with satisfaction. She had already begun to consider herself a British subject.

"No, miss, we had no need for a battle. The Treaty of Paris in '63 gave all of Florida to the Crown. The Spanish packed up and left, and in we marched." The lieutenant seemed to enjoy his own discourse. "Since early this year, we've been making the repairs you see in progress, including building a second floor beneath these battlements to hold more troops and supplies. We are prepared for anything the rebels might attempt." He waved his arm to take in the entire fort. "We're now the regimental headquarters, something you no doubt already know. The well has been cleaned out, and we can safely drink the water, which is particularly helpful in this hot weather, and the prison's been reinforced. Just in time, too, as we have a few rebels there who need a place to sit and behave themselves until things settle down up north."

Rachel shuddered, and her lips began to quiver. "You have pat...r-rebels right here in this fort?"

"Shh." Frederick put his arm around her. "I'm sure it's all right."

She looked up at him with a forlorn expression. "But—"

"Please permit me to assure you, miss." Lieutenant Cobb stepped closer, a solicitous frown on his brow. "They cannot escape. You are safe."

Rachel still stared at Frederick, her eyes wide. "Will they be e-executed?"

The lieutenant glanced at Frederick, questioning him with a grimace. Frederick shook his head. Rachel's tender concern for the prisoners was admirable and understandable, but she need not know the worst.

"No, miss, the commander has no orders to execute them, for they have not been accused of treason... or spying. Those would be the hanging offenses." He shrugged. "I'm not certain what the charges will be, or if there will be any charges. All I know is they were speaking in favor of the rebellion and stirring up local rabble in the taverns, and Governor Tonyn thought it best to keep them here so they could do no more mischief."

Again Rachel shuddered. But then she squared her shoulders and faced the officer. "May we see where they're being held?"

The lieutenant winced. "I'm not certain that's wise, miss."

"But we must know who they are." She looked at Frederick. "In case they manage to escape and come our way."

Frederick swiped his hand across his forehead. He wanted to please her, but this certainly was an unusual request. Still, it could do no harm. "Lieutenant Cobb, Miss Folger wishes to see the prisoners. Please take us there."

The lieutenant straightened. "As you wish, sir. This way, please."

Frederick offered Rachel his arm and squeezed her hand. "Your compassion for the prisoners is admirable, but please do not be overly concerned. I shall inquire of the governor regarding their treatment. You may trust me in this regard."

As they descended the broad stairway and crossed the courtyard, Rachel wondered how her trembling legs managed to carry her. She clutched Frederick's arm, but his encouraging words and agreement to her request revealed his misunderstanding of what had distressed her.

Spying was a hanging offense. She had never considered such a cost. And surely they would regard it as treason if she tried to help the imprisoned patriots to escape. Yet she must try to help them, must try to get information to help the revolution—somehow.

Lieutenant Cobb led them to the guardroom just inside the fort's entrance. They passed through a chamber where a raised platform held beds for off-duty guards. One of the two sleeping guards snored loudly.

In a second room—a dank, smelly chamber—Papa stood before a wooden door chatting with a prisoner on the other side. *Chatting*, as if talking with Frederick or Jamie, as if communing with an old friend. Only a tiny window in the door made their conversation possible.

At the same time, a quick survey of the room revealed she would not be able to likewise speak with the patriots, for she could hear from their murmuring that they were imprisoned in the windowless black room beyond the door.

In the dim candlelight, Rachel could barely make out the features of the man with whom Papa spoke. His complexion appeared swarthy, and the collar of his once-white linen shirt bore stains of sweat and dirt. She could not determine how tall he was. Yet, in spite of his imprisonment, he spoke in jovial tones thick with an accent Rachel did not know.

"I will take your advice, my friend." He stuck one hand through the small opening. "You have my promise."

Papa grasped it in both of his. "A good plan, sir. And ye may be certain I shall keep my end of the bargain." He chortled in his good-humored way.

Nearby, guards with muskets watched the exchange. But rather than appearing concerned, they seemed amused. Rachel wondered what Papa could have said to entertain them.

Frederick bent to whisper in her ear. "Your father makes friends wherever he goes. Perhaps he has extracted a promise from this Greek to mend his ways."

"Greek?" Rachel quizzed him with a look. "Do you know that from his speech?"

"Yes. No doubt he's from New Smyrna south of here. Dr. Turnbull brought Greeks and Minorcans to settle the area, but they've always complained about broken promises and ill treatment. In fact, I resolved to avoid Turnbull's mistakes in managing St. Johns Settlement."

From his whimsical look, Rachel guessed he wished for her approval. "You've certainly succeeded. Your diligence in your duties is one of your many admirable traits."

Playfulness lit his handsome face. "Shall I list all I admire about you?"

"Perhaps another time." She tilted her head toward the nearby guards.

"Yes, of course." Frederick looked toward the inner door. "Lieutenant, that room is black as night. How many men are in there?"

"Twenty-seven at present, sir."

"So many in such a small, dark space." Rachel shuddered at the thought of being thus locked away from friends and sunshine.

"Would it ease your mind," Frederick asked her, "if I inquired about sending oranges and other provisions for them?"

"Oh, how good of you." Even as gratitude flooded her, Rachel's heart twisted at the thought of her failure to explain matters to him. Why, it was nothing short of deception. As for the Greek whom Papa had befriended, he could hardly be interested in the revolution. But if Frederick sent the patriots some nourishing food, her ploy had a useful purpose, after all.

And, perhaps, the episode had one additional benefit. Despite her shaking knees, despite being frightened for her life, she had walked into this prison filled with determination. Now she knew beyond any doubt she would willingly die for the patriot cause. And now that Frederick's sympathies had been stirred, she would do all in her power to complete the work of turning his opinions toward freedom for the colonies.

Standing beside Frederick, Rachel took in the sights and smells of the large ballroom in the government house, an exquisite leftover from the days when Spain owned East Florida. The roses in her hair held secure, thanks to the skill of Mrs. Winthrop's maid.

Garlands of flowers vied with guests' perfumes for sensory preeminence. Some ladies wore tall powdered wigs like Lady Augusta's, but even she did not apply that horrid ceruse face covering she had worn at Frederick's dinner party. The ladies' low-cut gowns had wide panniers and a beautiful array of colors, from pink to green to blue, some with a lovely mixture of tones. Rachel decided she must be a little bolder in her color schemes. As for the gentlemen, most were dressed in embroidered coats and breeches, but none were as handsome as Frederick in his red brocade waistcoat and white satin breeches.

At the end of the large ballroom, a string ensemble sat on a raised platform and played music, and guests danced in the center of the room. At the other end, punch and cakes provided sustenance to last until dinner was announced.

Rachel glanced up at Frederick. He seemed somewhat distracted and kept looking about the room as if searching for someone.

"The music is lovely," she said. "I could listen to it for hours."

Frederick looked toward the musicians as if surprised to see them. "Yes, very nice. Forgive me, Rachel. Would you care to dance another set?"

"No. Two country dances are enough for me." She looked across the room at the musicians, trying to memorize the tunes so that she could play them on Frederick's pianoforte, soon to be *her* pianoforte. She exhaled a happy sigh in anticipation of that day.

Frederick took her hand. "The governor is approaching. Are you prepared for our announcement?"

A nervous flutter teased her stomach, but she nodded.

"Ah, there you are, Moberly." Governor Tonyn joined them, his wife on his arm. "As you requested, we will make the announcement at the end of this set."

"My dear, I wish you much happiness." Mrs. Tonyn squeezed Rachel's hands and took her place beside them.

"Thank you, madam."

As the music played on, Rachel located Papa and Mrs. Winthrop across the room. Papa was having a grand time, as he always did. After this evening, he would be able to remember the name and occupation of every person he met. Rachel had seen some guests snub him, but he forged on as if oblivious to the slights. One time she noticed Lady Augusta looking at Papa and whispering behind her fan to another lady, and both laughed. If Papa cared for their opinions, Rachel might have felt bad for him. But nothing ever seemed to hurt him. The joy in his face soothed away her anxieties on his behalf.

Deeper still, she admitted his bringing her to East Florida had been God's will for both of them. Loving Frederick and being loved by him was the fulfillment of her dreams. Papa's business was a success, and his feelings for Mrs. Winthrop made life in the wilderness even sweeter. And after Rachel and Frederick married, she could continue to look for ways to help the revolution among the few sympathizers who lived in the colony. With those happy thoughts, Rachel opened her heart to embrace her new life at last.

Papa and Mrs. Winthrop wended their way around the edge of the room to join Rachel and the others just as the music ended. The director bowed toward the gov-

ernor, who straightened his gold waistcoat and cleared
his throat.

"Good friends, it is always a privilege to announce
happy tidings, and this evening is no exception. Please
permit me to present to you Mr. Frederick Moberly and
his betrothed, Miss Rachel Folger."

Silence followed. Then several people gasped. Some
ladies murmured behind fans. The deep tones of several men carried across the room, filled with anything
but approval. Rachel looked at Frederick, and he gave
her a smile no doubt meant to reassure her. But chagrin
pinched his cheeks and darkened his eyes.

Chapter Twenty-Two

How long the room buzzed with shock and censure, Rachel could not guess. Then Mrs. Pilot, a plump, merry and influential matron whose husband was a regimental officer, hurried from the crowd to Rachel and embraced her. "Oh, my dear, how wonderful. I wish you much, much happiness." Her high voice rang across the room like a call to an assembly.

In her wake, dozens of other ladies and gentlemen surged forward to offer congratulations. Rachel noticed Papa's eyes had narrowed, as they did when he felt some strong emotion. How she wished she could discover his true feelings toward her betrothal. But he was a closed book, her only bit of sorrow in the midst of her joy.

Here she stood among all these Loyalists, who no doubt assumed she and Frederick could be counted in their ranks. While trading pleasantries with them, she thought of her loved ones in Boston who bore the revolution's weight. And, encouraged by Frederick's behavior as they toured the fort earlier in the day, she decided tonight would be her only chance to tell Mrs. Middlebrook of where her true loyalties lay.

Yet later, after Frederick had returned her to the

Baldwins' drawing room and she had whispered her thoughts to Mrs. Middlebrook, the other woman lifted her chin haughtily.

"I have no idea of what you are saying, Miss Folger." The woman's smile was tight, and her gaze did not meet Rachel's. "You must have had a dream. And of course, you were filled with romantic thoughts concerning your betrothal." She fanned herself with an ornate red-and-black fan. "Gracious, this heat."

Rachel glanced over her shoulder to make certain Mrs. Winthrop was still talking with their hostess on the other side of the room. The Middlebrook girls had already retired to the guest bedchamber.

"No, madam, I was not dreaming. I heard—"

"You heard nothing." Mrs. Middlebrook snapped her fan shut. "You are a silly girl. And, as if it were not enough that you, the daughter of a mere shopkeeper, have managed to ensnare a gentleman, the son of an earl, now you wish to stir up trouble in our peaceful colony. How dare you accuse me of...why, it is nothing less than treason."

Rachel's face flamed, just as it had earlier that evening when the governor's announcement had shocked the ballroom into silence. Never in her life had anyone spoken to her in this manner.

Mrs. Middlebrook leaned over her with a glare. "Your sort is reason enough not to mix the classes. Many of us will never forgive Mrs. Pilot for coming to your rescue this evening. To think that the wife of a noted regimental officer would rush to your side and countenance your betrothal, forcing us all to offer felicitations to Mr. Moberly, when all we felt for him was pity. Poor Mr. Moberly. To be shackled to a silly little gossip." She spun away and sauntered toward the other ladies, fanning herself once again. "Dearest Ida," she said to Mrs. Baldwin. "I am utterly wilted. Will you forgive me if I retire?"

Gulping back a sob of mortification, Rachel waved her own fan furiously to cool her blazing face. What a foolish mistake she had made. Of course Mrs. Middlebrook didn't trust her. A true patriot would not marry a loyal British subject. And Rachel could not, would not betray Frederick's sympathies for the cause. In truth, he had not yet voiced those sympathies to her. But his solicitous demeanor could mean nothing less than an agreement with her. They simply had not found the chance to talk about it.

Walking toward the tall, slatted veranda doors, she moved on legs rendered wooden by embarrassment. How could she redeem this situation? Never mind the shame of Mrs. Middlebrook's scathing rejection. If no one trusted her, she couldn't pass on information. Perhaps she wouldn't even be able to learn anything useful.

Outside, deep in the shadows of palm trees and fragrant geraniums, Rachel sat on a cast-iron bench and gazed up at the starlit sky through stinging tears. This should be the happiest night of her life, but her failure to find a contact spoiled it. Tomorrow morning after an early church service, their party would be returning to St. Johns Settlement. But what would she do at home? Nothing, simply nothing ever happened there that could help the revolution.

"Lord," she whispered, "please show me a way to serve the cause I hold dear." Conviction filled her. She must amend her prayer. "Please give me a way to serve Your righteous cause."

She leaned against the bench back and let the night breeze cool her face and soothe her bruised soul. After uncounted minutes, she grew drowsy and started to go inside, although she hated to think of facing Mrs. Middlebrook in the bedchamber. Before she could stand, something rustled among the palmetto bushes nearby. Fear clogged her throat. She never should have come out here alone.

"Did Odysseus give you the cylinder?" The hushed tones of a man's voice met her ears.

"Yes, I have it here." A second man answered in a low, gravelly voice. "All is well. They will put everything into place. We have only to get the cylinder to Perseus."

"You can do this?"

"Zeus will deliver it to Hermes. He will take it to Perseus on his next voyage."

A third man grunted his agreement.

The men continued to talk, but their voices grew softer as they moved away.

Rachel smothered a laugh. Now that surely was an interesting bit of information, but not a whit more useful than what she'd heard from the Middlebrook ladies that morning. What cylinder? What ship? And who were Perseus, Odysseus, Hermes and Zeus?

Too weary and disappointed to consider it further, Rachel returned to the upstairs guest room, changed into her night rail, and surrendered to sleep.

In the morning service, the bishop's homily did nothing to encourage Rachel regarding the revolution. He spoke of obedience, affirming that God's will could be found only in submission to His chosen authority, King George. Seated between Papa and Frederick, Rachel resisted the temptation to yawn.

That afternoon, the *Mingo* reached Mayport by dark, where they would spend the night on shipboard and continue by flatboat to the settlement in the morning.

Once again, Rachel had to sit in the cramped cabin while the other ladies hovered around Lady Augusta and chatted about frivolous matters. Rachel had given up trying to be a part of their society, but found solace in the warmth of Mrs. Winthrop's kind glances.

On Monday morning, her group parted company from the Amelia Island travelers, much to Rachel's relief. The two flatboats moved westward with ease due to the strong ocean tide flowing inland against the outflow of the wide, shallow St. Johns River.

In the early afternoon, everyone except the rowers had fallen into a lazy, heat-induced stupor. Rachel watched the passing scenery through half-closed eyes until she noticed Lady Augusta's arm hanging over the boat's side, her white dress's wide sleeve flapping like the wing of a wounded crane. A second later, movement in the water sent Rachel scrambling to her feet the instant an alligator rose from the river and clamped its massive jaws on the sleeve. The grunting beast twisted its scaly body as it dropped back, dragging Lady Augusta halfway over the side. She screamed and gripped the gunwale with her free hand.

"Help! Help us!" Rachel knelt and slammed her folded parasol on the beast's snout again and again. The wooden handle broke, and she stabbed at its eyes with the sharp splintered end. Numb to everything but the battle, she struck so hard that her broad-brimmed straw hat flew off.

Behind her, she heard scrambling and cries. Someone shoved her out of the way.

"Augusta!" Major Brigham grasped his wife's waist and tried to pull her into the boat.

"Shoot it. Shoot it," one soldier yelled.

A musket fired. The flatboat dipped dangerously.

"Balance the boat," Papa boomed out. "Moberly, over here, or we'll be swamped."

"Yes, sir," Frederick shouted. "Mrs. Winthrop, over here."

Rachel scrambled to join them.

"Shoot. Shoot." Major Brigham set his feet against the boat side, clutching and clawing to keep a grip on his wife's clothes.

The other two soldiers fired their muskets, then reloaded, a maddeningly slow process.

The battle seemed endless, but neither side surrendered. The five-foot alligator rolled again, and the sleeve became more entangled in its teeth and snout. Rachel could not believe the fabric had not torn loose.

At last the sleeve ripped from the dress. Major Brigham and Lady Augusta flew backward, landing in a heap. The soldiers fired again, and the beast disappeared beneath the murky surface. The boat continued to rock, and the rowers used their poles to steady it.

To her credit, Lady Augusta did not become hysterical. But her eyes were wide, and she shook violently as Major Brigham settled back into the seat and grasped her.

"Oh, my dear, my darling." The major seemed unaware of anyone but his wife. "Thank our merciful God that you are safe." He kissed her temple. "Let me see your arm."

Lady Augusta held out the scraped limb and gave him a trembling smile. "Only a little blood. There, I am the one wounded in battle, not you, my prince." Her expression was filled with sweetness such as Rachel had not imagined her capable of, and their endearments almost moved her to tears. Or perhaps it was her own hysteria, for a sob broke from her unbidden.

Frederick folded her in his arms. "Shh. You were quite brave, my love. We can thank the Lord you were alert and watching."

She nestled against him, still shuddering, still watching the woman whose life she had helped to save. All anger, all hurt feelings, all struggles not to mind Lady Augusta's rudeness floated away like Rachel's straw hat. Beneath her aristocratic exterior, she was a woman who loved and was loved by both God and the man He had ordained for her. Just like Rachel.

"Yes, thanks be to the Lord."

"Well done, Rachel." Papa's eyes sparkled.

She drank in his approval like a thirsty plant. She could almost feel water filling her. Looking down, she saw the river pouring into the boat through a small hole in the side.

"Water!"

Once again shouts filled the air.

"Row to the bank."

"Bail it out."

"Keep the powder dry."

"We're sinking!"

"Where's the other boat?"

Mrs. Winthrop dispensed cups and bowls from the picnic basket, and everyone except the rowers scooped out the water as quickly as they could. Even the Brighams joined the task.

Papa emitted a mild oath. "I never should have slept. Even then, I sensed we were off course."

"What do you mean, sir?" Frederick scanned the horizon.

"This river has many islands and creeks, as well ye know. From this level, they all look the same. It's easy to go down the wrong stream when ye don't set landmarks in yer mind." Papa tapped his forehead as he studied the area around them. "We've got to put in." He pointed toward a jut of land. "Over there. Put in, I say."

The rowers looked at Frederick.

"Do as he says." His tone was terse.

Amidst the disaster, Rachel felt a measure of pride that Papa still proved himself a worthy commander *and* that Frederick was not too proud to listen to him.

The two rowers gripped their poles and shoved the flatboat through the tall marsh grasses, coming at last to a sandy promontory. All the men jumped out and pulled the craft onto the little beach, then assisted Lady Augusta, Mrs. Winthrop and Rachel to dry land.

For several minutes, everyone looked around without speaking. Then Frederick grinned at Rachel. "Well, my dear, it looks as if we'll end the day with a stroll." He broke into laughter, and Rachel did, too.

The Brighams appeared unwilling to join the merriment, but the three soldiers and even the slave rowers guffawed.

Papa's gaze was directed toward the forest some distance away. Hands on hips, he faced the crowd. "We'll not be walking through that salt grass marsh. There'll be quicksand and water moccasins, not to mention more of those hungry alligators."

Major Brigham exchanged a look with Frederick, and they both turned back to Papa.

"What do you suggest, sir?" Major Brigham asked.

"I'd say Mr. Moberly and I should go for help. We'll take this lad along." He clapped one soldier on the back. "I'm fairly certain he's not the one who blasted that hole in the boat." He eyed the other two soldiers, one of whom appeared unwilling to meet his stare. "We can test our steps with one of these poles." He took one in hand. "And we'd best be off soon so the day don't get the better of us. Not all of the Indians in these parts think kindly of us."

Proud of Papa for taking charge, Rachel nonetheless moved closer to Frederick and looped her arm through his. She longed for him not to leave her.

"A good plan, Mr. Folger." Major Brigham shook Papa's hand. "Do you need any provisions?"

"A jug of water and a bit of bread should do it." Papa motioned to Frederick. "Come along, lad."

Frederick placed a quick kiss on Rachel's cheek. "Will you be all right? Silly question. Of course you will, my brave girl."

Despite his praise, it took all Rachel's inner strength not to beg him to stay with her. She noticed that Papa patted Mrs. Winthrop's hand, and the lady gave him an encouraging nod. Rachel decided she must be as brave as the older woman.

Lightly provisioned, the three men struck out on their venture. While the others made camp, Rachel watched the travelers on their zigzag course across the marsh. Several times Frederick turned back to wave, giving her an incentive to keep her vigil.

When at last they were out of sight, she searched for some task that might help the encampment, but all had been accomplished. The rowers had speared some fish and started a fire to cook them. Mrs. Winthrop had cleaned the cups and bowls and would ration the water. The beached flatboat sat drying in the sun. Even Lady Augusta joined the effort by bringing out the mosquito netting. All seemed in order.

After their humble meal, Major Brigham instructed the ladies to sleep within the boat's protection. The men would take turns standing watch.

Yet despite the comforts of a full stomach, the boat
cushions, mosquito netting and the fresh cool breeze
off the river, Rachel could not sleep. Alligators grunted
in the distance. Frogs and crickets played a discordant
symphony. Fish—or something else—splashed in the
river all too near them. Never mind that one could not
hear a snake if it approached. She could hear Major
Brigham ordering his men to keep watch for the Chick-
asaw, whose attacks on the English had led to many
deaths in recent years. Rachel shuddered, then shuddered again, thinking of the dangers Frederick and Papa
might encounter. She lifted up a prayer for their safety
before lying back to wait for whatever the dawn would
bring.

Chapter Twenty-Three

Following behind Mr. Folger, Frederick felt his admiration for the man grow, for he and Private Martin were forced to push themselves to keep up. Rachel once mentioned that her father limped due to an injury sustained on his last whaling voyage. The limp was not as noticeable today. With an optimism Frederick found contagious, the old man gamely led them across the salt grass marsh, both on sandy ground and through stretches of waist-deep water.

Folger had set their heading toward a thin spire of smoke curling into the afternoon sky, no doubt from the Timucuan village on the plantation's southeastern border. If the Indians would help them, they would be able to get back to Rachel and the others before daybreak.

The strenuous journey took its toll on Frederick. And from the haggard looks of the other two men, he could tell they also felt the stress. The sun beat down on them with fury, and their thirst raged. Folger rationed the water. Frederick and Martin bantered that they must match the older man's endurance. More than once, they sidestepped to avoid water moccasins, rattlesnakes, or snapping turtles, even juvenile alligators.

Startled cranes and cormorants took flight at their approach. Heat forced the men to remove their shirts. Then, shortly before sunset, mosquitoes swarmed over them, biting every bare patch of skin. They hastened to don their garments again.

But persistence proved rewarding, for they reached the tree line before twilight descended, albeit with torn, filthy, wet clothes. Summerlin would have a fit over Frederick's ruined boots, which were soaked both inside and out.

With what seemed to Frederick an uncanny sense of direction, Folger continued to wend his way through the palmettos and scrub that grew beneath the palm and cypress trees. At last they found a path to follow.

Ahead, the torch-lit village hummed with late evening activities. The smell of roasted meat met Frederick's senses, and his mouth watered. Beside him, he heard Martin's belly rumble.

Folger stopped and called out a greeting in the Timucuan tongue. The Indians sent the women and children to their palm-thatched huts, then grabbed bows, arrows and clubs. One man carried a musket, and several others brought torches. Most wore little clothing and bore many tattoos.

"Stop." A tall, burly, gray-haired man stepped from the group. "Who comes?"

"Greetings, Saturiwa. 'Tis yer friend Folger." He lifted both hands and spoke in his jolly, booming voice. "And my two friends." He moved forward.

"Folger." The old chief beckoned to Mr. Folger. "Come." He slapped him on the back.

As Frederick and Martin entered the torchlight, some men pointed to the private's red coat and began to murmur. Saturiwa hushed them.

"You come from the river," the chief said.

"Aye. Yes," Folger said. "Our boat got swamped. Can ye help us fetch the rest of our party?"

Not answering, Saturiwa now set his gaze on Frederick. "Moberly." The resonance in the chief's voice reminded Frederick of his father. When he had met the chief before, Frederick had been on horseback. Now the man's superior height, well over six feet, proved intimidating.

"Good evening, sir." Frederick shook away his edginess. The trip across the swamp had taken more out of him than he realized. "May we rely upon your help? I shall make it worth your while."

Saturiwa grunted. "When other English kill us, you let us stay on our land. That is enough. You will eat. Then we will talk."

Frederick and his companions sighed their relief as if one man. They followed the Indians into the center of the circled huts and sat beside an open fire, where remnants of the evening meal still hung on a spit. Two old women brought them springwater, roasted rabbit, and a tasty cornmeal mush. Soon Frederick felt his strength returning.

Across the campfire, Saturiwa and two other men conversed in their language. They appeared to reach some agreement, for the chief stared at Folger expectantly. Frederick dismissed the urge to speak up. An old man himself, the Indian no doubt respected age and regarded Folger as the group's leader.

Folger set down his wooden bowl and wiped a damp handkerchief across his lips. "Will ye help us fetch our friends, sir?"

Saturiwa nodded his affirmation. "We will *fetch*—"

he grinned using Folger's word "—your friends and take you to the plantation. We will go at first light."

Frederick and Folger traded frowns.

"Could ye consider going now?" Folger waved his hand toward the darkened path. "My daughter and the other ladies—"

"Ah." Saturiwa conferred with another man for a moment, then addressed Folger. "The little daughter of Folger must be safe, but travel in darkness is not wise. We will go before first light."

Frederick and Folger accepted his decision with reluctance. They would sleep beside the campfire and be rested for their journey.

As the Indians prepared for the night, Frederick noticed Martin's frequent glances into one palm-thatched hut. He nudged the soldier.

"That could be considered rude. Don't give them cause for offense."

"Yes, sir." Martin clenched his fists. "Thing is, sir, I see what looks like one of our uniform jackets hangin' in there. Why would these savages...'scuse me, sir, these people have a British soldier's jacket?"

Frederick took a step toward the hut but found his way blocked by two Indians.

"Moberly." Saturiwa called from across the camp. "Come."

Dreading a confrontation, Frederick walked around the fire. He'd noticed the chief's reference to "our land." If the Indians turned on them in reprisal for the suffering inflicted by other Englishmen, they might be slaughtered, as other white men had been during a recent uprising. The situation did not sit well with Frederick, but he must face up to the chief, whatever the outcome. "Why do you have a British soldier's jacket?"

Saturiwa regarded him for several moments, perhaps sizing him up. Frederick didn't lower his gaze, but he also kept his posture and expression neutral.

"A soldier came to us to flee his evil chief. He no longer wanted to soldier but to live among us." Saturiwa lifted his chin and narrowed his eyes. "We do not turn you away. We did not turn him away."

The hair on Frederick's neck prickled against his sweat-soaked collar. "Where is this man?"

"We do not betray those who put their lives in our hands."

"What's the trouble?" Folger approached, hands on hips, and cast a disapproving glare at Frederick.

Frederick bit back a retort. "I think we may have found the man who burned down the inn and almost succeeded in burning your store." He added that last detail for the chief's information.

Folger spat out an oath. "Where is he?"

Frederick turned back to the chief. "If my suspicions are correct, the man you are protecting murdered two innocent people in the great fire last month. He lied to you about fleeing an evil leader, Saturiwa."

"Ah." The chief looked toward the hut. "He has wounds and fights a fever. Come."

Saturiwa grabbed a small torch to light the hut's interior. The smell of infection and human waste assaulted Frederick, and he covered his nose with one hand. On a raised platform some four feet above the ground lay the soldier he had kept from harming Rachel, the one Brigham had identified as the vengeful arsonist. The sleeping man's pale face indicated his fever had broken.

"Buckner." Frederick reached out and shook him. "Get up, man. You're coming with me."

Buckner groaned but did not awaken.

Saturiwa stepped up beside him. "He cannot walk."

"What?" Frederick stared at the chief.

"Wild boar." The chief lifted his torch and pointed to Buckner's left leg, which was wrapped in blood-stained rags.

Frederick grimaced. "Will you keep him until we can send soldiers for him? I will make certain they do not harass you."

Saturiwa shrugged. "He will be here."

The chief's relaxed demeanor invited Frederick's confidence and soothed his earlier anxieties. "Thank you."

Frederick marveled at finding Buckner still on the plantation. He had ordered his people to leave the Timucua in peace, and no one ever came to this remote corner of the property. But by the strangest of circumstances, God had brought him here to find the miscreant, and Frederick would not rest until the man faced justice.

"Rachel." The impatient whisper came through the darkness from the flatboat's other end.

Rachel blinked away sleep and perceived the shadowed speaker's identity. "Yes, Lady Augusta?" Both drowsiness and impatience filled her voice. The first she could not help, but the second she regretted immediately. She sat up and rubbed her eyes. "What news, madam?"

Growing accustomed to the campfire's dim light, she could see Lady Augusta in silhouette and her husband beside her.

"Major Brigham has told me *you* are responsible for my rescue." Her tone resounded with annoyance.

"Augusta." Major Brigham spoke his wife's name so softly that Rachel could barely hear him.

"Oh, very well." Lady Augusta exhaled impatiently. "I thank you, Miss Folger. We shall reward you."

Raging heat rushed to Rachel's face. *Lord, give me patience.* She drew in a deep, cooling breath. "Your well-being is my reward, Lady Augusta. We may praise God for your deliverance."

Frogs croaked in the distance. The men standing guard murmured around the fire. A dove cooed its mournful night song. But no sound came from the boat's other end.

Rachel lay back down.

"Yes. Well. Nevertheless, I thank you."

With no small difficulty, Rachel held back a rush of tears. She would not have thought this woman could hurt her feelings again, but she just had. When Rachel could speak, she whispered "You are welcome."

She turned on her side and covered her head with her shawl to avoid hearing their quiet conversation. Soon they became silent, but Rachel could not return to sleep. Tears slipped across her cheek and ran down into her hair, but she did nothing to stop them.

Lord, please grant me kindness toward others, no matter what their station in this world, for You have made us all equal in Your sight. Grant me a stout heart and only courtesy toward Lady Augusta.

How like her arrogant English monarch this woman behaved. In spite of repeated attempts by the colonists to reconcile with King George, he had spurned their pleas for relief from mistreatment. While Lady Augusta held no such authority over Rachel, she certainly acted as if she did. And the woman continued to snub Rachel, even when Rachel had helped to save her life, and had lost her favorite hat while doing so.

A bit of Papa's playfulness entered her thoughts. *Lord, if You can find a reason to send Lady Augusta back home to England, she would be much happier there, don't You think?*

With the hope that her prayer did not sound too impertinent, Rachel sat up to await the soon-coming dawn. When she and Papa arrived in East Florida, the early arrival of daylight had surprised her. Dawn came early. Twilight descended late. Nights were short, especially in the summer.

Now a thin, horizontal glow split the eastern blackness, and with it a thick fog rose from the St. Johns River. Soon the small encampment became shrouded in gray. Rachel heard a haunting moan and saw hazy tongues of fire floating above the mists, as if the river were burning. Gradually, dark, blurred forms appeared and moved ever closer to the shore.

Major Brigham awoke and grabbed his musket. The two guards rushed to the flatboat and aimed their weapons toward the apparitions.

"Who goes there?"

Chapter Twenty-Four

Rachel gripped the sides of the yellow pine canoe as it flew through the water like an arrow shot from a bow, thanks to the muscular arms of the Indians at the slender vessel's front and back.

Frederick sat behind her, and she turned to see how he fared. Despite his puffy, bloodshot eyes and slumped posture, he gave her a reassuring smile. "Are you well, my love?" His voice croaked with weariness.

"Very well, thank you, now that the sun is up." She would not mention her lost hat or the heat scorching the back of her neck. This ordeal would soon be over.

What a fright he and Papa had given her, arriving through the heavy fog with a dozen or more torch-bearing Timucuans. Only by God's mercy did they not find themselves shot by the nervous soldiers guarding the encampment. Unlike the men, both white and Indian, who dismissed the incident once identities were established, the ladies had come near to fainting over what might have happened. Rachel hoped never to spend another night in this wilderness.

When the party arrived at the plantation in the late morning, Frederick ordered a carriage to take her home.

As a servant drove them toward town, she and Papa had little energy to talk, but she did find comfort in learning that Frederick had apprehended the man who started the fire.

Once home, they placed themselves in the capable hands of Mr. Patch and Inez. Rachel fell into bed and blissful rest.

She awakened to find the sun still up, only to realize by its morning position that Wednesday had arrived. She'd slept more than sixteen hours. Quickly washed and dressed, she hastened downstairs to the store. There Papa waited on customers as if he had never been away.

"There ye are at last." His light tone bespoke good humor. "Run along to the kitchen house, girl. I know ye're hungry."

"Have you eaten, Papa?"

"Enough for a horse, girl." His booming voice filled the store, to the amusement of the tanner's wife and another woman examining bolts of dress fabric. "Now, get ye along."

As she hurried to obey, Rachel shook her head, enjoying Papa's high spirits. Perhaps he and Mrs. Winthrop had come to an agreement and would soon announce their betrothal, too.

Crossing the backyard, she inhaled the aroma of cooking chicken, and her empty stomach cried out for satisfaction. Surprised to find the kitchen house door closed in such hot weather, she opened it cautiously in case Inez was bathing Sadie. Inside she found her servant at work and a young man seated beside Sadie on her bed. Dressed in rough brown breeches and a well-worn calico shirt, he had not shaved in some time, and his auburn hair needed to be combed.

Fear shot through Rachel. "Who are you?"

He jumped up, terror streaking across his face. With a quick glance about the room, he started toward the window.

"Rob, no," cried Sadie. "Don't leave us." She swung her legs to the floor and struggled to stand but fell back, wincing and crying out in pain.

"Sadie girl." The man hurried back to pull her into his arms. "Don't harm yourself, love." He stared at Rachel, fear widening his eyes. "I'm Sadie's husband, come to care for her."

Hoping to set Rob at ease, Rachel lifted little Robby. The child put his tiny arms around her neck and giggled as she kissed his forehead and nuzzled into his neck.

"You have nothing to fear. I'm merely surprised to find you here." She eyed the pot bubbling over the hearth fire, and her mouth watered at the aroma of the savory chicken. "Inez, I'm famished." Releasing the child to his play, she sat at the table. Although this could not be considered proper manners, she must eat something soon or risk becoming faint.

"*Sí,* señorita." Inez produced a crockery bowl and served meat, rice and bread.

"Does Mr. Folger know you are here, Rob?" Rachel spooned in a mouthful, endeavoring to appear detached. If he did know, surely he would have told her before she came out.

Rob and Sadie exchanged a look.

"No, ma'am," Sadie answered for her husband.

"Hmm." Rachel ate slowly. When Robby leaned against her, she fed him a bite of bread.

"Here, boy, don't annoy the lady." Rob pulled his son away.

"He is no annoyance." Rachel noticed that the others continued to watch her. "Have you eaten?"

"*Sí,* señorita, I feed them." Inez poured coffee for Rachel. "I know you are generous and would not mind."

"Very good." Rachel sent up a prayer for wisdom. Clearly Rob had deserted his soldiering duties, which would make him a criminal to some people. But unlike the horrid soldier who had set the fire, this one deserted for an honorable purpose—to care for his family.

After several minutes, Sadie and Rob seemed to relax. They whispered endearments to one another and talked about what they had done while separated. Rachel tried not to listen, but the room was too small to keep their conversation private.

"The boy's strong." Rob eyed his son with pride. "You've done a good job, love."

Sadie leaned against him. "He needs his pa, he does." Tears covered her cheeks. "Ya did good to come."

Rob kissed her forehead, but his eyes held concern, while Sadie's eyes radiated her love.

Their mutual tenderness moved Rachel. This was the depth of love she felt for Frederick. What would she do if they were forced apart? How could she bear it?

For Sadie's and Robby's sakes, Rachel must hide Rob, must help him avoid detection by the British soldiers who patrolled the settlement randomly day and night.

She finished her meal and stood. "Thank you, Inez."

"*De nada,* señorita." Inez came to clear the table, while Rachel walked toward the door.

"Beggin' your pardon, miss." Rob approached her. "Could you find it in your heart not to report that I've come here?"

Her heart welled up with sympathy. "Of course I'll not report you. But you cannot hide here for long. Do you have a plan?"

Rob glanced back at Sadie, and she nodded.

"We're going to Cuba."

Rachel stared at him. "Cuba? But why? And with Sadie's injuries, how will you travel?"

"Travel where?" Frederick appeared in the open doorway, his eyebrows arched with curiosity. He looked at Rob, then Rachel, then Sadie, and back to Rachel. "My dear, your father told me you were here. Who is this?" He stared at Rob, and his tone, while not forceful, rang with authority. His magistrate voice.

Dizzy with shock and a remnant of exhaustion, Rachel swayed, almost losing her balance. "Frederick."

Rob's face grew pale around the edges of his sunburn, and he began to tremble.

Rachel felt herself blanching, too. How tempting to lie about this situation, especially since she had promised not to betray Rob. But conviction blocked that wicked thought.

"This is Sadie's husband."

Frederick straightened and frowned. He stared hard at Rob. "Are you not in His Majesty's service?"

Rob gulped. "Yes, sir. That is, I was."

Sadie began to sob, and Rob hurried to her side. "It's all right, Sadie girl. I knew what I would face. But I had to come. I had to know about you and the boy."

A painful knot filled her chest, and Rachel could not contain her own tears. "Frederick, please, can we not let them go?" She grasped his arm and gazed up at him. "Please. Give this to me as a wedding gift, and I shall never ask anything else of you."

"Do you know what you're saying?" Frederick shook his head. "It would be treason."

She wiped a sleeve across her damp face. "Treason against whom? An unjust king who cares nothing for the suffering of common people?" If he did not help them, she wondered whether she would be able to forgive him. She stared into his eyes, wishing, praying for him to relent. "They will hang him," she whispered, "merely for loving his wife and child."

He looked across the room again, his struggle evident in his grinding jaw and deep frown. Anger stormed across his eyes. He stared at the floor, and his lips formed a thin line. At last, he slapped his hat back on and pointed at Rob. "Do not be here when I come back." Then he strode out the door, slamming it on his way.

Gulping back tears, Rachel refused to think of all this meant for their future. "You must have help. I'll go to my father." She opened the door.

"Oh, miss, what if he won't help?" Sadie began to sob again.

Rachel shook her head. "I don't know." *Lord, have mercy. Please soften Papa's heart and make him help us.*

She ran to the store and remained behind the burlap curtain until Papa's customer left. Driven by urgency, she rushed into the room and locked the door.

Papa stared at her with a bewildered expression. "What're ye doing, girl? 'Tis not yet closing time."

"Sadie's husband deserted and came here to see her. He's out in the kitchen house right now. Please, Papa, no matter how you feel about it, I beg you to help them get away from here. They want to go to Cuba and—"

"Hold on a minute." Papa held up his hands. "I'm getting yer meaning clear." He scratched his chin. "Go fetch Mr. Patch. He should be at the livery stable. I'll see what I can do."

Rachel reached up to kiss his stubbly face. "Thank you, Papa. I knew you would help."

He grunted. "Go on, girl. Don't waste time."

All the way to the stable, Rachel forced herself to walk instead of run, for she must not draw attention to herself. Now *this* was an adventure. This was something grand to do for someone else. Something so right that she risked displeasing Frederick, perhaps even losing him.

Dear Lord, please make him understand.

If he did not, she had no idea what she would do.

Frederick dug his heels into Essex's sides and bent forward in the saddle. The stallion leapt into a gallop and thundered along the road to the plantation. A good, hard ride would clear Frederick's mind and give the horse some much needed exercise.

He had come into town to make certain Rachel and Mr. Folger had recovered from their ordeal. He also wanted to deliver the news that Buckner had been brought to the fort and would face the ultimate punishment for his crimes, which included not only arson and murder but desertion. And now Rachel wanted him to help another man desert His Majesty's service.

How could she have put him in this position? From her disparaging remark about His Majesty, she appeared not to have changed her mind about becoming a loyal British subject. He had been foolish to think she would alter her allegiance merely because they were in love.

Love.

The word struck into his soul, and he reined Essex to a walk that he might have more time to ponder its meaning.

Indeed, he did love her, and all the more for her courageous generosity in helping the poor, unfortunate little family at the expense of her own happiness. Frederick had no doubt she would carry that same courage into their marriage and into their lives in this wilderness. Was this not the reason he had fallen in love with her in the first place?

An ironic chuckle broke through the knot in his chest, and some of his tension dissolved. His little darling would ask nothing but the soldier's freedom. Frederick recalled Mother asking something similar of Father, risking his wrath to acquire freedom for a mistreated slave. Mother and his beloved were much alike, a similarity that pleased him exceedingly.

He should have stayed to help her. Perhaps he should go back now. But this morning Oliver had requested an audience, and Frederick's every instinct required him to tend to that matter first.

He would return tomorrow morning, and they would talk about the disagreements that threatened their happiness, not the least of which was their conflicting loyalties. He must help her to understand that their lives would not be in danger here in East Florida, for the rebellion would not reach these shores. As for her other concern, he would convince her that the plantation slaves would always be treated with fairness. She herself could see to it.

Kicking Essex into a gallop again, Frederick whispered a prayer into the wind. "Lord, You know how much I love her. Please help us to work out our differences."

Chapter Twenty-Five

Frederick crumpled the letter and flung it toward the hearth. How tired he was of receiving nothing but condemnation from Father. The earl barely mentioned last spring's abundant shipment of indigo and rice. Instead, he harped on the expense of reinforcing the slave quarters and providing occasional meat for the plantation workers. Frederick wondered if it would be worth the effort to tell Father how well the quarters had withstood the recent storm or how the slaves worked harder in appreciation for his generous provision. No doubt the old man would still find some reason to call it wastefulness.

Leaning back in his chair, Frederick put his feet on the desk and toyed with the marble horse figurine Mother had given him before he left home. If not for her, he would have little trouble asking Father to replace him as the plantation manager.

No, that was foolishness. The people here thought well of him as magistrate, and in that position he had to answer to His Majesty, not Father. Furthermore, he would soon have a wife to care for, a fact that precluded any impulsive decisions such as leaving the plantation.

He sat up and retrieved the letter. It had been written

over six weeks ago, before Templeton had a chance to reach London. Perhaps now Father's opinion of Frederick had been improved by that worthy captain's recommendations. But what bitter medicine to swallow that the earl would listen to anyone but his own son.

The sound of labored breathing outside the library window interrupted his thoughts.

"No, sir, I won't do it."

Frederick recognized the voice of Betty, the housemaid. She sounded as if she had been running.

"I saved your life, you stupid little wench."

Oliver! What was the man up to now?

"Ow," Betty whined. "Twist me arm all you like, I'll not steal the—" Her words were cut off with a gasping cry.

Rage burned through Frederick's chest, but he managed to move quietly to the hearth and remove the crossed rapiers from their brackets.

"Shall I feed you to those alligators?" Oliver's voice held cruel amusement. "Ow. You little—" Had she stuck him? Bit him?

The unmistakable sound of a slap. A girlish whimper.

Frederick dashed from the library, down the hall, and then out the back door. There on the back lawn Betty knelt weeping with her hands to her face. Several slaves watched wide-eyed from the corner of the house. Oliver stood over Betty and drew back his foot.

"Kick her, and you are a dead man." Frederick raised one rapier and pointed it at Oliver.

The face his former friend turned to him resembled nothing Frederick could recognize—a dark, wild-eyed frown, an ugly grimace, cheeks contorted with hatred. He hurled out a blasphemous curse, words Frederick never permitted at the plantation.

"So you're home after all." Oliver's expression eased into a scornful scowl. "And playing with swords. My, my, Freddy, aren't we brave."

Frederick swallowed his fury and tossed the second weapon toward Oliver. It landed at his feet.

"Pick it up." *Lord, help me.* Perhaps this was not the best way to handle the situation.

Without removing his angry stare from Frederick, Oliver reached down to retrieve the foil. "You know, of course, that I am your better." He emitted an odd snicker. "At fencing, I mean." He bowed the blade slightly and swished it through the air.

Frederick looked beyond Oliver to see little Caddy helping the frightened housemaid to her feet. "What did he want you to do, Betty?"

"Keep your mouth shut, girl." Oliver kept his gaze on Frederick.

"For me to steal the keys from Mrs. Winthrop is what he wanted." Tears streaked her face. "But I wouldn't do it, no sir, not for him nor nobody."

"Good girl." Frederick felt a presence behind him and glanced back to see Summerlin, Cousin Lydie, Dr. Wellsey and several grooms. Old Ben held a pitchfork, and determination filled his black eyes as he glared at Oliver.

"Ah, me." Gratitude filled Frederick, followed by a twinge of disappointment. He truly longed to take Oliver on and prove him wrong about his swordsmanship. "Too much help for a fair fight. Shall we call it a draw?"

"Coward." Oliver flung down the sword and strode toward the stable.

Frederick stopped Oliver with the side of his blade. "We will talk in the library now."

Oliver jerked away and moved toward the house.

"Oh, dear, Frederick." Cousin Lydie touched his arm. "What if he—"

"It will be all right, dear." Frederick patted her hand. "You see to Betty." He motioned to Summerlin and Wellsey.

Inside, Dr. Wellsey closed the library door, and Summerlin leaned out the window and shooed away curious servants. Seated behind his desk, Frederick watched Oliver crumple into a chair and stare at the floor.

"Well, Oliver, out with it." Frederick had difficulty keeping a stern tone, for he would prefer to entreat his lifelong friend to explain his behavior. "Why did you need the keys?"

"Now, really, Freddy, if you had not taken my set of keys, none of this would have happened." Oliver rolled his eyes and shook his head. "I did not plan to take all of your money. Just enough for passage to Brazil. Oh, and a little food along the way." He brushed a bit of dirt from his shirtsleeve. "My needs are modest."

Frederick felt his jaw go slack. "Why did you not simply ask me?"

"I should not have to ask for what I have earned." His hands clenched, Oliver fidgeted, as if ready to take flight. "Simply put, I am leaving. I have depended upon *your* father's generosity for too long. It is time to make my own way in the world."

Frederick caught Oliver's emphasis on *your*. "What happened to prompt this decision?"

Oliver's face pinched into a grimace. "Your man Summerlin here has been with your family since he was fourteen." He glanced over his shoulder. "An excellent fellow, the epitome of uprightness. He, eh, informed me of certain happenings in the year before my birth that precluded some, uh, suspicions I have carried since boyhood."

Wellsey grunted, but Summerlin's neutral expression did not change.

"Ah." Both dismay and relief flooded Frederick. "Whatever the issue may be, I pray you will find peace in its regard."

"Peace? Ha." Oliver leaned back in his chair and stretched out his legs. "Lord Bennington has always treated me as a…treated me kindly and praised my business acumen. I thought to manage this plantation in your stead. But I could do that only if you failed." His eyes narrowed. "What do you think of that?"

At the affirmation of his worst suspicions, Frederick could hardly speak past the lump in his throat. "Did you plan that before we came here? No, I know you didn't. On our voyage over, we were friends as we always have been." He exhaled a labored sigh that hurt clear down to his belly.

Oliver snickered. "I really should consider an occupation in the theater." He rose and walked to the bookcase, where he pulled out the incriminating pamphlet Frederick had hidden in the pages of *Paradise Lost*. "I see your Miss Folger has left something for you to read. Perhaps Lord Bennington would be interested in it, as well."

Frederick felt the blood drain from his face. Rachel had never tried to conceal from him her sympathies for the insurrection. Was she the one who left the pamphlet the night of his dinner party in hopes of swaying his opinions? He glanced at Wellsey, who eyed the paper with curiosity. Summerlin maintained his disinterest.

"We have had numerous guests here, Oliver. Any one of them could have left it." He swallowed hard. "It's nothing but seditious nonsense."

Oliver's face took on a serpent-like slyness. "And yet here it remains, untorn, unburned."

"One does not burn evidence."

"Hmm." Oliver held the paper up as if reading it. "And yet you do not seek to find the guilty party?"

Anger flashed through Frederick—anger at himself, at Oliver and at Rachel. He crossed his arms. "You don't need to do this. You may go wherever you wish without trying to blackmail me." Boyhood memories of better times with this friend filled Frederick's mind. "In fact, you may have your mare, your clothes and thirty pounds to start your new life."

"What?" Oliver stared at him, clearly stunned. "After all I've done and said?"

Frederick walked around the desk and put his hands on Oliver's shoulders, forcing his adversary to look deep into his eyes. "Whatever you felt for me, I have always cared for you like a brother. In fact, closer than my true brothers."

Oliver's face grew pale, and his glance darted between Wellsey and Summerlin. "But—"

Soft rapping on the library door cut into his answer.

"Come," Frederick called.

The door cracked open, and the butler stuck in his bewigged head. "Sir, Major Brigham's in the drawin' room. May I say you'll see him?"

"Yes. Tell him I shall be there straightaway." Frederick eyed Oliver, but spoke to the other men. "Doctor, see Mr. Corwin out to the stable. Tell Ben to saddle the mare for him. Summerlin, pack his belongings and some food. He is not to set foot in this house again." A quick glance told him they would follow his orders forthwith.

"Oliver, I shall get the money for you shortly. I advise

you to take the King's Highway to St. Augustine. 'Tis a three-day ride, and there you will have your choice of ships."

"I—"

"Stubble it." Frederick left the room, swallowing the ache in his throat. He doubted he would ever know whether or not the pain in Oliver's eyes was genuine.

"A moment, sir." Summerlin stopped Frederick and fussed with his clothing and hair. "Now, sir, go meet the major."

Again Frederick tamped down his emotions. Summerlin's faithfulness stood in stark contrast to Oliver's betrayal.

At the drawing room door, he extended his hand toward his guest. "Major Brigham, I hope you and Lady Augusta have recovered from our excursion."

"Amazingly so." Brigham shook his hand. "In fact, I think she will take great delight in regaling her friends in London with her tale of being rescued from the jaws of a dragon." His eyes glinted with uncharacteristic cheerfulness.

"Very good, sir. Will you sit?" Frederick waved his hand toward an upholstered chair. "I'll send for lemonade." He made motions to the butler by the door.

"I will stay only a moment. I must return to the garrison and supervise the packing."

"Packing?" Frederick digested the thought for a moment. "Aha. Your transfer came through."

Brigham whisked a hand across his red jacket sleeve. "Yes. At last I'll have a purpose for wearing this uniform."

Frederick found his high humor a welcome relief. "Very good, sir. I'm pleased on your behalf. Did you come to take your leave, then?"

"Yes. I will leave in four days and wanted you to know of my good fortune."

"What of Lady Augusta?" Frederick asked. "Will she be regaling those friends in London sooner rather than later?"

A shadow passed over Brigham's brow. "I'd intended to send her home after the incident with the alligator, but the brave girl will have none of it. And there are other officers' wives in Boston. It shouldn't be a problem, as we will hold the city against the rebels. We have several thousand more troops arriving soon."

The butler carried in a refreshment tray and poured lemonade from a cut-glass pitcher into matching goblets. Both men partook.

"Well, then." Frederick eyed Brigham expectantly. "What other news?"

"Ah, yes." He drew out a sealed document from his jacket and handed it to Frederick. "From Governor Tonyn. He requires your presence back in the capital without delay. I've ordered a flatboat to take you to the coast this afternoon before the tides turn."

Frederick's heart sank. This would delay his getting back to Rachel to assure her he was not angry about the soldier and for them to have their long-overdue discussion about their differences. Yet he had no choice but to obey Governor Tonyn's orders, no matter what the personal cost to him or Rachel.

"The pony cart is almost packed." Rachel sat beside Sadie in the kitchen house while Papa and Mr. Patch helped Rob prepare for their departure.

"Thank you, miss." Sadie reclined on her cot beside her napping son. "With your help and Mr. Moberly buyin' the livestock, we'll be able to make it to Cuba."

Rachel ignored the disquieting emotion stirred by the mention of Frederick's name. Instead, she studied Sadie's expression. "You seem worried."

"Yes, miss. I ain't never known any Indians, and all I've heard is they like to kill us English for sport." She caressed her son's unruly hair.

"Do not be afraid. Papa has made friends with the Timucua people. They respect him, and for his sake, they will take good care of you until you are able to travel."

"I do hope so."

"And Inez will be there to take care of you, as well."

Sadie grasped Rachel's hands. "Oh, miss, will you ever forgive me? I never meant to take your servant. I never thought to *have* a servant, bein' one myself."

Rachel tried to smile, but her lower lip quivered. "But you can see God's goodness in this, can you not? Inez has been separated from her sons for twelve years, since England took possession of East Florida. Now she can go to Cuba with you and find them."

"You're good to look at it that way, miss." Sadie dried her face on her sleeve.

Soon Papa, Mr. Patch and Rob came to collect the other travelers. With last goodbyes said, Rachel watched the little band walk up the road toward the wilderness path.

How she wished she could go to the plantation. But seeking Frederick out, even though they were engaged, would be improper and might offend dear Mrs. Winthrop. He had said he would return, and while she awaited his visit with a measure of trepidation, she anticipated their long-overdue conversation about the revolution. For somehow she must persuade him to the patriot cause.

Chapter Twenty-Six

Frederick did not come to see her. Even Papa did not return from the Timucua village. At dusk, Rachel bolted the front door, secured the kitchen house and back door, and then carried her dinner upstairs. By candlelight, she managed to force down some stew, although her appetite had long ago been chased away by anxious thoughts.

The evening breeze blew in through the tall windows, carrying a refreshing pine scent and cooling the apartment. Raucous laughter and fiddle music came from the town's remaining tavern a half mile away. The haunting yelp of a dog wafted in from the salt grass marshes, and Rachel shuddered. No doubt some poor pup had fallen prey to an alligator.

She loaded one of Papa's muskets and laid it on the dining table. Other than the man who attempted to burn the store, no one had tried to harm them. But she would not be caught unprepared. New people came to the settlement every week, some like Papa fleeing the war up north, others perhaps to find wealth in the wilderness. But some might wish to cause trouble.

A slender crescent moon rose outside her window.

Papa still did not return. Rachel retired, but sleep would not come.

She prayed for Papa's safety, then reassured herself that he no doubt decided to stay the night in the village. He had proved his wilderness mettle, and her worries served no purpose.

She prayed for Frederick, but could find no such reassurance. The Lord remained silent. After a restless night, she rose to open her Bible at dawn. Her ribbon bookmark lay beside Psalm 51, where one verse seemed prominent. *Behold, Thou desirest truth in the inward parts: and in the hidden part Thou shalt make me to know wisdom.*

Certain she had been truthful with both the Lord and Frederick, she wondered why the verse lingered in her mind as she ate the remaining stew and went downstairs to open the store. Customers came and went. Clouds kept the sun's usual heat at bay.

Midmorning, Mr. Patch burst through the front door. "Miss Rachel, come quick." His terror-filled eyes sent fear coursing through her. She hurried outside after him.

"What—" At the front porch, she grasped the railing as light-headedness struck.

Papa straddled his mule and lay against its neck not moving, perhaps not breathing.

"Papa!" Rachel thrust away her weakness and rushed to him. "What happened?"

Small but sturdy Mr. Patch grasped Papa's waist and struggled to pull him down. "Snakebite. Rattler," Mr. Patch managed through clenched teeth.

"Is he alive?" Rachel choked out the question as she tried to help, to no avail. Papa weighed too much for the two of them and might be further injured if he fell to the ground.

"Aye, Miss Rachel, and flaming with fever. It happened early this morning as we made our way home." Mr. Patch blinked away tears. "After he was bit, he climbed up on old Kip here and passed out. I brought him as quick as I could without him falling off."

"You did well, Mr. Patch." Forcing aside the fear that paralyzed her, Rachel looked around for help. Several soldiers on their rounds appeared down the street, and she screamed out to them. Led by her acquaintance, Bertie Martin, the men hastened to pull Papa gently from the mule and carry him upstairs to his bed.

"I thank you all." Rachel wiped away her tears and stared at Papa's swollen calf and torn stockings. "Does anyone know what to do for a snakebite?"

"He'd do best to have a doctor, Miss Rachel." Private Martin's anxious expression spoke of his concern for Papa.

"Is it within your duties to fetch Dr. Wellsey from Bennington Plantation?" And Frederick. Surely he would come, even if he were still angry with her.

"Yes, miss. We can do that." Private Martin tilted his head toward the door, and the other soldiers followed him out.

"Mr. Patch, get fresh springwater and towels from the kitchen house." Rachel pulled off Papa's shoes.

"Aye, miss." Mr. Patch dashed out.

Her hands trembled as she removed Papa's knife from its sheath and cut away the stocking on his wounded leg. Two punctures scarred the outside of his calf, and the skin stretched tight over the red, swollen limb. Rachel examined the wounds, wishing she could squeeze out the poison that even now caused his labored breathing. Perhaps Dr. Wellsey would bring leeches.

"Lord, have mercy on Papa. Please do not let him

die without knowing You." Rachel bit back a sob. Papa would be all right. He was strong. He would fight off the poison.

Mr. Patch brought the water, and Rachel washed Papa's face and the wound. They replaced his shirt with a nightgown, and Rachel stepped into the hallway while Mr. Patch removed Papa's breeches. Mr. Patch paced the room and wrung his hands, stopping every few minutes to stare at him, as if willing him to be well. His nervousness made Rachel's struggle to stay calm all the harder.

"Mr. Patch, please go downstairs and manage the store."

Mr. Patch's face crinkled with worry. "Aye, miss." He cast a last glance at Papa before leaving.

Rachel paced for a few minutes herself, but then fetched her Bible and sat beside Papa's bed. She read aloud the third chapter of John's gospel, emphasizing verse sixteen, especially the last part, "whosoever believeth in Him should not perish but have everlasting life," willing Papa to hear and believe. Then she read Mother's most beloved verses, followed by her own favorites. Her voice grew weary from reading and praying.

If Papa heard any of her words, he didn't indicate it but continued his occasional groans and convulsions and his constantly labored breathing.

In the late afternoon, Dr. Wellsey marched into the room carrying a leather bag. "Good day, Miss Folger." He focused immediately on Papa, first checking the wound and then touching Papa's neck and lifting his eyelids.

"Rachel." Mrs. Winthrop entered behind the doctor. "I am grieved for your father."

"Oh, Mrs. Winthrop." Rachel hurried to the older woman's open arms and released her pent-up tears.

"There, my dear." Mrs. Winthrop patted Rachel's back. "We will do all we can." Her voice wavered with emotion.

Rachel lifted her head and peered around Mrs. Winthrop. "Frederick?"

She shook her head. "He could not come, my dear."

Could not or would not? Rachel had thought she could not endure any more heartache, but this cut even deeper.

While Dr. Wellsey studied Papa's wound, Mrs. Winthrop moved to the bed and leaned close, concern deepening the wrinkles around her eyes. "Mr. Folger." She reached a gloved hand toward his cheek, but drew back and seemed to swallow a sob. With a little sniff, she tore off her gloves and reached for the cloth and bowl of water on the bedside table, wiping sweat from his face with a tenderness that caused Rachel more tears.

Dr. Wellsey applied a green poultice to the snakebite. It smelled of bear grease and some sort of weed. Rachel almost gagged, and Mrs. Winthrop coughed discreetly.

All this time, a question nagged Rachel. Now it burned too much to keep it to herself.

"Mrs. Winthrop," she whispered, "you said Mr. Moberly could not come." She hoped her tone didn't convey an accusation of neglect. "Did plantation business keep him?"

Mrs. Winthrop arched her eyebrows. "Why, no, my dear. He is fond of your father and certainly would have come if he were home. But he was summoned back to St. Augustine."

"St. Augustine?" Hope lifted Rachel's heart. He had not disregarded Papa's life-and-death struggle, after all.

Mrs. Winthrop glanced at Papa. "Your father is in Dr. Wellsey's capable hands. Let us go to the drawing room." She led Rachel to a chair by the hearth and sat opposite her. "After our party left the city, Governor Tonyn received further information about the fighting up north. This is no longer a minor civil war easily dispensed with. The rebels are growing stronger. In May, they overran Fort Ticonderoga in New York colony and stole British cannons and ammunition to use against our own soldiers. In June, Boston suffered a siege, and many of our soldiers were killed or wounded."

Rachel's heart made several leaps. Praise God the patriots had conquered a British fort and secured weapons. And no doubt the siege of Boston included the Breed's Hill event Mrs. Middlebrook had whispered about in those early morning hours in St. Augustine.

"But why did that news require Frederick to go back to the capital?" A nauseating premonition swept through Rachel.

"According to the letter from the governor, more loyalists are coming to East Florida to escape the insurrection. Hidden among them are spies for the rebels. The governor has evidence that some are already here. Can you believe it? Spies, right here in our peaceful colony." She exhaled a weary sigh. "Why do people do such things?"

"But… Frederick?"

"Why, my dear, as His Majesty's representative in this area, he must learn all he can so as to apprehend those spies." Her tired eyes shone with pride. "When Mr. Moberly read the governor's letter to me, you could see his outrage. You can be certain no rebel sympathizer will go undetected. No spy will escape."

"He was angry?" Rachel's voice was thick.

Mrs. Winthrop nodded soberly. "You know our dear Mr. Moberly is a moderate, even-tempered young man, but he stormed about the house, slamming doors and muttering under his breath. Were he not such a gentleman and a Christian, I fear he might have, well, uttered an oath. He was quite upset."

Rachel swallowed hard, and the ache in her chest restricted her breathing. Frederick knew where her sentiments lay, and all this time he had hinted he had no quarrel with the patriot cause. What a fool she'd been. Now her morning verse made sense. God desired that truth should dwell in His children, and she had endeavored to be truthful. But Frederick had done nothing short of lying to her. He would never support the revolution, would do all he could to stop it. If she learned anything helpful and tried to relay it to her fellow patriots, Frederick would be required to have her arrested.

Sick with dismay, she forced her thoughts back to Papa, whose danger was more imminent than her own. "We must see how Papa is faring."

"Yes, of course, my dear." Mrs. Winthrop rose. "And let your heart be encouraged. Dr. Wellsey has used that snake-bite ointment on several slaves to good effect. He learned of it from the Indians."

When they returned to Papa's bedchamber, Dr. Wellsey was checking the poultice.

"It would have been more effective if I had applied this right after the bite." He seemed to speak to himself. "Nevertheless, we hope it will draw out the poison." He looked at Rachel. "I will be happy to stay with you until his crisis passes. Mrs. Winthrop insisted on accompanying me for propriety's sake."

"I'm grateful to both of you." Rachel's head and heart

had been buffeted from all sides, but she must see to her duties. "I'll order food from the tavern."

Throughout the rest of the day and into the night, Papa rolled about, sweating and vomiting. From time to time, violent seizures struck, and Mr. Patch came to help the doctor hold him to the bed. Everyone took a turn at sleeping and eating to maintain their strength. They also knelt in turn to pray for Papa's life and health.

After midnight, Rachel sat in the darkness of the drawing room, too weary to decipher all that Frederick's dishonesty meant to their future. Of course she could no longer think of marrying him. But how could she face him to break off their engagement?

The swish of Mrs. Winthrop's skirts interrupted her thoughts.

"Your father is not quite so restive now." She sat beside Rachel on the settee. "I thought I should come and give you another bit of news." The warmth in her tone generated Rachel's curiosity.

"Yes, ma'am?"

Mrs. Winthrop leaned toward her. "Major Brigham has been reassigned to Boston. He and Lady Augusta will be sailing there this Friday."

An unexpected giggle bubbled up in Rachel's throat, and she found it difficult to subdue it. The Lord had answered her selfish prayer for her adversary to leave.

But a sobering thought cut short her mirth. Now she had a new adversary, and he was none other than the man she loved with all her heart.

In the dim light of a whale oil lamp aboard the *Mingo,* Frederick studied the pamphlet, and his heart grew heavier with each reading, even as his mind became enlightened. Too long he had shrugged off the seriousness of the strife in the thirteen rebelling colonies. He should have comprehended what was to come when he learned the colonists had organized their auspicious-sounding "continental congress" in Philadelphia last September. That a large group of educated, landed gentry would gather to write such an articulate and well-reasoned appeal to His Majesty could not be dismissed out of hand. Especially when the war might now extend to East Florida, including his own settlement. Including his own upcoming marriage.

He could no longer lightly regard Rachel's passion for the colonists' cause, though he had dismissed his earlier concern that she might already be spying for the enemy. Her sentiments, whether serious or sanguine, always radiated from her dark brown eyes, a quality he valued, and she would have given herself away long ago.

The ship rose and fell in the undulating surf. The lamp swayed, casting grotesque shadows about the small cabin. The fetid odors of waste and dead fish reached his nostrils, and he longed to ascend to the deck so the fresh sea air might cleanse him inside and out. Simply reading this pamphlet befouled his soul and made him feel like a traitor.

Yet he could not argue with the colonists' claims to the historic rights of all Englishmen, rights he himself took for granted. Should not the present generation of English descendants on American soil have those same rights? It all made sense to him and was, in fact, the way he dispensed his own authority.

As manager of his father's plantation, he held a kinglike power and endeavored to wield a temperate scepter over the servants and slaves. They responded by working harder, thus producing more and finer crops than they had under Father's imprudent former agent or would have under Oliver's iron hand. Why could His Majesty not treat his colonies in like manner? Did not the Scriptures teach that a laborer was worthy of his hire? Moreover, a king should serve his people rather than bleed them dry through taxation. He should permit them to gather lawfully in order to deliberate on how to present "their dutiful, humble, loyal, and reasonable petitions to the crown for redress." The men who wrote this document were articulate, God-fearing gentlemen.

Exhaling a weary sigh, Frederick folded the pamphlet, tucked it in his coat, and then retrieved the governor's letter. This missive convinced him that, instead of a civil conflict propagated by a few unruly dissidents, a full-blown war raged between his homeland and thirteen of her American colonies. The rebels' successful raid on Fort Ticonderoga and the many British losses at Breed's Hill demonstrated that the colonists were endeavoring to sever their ties with England. The news that they might bring their rebellion to East Florida portended many unpleasant days ahead. Before he could decide what part to play in this tragedy, Frederick had much to consider and much to pray about, not the least of which was how it affected his marriage to Rachel.

Chapter Twenty-Seven

"Perseus."

Rachel jolted awake in her chair beside Papa's bed and rushed to his side. Darkness shrouded the room, but she could make out his form.

"What is it, Papa?" She caressed his brow, grateful his fever had broken earlier.

Mumbling unintelligible words, he tried to roll toward the side of his injured leg, but returned to his back with a deep groan.

"Shh. It's all right, Papa."

Unshaven but wearing a clean nightgown, he smelled of lye soap from the bath Dr. Wellsey and Mr. Patch had given him.

"Take it to Perseus."

There. He said it again. She hadn't dreamed it. Her scalp tingled, and a shiver ran down her neck.

"Who is Perseus, Papa?"

"Uh?" He rose slightly. "Water."

She struggled to lift him while raising a glass to his lips. He drank greedily, then fell back on the pillow and began to snore. His noisy but even breathing mitigated her disappointment that he hadn't answered her question. The crisis had passed, as Dr. Wellsey informed her before he and Mrs. Winthrop returned home.

Once Papa awoke, however, she would hound him until he confessed. She had not the slightest doubt he was the third man she heard talking in the night in St. Augustine. In spite of her constant grief over Frederick, this truth about Papa tickled her insides. To think, Papa was a patriot. Why, that must mean Cousin Jamie was, too. Though exhausted, she remained by Papa's bed, shaking her head over the absurdity. All this time she had never suspected either of them.

Then another thought took hold. Why had he never told her? Why had he not let her stay in Boston to spy on General Gage? He and Jamie had shut her out, calling their secret discussions "men's business." Pain ripped through her, rivaling her agony over Frederick's lies. She didn't have to ask Papa why. Their exclusion of her in their plans said it all. They did not trust her.

Tears scalded her cheeks, and her body ached. Minding Dr. Wellsey's instructions to get her own rest, she lit a candle and examined Papa's color. As best she could see, it appeared normal. Now she could safely leave him and go to bed.

Once there, she still could not surrender to sleep for the turmoil in her mind. She had heard at least three men in St. Augustine, but one only grunted rather than speak. *Zeus.* Why, that was the ruling god of Greek mythology. If Papa had chosen that name for himself, he must be the leader. And that meant he had the cylinder. He was to deliver it to… *Hermes.* Hermes, the messenger god. That must be Jamie! Who would take it by ship to… *Perseus.* But who was Perseus? And why had they chosen these names from Greek mythology? Could it be to show that some Greeks in East Florida supported the revolution? That must be the reason Papa had spoken with the Greek prisoner. She wondered what he had told the guards to gain such a privilege.

With Papa likely to be sick for some time, with Jamie in England for who knew how long, someone needed to deliver the cylinder to Perseus. If only she knew where it was and where to take it, she could prove herself worthy of helping the revolution.

She would search Papa's belongings at first light. As a child, she'd discovered a false bottom in his sea trunk. She also knew of a hollow chamber beneath the finial on one of his bedposts. A brick on the hearthside had been loosened and might hide a cavity. She had no doubt Papa would keep something that valuable close by. She would find it somehow.

Lord, please show me where it is. Please reveal to me who Perseus is and how I can find him. And help me to forgive Papa and Jamie for treating me like an inconsequential child.

A map. Of course. Rachel marveled at the clever ploy. The topography of northern East Florida drawn on doeskin as thin and pliable as a lady's gloves, then rolled tightly into a brass cylinder resembling a sea captain's collapsible telescope, lay in the top drawer of Papa's chest. If Rachel had not grown frustrated in her search and retrieved the supposed telescope to stare out the window for amusement, she never would have found the map.

What amazed her even more was the discovery of a fake red beard and a heavily lined coat under the false bottom in Papa's trunk. But Papa could not be the patriot who had tried to stir up the settlement, for he could never hide his limp. And dear Mr. Patch was far too short.

But now she must discover the identity and location of Perseus. If Jamie was to take the map to the man on his next voyage, the place could be anywhere, but most likely in the colonies. Most likely Boston. But Rachel could not be certain.

Still, the idea of Boston grew with such strength that she began to think it was God's leading. She must find a way to get there, even if forced to humble herself and ask to travel with Lady Augusta. Providing, of course, Papa felt well enough by Friday for her to leave him in Mr. Patch's care. If Frederick would stay away until then, she would not have to face him to break their engagement. By implying he supported her belief in the revolution when he actually stood against it, he had hurt her too much to deserve an explanation. Indeed, how could she explain to him that, now and forever, they were enemies?

In the afternoon, Rachel read to Papa, interspersing prayers with Bible verses. His even breathing encouraged her regarding his health, but his lack of faith still concerned her. She had just begun a passage in James, when he mumbled, coughed and opened his eyes.

"Rachel." His gravelly voice sounded like music to her.

"Papa." She set aside her reading and kissed his unshaven cheek. "Dear Papa." She laid her head on his chest and wept.

For once, he didn't dismiss her display of emotion, but patted her hair and coughed. "There now, daughter. All's well 'cept for my voracious thirst."

She dried her tears and poured water, which he managed to drink by himself.

"Are you hungry?" Rachel straightened his sheets, trying to anticipate what he might need.

"No." His reddened eyes turned toward his chest of drawers, and a worried frown crossed his brow. "Doubtless I will be soon." He grimaced. "'Tis a frightful thing, a snakebite. Never have I felt such pain."

"Not even when you broke your leg?"

"My what?" His eyes widened briefly. "Ah, yes. Even more painful than the broken leg."

"Oh, dear Papa, I'm so sorry." Rachel glanced toward his once sturdy limbs. "My heart grieves for your suffering, but we may thank God for your life."

She braced herself for his usual dismissal of her faith, but he merely grunted, even gave her a little smile. "Well, I suppose this'll go down in the family lore about yer old father. Do be sure to write yer sister all the details." Now his eyes lit with a bit of their old sparkle, though dark shadows hung beneath them.

Rachel's mind turned. This could be the answer to everything. "Papa, what would you think if I went to Boston and told her myself?"

"What?" He tried to sit up, but fell back against the pillow. "Hmm. Aye, aye. East Florida's turned out to be a dangerous place. Not that Boston's any safer these days." He closed his eyes for a moment, then stared at her with tender concern. "But what of Mr. Moberly?"

She looked away, forbidding herself to cry. "Haven't I been foolish, Papa? You saw it, I am certain. That is why you were reluctant to approve our engagement. Mr. Moberly is a Tory, a loyalist. We would not make a good match." Another thought intruded. "Nor will you and Mrs. Winthrop."

"Me and Mrs. Winthrop?"

"Of course. I know you are fond of her, but you must

not deceive her about who you really are." Rachel fussed with his sheet corner. "You see, Papa, I know you are a patriot... Zeus."

Papa inhaled sharply. "Did I speak that name in a delirium?"

She patted his shoulder. "Don't worry. You and I were alone when you mentioned Perseus." Briefly, she told him all that had transpired during their trip to St. Augustine, including when she had overheard him with his cronies. "If you had spoken that night, I would have recognized your voice right away. But I did not realize until you said 'Perseus' in your sleep that you were the third man."

With each incident, his eyes widened and his mouth hung open. "Rachel, my girl, I'd have never thought..." Perspiration beaded on his forehead, and his face grew pale.

"Please rest now, Papa. We can talk more later."

He rolled his head from side to side on the pillow. "No. This must be decided." His gaze became steady, even harsh. "Ye must go to Boston to deliver a gift to Charles, but ye must tell no one of it. Keep it deep in yer travel bag, and never let it out of yer sight. Can ye do this, girl?"

"Yes, of course." Excitement spun through her like a storm. Now he would trust her. Now she had a chance to prove herself. "May I assume Charles is Perseus?" She never dreamed her sister's mild-mannered husband possessed such courage.

Papa's eyes narrowed into a wily expression. "I know not what ye mean, girl. Have ye been reading Greek myths again?"

At last, she permitted herself to laugh. "No, sir." But she must make one more attempt to win his soul. "These past few days, I have found great comfort in the Scriptures."

"Ah, that answers it." He scratched his scruffy chin. "Many a dream I had these nights of yer mother reading those same Scriptures to me. But ye left out my favorite passage, John 6:68–69. In my travels to many ports of this world, 'twas the one that kept me from the seductive spells of strange religions."

Her pulse racing, Rachel snatched up her Bible and quickly found the passage. "'Then Simon Peter answered him, Lord, to whom shall we go? Thou hast the words of eternal life. And we believe and are sure that thou art that Christ, the Son of the living God.'" She could barely finish for weeping. "Oh, Papa, you believe. Why have you never told me?"

Weariness seemed to overtake him, for he closed his eyes and sunk deeper into the pillow. "Not every man wears his opinions…or his faith on his face. Sometimes 'tis better not to bare yer soul."

As she considered his words, she longed to discuss them further. But he had drifted back to sleep, and she would not disturb him. Nor would she urge him to reveal the identity of the other local patriot.

How often he had chided her for her emotional displays, which she rarely tried to contain. Could such a person be trusted to spy or even keep a secret? Not likely. Even falling in love with Frederick had been fraught with too much emotion and too little temperance. Had she been wise, she would have required a definitive answer regarding his sentiments on the revolution. But she had disregarded the proverb to keep her heart with all diligence and blinded herself to the truth, seeing only what she wished to see.

Now she had the opportunity to do something truly

important for the cause she held dear, but only if she could hide her deepest feelings. That might not be possible if Frederick returned from St. Augustine before she left.

"You have made a wise decision, Rachel." Lady Augusta fanned herself as they sat in the cabin of the British frigate three days later. "Marital happiness cannot last when the wife's rank is inferior to her husband's."

Bracing herself against the woman's hurtful remark, Rachel ran a finger over the ornately carved arm of her mahogany chair beside the captain's desk. "But isn't Major Brigham the son of a baronet, while you are the daughter of an earl? I do not pretend to understand much about English rankings, but doesn't that mean you married beneath your station?" She smiled sweetly and blinked several times.

Lady Augusta's eyebrows lowered, and her pretty mouth twisted into a snarl. "My connections have made it possible for my husband to advance in His Majesty's service, whereas an inferior wife will always be a detriment to her husband's aspirations."

Rachel stared down and bit her lower lip to keep from responding. She was no match for this woman's cruel tongue. Further, any discussion of her former engagement to Frederick would be pointless. She inhaled deeply to soothe her ravaged emotions, drawing in the mouthwatering aroma of beef stew. They would soon be dining with the captain here in his quarters, and Rachel consoled herself that during the meal she might gather some helpful information to pass on to Charles. Posing as a loyalist rankled, but it also gave her a heady sense of dangerous excitement.

Her emotions now under control, she again looked

at Lady Augusta. "I hope you will find Boston more pleasant than St. Johns Settlement."

Lady Augusta sniffed. "At the very least, the society will be an improvement."

At a knock on the cabin door, Lady Augusta said "You may enter."

The captain's uniformed steward stepped in and bowed. "Ladies, if you will excuse us, we must prepare the cabin for supper." He turned to Rachel. "Will you be joining us, miss?"

"Don't be ridiculous." Lady Augusta marched toward the door, her wide panniers brushing against the desk and almost knocking over the chairs. "She will eat with the servants."

Trailing after Lady Augusta as she left the cabin, the scent of orange blossoms struck a double blow to Rachel's already aching heart. The sweet, delicate fragrance would always remind her of this unfeeling woman, but worse, of pleasant walks with Frederick in his orange grove. Papa had promised that the pain would lessen one day, but Rachel doubted she would ever stop hurting.

"To Boston?" Frederick stared at Mr. Folger, not believing his words. "Sir, why would you send her back there when the city is under siege?"

Mr. Folger sat propped against his pillows, pale and sweating. But he had assured Frederick he was on the mend.

"Would she be any safer in this wilderness?" Mr. Folger pointed to his leg. "Snakes, alligators, mosquito hordes… I was wrong to bring her here."

Frederick paced the wooden floor, trying to make sense of all that had happened while he was away. Mrs. Winthrop had related the horrifying news of Mr. Folger's snakebite, but she made no mention of Rachel's leaving. This news would break his cousin's gentle heart.

He stopped beside the bed, his mind torn between wanting to shake more information from Mr. Folger and sending for Dr. Wellsey to be certain the old man was indeed improving.

Feeling as if someone had sliced open his chest and ripped out his heart, Frederick dropped into a bedside chair and lifted his hands in supplication. "Sir, I implore you to tell me the reason she left. Did she fear I would not forgive her for harboring the deserter?" He stood and paced, then reclaimed the chair. "We agreed we must talk about our differences regarding the revolution. Why would she leave before we could do that?"

Mr. Folger shrugged. "Ye knew of her devotion to that cause. Did ye think she would lightly abandon it?"

Frederick ran a hand through his hair, loosening several strands from the queue. "I know you have no interest in the conflict, sir, but I do. Rachel's passion for it has forced me to examine the issues more deeply." He paused, wondering how much to trust Mr. Folger. "This second trip to St. Augustine was…enlightening."

Mr. Folger's eyes flickered. He yawned and stretched. "Yer pardon. These past few days, I'm not myself."

Shame filled Frederick. "Forgive me. I will take my leave and let you rest." He stood and walked toward the door.

"Sit down, boy." Mr. Folger's hoarse tone resounded with authority.

Frederick did as he ordered. "Yes, sir."

"As ye said, Rachel's passion for the revolution makes a man think, that and my comin' near to death's door.

Mayhap I've been a coward not to choose sides. What think ye?"

Frederick stared into the old whaler's dark brown eyes, searching for some indication of his opinion. Now who was the coward? Perhaps the time had come for him to state his own opinion regardless of what others thought, regardless of the outcome.

"My visit with Governor Tonyn was informative, but not the way he intended. All of England's colonies in this hemisphere are feeling the same pressures, may I say, *injustices* from the Crown. Only thirteen of them are willing to do something about it. It takes courage to break off from one's parent, especially when that unjust parent tries to control his child by any possible means." As he said the words, Frederick's heart swelled with affirmation. His course of action had not yet become clear, but he knew where he would stand.

Mr. Folger grunted. "Speak ye of the colonies or yer own father?" A grin lifted one corner of his lips.

Frederick returned a rueful grimace. "I should go to her."

Mr. Folger's gaze grew intense. "Aye. Ye could do that…if ye've no doubt about yer sentiments bein' equal."

The sly old fox. He had said nothing to incriminate himself, yet everything to bestow his blessing on Frederick.

Yes, he *would* go. For he could not think of staying in this wilderness without Rachel by his side.

Chapter Twenty-Eight

"Mind your stitches." Susanna studied eight-year-old Eliza's handiwork. "Loose stitches lose his britches."

Rachel and the four other ladies in the sewing circle hummed their agreement to the instructive rhyme and continued with their harmless gossip.

Susanna mentioned a stray sow in someone's garden and warned everyone to keep their gates closed. Mrs. Arthur told of her concern for a peacock whose hen had vanished. Mrs. Brown expressed the wish that someone would shoot a mad dog causing distress in the city. With the British controlling Boston, those who favored the revolution needed to avoid drawing attention to themselves. Thus, gossip about minor things became the only fodder for wagging tongues, other than an occasional outburst by a passionate patriot.

With the map safely in Charles's hands, Rachel felt adrift, no longer important to the cause. Her brother-in-law had forced a promise from her not to attempt anything on her own.

"But I might be able to gain a position in General Gage's house," she said. "Mrs. Gage hired me before. Think of what I could learn as her servant."

"All of the necessary people are in place," Charles said. "We're relaying information to General Washington daily. You've done your part. In due time when we've built our strength, we'll pass this map to the patriots in Georgia and South Carolina. Taking the revolution to East Florida will be their responsibility." He patted her shoulder. "I am proud of you, sister. You have done well."

After that, no one in the family mentioned the war, and the red-coated soldiers who patrolled the city received their every courtesy.

Rachel sometimes saw Major Brigham at a distance but avoided him. He had been kind to her in East Florida and on the voyage to Boston, but now he was the enemy, just like Frederick. At least the officer had never deceived her, but Frederick's lies still pained her. Many nights she fell asleep with tears drenching her pillow.

With October approaching, Rachel consoled herself by sewing winter clothes for her nieces and nephew and helping to harvest her sister's kitchen garden. As a supposed Tory, Charles did not suffer as many others in the city. The family sat in church side by side with known loyalists. Unlike years past, no soldiers quartered in their home, and a rare shipment of goods reached Charles despite privateers lurking at the mouth of Boston Harbor.

The leaves turned bright red and orange, then faded to brown and fell to the ground. November arrived, and hearth fires were lit, filling the air with the smell of burning wood. One afternoon, Rachel donned the long woolen shawl she had left behind when she and Papa sailed to East Florida.

"I'm going to Granny Jones's house with her dinner." Rachel lifted the covered basket, enjoying the aroma of chicken, spiced apples and pumpkin pie. "She'll want me to eat with her."

"Come home before dark." Susanna frowned. "The soldiers..."

"Yes, I know." Rachel shuddered. Once darkness struck, not all British soldiers behaved as gentlemen toward the ladies of Boston.

She hurried through the narrow cobblestone streets toward a poorer section of town. Granny Jones lived alone and always enjoyed company. Rachel could not be certain, but she guessed that the widow's sons had joined the Continental Army encamped around the city. If they invaded, Rachel wondered who would keep the feeble woman safe.

They sat at a rough-hewn old table, and Mrs. Jones devoured her meal while Rachel munched some chicken.

"Shall we have pie?" Rachel lifted the pie tin from the basket.

"No, dear. I'll save it for later." Mrs. Jones blinked behind her spectacles, her eyes not focusing.

"Since I must go before dark, I'll eat some now." Rachel plunged a knife into the creamy orange pumpkin.

"Don't—"

"What on earth?" Rachel pulled a small square of oilcloth from beneath the piecrust. Wrapped inside was a piece of parchment containing dates and names of familiar places. "Why, Mrs. Jones, what is this?"

The widow's eyes focused sharply on Rachel. "Tell Charles it'll be delivered."

Rachel stared at her for a moment, her heart racing. That rascal. He *was* using her for the cause. How many other messages had she unwittingly delivered to this *bright* old woman?

"Now get on home."

Rachel wrapped a blanket around the woman's feet. "Yes, ma'am." She took her basket and hastened from the cottage, shoving away the hurt feelings that tried to take hold. With every person under suspicion by the British, Charles was wise to keep secrets from her.

Two blocks from home, she cut through an alley to save time, almost bumping into Mrs. Arthur from the sewing circle.

"Oh, good evening, Mrs.—"

The words froze in her throat as Major Brigham stepped from the shadows. "Good evening, Miss Folger. What a surprise to see you out so late."

"Oh. Yes. It is." Rachel stared at Mrs. Arthur, the plump, pretty wife of a church deacon. Had she interrupted an assignation?

The woman's eyes narrowed. "Miss Folger, you should be at home at this hour." Her lips formed a thin line, and she stared up at the officer. "Major Brigham, perhaps you should escort this young woman to Charles Weldon's house. He is her sister's husband."

The sly look of understanding that passed between them could not be regarded as lovers' gazes. No, this woman, who just yesterday had sat in Susanna's house and whispered with passion about the revolution, was conspiring with the enemy. Why, she had been baiting Susanna.

"Tell me, Miss Folger, why do you look so alarmed?" Major Brigham cocked one eyebrow and gave her a smile that sent a shiver of fear down her spine. "And where have you been just now?" He took her basket and lifted the embroidered linen napkin. "Empty." He glanced at Mrs. Arthur.

"I, uhm, that is, I took supper to an old widow." Rachel forced a smile but could feel her lips trembling.

"Ah, yes. Granny Jones." Mrs. Arthur snickered.

"Yes. Poor dear." Rachel swallowed. "Well, if you will excuse me—" She turned to go.

Major Brigham caught her arm. "I think you should come with me."

"Ouch." Rachel leaned away from him, longing to run. But he would easily catch her.

"Come along, my dear." From his tone, he might be asking her to tea. He handed the basket to Mrs. Arthur. "Take this to Weldon and tell him you found it on the street."

"Poor Susanna." Mrs. Arthur muffled her laughter with her hand. "She will be in such despair over her sister's disappearance."

"But why—?" Rachel's eyes stung, and she struggled not to give way to tears.

"Really, Miss Folger, do not be tedious. We're merely going to visit General Gage." Major Brigham gently shoved her along the street, glancing back at Mrs. Arthur. "I'll see that someone calls on Granny Jones."

"Thank you for bringing these letters, Captain Templeton." Frederick held a stack of correspondence from his family. "I trust Mr. Folger has apprised you of the situation here." He moved closer to the fire blazing in his drawing room hearth, thankful for the warmth this chilly November morning. After three years, he preferred East Florida's warmer days.

"I surmise you're referring to Rachel removing to Boston." Templeton lounged in a wingback chair, a frown of concern darkening his eyes. "You have my sympathy, sir."

Frederick took a seat opposite his guest. "Thank you. I trust you found my family well."

"I did. You come from hospitable people. They were eager to hear of your endeavors." Templeton puckered his lips as if smothering a smile, and his eyes now radiated high spirits. "Your sister sends a particular greeting."

"Marianne." Frederick glanced at her unopened letter, eager to read what the little darling had written. She'd been almost seventeen when he left home and would soon turn twenty. "Did she say something that is not in her letter?"

Templeton shifted in his chair. "It would be better if you read the letter first, but may I say that I found... that is, she is, I, uhm—"

Comprehension filled Frederick, and he burst out laughing. "Good show, Templeton. You know a true gem when you see one."

Templeton's eyebrows rose. "That sounds very much like approval."

Frederick shrugged. "My approval is not required." Yet this man could become a closer brother to him than the three with whom he shared Lord Bennington's blood. "But I will gladly grant it if you like."

Templeton's high humor returned. "That's all we need. God willing, we'll find our way to happiness."

"You understand my father will never approve."

Templeton flung out his hands, palms up, and shrugged. "Nor will he approve your marriage to Rachel."

Frederick noticed the calluses on Templeton's broad, work-roughened hands, unlike those of the dandies who graced London's balls, but much like Frederick's own since he had been in East Florida. "I suppose Mr. Folger told you she broke our engagement. I hope to change her mind."

"Yes, he told me." A sympathetic frown furrowed Templeton's brow. "He also said you hadn't yet found a ship willing to brave the privateers outside Boston Harbor."

"No." The old wound broke open, flooding Frederick with pain. "Furthermore, I could not in good conscience leave the plantation before the last harvest. Then a fever struck the settlement, requiring me to stay. But now, if winter were not upon us, especially in the north, I would ride the length of the continent to pursue her."

Templeton stood and strode to his side, thumping him hard on the shoulder. "What's the matter with you, man? Settle your affairs here, and we'll sail for Boston."

Objections flew through Frederick's mind, but hope quickly dismissed them and lifted him from his chair. "If you're willing to run the gauntlet, so am I."

"Ha. That's the spirit." Templeton clapped him on the same shoulder, almost knocking him over. "That's the man who's worthy of my cousin Rachel."

Recovering from the friendly battering, Frederick felt less eager to read his parents' letters. Had Templeton persuaded Father that Frederick was no failure? Had Mother been aware of the romance blooming in her own drawing room? Of only one thing was he certain: Marianne's words would feed his soul in unexpected ways.

Not until Templeton left did Frederick realize he had no idea where the man stood regarding the revolution.

Chapter Twenty-Nine

Standing tiptoe on a crate, Rachel peeked out the small round window at the gray sky. If she were a little taller, she could see down to the street or perhaps as far as the harbor. As it was, she saw only an occasional airborne seagull or wren. She heard only horses' hooves clopping past General Gage's house and the muffled voices from the rooms below. Try though she might with an ear to the floor, she could not distinguish one word from another.

Since her imprisonment almost a month before, Rachel had dredged up memories of sewing circle conversations and prayed none of the other ladies had revealed important information to the traitor. Only one clue surfaced. The peacock had lost his hen, and Major Brigham's dreadful wife had sailed home to England. Perhaps the stray sow in the garden referred to none other than Mrs. Arthur. Had Susanna suspected her?

To furnish Rachel's tiny attic prison, Mrs. Gage had provided a narrow cot with a feather mattress and two blankets. Three times a day, either a British lieutenant or Major Brigham himself brought her meals and hot water, no doubt to keep her from talking to servants or kind Mrs. Gage to beg that a message be sent to Susanna. Rachel's poor sister must be worried sick. Charles might make a few inquiries about her, but his position must not be compromised.

With only a borrowed Bible for comfort, she spent her days and weeks reading and praying for a way to escape. Once she had tried stacking the crate on a trunk to reach the window and climb out. But the scraping sound had alerted the soldiers, and they took away the trunk. After many tears and prayers, Rachel decided her post in the revolution was to be a prisoner. By delivering the map to Charles, she had done all that she was supposed to do. One thing was certain: her face would always betray her heart, as proven by her confrontation with Major Brigham.

Snow brushed over the round window, dimming the attic. Huddled against the chimney's warm bricks, Rachel pulled her woolen shawl closer. Soon winter would arrive in full force. Never had she expected to miss the heat of East Florida, but oh how she would welcome it now.

The key turned, the door opened, and Major Brigham stepped into the attic. "Miss Folger, gather your things." His placid expression gave her no indication of whether or not she was in imminent danger.

She glanced about the attic. "I have nothing to gather." Hugging her shawl, she toddled across the room on legs aching from want of exercise and stopped in front of her captor. "Am I to be p-punished?" Would they hang a woman? "If so, would you please explain why?"

Amusement rippled across his aristocratic face. "No, my dear, you will not be punished. You have been our guest these weeks past to prevent your divulging, ah, how shall I say it? A certain friendship of mine. Now you will be delivered into the hands of a loyalist sea captain who in turn will deliver you back to your father, from whom I never should have separated you."

"Sea captain?" Irrational hope sprung up within her.

"Yes," Major Brigham drawled. "I believe you know the chap. This way, Miss Folger."

Her legs shook as she descended two flights of stairs to the drawing room. Near the door stood Frederick, and he took a step in her direction.

"Rachel!"

Her heart seemed to rip in two. She pushed past him and flung herself into Jamie's arms.

"Oh, Jamie, take me home."

To her shock, Jamie gripped her upper arms and stared sternly into her eyes. "Cousin, do you not wish to greet your betrothed?"

The imperative message in his gaze penetrated her cloudy mind.

"Oh." She turned around. "Frederick. Darling." Surely no one would be fooled by her cold tone. She walked across the room on wooden legs, seeing beyond him that Major Brigham stared at her through narrowed eyes.

Frederick pulled her into his arms and kissed her forehead. "Dearest," he whispered, "trust us."

She nodded her assent, but only because Jamie had come, too.

"Enough." Major Brigham moved closer. "Our bargain is that you will return her to East Florida forthwith and keep her out of trouble once she's there." He leaned so near that Rachel could smell cherry tobacco on his uniform. "Understand, Miss Folger, I am releasing you only because—" Abruptly, he stepped back. "Really, I am not a brute. But we are at war, and—" He exhaled impatiently. "I owe you much for saving Lady Augusta from the alligator. This should balance our accounts."

Rachel's knees buckled, but Frederick held her fast. She tried to form a response.

"Furthermore," Major Brigham continued, "your courage during the fire impressed me. Take that boldness back to the wilderness and raise loyal British subjects—"

"Enough!" Rachel straightened and stepped out of Frederick's embrace. "You have prattled on far too long." She glanced at Jamie. "Shall we go?" Forcing strength into her legs, she strode toward the hallway door.

"Sir, forgive her." Jamie's voice reached her. "Naturally, she's a little overwrought."

"Naturally." Sarcasm laced Brigham's tone. "As I told you, you will have an armed guard until your ship sails, in case she tries to—"

"She will behave, Major Brigham." Frederick's voice sounded like music to her traitorous heart.

No, she would not behave. Not if she could help it.

"Please believe me, Rachel." Frederick stood beside Jamie, blocking the door of the ship's cabin. "Your sister and her family are in no danger."

Rachel looked at Jamie, wondering what safe response she could give. Anything she said to Frederick might cast suspicion on her cousin. Like Papa, Jamie had never claimed to be a patriot, thus keeping their revolutionary activities secret. But Jamie's brotherly smile gave her no indication of what she should say.

"It's true, Rachel." Jamie nodded. "We visited with Charles. He said to tell you the stray sow in the garden has been put back in her pen."

Cautious relief crept into her. "That is good news. Do you know what happened to…to a certain old woman?" Rachel could not bear to think of Granny Jones being imprisoned, too.

Jamie put a warning finger to his lips. "When we're out to sea, I'll tell you everything. For now, will you please stay here and not try to jump ship?" His face creased into a pleading expression.

Rachel pursed her lips at his humorous remark. "I won't jump ship." But only because she could not swim.

The two men traded a look of relief.

"I'm going on deck," Jamie said to Frederick. "We'll want to sail beyond the harbor before sunset."

Once he left, Frederick sat behind the oak desk and toyed with a long, slender package.

Rachel fussed with her shawl. "This is against all propriety."

He glanced up. "What is?"

"Our being alone. Is there no other woman on board?"

Frederick set aside the package. "Tsk. An oversight. How shall we amend that?"

Despite the cold, heat filled Rachel's cheeks. "*You* could jump ship."

Merriment lit his face. "Ah, but I promised your esteemed father that I would deliver you safely home."

"Nonsense. Jamie can do that." She could not comprehend why Jamie seemed all too willing to leave her alone with Frederick.

"Or we could secure the services of a vicar, who could marry us before we are out to sea. Then you would be safe in my care."

"What?" Rachel crossed her arms and glared at him.

"Oh, forgive me. I forgot to tell you. I have released you from our engagement."

Hurt clouded his gaze, but his smile remained. "Rachel, I know of no other way to tell you this. I have come to believe the revolution is the only right and righteous course for England's American colonies—all of them." Fervor burned in his eyes, and he came around the desk to kneel in front of her. "Believe me, my darling. You and your father have convinced me."

Shivers swept down Rachel's back, and she drew her shawl tighter around her. "You expect me to believe you? You implied all this before, yet it was a lie."

Frederick moved to the chair beside her and grasped her hand. "I did not intend to lie, but I know I misled you. By doing so, I failed to respect your opinions, your most cherished beliefs. But your father and I have had many talks these past months. We are convinced that the revolution will come to East Florida after all. Every man will have to decide where he will stand. I have made my decision."

Tears coursed down Rachel's cheeks. "You have?" Hope burst through her grief like sunlight through the falling snow, but caution gripped her once more. "How will I know you're telling the truth this time?"

Frederick stared at the floor for several moments, then rose and left the cabin. Within minutes, he returned with Jamie.

"Captain Templeton, we have often skirted this discussion, but the time has come for me to tell you that I support the patriots and their revolution. If you do not, then kindly permit Rachel and me to leave this ship... or return us to Major Brigham."

Rachel gasped. "No, Jamie. He does not mean it."

"Shh." Frederick grasped her hand once more. "I do mean it. Captain, what say you?"

Jamie chuckled. "I wondered how long it would take for you to tell me."

Frederick chortled, obviously not surprised by his response.

"You have known?" Rachel thought she might like to smack her cousin.

Jamie crossed his arms and leaned against the door. "Yes, since returning from England."

"All this time." Frederick scratched his head. "You see, my dear, everyone except you has been reticent to expound on their opinions. You have more courage than all of us." He glanced at Jamie. "Or perhaps just more than I."

Her face flamed again, this time with pleasure at his praise. "Oh, Frederick, I have missed you so much."

He brushed a hand across her cheek. "Will you make me the happiest of men and become my wife?"

Sniffing back her tears, Rachel whispered, "Yes."

"Ahem." Jamie shuffled his feet. "May I take my leave now?"

Rachel shook her head. "We cannot sail until Frederick and I are married. We must go ashore and find a minister."

"Hmm." Jamie scratched his chin. "I think I might have a stray parson somewhere on board." He hastened from the cabin.

"What?" Rachel started to follow him.

"Wait." Frederick gripped her hand and gently tugged her back into her chair. "You see? We came prepared."

She huffed out a bit of artificial indignation. "You are very sure of yourself, are you not?"

His rueful wince contradicted her. "Not when it

comes to you." He leaned his forehead against hers. "Beloved, the coming days will not be easy."

"But God will be with us and guide us."

"Yes. And I believe He will bring about a new day for all of the colonies."

Rachel searched his eyes. "Do you think the people of East Florida will join the revolution?"

He shook his head. "There's no way to know right now. We only know that each of us must do his part."

Jamie returned with his first mate and Rachel's former minister.

Rachel jumped to her feet. "Reverend Wentworth, how kind of you to come."

The elderly vicar gave her a gentle smile. "My dear, it gives me great joy to unite you and this young man in marriage."

He opened his well-worn prayer book. "Dearly beloved, we are gathered together here in the sight of God, and in the face of this congregation." He glanced around the small cabin and chuckled. "Wherever two or three are gathered in His name." He continued with the rites and led Rachel and Frederick through their marriage vows, then invited them to sign his Bible, gave them a blessing and thereafter took his leave.

Jamie embraced Rachel and shook Frederick's hand. "God bless you both." He hustled the first mate from the cabin. "See you in the morning."

Her face burning, Rachel could not look at her new husband until he cleared his throat.

"My dear, I have a wedding gift for you." He retrieved the package from the desk.

"Oh, my." She took it in hand and tore off the paper, revealing a white lace parasol. "Why, it's beautiful." Her heart pounded as she began to push it open.

"Ah, ah." Frederick stayed her hands. "Tomorrow is soon enough."

She started to reach up and kiss him. But the memory of their first such encounter held her back. "You may kiss your bride, Mr. Moberly."

The love shining from his eyes swept away the last of her doubts. "Why, Mrs. Moberly, I think I might just do that."

Chapter Thirty

"Papa, I am exceedingly displeased with you." Rachel spoke in soft tones and kept an eye on the drawing room doorway, lest a servant should happen by. With one hand on her well-rounded belly, she shifted in discomfort on the red brocade settee. "How can you marry Cousin Lydie without telling her of your nighttime activities on behalf of the revolution?"

Seated in the adjacent wingback chair, Papa leaned toward Rachel with a glower. "What makes ye think I haven't told her? Do ye think I lack the integrity to be honest with yer future stepmother?"

"But she has never mentioned—ah!" Rachel gasped as the new life within her made his presence known with a pointed kick to her rib cage.

Papa's glower turned to a playful smirk, the only indication that he noticed her plight. "O'course she hasn't mentioned it nor even given anybody a hint. As I've told ye before, not everybody wears their feelings on their faces."

Rachel did not acknowledge Papa's comment, for Frederick often told her how much he loved her openness. Not a helpful trait if one wished to be a spy, but then God had made clear His will for her in that regard.

To think that dear Cousin Lydie did not oppose the revolution. In the eight months of living here at the plantation, Rachel never would have guessed the old dear's views had changed. Indeed, it was a topic Rachel and Frederick discussed only in whispers, only to each other. If the war came to East Florida, many families might find their loyalties divided.

"Where is my bride?" Frederick's voice echoed down the front staircase, and soon he strode into the drawing room. "Ah, there you are, my darling." He bent over the back of the settee and kissed her cheek. "Mr. Folger, welcome." He extended a hand to Papa, who shook it with his customary enthusiasm. "Cousin Lydie will be down in a moment." He sat beside Rachel and flung an arm behind her across the back of the settee. "Darling, are you certain it is wise for you to take a turn around the grounds?" He glanced at her belly, then at Papa and his ears reddened. "I mean—"

"Oh, yes." Ignoring his chagrin, Rachel drew in a quiet breath so he would not see her discomfort. "Walking is the very best thing for me these days."

"And for me, as well." Papa patted his left knee. "Disuse makes a body unusable."

Rachel puckered away a giggle. "Just make certain you do not forget to limp." She still had difficulty comprehending that Papa's claim to have broken his leg while whaling had been a ruse so that he could walk naturally in his patriot disguise. And now that his snake-bitten limb had healed, he could walk without difficulty.

"Indeed." Papa clicked his tongue. "Do keep reminding me, daughter. I fear these days my mind's on other things."

One of those *other things* walked into the room, her lightly wrinkled face smoothed by a radiant glow. "Good morning, Lamech."

Papa stood and hurried to her—without a limp—and kissed both of her hands. "My dear Lydia, how beautiful you are this fine day."

Rachel traded a look with Frederick. They had discussed how Papa's speech improved in Cousin Lydie's presence, as did his manners, and his changes amused them both.

"Shall we go?" Cousin Lydie grasped Papa's hand and led him from the room.

Frederick helped Rachel rise from the settee. She placed a hand on her aching lower back and was grateful for the loving sympathy emanating from her husband's eyes.

Little Caddy opened the front door for the party, and Frederick rewarded her with a confection. Rachel touched the child's shoulder as she passed by.

As she descended the front steps, with Frederick's hand cupped under her elbow, she surveyed the distant indigo fields where most of the plantation's two hundred slaves bent over the tender green plants. Rachel prayed that when the British were driven from these shores, freedom would come for these slaves as well as for the white colonists.

"You are frowning, my love." Frederick kept a supporting hand under her arm. "Are you in pain?"

She gave him a little smile. "No more than usual."

"But you are not happy, are you?" He bent and kissed her forehead.

Rachel leaned against him. "I am happy with you, my darling. But—" She looked toward the fields again. "If East Florida joins the other colonies in their fight to dissolve its ties with England, what will become of these people when the revolution succeeds?"

When Frederick gazed down into his beloved's dark brown eyes, the love that welled up in his heart felt almost painful. How he longed to grant her every wish, even going so far as to free the slaves. Yet until Father responded to Frederick's news, it would be madness to make such a drastic move as to set the slaves free.

"Perhaps we will have our answer when Jamie returns from London." Frederick expected it to take a long time to straighten out the lies Oliver had told Father. If Father would listen to reason about that tangled matter, perhaps he would look favorably on other matters.

Frederick had spent much time on his knees imploring the Almighty that his marriage to Rachel might find favor in Father's eyes. Whether or not the earl forgave him for following his heart, Frederick would never regret doing so. Further, he had proven to himself that he could work with his hands, that he could manage money without wasting it, and that he could be a loving husband. If Father banished him from the plantation, Frederick and Rachel would be able to face whatever challenges life might bring them. What more should a parent ask of his child than that he might be self-determined and capable? Much like the colonies who strove for freedom from their mother country, England.

Frederick had written all his thoughts in a diary to keep until the day when his son—or daughter—found someone to love. Simply reading his own words on the page deepened his convictions.

"Would it not be wonderful if Jamie brought Lady Marianne back with him?" Rachel gave him a playful grin. "Married to her, of course."

"Of course." Frederick tweaked her pretty little nose. "But have you no mercy? My father may be a tyrant, but Mother should not be bereft of both of her children." He would await their child's birth before telling her of his letter to Marianne. He wrote that his sister must accept with grace Captain Templeton's decision to break with her. One day, both she and Rachel would understand.

"Jamie deserves to marry the woman he loves." Rachel's eyes twinkled. "As you did."

Frederick observed that Mr. Folger, whom he had not found courage to call Father, had found a wrought-iron bench under a spreading oak tree. There he sat with dear Cousin Lydie, both of them clearly besotted with love, if one could judge by the tender expressions passing between them. Frederick leaned down and placed a gentle kiss on Rachel's lips.

"Will you always have the last word, my little rebel?"

"Why, Mr. Moberly, I certainly do hope so."

And Frederick found that admission not at all discouraging.

* * * * *

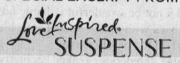
The steady rhythm of the bicycle did little to calm her nerves. Ominous dark blue clouds propelled Katie Schwartz forward.

A slight breeze ruffled the leaves, sending a few skittering across the road. But then it died, leaving an unnatural stillness in the hush of the oncoming storm. Beads of perspiration dotted her forehead.

Should she call out? Announce herself?

Gingerly, she got off her bicycle and stepped up to a window, clutching her skirt in one hand and the window trim in the other. Through her shoes, her toes gripped the edge of the rickety crate. Desperation to stay upright and not teeter off sent a surge of adrenaline coursing through her as she swiped a hand across the grimy window of the hunter's shack. The crate dipped, and Katie grasped the frame of the window again.

"Timothy?" she whispered to herself. "Where are you?"

With the crate stabilized, she swiped over the glass again and squinted inside. But all that stared back at her was more grime. The crate tipped again, and she grabbed at the window trim before she could tumble off.

Movement inside snagged her attention, although she couldn't make out figures. Voices filtered through the window, one louder than the other. What was going on in there? And was Timothy involved?

Her nose touched the glass in her effort to see inside. A face suddenly appeared in the window. It was distorted by the cracks in the glass, but it appeared to be her *bruder*. A moment later, the face disappeared.

She jumped from the crate and headed toward the corner of the cabin. Now that he had seen her, he had to come out and explain himself and return with her, stopping whatever this clandestine meeting was all about.

A man dressed in plain clothing stepped out through the door.

"Timothy!" But the wild look in his eyes stopped her from speaking further.

And then she saw it. A gun was pressed into his back. "Katie! Run! Go!"

Don't miss
Amish Covert Operation *by Meghan Carver,*
available July 2019 wherever
Love Inspired® Suspense books and ebooks are sold.

www.LoveInspired.com

WE HOPE YOU
ENJOYED THIS

LOVE INSPIRED® SUSPENSE BOOK.

Discover more **heart-pounding** romances of **danger** and **faith** from the Love Inspired Suspense series.

Be sure to look for all six Love Inspired Suspense books every month.

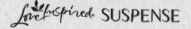 *Love Inspired.* SUSPENSE

www.LoveInspired.com

Any day she could see Sammy was a good day. But she was pretty sure Jack was about to turn down her nanny offer. And then she'd have to tell Penny she couldn't take the apartment, and leave.

The thought of being away from her son after spending precious time with him made her chest ache, and she blinked away unexpected tears as she approached Jack and Sammy.

Sammy didn't look up at her. He was holding up one finger near his own face, moving it back and forth.

Jack caught his hand. "Say hi, Sammy! Here's Aunt Arianna."

Sammy tugged his hand away and continued to move his finger in front of his face.

"Sammy, come on."

Sammy turned slightly away from his father and refocused on his fingers.

"It's okay," Arianna said, because she could see the beginnings of a meltdown. "He doesn't need to greet me. What's up?"

"Look," he said, "I've been thinking about what you said." He rubbed a hand over the back of his neck, clearly uncomfortable.

Sammy's hand moved faster, and he started humming a wordless tune. It was almost as if he could sense the tension between Arianna and Jack.

"It's okay, Jack," she said. "I get it. My being your nanny was a foolish idea." Foolish, but oh so appealing. She ached to pick

Sammy up and hold him, to know that she could spend more time with him, help him learn, get him support for his special needs.

But it wasn't her right.

"Actually," he said, "that's what I wanted to talk about. It does seem sort of foolish, but…I think I'd like to offer you the job."

She stared at him, her eyes filling. "Oh, Jack," she said, her voice coming out in a whisper. Had he really just said she could have the job?

Behind her, the rumble and snap of tables being folded and chairs being stacked, the cheerful conversation of parishioners and community people, faded to an indistinguishable murmur.

She was going to be able to be with her son. Every day. She reached out and stroked Sammy's soft hair, and even though he ignored her touch, her heart nearly melted with the joy of being close to him.

Jack's brow wrinkled. "On a trial basis," he said. "Just for the rest of the summer, say."

Of course. She pulled her hand away from Sammy and drew in a deep breath. She needed to calm down and take things one step at a time. Yes, leaving him at the end of the summer would break her heart ten times more. But even a few weeks with her son was more time than she deserved.

With God all things are possible. The pastor had said it, and she'd just witnessed its truth. She was being given a job, the care of her son and a place to live.

It was a blessing, a huge one. But it came at a cost: she was going to need to conceal the truth from Jack on a daily basis. And given the way her heart was jumping around in her chest, she wondered if she was going to be able to survive this much of God's blessing.

Don't miss
The Nanny's Secret Baby *by Lee Tobin McClain,*
available August 2019 wherever
Love Inspired® books and ebooks are sold.

www.LoveInspired.com

Love Inspired®

Inspirational Romance to
Warm Your Heart and Soul

Join our social communities to connect
with other readers who share your love!

Sign up for the Love Inspired newsletter
at **www.LoveInspired.com** to be the
first to find out about upcoming titles,
special promotions and exclusive content.

CONNECT WITH US AT:

Facebook.com/groups/HarlequinConnection

 Facebook.com/LoveInspiredBooks

 Twitter.com/LoveInspiredBks